S0-BZX-950

NEAR DEATH

A Raney/Daye Investigation

Rich Hosek
Arnold Rudnick
Loyd Auerbach

nifni
PRESS
Sherman Oaks, California

Visit **RaneyAndDaye.com** for more information about
a free audio version of this book,
special editions and offers,
future Raney/Daye Investigations
and resources about the paranormal.

Copyright © 2020 Rich Hosek, Arnold Rudnick and Loyd Auerbach
Based on the screenplay *Raney & Daye: Supernormal Sleuths*
Copyright © 1992 – Registered 2005
All rights reserved.

No part of this book may be reproduced in any form whatsoever
without written permission from the publisher.

Nifni Press
a Paraphrase, LLC imprint
P.O. Box 56508
Sherman Oaks, CA 91413

Read a Book, Read a Mind

ISBN: 1-953566-00-6
ISBN-13: 978-1-953566-00-3

Printed in the United States of America
First Printing: October 2020

For my big brother.

—*Rich Hosek*

Thank you, Rich, for making this book possible and ensuring Jennifer and Nate reach a wider audience. Loyd, for helping all of us understand the amazing paranormal world. And ESPecially, Kathryn, for making my world supernormal.

—*Arnold Rudnick*

To the memory of the late great science/science fiction writer (and mentor) Martin Caidin—who told me I should be involved in fiction.

—*Loyd Auerbach*

also by Loyd Auerbach

ESP Wars: East & West (with Edwin C. May, Victor Rubel, Joseph W. McMoneagle)
Self-Publishing: It Ain't Rocket Science (with Richard L. Wren)
Mind Over Matter
Psychic Dreaming: Dreamworking, Reincarnation, Out-of-Body Experiences & Clairvoyance
A Paranormal Casebook: Ghost Hunting in the New Millennium
Ghost Detectives' Guide to Haunted San Francisco (with Annette Martin)
ESP, Hauntings and Poltergeists: A Parapsychologist's Handbook
Ghost Hunting: How to Investigate the Paranormal
Psychic Dreaming: A Parapsychologist's Handbook
Hauntings and Poltergeists: A Ghost Hunters Guide
Reincarnation, Channeling and Possession: A Parapsychologist's Handbook

also by Arnold Rudnick

ESPete: Sixth Grade Sense
ESPete in ESPresident: Featuring *ESPete's Psychic Joke Book*
Little Green

also by Rich Hosek

Beyond the Levee and Other Ghostly Tales (contributor, edited by Peter R. Talley)
The Dead Kids Club (2021)

PROLOGUE

San Francisco - 1958

Luther Laramie looked down at Sarah Montgomery's lifeless body. She was laid out before him, her head nearly severed and deep gashes cut into her chest, shoulder and hip. Blood clung to her naked form like a skin-tight scarlet dress.

The axe dropped from Luther's hand. It made a loud thunk when its head hit the hardwood floor. The handle smacked into the growing pool surrounding Sarah's body and a splash of crimson sprayed across his shoes.

He kneeled, oblivious to the blood and stroked Sarah's lifeless cheek. Her dead stare looked past him as his own eyes started to tear. Luther sucked in a breath, his body now shaking with sobs. He lifted her head and cradled it against his chest. A low moan escaped his lips, then he raised his head and howled.

How could this have happened? he asked himself.

He caressed Sarah's hair, that dark brown almost black mane, so soft, now matted and soaked with blood. His dreams of someday marrying her were cut short just like her young life.

A siren wailed in the distance.

Luther gently laid Sarah back down on the floor. He stepped to the window overlooking the street.

A police car, its light flashing, raced down the dark streets toward the building. Two more approached from the opposite direction. Were they coming here? Had someone heard what happened in Sarah's apartment and phoned the police?

Luther looked down at his hands and clothes. They were covered in Sarah's blood. He didn't want to think what they would do if they found him like this. The deaths of the other girls by the hand of the killer known in the papers as "The Axeman," had created a vigilante mood in the city. He knew if anyone connected those heinous crimes to him there would be no trial, it would end in the streets.

He headed for the front door stopping at the chair where he'd left his fireman's turnout coat. He didn't have a cold weather jacket of his own and often borrowed the heavy garment from his locker at the firehouse on cold, wet nights like this one. He slipped it on. It hung almost down to his knees, and the sleeves covered most of his hands. If no one looked at him closely, didn't see his blood-spattered shoes, he might be able to make it out unnoticed.

Luther opened the apartment door and peeked out into the hallway. It was empty. He walked quickly but quietly down the hall to the stairwell, opened the door and slipped inside.

The door across from Sarah's apartment opened and a young blond woman peeked out. She looked across at Sarah's door, then down the hallway to where she noticed the stairwell door close with a gentle click. She seemed puzzled, almost curious and stepped across the hall toward Sarah's door.

The blue light from the police cars outside flashed through the window at the end of the hallway between the two apartments. She glanced down at the gathering police cars and decided to retreat back to her own apartment. Whatever was going on, she was going to leave it to the police to sort out.

Luther took the stairs two at a time, hanging on to the railing, oblivious to the trail of blood smears he left behind. He made it to the ground floor and opened the lobby door enough to peek out from behind it.

There was a policeman in the front of the elevators speaking to the old janitor, Shoetensack. Sarah had often told him how kind and helpful the building superintendent was. He had been working at the Oakley Arms since it was built after the Great Quake. The old man was in his seventies now and probably knew every nook and cranny of this place like the back of his hand.

Luther decided to take a chance and see if he could slip past the two men, just an off-duty fireman heading off to start his shift, if anyone asked. The police and fire departments had a good relationship, they would afford him professional courtesy without any cause for suspicion.

Luther turned up the collar of his coat and pulled his hands up into the sleeves, then strode purposefully toward the front door. There was a growing crowd of police outside. As he passed the elevators, the old man caught his eye. "Good evening, Mr. Shoetensack," Luther said, "how are you tonight?"

"Right as rain and feelin' no pain," the old man answered.

The policeman gave Luther a curious glance, saw his jacket then offered a deferential nod. "Be safe out there," the policeman said.

"You too," Luther said and nodded back.

As Luther continued toward the entrance, the front doors opened, and a group of policemen entered. Luther stepped to the side to let them by. They seemed on a mission, and a fireman passing by wasn't worthy of their notice. He offered them a friendly nod, and some of them nodded back.

But one cop, the youngest of the bunch, a rookie in his freshly issued blues, reached into his pocket for his notepad. Jostled by another officer, he dropped it to the floor and bent down to pick it up as Luther passed. The rookie's eyes were drawn to still glistening drops of blood on the fireman's shoes.

The cop stood up and his and Luther's eyes met.

"Come on, Raney, let's get a move on! I want you and Kendall to secure the stairwell," ordered the detective in charge.

Officer William Raney kept his eyes on Luther. He let the notepad slip out of his hand, then slowly reached for his revolver.

The other policemen noticed Raney's subtle movements and shifted their attention to the fireman.

Luther looked to the front door just ten feet away. There was now a crowd of a dozen or more police officers, and nearly as many cars with their lights flashing.

"Mister, you mind putting your hands up?" Raney asked.

"Sure," Luther said as he slowly raised his arms, careful to keep his hands in his sleeves. He nodded outside. "You mind telling me what's going on?"

"Turn around and put your hands behind your back, slowly," Raney ordered.

Luther saw no way out. His mind raced. Did he even care now that Sarah was dead? Did anything else matter? He spun around and slowly lowered his hands and placed them behind his back.

The detective and the other policemen relaxed, seeing that Luther was cooperating. "What you got there, son?" the detective asked Officer Raney.

"I think there's blood on his shoes," the nervous rookie replied. He grabbed the handcuffs from their case on the back of his belt and reached for Luther's hand. He hesitated when he saw that it too was covered in dark, sticky blood.

Luther sensed the hesitation in the young officer's actions. He grabbed Raney's hand and twisted it around, forcing the young cop to his knees, then let go of the stunned officer's wrist and ran straight toward the detective and the other officers.

Surprise slowed their reactions. Some reached for their guns, others tried to grab the fireman. Instinct drilled into Luther from his days as a running back on his high school football team kicked in. He threw a shoulder at one man, taking out two others like human bowling pins. Then he spun past another two and raced through the lobby, past the elevators and back to the stairwell door.

Shots rang out and bullets slammed into the wall in front of him.

None of them hit Luther.

He pushed open the door and started bounding up the steps. His experience as a fireman allowed him to race easily up the stairs, but to where? Back to Sarah's apartment? End it all there? The building was surrounded by now. It was just a matter of time. But maybe there was a chance he could get out of this.

He raced on past the tenth floor where Sarah's apartment was and up toward the roof.

In the building lobby, the detective helped Officer Raney to his feet. "What did you see son?"

"There was blood on his shoes and hands. A lot of it. When I went to put the cuffs on, he took me by surprise. I'm sorry sir, I let you down."

"Nah, you did good. He didn't get out of the building. That was all you. There's no way out now."

"It's him, sir, isn't it? The Axeman?"

The older detective nodded. "Gotta be."

Officer Raney couldn't help but notice the older detective's suit. It was remarkably clean and well pressed for someone who had either been working all day or had been called in from his home in the middle of the night. The detective noticed the younger policeman's gaze.

"Always wear a good suit and a fresh shirt. Everyone respects a man who dresses well."

"Yes, sir," Raney answered, accepting the advice from the detective like an eager student.

"Come on," the older detective said, "you're with me."

The detective marched toward the elevators where the rest of the police were gathering. He pointed at a couple other uniformed officers and motioned for them to follow as he barked commands to the rest of the growing crowd. "All right, listen up. This is our man, five-ten, one-seventy, brown hair, last seen wearing a fireman's coat. I want units on every floor at the elevators and the stairwells and fire escapes. No one comes in or out of this building unless they have a badge. All civilians are to remain in their apartments. If they don't comply, cuff them to their radiators. If you see the suspect, do not let him get away. Use whatever force is necessary to capture him. Dead or alive."

The officers all nodded.

The detective, Officer Raney, and the two other policemen headed toward the stairwell door. They burst through, guns drawn but Luther was nowhere in sight. Raney pointed to the blood smears on the handrail.

"Okay, boys, heads up. Nothing more dangerous than a cornered animal." The detective led the way up the stairs.

As they reached each landing, the detective swung the door open quickly as the rest of them trained their guns on the hallways. On the second and third floors, the detective ordered one of the uniformed officers to take a post at the door. By the time they reached the fourth floor, there were guards already stationed at the elevators and the stairwell door.

They continued that way, methodically sealing off each floor as they reached it until they arrived at a heavy door marked "Roof Access."

The detective checked the door. It was unlocked. He turned back to Officer Raney.

"Did you get a chance to pat him down? Did he appear to have a gun?"

"I didn't, but…"

"But what?"

"Well, he's the Axeman. Why would he carry a gun?"

"Son, never take anything for granted. As far as you know, he had a Tommy gun and a half dozen grenades under that coat. Got it?"

"Yes, sir."

"All right. Stay in sight, follow my directions."

"I'm ready, sir."

The detective drew his gun, then silently counted to three with the fingers of his free hand and opened the door to the roof.

Officer Raney held his weapon out, ready to fire if Luther came at them. A quick sweep told them there was no one on the roof—or at least the part of it they could see. The stairs came up out of a small raised room tacked on to the roof. It looked like some residents had set up private gardens, though nothing was growing except wilted weeds.

The detective stepped through the doorway, leading with his gun. He eased slowly around the corner, then motioned for Raney to stand guard at the door while he looked around.

A drop of water splashed onto Officer Raney's cheek. He looked up and saw dark, menacing clouds ready to let loose at any moment.

A gust of wind swept across the roof, blew into the stairwell entrance and slammed the metal door against the wall with a loud bang. A couple pigeons who had settled in for the night under a table took off with a flurry of wings. Officer Raney instinctively swung his gun around toward the commotion.

There was a flash of lightning.

For a moment, the rookie thought he saw Luther standing on the edge of the roof. But the lightning must have played some sort of trick on his eyes because to Officer Raney, it looked like he could see right through him.

"Don't move," the young policeman ordered.

In the next flash of lightning, there was nothing. The roof was empty.

"Did you see him?" the detective asked.

"Over there, sir. I saw something."

"The rest of the roof is clear. Remember what I told you. Assume he's armed and dangerous and knows you're coming."

Raney nodded. They proceeded to the far end of the roof where it abutted another building that was four or five stories shorter. As they walked, they checked behind each raised flower bed, cleared each table and chair. Raney noticed the older officer keeping the stairwell entrance in his peripheral vision.

They reached the end of the roof.

"Maybe he didn't come up here after all," Officer Raney suggested.

"We have this building locked down. Nowhere else he could be."

Officer Raney looked out over the city. Another flash of lightning lit up the sky. Something caught his attention out of the corner of his eye. Something below them.

He peered over the edge and thought he saw a shape on the adjacent roof four stories below. "Detective, I think there's something down there," he said.

The detective looked down. "Give me your flashlight," he ordered.

Raney pulled a long, bulky flashlight off his belt and handed it to the detective. He switched it on and cast the beam down to the neighboring rooftop.

A low rumble of thunder rolled by.

In the beam of the flashlight was the twisted and lifeless body of Luther Laramie.

It started to rain.

CHAPTER ONE

Present Day

It started to rain.

Dr. Jennifer Daye guided her Volkswagen Bus through the steep and narrow streets of the city. She was an attractive woman in her mid-thirties, her blond hair pulled back. She wore a vintage raincoat over a dark turtleneck sweater. Around her neck hung a gold chain with a pendant in the shape of the Greek letter Psi. Tweed slacks and a pair of red Vans completed her outfit giving her a decidedly bohemian look.

"Are we there yet?" asked the younger man sitting in the passenger seat. Dave Edwards was a graduate student and Dr. Daye was his thesis adviser. He found her interesting and brilliant, an expert in his chosen major of Anthropology, but she also expected him to help her with research that fell outside the traditional bounds of the field. He discovered to his frequent dismay that those duties included accompanying her on midnight outings to rundown parts of the city.

"Allegedly," she answered, nodding at the navigation app on the phone attached to the dashboard. "There should be a big sign out front. It's not like we're looking for some hole-in-the-wall video rental shop, it's the Palace Theater. It's an architectural landmark."

The rain picked up. The minibus' headlights had trouble piercing the veil of water pouring down from the sky. Jennifer slowed down, scanning the buildings lining the street while keeping one eye on the road.

"Yeah, well, everything is just another wet gray building in this weather," Dave complained. "Wait, there it is," he said suddenly, pointing at a building with a large unlit sign with the name "Palace" spelled vertically sticking out over the sidewalk.

"We're supposed to go around to the rear entrance. Do you see an alley or something?" Jennifer asked.

"You have arrived," the app informed her.

"Yes, I know we're here," she said to the phone, "but I want the back door." She plucked the phone out of its mount and shoved it into a pocket.

"I think there's an opening up there," Dave said, pointing down the street.

"I see it," Jennifer said. She drove up to a narrow alley between the theater and an office building.

"It's too narrow," Dave warned.

"I've got it," she insisted, then made a sharp turn into the alley.

The passageway was clearly created before the widespread use of cars and trucks. A narrow horse-drawn cart might easily fit through the gap, but Jennifer's minibus had barely enough room to squeeze by.

"See, told you," Jennifer said.

"What if you need to back out?" Dave asked.

"You are always such a downer, Dave. Why can't you be more like Emily?"

"Here's an idea, next time take Emily with you."

"She's only an undergrad. I need graduate level help for this one."

Dave sighed. This was a conversation he'd had many times, and one he was not eager to repeat because at the end of it he usually ended up doing even more of what he was complaining about. He sucked in a breath as they passed a carriage light hanging off of one wall that nearly scraped the window on the passenger side.

The narrow alley opened up into a loading dock area that the theater and other buildings on the street backed up to. There were a couple cars parked here and there, and a large panel van.

"See," Jennifer said, "that truck made it through."

Dave pointed to a large, well lit opening between the buildings on the opposite side of the parking lot.

"Ah, that makes all kinds of sense."

She steered the VW to a spot near a door marked "Stage Entrance" and parked. From a deep pocket she pulled a rumpled paper sack and dumped out a handful of candy corn. She offered the bag to Dave. He peered inside and shook his head.

"Suit yourself. Get the gear," she said to Dave.

"Of course, that graduate level task of getting the gear. So glad I'm here." Dave got up and worked his way to the back of the minibus to gather the equipment.

Jennifer retrieved a compact umbrella from another of the raincoat's pockets and opened the door a crack. She pushed the umbrella out through the opening, pressed the button on the handle and it shot out into a bright red dome that matched her shoes. She opened the door the rest of the way and stepped out. Her canvas sneakers were of little protection against the water gathering in the alley, but she didn't seem to mind, and soon even the high cuffs of her pants were soaked as well.

With a scientist's eye, Jennifer looked around the area behind the theater. The alley was paved with cobblestones even though many of the buildings surrounding the theater superseded them by decades. She sniffed the air, searching for some telltale scent underneath the smell of the rain. The rear of the building was constructed from rough bricks, a material that saved money on construction which was lavished on the front façade of the building and in the lobby, she presumed. Her fingers reached out and brushed the wet stone, stroking the bumps and crevasses like a blind person reading braille. She looked up. The rear of the building was mostly featureless, a few small windows here and there and vents jutting out at odd locations, modern add-ons, obviously not part of the original architecture.

She walked along the wall toward the stage door, her fingers tracing the mortar lines between the bricks. In her mind's eye she pictured fans and reporters gathered around the stage door, dressed in suits and evening gowns, everyone wearing hats. She wished people would wear hats more. Not the backward baseball caps that were popular among the kids on campus, but fedoras and bonnets adorned with feathers and bows. She was definitely born in the wrong century.

"Can I get a hand back here?" Dave shouted.

Jennifer turned toward the VW and danced between the growing puddles until she made it around to the back of the minibus.

Dave was struggling to close the doors of the vehicle while holding a large case in each hand, and a smaller one tucked under his left arm. He had on a yellow rubber raincoat with the hood pulled up over his prematurely balding head. His feet were clad in thick rubber galoshes.

"I got it," Jennifer said and swung the doors shut.

Dave turned to offer her the case under his arm, but Jennifer either didn't see his gesture or—more likely—ignored it and started leaping her way back over the puddles to the stage door.

"You know, if you invested in a decent pair of boots, you wouldn't have to worry about getting your feet wet," he said, then took a step into the nearest puddle and almost dropped all the cases as he found himself with one leg knee deep in a water-filled hole. His face registered the shock his body felt as his waterproof boot filled with icy water. "A little help?" he asked feebly, knowing that even if Dr. Daye did hear him, she would assess his situation as manageable and leave him to fend for himself. He lifted his foot out of the hole, got a firm grip on the cases and followed after her.

Jennifer pounded on the old steel-clad door.

Dave waited while the rain smashed against his raincoat.

Jennifer checked her watch. "He said he would meet us at one."

"Sure we have the right building?" Dave asked sarcastically.

The door swung open revealing a short, bald man, wire-rim glasses perched on a nose that was too small and anchored by ears that were too large. He was dressed in a suit that had seen more years than Jennifer and Dave put together. A bow tie cinched his neatly pressed collar close to the loose flesh at his neck. He regarded the professor and her assistant suspiciously. "Can I help you?"

Jennifer raised her eyebrows in surprise. "I'm Dr. Daye, the parapsychologist from the University."

"You?" he said. "I spoke to a man."

"That was me," Dave said. "Do you mind if we come in? It's really raining out here."

"Hmm," he considered, "all right. Try not to get everything wet." He stepped aside and held the door open while Jennifer entered, collapsed her umbrella, shook it out and returned it to her pocket.

Dave followed, dropped the cases, then turned back to the door where he removed one boot and emptied it out onto the rain soaked cobblestones.

Once they were safely inside, the old man closed the door against the storm and took on a completely different air. "Welcome to the Palace Theater," he said with a slight bow. "I am Victor Nagel, manager." He extended his hand to Jennifer.

"Jennifer Daye, pleased to meet you," she said, shaking his hand. His grip was firm yet gentle.

Then he extended his hand to Dave. "Victor Nagel," he repeated.

"Dave Edwards. Thanks for letting us in," Dave said, grateful to be out of the rain at last.

"My apologies for the late hour," Victor continued.

"It's all right, we're used to working the graveyard shift," Jennifer said.

Dave rolled his eyes at her joke, adding a tick to his mental tally of how many times she'd used it.

"I didn't want word to get out that the place was... you know... haunted. It's hard enough to get people in the doors as it is. They'd rather watch movies on those tiny phones instead of the silver screen."

"I know," Jennifer agreed. "You can't expect to take in the full glory of 'Casablanca' on a six inch rectangle."

"Oh, it pains me just to think about it," the old man said, putting a hand to his heart.

"I like watching movies on my phone," Dave said.

Jennifer and Victor both gave him a reproachful glance.

"You'll have to excuse Dave, he may lack an appreciation for the cultural masterpieces of the past, but he can be useful."

Victor considered her words, regarding Dave suspiciously. "Yes, I do find children today do lack a degree of respect for their elders."

"I'm twenty-five," Dave responded. "Not really a child any more."

"That's to be determined." He winked conspiratorially at Jennifer and she grinned back. "So, how does this work? You put on those ray gun backpacks and capture whatever ghost has decided to make me miserable in my waning days? Let me tell you, when I die I'm not sticking around."

"That's a shame, you'd make a really annoying ghost," Dave remarked off-handedly.

Jennifer shot Dave a look, her usual playful expression was gone, replaced now with disappointment and admonishment.

Dave turned to Victor. "I'm sorry, I didn't mean that. I get cranky when I get tired, and I'm not only tired, I am very cold and wet. My apologies."

"For you, I might make an exception and follow you around singing 'Henry the Eighth,'" Victor replied.

Jennifer smiled. "Nice 'Ghost' reference."

"Thank you. I may manage a classic cinema theater, but I do appreciate the modern films as well."

"That movie's like thirty years old," Dave remarked.

Jennifer ignored him. "Well, we don't actually do things the same way they did in 'Ghostbusters' with proton packs and electronic traps."

"You know, I didn't think the remake got as much appreciation as it deserved," commented Victor.

"I agree," said Jennifer.

Dave yawned. He had the two larger cases on the floor already opened up. Each had a foam lining that had cutouts for a variety of devices as well as tripods and battery packs. The smaller case contained a laptop computer. The graduate assistant turned it on and began syncing the various devices to data widgets on the screen.

"Not to disappoint you, but chances are you don't even have a ghost. Most of the situations we investigate turn out to have rather mundane and ordinary explanations," Jennifer explained.

"Well, I've never seen anything like this before, except maybe on the big screen."

"We'll take a look around, get some readings and if we find any indications of unusual activity, we'll set up some recording gear and see if we can verify that you do have something paranormal going on here."

Dave handed Jennifer a device that looked like a short pole with a pistol grip and a variety of different shaped protuberances along its length. Some were spheres, others cones, one at the end looked like a miniature satellite dish. Jennifer flicked a switch at its base and a series of LEDs along the top lit up in sequence, flashed, then settled in to a steady yellow glow. She pulled out her phone and opened up an app. The screen told her it was attempting to pair, then displayed a success message, and the LEDs shifted in color to green.

Dave was wearing a harness adorned with a variety of sensors. He had a body-cam clipped to one strap, an omni directional microphone on his shoulder and two cameras with bulky lenses slung around his neck, one film and one digital. "Ready," he declared.

Victor regarded him with deserved disdain and smiled at Jennifer. "Where would you like to begin?"

Jennifer glanced around and spotted a dark stairway. "What's down there?"

"Used to be dressing rooms back in the days when they did live shows here. Just storage now. Come, I'll show you."

Victor led them down the stairs to a dimly lit hallway that had a dozen doors along its length on either side and at regular intervals. There was a faded star painted on the nearest one. "Oh, the names that graced these doors. Mae West, Eddie Foy, Will Rogers, Bob

Hope, Fanny Brice… My father came when he was a boy. Then the big stars moved to the big screen and the days of Vaudeville were over. We used to come here for double features on Sundays. I got my first job tearing tickets at the door."

"Jeez, how old are you?" Dave asked.

Jennifer elbowed Dave in the side.

"I'll be ninety-eight this year," Victor said. "Going to make it to one hundred, just like George Burns. He played here, too!"

Jennifer checked the screen on her phone while she slowly swung her device around.

"Anything?" Dave asked.

"Not yet."

She reached out and pushed open the door to the nearest dressing room. She took a compact flashlight from one of her pockets and flicked it on. The beam illuminated a collection of furniture, broken down concessions equipment, posters, cardboard stand-ups from blockbuster movies and racks of usher uniforms.

"Just storage in here. People tell me I could get a lot of money for some of this stuff on ebbie."

"E-bay," Dave corrected.

"Hmm, yes, well, I'm not quite ready to part with it, but it may come to that soon."

Jennifer's flashlight continued exploring the dusty memorabilia. She stopped, her eyes widened, and she screamed.

Dave snatched up one of the cameras on instinct and started snapping photos of the inside of the crowded dressing room.

Victor leaned against the wall, clutching one hand to his heart.

"What is it? What did you see?" Dave asked, suddenly wide awake.

"Oh my God!" she exclaimed, then pushed her way into the room to a corner where a framed poster was hidden behind a cardboard cutout of Clint Eastwood from one of his spaghetti westerns. She pulled it aside and shined the light on the piercing eyes and distinctive haircut of Harry Houdini.

"My dear," said Victor weakly, "I did mention I wanted to make it to one hundred, didn't I?"

"It's Houdini," she said, as if it explained everything.

"Yes, yes, he played here many times. They had to reinforce the stage to accommodate his water tank."

"How much do you want for it?"

"Get rid of my ghost and it's yours," Victor answered.

"Deal. Come on Dave, we have to check out all these rooms down here."

"I expected nothing less," he sighed.

Jennifer led Dave on a meticulous examination of the dressing rooms. Victor informed them he would be making tea in his office, then he excused himself and made his way back up the stairs.

"What do you think?" Dave asked.

"I think there's a lot of great stuff down here."

"You know what I mean. The guy is pretty old. Could just be dementia."

"I doubt it. He has a very sharp memory, no problems expressing himself, I'd say he has another good decade left. And if he claims there's something strange going on here, I am inclined to give him the benefit of the doubt."

"Okay. But is it a haunting?"

Jennifer shrugged. "Look around you. A lot of history inside these walls, a lot of drama, emotion, probably a good number of deaths as well."

"You always have the cheeriest thoughts," Dave chided.

She smiled. "Nothing like a good murder to leave a psycho-emotional imprint on a place."

They continued on, Jennifer leading the way with her sensors, indicating with her flashlight what she wanted Dave to photograph.

When they completed the survey, Jennifer sighed, disappointed. "Well, nothing down here. Let's go get a cup of tea."

Jennifer and Dave found Victor's office with no trouble. The manager had a formal Wedgewood service. He served Jennifer and

Dave hot cups of tea.

"So, did you find any ghosts in my basement?" Victor asked.

"No, but there were a few lobby cards I may add to the bill," Jennifer said. "What kind of disturbances have you experienced down there?"

"In the basement? None," Victor said.

"Then why did you take us down there?" Dave asked.

Victor looked to Jennifer with a smile, "She asked."

"He's right, I did," Jennifer confessed. "I can never pass up a good basement."

"What a waste of time."

"Hardly, that Houdini poster is going to look awesome in my office."

"Yeah, I'm guessing it's a graduate level task to get it from that dressing room back to the University." Dave muttered regrets under his breath while he sipped his tea.

"So, Victor, where exactly have you encountered your 'ghost'?"

He glanced around the office. "In here. Up in the projection room. In the theater itself."

"Did you see anything?"

Victor shook his head. "Sometimes it's just an uneasy feeling. Other times, things move on their own, pictures fall off the wall."

"Poltergeist?" Dave asked.

"Too soon to tell," Jennifer answered. "This tea is wonderful. Ceylon Sonata?"

"You know your teas," Victor said, impressed.

"I worked as a nanny for a British family in college. But I never made tea this good."

"The secret is to use spring water. The minerals bring out the flavor."

"They do indeed." She set her cup down. "Shall we check out the projection room?"

The projection room was an obvious afterthought to a theater originally designed in Vaudeville's heyday. There was an iron spiral staircase tucked in a corner of the theater that ended at a catwalk connecting it to the projection room. Victor led them across the rickety walkway to the door and opened it.

Inside were two enormous seventy millimeter projectors that had been moved aside to make room for more economical thirty-five millimeter machines. They came in pairs so that one reel could be projected while a second was cued up. A feature length presentation came on five, six or more reels.

"You run this yourself?" Jennifer asked.

"I can barely afford to pay the kids at the ticket window and concession stand, let alone a projectionist. It's not hard. And I love doing it. Something about the sound of the projector clacking away that I find soothing."

"You know if you went digital, you could—" Dave stopped talking when he saw the reaction his suggestion created on the faces of Jennifer and Victor. "Never mind."

Jennifer's face shifted from disdain, to unease. "Whoa," she said. "Do you feel that?"

"I didn't want to say anything," Victor admitted, "I'm glad it's not just me."

"What?" Dave asked, then a feeling of nausea swept over him.

Jennifer pulled out her sensor and tapped her phone awake. The screen was showing some sort of activity.

Dave tapped her on the shoulder and pointed to a workbench where a film cannister slowly crept along the surface toward the edge. He grabbed one of the cameras, the digital one, and switched it to video mode and zoomed in on the can. It fell off and hit the ground with a clatter.

Jennifer walked over and inspected the cannister, waving the sensors over every surface. She set it back down on the floor, then pulled out her bag of candy corn and spread a few of them on the workbench. The colorful candies started to dance around. "Interesting," she said. And then they stopped.

Dave took a deep breath and realized his nausea had abruptly vanished.

Jennifer turned to Victor. "Where else did you say you've experienced this?"

"In the lobby at the concession stand. In the theater itself."

"Let's go," she said, then quickly walked out of the projection room and along the catwalk toward the spiral staircase.

The lobby of the Palace Theater showed evidence of several makeovers while retaining a grandiose quality missing from modern multi-screen cinemas. There were gold flourishes around every doorway and in every corner. The wallpaper had a textured pattern, and the red carpeting, though worn and stained, still gave the lobby an aura of luxury.

"This way," Victor said, leading them behind the popcorn counter.

Jennifer found a container of unpopped popcorn kernels and spread a handful of them across the counter. She stared at them. Dave took this as his cue to start recording the scene.

Nearly a minute later, their patience was rewarded. The kernels started sliding toward the edge of the counter. Jennifer let them drop into her hand, then consulted the screen of her phone. It showed a similar reading to what she registered in the projection room.

"It is a ghost, isn't it?" Victor asked. "It's following us."

Dave looked around the lobby, a little creeped out.

"In the theater as well, you said?" Jennifer asked.

"Yes, follow me." Victor led them out from behind the concession stand to the entrance to the auditorium.

The space was cavernous and even more opulent than the lobby. A spectacular chandelier hung from the ceiling which was adorned by a mural of angels and demons. Great velvet curtains hung from the walls.

Jennifer started walking down the aisle toward the stage. The enormous screen lay unlit before her with the promise of brooding film noir or spectacular Technicolor musicals.

"Over here," Victor said, directing them to the east wall of the theater.

Jennifer followed him, glancing up at the intricately cast sconces and the delicate plaster cornices. She pulled out her phone, then checked her watch. She looked at Dave, then with a mischievous smile, started counting down. "In five... four... three... two..."

At the point where she would have said "one" Dave felt nauseated again. The Chandelier rattled. A piece of plaster broke off from the wall and landed at Victor's feet.

"It's periodic!" Jennifer announced excitedly. She pressed her ear against the wall and listened, her smile growing broader. "What's next door?" she asked.

"A delicatessen," Victor answered. Then, "No, wait. They moved out. I think it's a laundry now."

"When did it change?"

"About seven months ago."

"And when did you start noticing the disturbances?"

Victor thought for a moment. "About six months ago."

Jennifer stuffed her sensor and phone into her raincoat pockets and raced back to the aisle of the theater. "Come on," she said to Dave and Victor. "Follow me!"

She raced out of the auditorium. Dave started to follow, then noticed Victor was not even trying to move as fast as she was. "Does she do this often?" Victor asked.

"Oh, yeah. It's a regular cross-fit class working for her."

"You go on, I'll catch up."

"You sure? I can help you—"

"Thank you, young man, but I can manage. Go, catch her. I'll be right behind."

Dave nodded. He ran after Jennifer, holding onto his cameras so they wouldn't bounce around.

He reached the lobby just in time to see the front door close. He jogged across the red carpet, pushed open the door and stepped out into the street. The rain had stopped, but the threat of its return hung heavy in the air. He looked down the street in one direction, then the other and saw Jennifer pounding on the door to a neighboring business. He caught up to her just as a frazzled young man, tall and lean, entered the business' lobby from behind a curtain followed by a hazy cloud of smoke. Dave spotted a marijuana pipe in his hand. "This is going to be interesting," he said.

"We're closed," the attendant shouted from behind the counter.

"I know," Jennifer replied. "But you have to let us in. It's a matter of life or death."

A look of concern crossed the man's face. He considered for a moment, then decided to err on the side of caution and walked around the counter and let Jennifer and Dave into the laundry.

"What is it? Is someone hurt?"

"Your machines. You do have machines here, don't you?"

"Yes, of course. Washing machines. We're a laundry."

"I need to see them. Now."

A panicked look crossed his face. "What's wrong?"

"That's what we're here to find out," Jennifer assured him.

"Okay. Back here," he said, then disappeared behind the curtain.

Dave waved away the remnants of the smoke cloud. "Wow, I think I'm getting a contact high."

"Don't judge," Jennifer admonished him. "It could be medical."

There was a knock on the outside door.

Victor waved to them from the street.

"Let him in, Dave," Jennifer said.

Dave crossed back to the front door and let Victor in.

"What's going on?" he asked.

"I think Dr. Daye's on to something."

"Come on, this way," Jennifer said, then disappeared behind the curtain.

Dave and Victor followed. The back room was hot and steamy. Along the wall that the laundry shared with the theater there was a bank of enormous washing machines, humming and spinning away.

The young man waited patiently for more instructions.

"Do you have the inspection certificates for these?" Jennifer asked.

"I don't know. I can check in the office," he answered, exhaling another cloud of smoke with the words.

"Well, hurry up then."

The man nodded and ambled away.

Victor stopped and sniffed the air. "What is that smell?" he asked.

Jennifer ignored his question and walked slowly past the machines. She noticed the mounting bracket on one of them was missing its bolts. "Take a look at this," she said to Dave.

He automatically started shooting photographs.

Jennifer glanced at her watch. She held up her hand to silence her companions and then did her countdown again. "Five... four... three... two..."

The machine in front of her started a spin cycle. As it got faster and faster, Dave could feel the wave of nausea again, this time mitigated by the second hand cannabis. "No wonder that guy is hot boxing himself."

Jennifer hit the red stop button on the machine and it quickly ground to a halt. The door popped open.

Everyone felt immediately at ease.

"What was it?" Dave asked.

"Infrasonic sounds," Jennifer explained. "You can't hear them, but they jiggle your insides—among other things." She reached inside the washing machine, grabbed a sheet from inside and draped it over her hand. "I think we found your ghost, Victor."

The laundry attendant emerged from the office with a framed certificate in hand. He saw the machine stopped and open. "I couldn't find anything for the machines, but I found this old elevator inspection certificate."

Jennifer took it and looked at it. "Inspected by number forty-three. He's good."

"I don't think we have an elevator," he added.

"Does anyone feel really good about this?" Victor asked. "For some reason I feel really good." He took a deep breath.

Dave looked over at Jennifer. "Emily would have liked this one," he told her.

Jennifer nodded. "Yes, she would."

CHAPTER TWO

The police car went airborne for a second and a half when it crested the top of the hill. The blaring siren and the flashing blue and white lights mounted on the dashboard gave just enough warning to the other cars and pedestrians in its path to get out of the way.

The passenger, Detective Nate Raney, sat passively as if this was a Sunday drive in the country. He wore a bespoke suit with a clean white shirt and a silk tie that gave him the look of someone older than the thirty-odd years he'd been kicking around.

The driver was a stark contrast to Nate. Max Lee was a younger Asian man, his hair was spiked in place with gel and a sparse week's worth of beard covered parts of his chin, jawline and upper lip. He wore a sport coat, but it was clearly something off the rack, and the t-shirt he wore under it declared that he would wear the jacket, but screw the tie. His eyes had the look of a maniac on a mission.

"You know," Nate said to his partner, "you're really not supposed to use the siren unless we're on official business."

"Yeah, I think you've mentioned that before. But I remind you, we are on official business," Max insisted. "We're buying a birthday present for the Captain. Doesn't get any more official than that."

Nate sighed, knowing better than to argue with the headstrong detective. He was a good cop who had just seen one too many "Lethal Weapon" movies. "That's the place up there," Nate told him, pointing to a storefront for a high-end gift shop.

"Got it," Max said. "You see any parking spaces?"

"Kind of hard to tell while we're going sixty miles per hour."

"Never mind, I see one."

Max cut the wheel hard to the left, swinging the back of the car around and sliding it into a spot on the opposite side of the street.

Nate reached over and killed the siren and lights. "You are one police procedure savvy citizen away from a disciplinary hearing."

"I had a girlfriend once who was into discipline. She was hot."

"Not at all the same thing," Nate said as he got out of the car.

"I wonder if I still have her number?" Max unbuckled himself, then stepped out of the car right into traffic.

Seymour Bertrand, a heavyset man in his forties with greasy hair attempting to cover a balding head, slammed on the brakes. His passenger, Freddie Harding, thinner, older and with a military style buzz-cut, nearly slammed into the windshield.

"Hey, watch it?" Freddie complained.

"It's not my fault some asshole just walked into the middle of traffic. And I told you to wear your seatbelt. We don't want to get pulled over for some stupid traffic violation."

"Whatever. Let's just do this job, pay off Deuce and get the hell out of this city. Hell, this state."

"Yeah, I'm with you on that."

"That guy's leaving. It's perfect."

Seymour waited for a car just ahead of them to pull out from its parking space and gently eased the old Cadillac into the spot. He turned off the car, but left the key in the ignition. It wasn't on a key chain, so it was hard to see that the key was there and unlikely that someone would jack it while they were inside.

Both men wore long, bulky overcoats that hid shoulder holsters keeping their Glocks at the ready. "Remember," Seymour told his partner, "watches, wallets, phones and rings. We don't have time for anything else. We've got four minutes tops once we have their attention."

"Yeah, yeah, I know. Remember, I'm the one who found this job.

High end merch, lots of fat wallet tourists and rich assholes from the financial district."

"You want a medal? One more time. What's the approach?"

"I know what to do," Freddie assured him.

His partner stared him down.

Freddie relented and answered Seymour's question. "You go in the front, I'll enter through the back."

"What do you say if someone asks what you're doing back there?"

Freddie repeated his reluctantly memorized line, "I'm picking up my girlfriend who works there."

Seymour was not impressed. "Let's just hope they believe you would actually have a girlfriend."

"I could say boyfriend if that would make you feel better."

"They'd be even less likely to believe you're gay."

"I got this," Freddie insisted. "You do your part and I'll do mine."

"All right. You go first, I'll head out in a minute."

"Whatever." Freddie stepped out of the car, then reached in to the back seat and pulled out a large empty duffel bag. He shut the door, then walked up to the corner, crossed the street and made his way to the alley behind the shops.

Seymour took a deep breath. "This is the last time I work with that guy," he promised himself.

In the shop, Nate browsed an assortment of gadgets lined up on a table in the middle of the store. He picked up a GPS enabled watch, tapped at its screen and pressed its buttons.

Max walked up behind him and slapped both hands on Nate's shoulders, nearly causing his partner to drop the watch. "No gadgets, buddy. That's your thing, not hers."

"She runs. Might like something to keep track of where she's going."

"Partner, that lady knows exactly where she's going, and its initials are City Hall."

"Not initials, Max. Did you even go to school?"

"School of hard knocks, my friend. The street was my school. Say, what's the budget on this gift?"

"The squad kicked in just over six hundred dollars."

"Wow, I say we take half, get massages and a couple rare steaks, then get her a gift card."

"Classy," Nate replied.

"Just a thought. We can spend it all on the Captain if that's what you really want to do."

"Yes, that's what I and the rest of the squad want to do."

"All right, just asking," Max said. Something across the room caught his eye. "Hey, what about those?" He indicated some hammered copper planters.

"Planters?"

"Don't chicks like plants?"

"First of all, the Captain is not a chick, she is our superior officer, and second, over my dead body."

"Relax. Anyone ever told you you're uptight, Nate?"

"Just you, Max. Just you."

"I'd listen to me. I do and I'm a pretty happy guy."

"I think I'll stick with common sense, respect for others and obeying regulations."

"All right. Let's keep looking."

Max checked out an assortment of collectible figurines.

Nate noticed a heavyset man enter the store. He wore a bulky overcoat, but it still fit him tightly enough that Nate thought he could make out the familiar outlines of the straps from a shoulder holster. The man scanned the store, checking out the customers rather than the merchandise.

"Oh, shit," Nate said to himself, hoping he was wrong. "Max," he whispered. "Max!"

"You find something?" Max asked.

"Guy in the overcoat by the front door. Looks like he might be casing the joint."

"For what?" Max caught a glimpse of the fat guy. "Oh, yeah. He's not here for the planters."

Nate looked around. "Big place, you'd need at least two people to pull it off."

"Yeah, a partner would make sense."

"Call it in, get some backup over here."

Max pulled out his phone.

"Not in here," Nate told him, "I don't want to scare anyone or tip him off. Take it outside. If you don't see anything, circle around back."

"Okay, boss, I'm on it." Max made his way to the front of the store, passing the heavyset man on his way. The man watched Max leave, then reached inside his coat.

Nate turned his attention to the back of the store and saw a second man, much thinner, wearing an identical coat and carrying a duffel bag emerge from the employees only door. "On second thought, Max," Nate said to himself in a low voice, "why don't you wait here with me in case this thing goes down right now?"

Seymour pulled his gun out and fired a shot into the air. It was a dramatic move, but in his experience it scared the shit out of everyone around him, and scared people made terrible witnesses and generally did what they were told.

Freddie fired his gun as well, adding confusion to the fear, effectively causing everyone who thought about fleeing out the back of the store to freeze in place.

"Sorry to inconvenience anyone," Seymour announced, "but this is a robbery. If you do what we say, you can be on your way quickly and alive. If you don't, I can't make that promise. Everyone get into the center of the store, form a line." No one moved. Seymour fired another shot into the air and the shoppers hurried to gather haphazardly between the two gunmen. Seymour knew the gunshots would cause someone to call the police, but all of that was anticipated. They would have what they wanted and be out the door in less than three minutes, half the average response time for this neighborhood.

Nate considered reaching for his gun, but without backup and a store full of civilians, that scenario just did not play. Instead, he mingled with the other shoppers, waiting for backup. Since Max hadn't come bursting back in with his gun drawn, he assumed he was still making his way to the rear entrance, unaware that the situation had escalated. Nate slipped his phone out of his jacket pocket and started tapping out a message to Max on the screen.

"Hey, you," the skinny man said, tapping Nate on the shoulder with his gun. He held out his over-sized gym bag. "Let's have that."

Nate managed to hit the send button as he dropped the phone in the bag.

"Get in line," the skinny man ordered.

Nate fell in with the others, positioning himself in the middle.

"Come on, shoulder to shoulder. No funny business. Have your phones, wallets, watches and rings ready when I walk by."

As the skinny one walked along the line collecting everyone's personal possessions, the fat one watched over them from the opposite side. Smart. With everyone lined up shoulder to shoulder, if anyone made a move, he could easily see it. Nate was glad that no one so far was stupid enough to try to be a hero.

The skinny guy reached Nate. "All right, let's have the rest of it."

Nate stripped off his watch, confident the gift he had received from his great uncle when he graduated from the police academy would soon be back in his possession, and dropped it in the bag. He pulled out his wallet and added it, too. When it landed, it popped open, revealing the detective's shield inside.

Freddie saw a flash when the guy in the nice suit dropped his wallet in the bag. He looked inside and saw a gold badge affixed to the black leather wallet. He looked back at the guy who smiled awkwardly. "No need to do anything crazy. I want to get out of here with no one getting hurt as much as you guys do."

Freddie dropped the bag and held his Glock on Nate with both hands. "We got a cop," he shouted to Seymour.

"Shit. Does he have a gun?"

"I don't know. I guess so. He's a cop." Then he spoke to Nate. "Put your hands up! Slowly!"

Seymour walked over behind the line of frightened shoppers to join his partner. When he reached the cop, he patted him down and found his gun in a shoulder holster. He pulled it out and tossed it in the bag. "Any more?"

"No," the cop promised.

But Seymour continued to pat him down, checking his waist band and his ankles.

"Shit, what do we do now?" Freddie asked.

"Stick with the plan. Get the rest of the stuff and we're out of here."

Freddie nodded, picked the bag back up and continued walking down the line accepting each person's valuables, speeding up the process by making threatening gestures with his gun.

A siren wailed in the distance.

"They're early," Seymour cursed. "Let's get out of here."

Freddie spied a gold locket hanging around a young woman's neck. It looked like it had some rather decent sized diamonds in it. "Let's have that," he insisted.

The woman put a hand to her chest to cover the locket. "No, please. It's very special to me."

"Then I'll be sure to take very special care of it," Freddie promised.

He ran his thumb over the top of the locket and as he brushed over a latch, it popped open, revealing a photo of a baby inside.

"That's my baby," the woman pleaded.

"I wouldn't brag about that," Freddie replied. He snatched it from her neck. The clasp didn't break easily, and it pulled her forward, knocking her off balance.

"Hey, give that back," said a young man who was obviously the woman's companion. Freddie couldn't remember if they had put wedding rings into the bag or not.

"Shut up," Freddie said, then whipped his gun across the young man's face, momentarily dazing him.

"Let's go!" Seymour shouted.

Freddie shifted his attention to his partner, and that was all the young man needed to make his move. He lunged at Freddie, knocking him to the ground.

The duffel bag of valuables spilled half of its contents.

Freddie's gun went off.

The young woman screamed.

Nate reached for his gun before remembering it was no longer tucked away in his shoulder holster. He raced toward the two men who were struggling on the floor. A shot from the front of the store rang out and Nate could hear it zip past his head, missing him by inches.

"Stay where you are," the fat man warned.

Nate froze.

"Let's go, asshole!" the fat guy yelled at his partner.

The skinny guy managed to elbow the young man on the side of the head, tossed him aside and scrambled to his feet. He kicked the man in the ribs, then grabbed the bag.

"Freeze, police!" Max yelled from the back of the store.

Nate looked to his partner. He opened his jacket and showed him the empty holster.

Max realized his mistake. Instead of he and Nate having the upper hand, he was now outnumbered.

The skinny guy fired at Max, causing him to retreat.

The siren sounded like it was still a couple blocks away.

"Come on!" shouted the fat guy.

Nate had to give him credit. He obviously wasn't pleased with his partner's screwup, but wasn't going to leave the man behind and knew they only had seconds left to make an escape.

The skinny guy scrambled to pick up the spilled valuables.

"Leave it," the fat guy ordered.

The skinny guy reluctantly grabbed what he could and turned toward the front of the store while the fat guy held his gun on the customers. Both of them were now on the other side of the civilians from Max, who couldn't possibly have a clear shot.

Then, Nate's worst fear materialized. The young man who moments ago lay incapacitated on the floor, was now getting to his feet. His hand found a heavy paperweight, and he picked it up and hurled it at the skinny guy as he ran toward the door. It hit him square between the shoulder blades.

In a moment of blind rage, the skinny man swung his gun around toward the young man. "You stupid mother-!"

"Forget him!" the fat man shouted. "Let's go!"

But Nate could see in the skinny guy's eyes that he would not let it go. Nate took two giant steps, then launched himself into the air.

A shot rang out.

Nate smashed into the young man, taking them both to the floor.

A sudden pain burned in Nate's chest. He must have landed funny.

"Nate!" Max shouted from the back of the store.

Nate looked to the front entrance and saw the two men exchange a few words as they fled out onto the street.

Nate got to his knees. It took a lot more effort than it should have.

Max rushed to his side, put his arms around Nate to steady him. "Easy there, partner. Just lie down."

"I'm fine. Just had the wind knocked out of me." He looked into Max's eyes. The Asian man's bravado was gone, replaced with fear.

"You're shot, Nate. Lie down."

Nate looked down at the spot on his chest that now burned as if someone was sticking a red hot poker into it. There was a hole in his suit, surrounded by a growing spot of blood. He suddenly felt dizzy and allowed Max to lower him to the floor.

"Someone call nine-one-one," he said. "Tell them there's an officer down."

No one moved.

"Sounds like they're already on the way," someone said.

"That's just more cops. I need an ambulance."

"They took our phones," one of the other shoppers told him.

Max pulled out his own phone and tossed it to the shopper. He returned his attention to Nate, peeled back his jacket to inspect the wound. Blood pumped out in weak spurts. Max placed his hands over the wound and applied a hard, steady pressure. "Stay with me, Nate. Hang on," he pleaded.

"You were right," Nate said.

"Right about what?"

"We should have gotten a gift card."

Max laughed.

Nate felt the world fading away. His eyes closed and his head fell to one side.

CHAPTER THREE

Nate looked down at the street.

Wait, that wasn't right. He couldn't have been looking down, because he was lying on a stretcher being rushed out of the gift shop. One paramedic was pushing the gurney, while a second was astride Nate pressing down on a stack of blood-soaked gauze over the wound in his chest.

Yet somehow he was watching it all happen.

"Get him to county. I've got an escort for you and the trauma team is waiting," Max ordered the paramedics.

"You got it," one of them replied.

Max put his phone to the side of his head, "He's on his way, Cap. I'll meet you at the hospital. Someone should call his mother." He ended the call and stopped to watch the paramedics slide Nate into the back of the ambulance. He ran a hand through his spiked hair and turned away.

Nate knew that Max—despite his current outward appearance and action—was lost. He was taking control of the situation because he had lost control of his feelings. His partner had just been shot and the poor kid was probably blaming himself, replaying the scene in his head a hundred different ways, trying to figure out how he could have stopped something that had already happened.

"Wasn't your fault," Nate said—or rather thought. No one seemed to react to his words.

The street grew brighter, as if someone had shined a huge spotlight on it. No one else seemed to notice. Nate looked behind him and saw a bright light. It wasn't blindingly bright, but rather inviting and comforting. He wanted to go toward it, to go into it.

For a moment, he thought he saw a shape in front of the light, a silhouette, and heard someone saying faintly, "Not now."

He turned away. The cop in him took over. He searched the street for any sign of the two gunmen. They were probably long gone, but he felt a strong drive, a powerful need to find them. Oddly, he realized he didn't so much want to find them for himself, but so that Max could be at peace.

The ambulance arrived at the trauma center and a team was waiting to transfer Nate from the stretcher to a hospital gurney. They wheeled him inside while the paramedics fed information about their patients vitals to the doctors and nurses. "Take him directly to surgery," one doctor ordered. "They're waiting for him."

The trauma team raced through a series of doors, each held open by a nurse or orderly so that their progress to the elevator was unimpeded. The ride up to the third floor surgery suites took longer than any of them liked.

Another cleared path was waiting when they exited the elevator and he was handed off to the surgery team.

The lead doctor inspected the wound. "Let's get some more blood in him right away. He's going to need it."

A portable X-Ray machine gave them a look at what they were dealing with. The bright, white lead of the bullet lay just a fraction of an inch from his heart.

"Lucky son of a bitch. He's got a chance."

Nate watched the doctor open his chest while a nurse suctioned away excess blood. Clamps were applied to vessels as they dug their way down through his flesh to where the bullet that killed him sat.

Killed him was the right way to think about it, Nate realized.

He was dead.

Wasn't he?

The pain from the gunshot wound was gone—though that could be the anesthesia. Maybe there was a mirror above the operating table, and he was one of those rare patients who was awake during surgery, but paralyzed and unable to speak.

"Got it," the doctor announced and dropped the bullet into a waiting tray with a solid clink. The operating room team knew what to do next. They sealed it into an evidence bag they kept on hand for such occasions and a nurse walked it out of the operating room and handed it to a police detective who had watched the entire process and could and would verify the chain of custody in a court of law.

"Let's get his heart started. Paddles," the doctor ordered.

A nurse handed him the small, thin defibrillator paddles used on an exposed heart. The doctor placed them carefully inside Nate's chest. "Clear," he said, then pressed the small button that applied the electric shock.

Nate's heart jumped, but didn't beat.

"Okay, again. Clear," the doctor ordered.

Another surge of electricity flowed through the paddles into Nate's heart, and this time it started beating.

The doctor waited patiently, observing the EKG screen as the jagged but regular lines from Nate's heartbeat traced across it.

Then they stopped and the steady beats of his heart changed to a flat tone.

The doctor looked inside Nate's chest. "We have another bleeder," he said dispassionately. "Suction!"

The room grew bright.

Again Nate turned and saw the light beckoning him, promising peace. He could see the shadowy figure more clearly now. There was something familiar about it.

Nate fought the compulsion to move toward the shape into the light and turned away from it. He found himself once again on the street in front of the gift shop.

No, not on the street, above it.

He heard a familiar voice. The frustrated tones of the fat guy from the robbery. "A cop. You shot a cop. You idiot. We are so screwed."

Nate turned around, but the robber was no where in sight. He realized he wasn't in front of the store anymore. He was in a decidedly different neighborhood. It looked like somewhere in the Tenderloin district. He was in front of a house with an unkempt yard bordered by a low, stone fence and a decades-old Cadillac parked under a carport that had no roof. He looked at the car, thinking there was something he should do. Something a cop would do.

"I wasn't aiming for the cop, asshole," the skinny guy said.

"Oh, well as long as you weren't trying to kill him I'm sure they'll just let the whole thing go."

Nate followed the sound of the voices, but it wasn't like they were nearby. It was as if he could hear through the walls. He looked at the house, searching for a way in other than the front door.

Then he was inside, looking at the fat guy and his skinny partner. The fat guy was pacing nervously, while the skinny one was sorting the take from the robbery. "Should have stayed and grabbed the rest of the loot. This isn't enough. I say we fence it and get out of town," the skinny guy said.

"The cops are going to be putting pressure on every fence in the city. No one is going to want to handle this stuff. It might as well be radioactive."

"Then we leave town and fence it out of state."

"And if Deuce gets wind that we slipped out of town without paying him, the cops will be the least of our worries. Besides, we can't show our faces right now."

"Why not? You said those suckers in the store would be so scared they wouldn't be able to give a decent description."

"Yeah, they can't, but that other cop can. They're trained for that shit.

"I certainly can," Nate said.

But neither man heard him.

"So, we wait a couple weeks. Grow beards. I let my hair grow, you shave yours off, maybe drop a few pounds. It'll be fine."

The fat man shook his head, then dropped down on the sofa and covered his face with his hands.

He opened his mouth and beeped.

The skinny man beeped back at him.

Nate looked around, wondering what the hell was going on, only now he was back in the operating room where the EKG was beeping out a steady rhythm.

"Got him back," the doctor announced.

The other doctors and nurses sighed with relief.

CHAPTER FOUR

Jennifer admired the poster of Harry Houdini mounted on the wall of her office. It hung behind her desk, displacing dozens of other photos, diplomas and various examples of indigenous art she had collected during her travels, all of which now were stacked on top of a pair of file cabinets.

It mirrored another poster hanging across from it. In this one, there was a picture of a woman identified as "The Mysterious Professor," Jennifer's alter ego. A variety of magical accouterments floated around her while she stared straight ahead with just the hint of a mischievous smile. It had been years since she had performed professionally, the demands of teaching left little time for it to be more than a hobby, now.

Emily Vargas, a young undergrad, borderline goth, walked in. She froze in place when she saw the eerie face of the master magician staring at her. "That is so creepy," she said. "And not in a fun way."

"No it's not," insisted Jennifer. "It is most awesome."

"BTW, no one says awesome anymore."

"Awesome sauce?" Jennifer inquired.

"Not even," Emily replied.

"Well, I like it, he's one of my heroes and he's staying."

"I thought Mary Leakey was your hero."

"I said one of them."

"Did you read your messages?" Emily asked.

"No, that's your job."

"Yes, I read them and then leave the important ones for you to read so you can respond and make sure the dean doesn't fire you."

"That's ridiculous. Why would he fire me? The dean loves me."

"Actually I don't think that's accurate."

Emily dropped a newspaper on her desk. It was open to a story with the headline, "Local Ghostbuster Exorcizes 'Spirits' from Historic Palace Theater." "And I know he doesn't like it when you associate the University with your side hustle."

Jennifer looked at the article and smiled. "I'm glad Victor got some publicity out of the whole thing. Maybe he'll be able to keep the place going. Though I wish they wouldn't refer to it as an exorcism. There wasn't even really a spirit."

"They put 'Spirits' in quotes," Emily pointed out.

Jennifer glanced back down at the newspaper. "Still, quite a lot of editorial license in that headline."

Then another story caught her eye. "Local Cop Recovering After Shootout." She skimmed the article which focused mostly on the fact that the perpetrators were still at large, but she did find buried in the final paragraphs what she was looking for. "Surgeons managed to save the detective's life after his heart had stopped repeatedly on the operating table."

"Yes!" she exclaimed excitedly.

"What is it now?" Emily asked.

"Possible NDE," Jennifer replied.

"Oh, God," droned Emily. "They're never going to let you in to see him."

"I need more cases for the book," she insisted. "Besides, you'll be there to help me."

"I have classes over the next three days, finals are next week and I have a major paper due in your class."

Jennifer scribbled a large letter A on a pad of paper and ripped off the sheet and handed it to Emily. "I loved your paper, it was well reasoned, carefully researched, and the grammar was spectacular. We'll go on Friday. He just had major surgery, we should give him a couple days to rest."

"You think?" Emily asked, sarcastically. Then she handed back the A to Jennifer. "I'm going to write that paper. I like writing papers. It's fun. I like doing research."

"That's why I like you Emily, you like doing the things I don't have time for."

CHAPTER FIVE

Nate opened his eyes.

Judging from the smell, the television set up high in one corner playing an episode of "Judge Judy" and flowers and balloons crowded around the perimeter of the room, he guessed he was in a hospital.

The sensation of an elephant sitting on his chest reminded him why.

He had been shot.

And then he had that strange dream, one he wanted to forget.

A soft, gentle hand squeezed his own.

Nate looked to his right and saw the smiling, yet concerned face of his mother, Eleanor. He tried to speak, to say something comforting to her, but he realized he couldn't. There was a breathing tube down his throat.

"Don't try to talk," she said to him. "I'll call the nurse." She reached over to the panel on the bed and pressed the button marked call. "You had me worried for a while, but then I spoke to your father and he told me everything was going to be all right. It's not your time," she said to him.

Nate rolled his eyes and shook his head slowly. Moving it at all hurt like hell.

His father, Ben, had been dead for fifteen years now. But his mother spent a good portion of his social security benefits and her own meager teacher's pension on psychics and mediums who convinced her they could speak to him. It was a constant struggle between his mother and him.

The nurse entered and walked over to Nate with a broad smile on her face. "Welcome back, Detective," she said cheerily. "How are you feeling?"

Nate offered her a forty-five degree thumbs up.

"Let me talk to the doctor," she said. "I'll see if we can get that tube out."

Nate nodded slowly, his eyes signaling his eagerness.

The nurse checked his pulse with her warm, slender fingers. An act that was unnecessary since he was hooked up to multiple machines that could give her that information. "By the way, I'm Izzy. I'll be right back," she promised.

Once she left the room, Eleanor leaned in to Nate and whispered. "I think she likes you."

Nate's status as an unmarried, childless man was the other topic of conversation that generated conflict between him and his mother.

The nurse returned with a small cart and started unstrapping the ventilator mask.

"Hey, look who's awake!" said Max's exuberant voice from the doorway. He noticed Eleanor sitting at the bedside and stepped over and put a comforting hand on her shoulder. "How's he doing Mrs. R.?"

"He's awake," she said.

The nurse proceeded to remove the breathing tube from Nate. He tried to speak, but ended up coughing instead.

"It may be difficult to talk for a little while. Do you have a sore throat?" Izzy asked.

Nate shook his head. He cleared his throat, then turned to Max. "My rabbit ate twenty-two Easter eggs."

"What?" asked Max confused.

"What?" Nate answered, equally confused.

"You said your rabbit ate some eggs? You have a rabbit?"

"Did you get a pet, dear?" Eleanor asked.

"What are you two talking about? I asked if you caught the bastards who shot me."

"Sometimes the anesthesia does funny things," Izzy offered.

Max shook off his confusion, "Okay, my bad. We haven't captured them yet, but every cop in the city is on it. We'll get them."

Nate nodded.

A doctor entered and stepped up to the bed. "Hello there, Detective Raney. I'm Dr. Cullen."

Nate recognized him as the doctor he saw in the operating room in what he remembered as a foggy dream. "Have we met before?" Nate asked.

"The first time I saw you was when I pulled a bullet out of your chest. You gave us quite a scare, thought we lost you a couple of times on the operating table, but you kept coming back."

"Thank you for saving my son," Eleanor said.

"From what I hear, he was the hero," the doctor added. He turned back to Nate. "From one to ten, how is the pain."

Nate considered the question. The pain in his chest was constant, but as he tried to lift his right arm, he realized it was in a sling. A sharp twinge shot through his shoulder. He winced. "I was going to say five, but I think I just bumped it up to an eight," he answered hoarsely.

The doctor gently positioned Nate back on the bed, adjusting his arm to an angle that offered immediate relief to the discomfort. "When the bullet entered your chest, it essentially split into two fragments. One ended up about two millimeters from your heart, the other ended up in your shoulder. We removed it, but you're going to need some additional surgery before you can experience the kind of mobility you had before."

The words took a moment to sink in. Nate shot a look to Max, who looked away. He, too, knew the consequences of what the doctor said. Nate's right arm was his shooting arm. If he couldn't qualify on the range, he would be removed from active duty. They both knew fellow officers who had experienced career ending injuries. Putting it into perspective, Nate knew he was lucky to be alive, but the prospect of sitting behind a desk for the rest of his career was not appealing.

"Thank you, doctor," was all Nate could manage to say. But the disappointment in his voice was apparent to everyone in the room.

"All right, everyone," Izzy announced. "He needs rest."

"I'll make sure the orthopedist stops by to explain things to you more completely," the doctor assured him.

"Come on, Mrs. R., let me take you to lunch," Max offered.

Eleanor considered, then turned to Izzy. "Will you take care of my boy while I'm gone?"

"Absolutely," Izzy promised.

Eleanor stood and took Max's proffered arm. "Then I accept your kind offer," she said.

"Don't worry, Nate, I'll be a gentleman," Max assured his partner.

"Why start now?" Nate asked sarcastically.

Max escorted Eleanor out of the room. The doctor offered Nate a reassuring nod and followed them out.

Izzy made one last check and positioned the remote with the call button near his left hand. "Let me know if you need anything."

Nate nodded. Two thoughts swirled in his mind. First, the men who shot him were still at large. And second, he would likely not be able to participate in tracking them down.

In one moment his life had changed direction. The question remaining was where that change would lead him.

CHAPTER SIX

Diane Collins walked up the sloping street toward her apartment building. An overcast sky obscured the full moon, visible only as a bright spot behind the clouds. The threat of rain was in the air, but the streets were still dry. Diane hurried toward her building, worried that she would be caught in the coming downpour before she made it there. She had left her umbrella at home that morning, a decision she was starting to regret.

The Oakley Arms was an older building and lacked the modern amenities of other apartment complexes, but it was within walking distance of her paralegal job at a mid-sized law firm. She enjoyed the work and knowing she wouldn't have to deal with traffic was a big plus. She had previously lived on the other side of town with her boyfriend, but when that relationship ended, she decided to move. So many things in her life had improved when she and Jerry split, though they did remain friends.

The outer door wasn't locked, but to get into the lobby you had to either be buzzed in or use a key. Originally, the building had a doorman and a concierge who accepted and sorted the mail, but now there was a bank of steel mailboxes. She paused to check the one assigned to her apartment. It was empty.

Diane moved on to the inner door, unlocked it and pushed it open. She waited for the door to close and the lock to catch before she moved on. There had been times when she had seen strangers hanging around the front of the building, and the management frequently sent messages to the tenants reminding them not to allow strangers in, or buzz in someone without verifying who they were.

The elevators were ancient, noisy and slow, but they were fairly reliable, especially compared to the old freight elevator she had used when she moved in. She was just grateful she didn't have to climb up ten flights of stairs after a long day. She did a lot of walking at work. Many of the records and filings were electronic these days, but she attended a lot of meetings and made frequent trips to the courthouse.

She was alone on the elevator which allowed her to kick off her shoes and wiggle her toes. Like most nights, she had eaten takeout at the office and was ready to just go to bed and fall asleep.

The doors opened on her floor and Diane stepped out into the hallway, shoes in one hand, the key to her apartment door at the ready in the other.

The door across from her apartment opened as she approached. Rose Walton, Diane's insomniac octogenarian neighbor poked her head out and smiled. Diane suspected that Rose kept her eye pressed against the peephole so she could "run into" Diane at moments like this.

"Oh, hello dear. Working late again?" Rose asked.

"Yes, Mrs. Walton. How was your day?"

"Oh, you know. The usual. I watched my programs. Wrote my letters. Went to the market."

While Rose spoke, Diane unlocked the door to her apartment and slowly opened it, hoping it was a clear sign to Rose that she wanted to keep the conversation short.

"That's nice. I don't mean to be rude, but I really need to get to sleep, long day," Diane said with a friendly smile.

"Is it raining yet?" Rose asked. "The TV has been saying that it was going to rain all day, but I haven't seen a drop yet."

"No, not yet," Diane answered.

"Bad things happen when it rains," Rose added with a note of foreboding.

A flash of lightning lit up the hallway, followed shortly by a clap of thunder that was strong enough to shake the old building.

Rose jumped, put a hand to her chest. "Oh, dear. I guess that answers my question. Good night," she said to Diane, and retreated into her apartment.

Diane took a moment to look out the window at the end of the hallway. Drops of rain started to dot the glass, then all of a sudden, there was a sheet of water sweeping down the pane, followed by more thunder and lightning. It gave Diane an odd chill, as if there was something out there besides the storm.

The apartment was a mix of the old and the new. The classic moldings, tall ceilings, imposing iron radiators and broad wooden framed windows were juxtaposed with modern furnishings and a large, flat screen television. Diane tossed her coat and purse onto a nearby chair and let her shoes fall to the floor. She didn't have the energy to be tidy tonight.

She flicked on the bathroom light. At some recent point in the building's history, the bathrooms were updated with modern fixtures, tubs and vanities. It was one of the things that sold Diane on the apartment. She started the shower at the highest temperature so the room would fill with steam. She enjoyed the sauna-like experience it created. Her bedtime routine began with washing the modest makeup from her face, then brushing her teeth before stripping out of her work clothes and stepping into the shower.

Diane adjusted the temperature to just below scalding and let the water cascade over her. She hated the rain, but loved a hot shower.

After a while, she turned the water off and wrapped herself with a large, soft towel. At the vanity, she reached for some lotion and began applying it to her arms, and neck. She dabbed some on her cheeks, then wiped the mist from the mirror so she could see her face.

She saw something moving behind her.

No, not something, someone.

Standing in the tub was a man. He mouthed something to her.

Diane spun around. Her foot hit a wet patch, and she lost her balance. As she fell, her head smacked against the toilet seat and a moment later she faded to unconsciousness.

CHAPTER SEVEN

Jennifer and Emily entered the lobby of the hospital. Jennifer was carrying a large shopping bag and nudged her reluctant intern to approach the woman stationed at the reception desk.

"Are you visiting someone?" the woman behind the circular station asked.

"Yes," Emily replied. "Nathaniel Raney."

"Oh, the policeman," the woman said. "Are you family?"

"Yes," Emily answered without thinking.

The woman typed the name into her computer and found the room he was in. "It's five-oh-five, dear. Niece?" she asked.

"Excuse me?"

"Are you his niece, dear?"

"Oh, yes. Once removed," she added, then took the visitor passes the woman offered and returned to Jennifer.

Jennifer led Emily to the elevators. She pressed the up button and waited for the first car to arrive. They stepped inside and pushed the button for the fifth floor. Just as the doors were closing an old couple shuffled up to the elevator. The man stuck his cane in between the doors causing them to reopen. "Sorry, this one is full," she told them, then pushed the close button. The couple was confused enough that the doors closed fully this time before they could react.

Jennifer opened the shopping bag and handed Emily a Candy Striper apron and slid into a white lab coat.

"We have guest passes, why do we have to dress up?" Emily asked.

"He'll be more likely to talk if he thinks we're with the hospital."

"That sounds borderline unethical," Emily suggested.

"No, not at all," Jennifer insisted. "The police use deception when interrogating suspects all the time. He'll totally understand."

"Totally," Emily echoed sarcastically.

Jennifer loosened her hair and undid a few buttons on the blouse she wore under her white lab coat. "Well, when you have a Ph.D. we can have a philosophical discussion about the ethics of my research methods."

"Oh, right," Emily replied, "because I'd be a doctor of philosophy as well."

"Another reason I like you," Jennifer added. She slipped on a pair of black-rimmed glasses and pulled a clipboard out from the shopping bag.

The elevator opened, and they stepped out. Jennifer led her assistant confidently through the corridors, heading directly and purposefully toward room five-oh-five.

Nate heard a knock at his hospital room door and looked up to find an attractive blond doctor standing in the doorway. A girl in a pink and white striped smock stood just behind her, somewhat nervously looking up and down the corridor.

"Detective Raney," she said as she walked into the room. "I'm Dr. Daye. How are you feeling today?"

"Well, I have to say I'm feeling good today, Dr. Daye, ready to be on my way."

"Great," said the candy striper with a roll of her eyes, "now we're in a Dr. Seuss book."

The comment made Jennifer and Nate laugh.

"Good to see a positive attitude, I hope I'm not interrupting your lunch," Jennifer said, noticing the tray in front of him.

"More like rescuing me from it," Nate said. He pushed the tray aside with his left hand and sat up straighter in the bed.

"Well," Jennifer continued, "I was hoping to talk to you about your experience." She took a seat next to the bed and set the clipboard on her lap.

Nate seemed confused. "You mean my stay at the hospital?"

"Not exactly. I'm more interested in your experience before you came to the hospital." She consulted something on her clipboard. "It's my understanding that you were clinically dead in the ambulance, and then also while you were being operated on. Did you experience anything unusual?"

Nate regarded Jennifer suspiciously. "I was unconscious. I didn't experience anything."

Jennifer leaned forward. "I'm sure you've heard the stories about people who die and are brought back to life describing a bright light, or momentary contact with relatives who have passed on. They're called near-death experiences."

Nate recalled the dream he had while recovering from his surgery. The bright light, the shadowy figure.

"Sometimes," Jennifer continued, "it's coupled with an out-of-body experience. A sensation of viewing yourself from a distance."

Like when I could see the doctor opening my chest, thought Nate, *or visited fat guy and skinny guy at their hideout.*

Nate shook his head. "No, nothing like that. I remember getting shot, then waking up here in this room. Nothing else."

"It may feel like a dream," she went on. "You may not remember it right away, but it could come back to you. Has anything strange happened since you woke up? Any behaviors that seemed odd, maybe something you weren't aware of at the time, but that now feels out of place?"

Nate remembered how Max and his mother had misheard the first words he said when he was extubated. He clearly remembered asking Max about the case, but Max claimed he had said something about a rabbit eating eggs. *My rabbit ate twenty two Easter eggs,* echoed in Nate's mind. That was strange, but he was reluctant to share that with this doctor sitting at his bedside. "Who did you say sent you?" Nate asked.

The woman looked away for a second, then smiled. "Dr. Cullen," she answered. "You looked like you were going to say something just then," she pressed.

Nate studied her for a moment, then looked at the candy striper, who seemed to be standing guard at the door. "You're not with the hospital, are you?" he asked.

Jennifer sat back, smiled slyly. "I never said I was," she replied.

He thought back over their conversation. That was certainly true. When he had questioned whether she was asking about his hospital stay in general, she had deflected and steered the conversation in another direction.

"What gave me away?" she asked.

Nate shrugged, "A lot of little things. You don't have your name embroidered on your jacket like the other doctors in the hospital. You had to glance over at the whiteboard the nurses use to keep track of whose patient I am when I asked who had sent you. And the candy striper is acting more like a sentry than a volunteer. She never once asked if I wanted a magazine or whatever it is they do. Come to think of it, I don't think the volunteers I have seen wear those striped smocks. Second hand store?"

"You'd be surprised what you can find there," Jennifer answered, almost bragging.

"Who are you really?" he asked.

"Oh, I'm Dr. Jennifer Daye, just like I said."

"Not a medical doctor, though. Psychologist?" he guessed.

"Parapsychologist."

"I didn't see that one coming."

"I teach Anthropology at Cal State Hayward, the candy striper is my undergrad intern, Emily."

"Nice to meet you," Emily said. "Please don't arrest me. She made me do it."

"I'm pretty sure there aren't any laws on the books for impersonating a candy striper," Nate assured her. He turned back to Jennifer. "Sounds like you're a legitimate scientist. What's up with all the bright light and out-of-body questions? Why the interest in this...

what did you call it?"

"Near-death experiences."

"Doesn't seem very scientific," Nate noted.

"Well, as an anthropologist I developed an interest in death."

Nate raised an eyebrow.

"From an academic perspective, not causing it."

"Thanks for making that distinction."

"Every culture has their own mythology and beliefs centered around death and the afterlife. The idea that something of the person—the soul for lack of a better word—continues on after we die is a universal idea. Those types of memes must come from somewhere."

"Well, if you're referring to memes in the Dawkins sense rather than the social media definition, you could make the case that such an idea was inevitable as a way to control populations with the threat of punishment in an afterlife for misdeeds in this life," Nate countered.

Jennifer sat back as if his words had physically pushed her. "I'm impressed. Not many policemen I've met are so well read."

"A habit I picked up from my dad."

"I'd like to meet him sometime."

"Well, if you truly believe in an afterlife, then maybe you will."

Jennifer realized the implication of his reply. "I'm sorry for your loss."

"Fortunately, where he left off, my great-uncle took over."

"See, this is exactly why I wanted to interview you. First, you're a cop so you're trained to observe and take note of things other people might miss. And second, you're a skeptic, so I can get an unfiltered account of what you saw."

"You're forgetting third. Nothing happened to me. No angels singing, no pearly gates, not even the other guy with his pitchfork and brimstone."

Jennifer looked at him. Her lingering gaze made him uncomfortable. "I thought so," she said. "You did see something, but you're embarrassed to admit it."

"Or, I saw nothing and I'm getting a little annoyed by the pesky pseudo-scientist who sneaked into my room under false pretenses."

"Actually," Jennifer said in her defense, "I didn't have any pretenses at all. And there is something you're not telling me."

"No," Nate protested.

"You should do a ride-along with me."

"What?"

"Come with me on an investigation. Looks like you're not going to be chasing bad guys for a while. If I can show you something you can't explain with your skeptic's mind, you tell me what you saw."

"No," Nate repeated.

"Hmm," Jennifer said with a note of disappointment. "You didn't seem like the kind of man who would turn down a challenge."

"Kangaroo!" Emily said.

"Kangaroo?" Nate asked.

"That's our code word for someone is coming," Jennifer explained.

"Kangaroo, kangaroo, kangaroo," Emily repeated with more urgency.

Before they could make a move to leave, Nurse Izzy entered the room.

Jennifer tried to hide her face.

"Sorry to interrupt, Doctor, it's time for Nate's medication." Izzy brought Nate a glass of water and a collection of pills in a small paper cup.

Everyone was silent while Nate took a sip of water, handed the glass back to Izzy, then took the pills and dumped them into his mouth and swallowed. He smiled and handed the empty cup to the nurse. Izzy became aware of the awkward silence. She turned to Jennifer, who did her best to avoid looking her in the eye. Then recognition and annoyance erased the smile on the nurse's face.

"Ms. Daye. You're not allowed to be in here."

"It's Dr. Daye," Jennifer corrected.

"I don't care if it's Pope Daye, you know Dr. Cullen doesn't want you disturbing the patients."

"I'm not disturbing the patients. Tell her, Detective," Jennifer begged of Nate.

"She's disturbing me," Nate said.

Jennifer looked at him, surprised. "I thought we had something, Nate."

"Don't make me call security," warned Izzy.

"All right, we're going." She slipped her clipboard and glasses into the bag and started for the door. Before she left, she turned back to Nate. "The offer still stands. I'd love the opportunity to open your eyes to other possibilities."

"No, thank you," said Nate. "Bye."

"Ms. Daye…" Izzy said with a tone of impatience.

Jennifer shook her head, then left the room, Emily close behind her.

Izzy turned her attention back to Nate. She fluffed his pillow and gave his good shoulder a comforting squeeze. "Sorry about that. She has a nasty habit of sneaking into the hospital and pestering the patients."

"She wasn't really a bother. Interesting woman. Do any of them ever have anything to tell her?"

"You mean that whole 'near-death' thing?" She shrugs. "People sometimes really want to believe, especially after a stay in the ICU. Being close to death makes you hope there's something more."

"What do you think?"

"I'm Catholic. I know I'm going to hell," she said with a wink.

Nate smiled. His mother was right, she was cute, and a little more attentive than she needed to be.

Izzy took a look at his lunch tray. "Are you done with your lunch?"

"Yeah, unless you have a Kobe slider with asiago tucked somewhere in those scrubs."

"No cheeseburgers," she said with a flirtatious smile. "I'll have someone pick up the tray. You should be getting out of here tomorrow, you really should try to eat more."

"I know," Nate said. "Thank you."

Izzy left the room, leaving Nate alone with his thoughts. He was sure that what he remembered was a dream. It had to be. There was no such thing as an afterlife, or souls, or ghosts. We got one shot at this life, and this was it. And he was determined to make the best of it.

The doctors had been conservative in their assessment of his recovery. They were wary to promise him that he would be able to return to active duty, even after the reconstructive surgery that was scheduled for his shoulder. But they didn't know Nate. He would work as hard as he could to get his body back to one hundred percent. He was born to be a cop, and one unlucky bullet wasn't going to stop him.

CHAPTER EIGHT

Diane sat at her desk, typing in changes marked up on a contract by a lawyer with a love of red ink and near illegible handwriting. A dark purple bruise was visible above her right eye. She did her best to cover it with makeup and an adjustment to her hairstyle, but she still had to deal with the well-meaning inquiries from her coworkers. She told them the truth—minus the part about seeing a ghost in her bathroom.

It was obvious to her that the apparition of a young man she saw was a ghost. She was previously agnostic on the subject, but when she had first moved into the Oakley Arms, many of the tenants warned her that there were lost souls tied to brutal incidents in the building's history. But everyone spoke highly of the ghost of the long-time superintendent, old Mr. Shoetensack. They claimed he was the reason the elevators rarely broke down despite their age—except the old freight elevator, though that was apparently installed after he died.

The spirit she saw in her bathroom, however, was not an old man. She only saw him for a moment before losing her footing and knocking herself unconscious, but she was certain he was young, perhaps in his twenties. And she had an impression that he was from a decade long before she was born. Diane was fortunate that she hit the side of her head instead of smashing her face into the toilet bowl. She woke with her hair matted in dried blood. She showered again, discovering that her injury was not serious enough to require medical attention, though it did necessitate a handful of ibuprofen.

She looked at her bruised face in the mirror the next morning and decided to call in sick. The bruise was brightly colored, a deep purple at the center and various shades of red, blue and yellow at the edges. That would have been enough to keep her from making an appearance, but a deep, blinding headache had set in as well. She spent the day lying on her couch with an icepack on her face, the television on as a distraction.

She returned to work the day after and found some coworkers skeptical of the explanation for her injury. A lot of them knew of her ex, Jerry, and his history with the law. He'd never been arrested for anything violent and she certainly never felt physically threatened by him, but regardless of the facts, many of them now looked at her injury wondering if it was the result of a reunion between the estranged couple. Diane didn't blame them, it was what she would have thought if a friend was in a similar situation, and it was oddly much easier to deal with than if she were to tell stories of seeing a ghost.

It was well past midnight. Most of her coworkers had long since left. She only noticed because the cleaning crew had started vacuuming around her. She turned off her computer, locked the files in a drawer and grabbed her coat.

She smiled a goodbye to the woman cleaning the floor and, somewhat reluctantly, headed home.

Diane stretched out the walk between work and her apartment, the dread growing in her as she approached the imposing edifice of her building. The night was clear and that meant the homeless people who claimed this stretch of Pine Street were out, sleeping under tents and tarps.

She paused at the outer doors to the building and looked up at the façade. The entrance was surrounded by a giant stone cornice and a few floors above it an enormous flagpole, with the stars and stripes dangling limply in the still night. Diane took a deep breath and pulled open the door. She checked her mailbox, then placed her key into the lock of the inner door, turned it, and put her hand on the handle to open it.

A chill ran across her arm and down her back. It made her shudder.

She peered through the glass of the door across the lobby to the elevators.

The lobby was empty, but Diane thought she saw a shadow move across the floor even though there was nothing around to cast it. She let go of the door, tossed her key into her purse and pulled out her phone. She dialed a number and put it to her ear. It rang almost eight times before someone answered.

"Hi Julie, I'm really sorry to wake you."

She listened for a moment.

"No, nothing like that. I was just wondering if I could crash on your couch tonight. The power's out at my apartment." Her concern changed to relief. "Thank you. I'll be by in ten minutes. You're a lifesaver. Bye."

Diane stuffed the phone back into her purse and stepped quickly across the mailbox foyer and out the main doors, moving briskly as she put the dread of returning to her haunted apartment behind her.

CHAPTER NINE

The elevator opened and Jennifer side-stepped around the men laden with boxes and furniture as they walked by her. She spotted Dave and Emily and walked up to them. "What is going on?" she asked.

"Apparently we're moving," Emily replied.

"Why?" she asked.

"Orders from the dean," Dave answered.

"You never called him back," Emily scolded.

"I was going to," Jennifer said. "Why didn't you stop them?" Jennifer asked Dave.

"Because," he said, pointing at the phalanx of large, burly movers as his explanation.

"Well, I'll just have a word with Dean Patterson," Jennifer said. She pulled out her cell phone and noticed her voicemail already had several messages from her department head. "Or maybe I'll just call him later."

"The talk is they're moving Crenshaw in," Dave mentioned.

"He's been here all of six months. I have tenure. And classes to teach. Where am I supposed to do office hours?" she asked.

"Maybe they're giving Crenshaw your classes, too," Emily guessed.

"They can't do that. It's the middle of the semester."

"I think Dean Patterson is punishing you," Dave suggested. "All the ghostbusting stuff is coming back on him. He's trying to get you to fall in line."

"That's ridiculous. This is a university. It's supposed to be a place of academic inquiry."

Dave shrugged. "I guess he doesn't like the questions you're asking."

Two movers exited the office carrying the poster of Harry Houdini.

"Careful with that!" Jennifer warned. "Where are you taking it?"

Another mover answered her question by taking a folded piece of paper from a back pocket and handing it to her.

"B-one-eleven? Where's that?"

"B is for basement," Emily told her.

"Oh," Jennifer said. Then, looking on the bright side, "Well, at least it will be cool in the summer."

Emily shook her head and went into the office to make sure her personal belongings didn't get crated up and carted away.

"Should I start looking for another adviser?" Dave asked.

Jennifer looked at him as if he was certifiably insane. "Of course not. This is just a little setback. I'm going to land a grant that will set us up for the next ten years. This would be the worst time for you to find someone else."

"It kinda feels the exact opposite of that."

"Dave, trust me, when have I ever let you down?"

Dave started to speak, but Jennifer cut him off.

"Come on, let's go check out our new digs," she suggested, then followed her poster of Houdini into the elevator. Dave hurried after her, reluctant to be left on his own.

CHAPTER TEN

Max pulled up to the curb on the quiet street in front of an old two-story bungalow. Nate looked out the passenger window at the home he hadn't seen in over a week.

The house had once belonged to his Great-Uncle Bill and Great-Aunt Lillian. They never had children of their own, but judging from the size of the place, they had at one time at least hoped for a big family. Nate and his cousins had filled the extra rooms on weekends and extended summer stays, giving their parents a needed respite and Bill and Lillian an occasional house full of children. The way home values had skyrocketed over the last couple of decades, Nate could have never afforded such a residence on his detective's salary. Even without a mortgage, the property taxes were straining his budget, but selling wasn't something he'd even consider while Uncle Bill was still alive. Besides, there were a lot of great family memories in the big old house.

Nate's mother had insisted on keeping her own home and even offered to let Nate have his old room, but he did not buy into his generation's practice of living with their parents. His father had instilled in him a sense of self worth and self respect that he carried with him. When Uncle Bill had to check into an assisted living facility a few years back, he let Nate move in and take over the taxes and utilities. That allowed Nate to take care of some of his mother's expenses in addition to his own.

Nate sat in the passenger seat, staring out the window, his mind somewhere else.

Max couldn't imagine how his partner felt, but he knew if anyone could come back from this, it was Nate.

"Thanks for sticking close to the speed limit," Nate said to Max.

Max smiled. "I promised Eleanor I'd get you home safely."

"You know," Nate said, "it's kind of weird that you call my mother by her first name."

"I'm good with moms."

"It doesn't help for me to hear that."

"What? She's nice. I'd totally—"

Nate cut him off. "Okay, let's stop this conversation right there. Thanks for the ride."

"No problem. I was going to say I'd totally like her to be my mom, but that would make us brothers, and I already have too many brothers."

"I should've called an Uber." Nate reached over with his good arm to try to open the door.

"Wait, let me get that," Max said as he jumped out the driver's side and ran around to assist Nate.

Nate somewhat resented the fact that he needed help, but when he got to his feet and felt momentarily dizzy, he realized that he was not going to be able to just pick up where he left off. It was going to take time. And how he was going to spend that time was what he needed to figure out.

Max walked him up the path to the front door and collected the mail from the overflowing box affixed to the wall next to it. Nate managed to work the lock successfully with his left hand and they entered to an immaculately clean living room.

"Looks like the maid's been here," Max commented.

"I don't have a maid."

"Oh, so the whole neat freak thing extends all the way back to your crib."

"You know, it's not that hard to do, Max. You just put things away when you're done with them instead of leaving them in a pile on your desk."

"I like having everything within reach," Max said defensively. "So, what can I do for you? Need any groceries? Bring some of the boys by later for poker? I draw the line at helping you out in the bathroom."

"I'm fine," Nate insisted. "I'm just going to follow the doctor's advice and get some rest."

"You still plan on stopping by the office tomorrow?"

"Why, you guys got some welcome back thing planned?"

Max was uncharacteristically silent.

Nate smiled. "Yeah, I'll be there."

"Great. Call me if you need anything."

"Thanks, Max. Really. You're a good partner."

"Aw, shucks, Nate. You've never told me that before."

"Still on the pain meds. I'll forget and deny I ever said it by tomorrow."

Max laughed. "Okay, boss. See you tomorrow."

"Wait. Did you bring it?" Nate asked.

There was a pause before the younger man answered. "I was hoping you'd forget about it."

"I just want to get up to speed. I need something to do."

Max nodded, understanding. "It's in the car. I'll be right back."

"Thanks."

Max nodded and dashed back out to the car.

Nate walked slowly into the kitchen and opened the refrigerator. He took a mental inventory of its contents, noting the produce he'd have to replace after over a week in the hospital. He reached for a beer, then remembered he was still on medications and decided against the risk of mixing alcohol with whatever narcotics were keeping the pain in check. He instead grabbed a bottle of Perrier, managed to get it open with his left hand and took it to the couch in the living room.

Max popped back in and tossed a thick file on the coffee table in front of Nate. "Here you go partner. If the Captain asks, you stole it from me while I was rescuing some orphans from a fire."

"Orphans. Nice touch."

"Hey, I'm a hard-nosed cop with a heart of gold." Max pushed a fist out and Nate, who usually shied away from what he considered such a juvenile replacement for a handshake, bumped it with his own.

"I appreciate it," Nate said sincerely.

"Oh, that reminds me. I almost forgot." He reached into his pocket and pulled out Nate's watch. "The robbers left this behind. They got your wallet and gun, but this fell out when the skinny guy dropped his bag."

Nate took the watch and turned it over. On the back was a simple inscription. "Welcome to the force. Uncle Bill."

"I appreciate you bringing this back. I owe you one."

"Don't think I'm not keeping track," Max said. He let himself out.

Nate leaned over and opened the file. He flipped to the photos first. Most of them were evidence shots of shell casings and broken merchandise. Then there were a series of different angles on the pool of blood that Nate left behind. He closed the folder and pushed it away. There would be time for that later. He couldn't focus right now. He hadn't had a decent night's sleep since the shooting.

On the mantle above the fireplace were several photos that helped anchor Nate. One was of him with his father when he was a teenager about a year before his dad passed away. There were no signs of the brain cancer that would take him all too early. His father was an engineer and had encouraged Nate to keep his eye on the burgeoning activity in Silicon Valley. His advice led to some strategic stock purchases. He had a nice little nest egg thanks to his father's foresight.

Another was of his graduation from the police academy, his mother on one side, his Great-Uncle Bill on the other, wearing his old uniform from when he was on the force.

Nate had always been drawn to law enforcement and believed he would have made his way to that career regardless of whether his grandfatherly great-uncle had been a policeman as well. But Uncle Bill's stories of his days on the force, the "hard old days" he used to call them, before the age of DNA and computers and even hand-held radios, had sealed the deal.

When Bill retired from the force, he had hung out his shingle as a private eye for a while. Nate wondered if he might follow in those footsteps as well. Maybe going private was what he might need to do if he didn't recover from this injury.

He tentatively lifted his right arm, wincing from the pain that shot from his shoulder up his neck to the base of his skull. Riding a desk was not in his character. He'd rather collect whatever disability benefits he'd accrued and strike out on his own than end up in the records room, or some other paper-pushing job.

But that decision was a long way off. He had at least two surgeries to look forward to according to his orthopedist, and at least six months before they'd know anything for sure. All he had to do was not make things worse.

For now, that meant taking it easy.

He grabbed the remote for the television and found a midday local news show, but after a few minutes of stories about the growing homeless problem, the need for new taxes to fight climate change and the obligatory feel-good story, he fell asleep.

CHAPTER ELEVEN

In the dream—and he knew it was a dream right away—Nate was back at the scene of the shooting. It didn't feel exactly like the dream he had during his surgery, though. This time, he wasn't just standing among the shoppers, he was watching from a different point of view. From above.

He could clearly see the layout of the store. How the robbers had positioned themselves so that the store patrons were between them and Max.

Then he saw the young man scuffle with the thin man. He could even see himself willing the man to back off. Nothing was worth his life. Things could be replaced.

But the young man was headstrong, emotional, unstoppable.

Nate could see himself watch the paperweight fly through the air and hit the skinny man in the back. He knew at that moment what the reaction would be and that he had only a matter of seconds—no, less than a second—to react. He sprinted at the young man as if launched from the starting blocks of a hundred yard dash.

He tried to tell himself to stay low. To tackle the man at his waist, to cut his legs out from under him, to stay out of the path of the bullet. But he knew it was too late. The bullet was going to hit the young man in the chest. The only thing he could do was put his own body in its path.

Nate watched it all happen in slow motion. Even though he was watching, he could feel the sharp, burning pain of the bullet enter his chest as his body took the place of the young man's.

Then the pain was gone, and he was just an observer again.

He saw the thin man taking aim at the young man.

He saw the fat man stop him and say something in his ear. The words were loud and clear in Nate's dream. As if it was the only sound in the room.

"Leave him. Get in the catty."

Get in the catty?

Nate woke up.

It was dusk.

The dream hung on the edge of his consciousness. More than a dream. A memory.

Only, that wasn't quite right. He couldn't have remembered anything that happened after he was shot. The only thing he could recall was the pain. Max's face leaning over him. The lights of the ambulance. A cacophony of sounds, but he was absolutely certain that he never heard one gunman called the other "catty."

No, he didn't call him catty. He said, "Get in the catty."

Get in the catty.

Get in the Caddy? Cadillac?

Then he remembered the echos of another dream. The one he had when he was waking up from his anesthesia. That weird moment when he thought he was outside and then inside the robbers' hideout. Somewhere in The 'Loin, he thought. Which was crazy.

But wasn't there something outside the house? A car in the driveway?

A Cadillac?

Now it made a bit of sense to Nate. He had fallen asleep thumbing through the file Max had given him. His mind had married those last waking thoughts with the dream of the robbers' hideout. He saw a Cadillac in his dream, and his mind had created dialog for him.

Dreams could do that.

He stood and immediately sat back down again. He felt light-headed. He felt hungry.

Nate rose again, more slowly this time. He stood still for a moment until he felt his balance return. He went into the kitchen and fixed himself a dinner of canned soup and a sandwich. He wanted to open a bottle of wine. There was a nice Pinot Noir that would be perfect for such a casual dinner, but the meds...

After he ate, he went into the bathroom and organized the various prescriptions the hospital pharmacy had sent him home with. He was especially careful with the pain medication. He had known fellow officers on the force who had fallen under the influence of opioids and it was not a battle he wanted to take on. He swallowed the combination of analgesics and antibiotics with a glass of tepid water.

It was a challenge completing the rest of his bedtime routine with his left hand. Funny how something as simple as brushing his teeth became a test of his dexterity. Keeping his right arm still and in the sling made it even more difficult.

Undressing was particularly hard. He managed to get down to his underwear and stopped there. Normally he'd slip into some sleeping pants and a fresh t-shirt, but he'd already struggled to take off the shirt the nurse had helped him slip on at the hospital. He figured that was enough stretching and bending for his battered shoulder for one day.

Nate lay in the bed for a while, but sleep wouldn't come. He got up, went to the living room and gathered up the file on the robbery and what the police were classifying as his own attempted murder. He brought it to the dining room table and began to lay out pages from the file along with photographs and copies of handwritten statements. He found a floor plan of the store and attached little sticky flags on it, the type you'd see pointing to the parts of a contract you were supposed to sign or initial. He always kept a supply of them nearby, he found them tidier than scribbling in the margins as Max often did—when he could be bothered to read the reports.

Max claimed that it was much more efficient for him to let Nate digest the material and summarize it for him. Nate didn't complain. This was the part of police work he enjoyed. Pouring over the details, finding the inconsistencies, the hidden clues. It was like a puzzle.

So many of his colleagues, Max included, wanted to be out on the streets, banging down doors, putting the squeeze on snitches. But detectives rarely did more than ask a lot of questions, read a lot of reports and write even more.

The robbery was the most action Nate and Max had seen in years. His days of chasing junkies or working crowd control at one protest or another were over. He kept himself fit, but not because he expected to get into a fight with a suspect, or do some crazy parkour chase through a Knob Hill construction site.

Nate started by reading the reports submitted by Max and the other officers from the scene. These included interviews with all the witnesses inside the store—more than thirty of them—and employees from a few neighboring shops who thought they might have seen two men in long, loose coats hurry by carrying a large duffel bag. What was conspicuously missing was any information about what kind of car the men had left in or if they even left in a car. They could've hopped on a bus. It wouldn't be the first time criminals had used public transportation as their getaway ride.

The reason for this became apparent when Nate came across an addendum to one of the reports describing two long coats found stuffed into recycling bins two doors down from the gift shop. It was clear the men had ditched the overcoats and likely donned caps or sunglasses or some other accessories that changed their appearance. Possibly the duffel converted to a wheeled configuration, so they'd look like a couple of tourists trying to catch a ride to the airport. Maybe one of them got the car and picked up the second robber down the street. Or maybe they just strolled down the street with thousands of dollars in stolen goods, cash and saleable identities and no one paid them any mind at all. People's attention was so diverted to phone screens and other distractions that canvassing for eyewitnesses was an exercise in futility.

But occasionally there was someone who saw something that was relevant—though not initially recognized as such. So, he poured through every word of every witness statement, cursing when each one ended with unasked questions that were relevant to the case. Of course with hindsight, it was easy to fault the interviewers for not following up. At the time the statements were taken the fact that the robbers had discarded their coats was not yet known, so they focused on the description Max had provided. It would have taken mere seconds for the robbers to slip out of their coats and shoulder holsters. The fact that the guns were not also found led Nate to believe that they took those with them, likely stuffing them into the duffel with the loot. But the coats were easily balled up and dumped into a nearby bin. No one would take notice of someone throwing something away.

However, they were likely wearing the coats when they arrived, by whatever mode of transportation they had used, to hide their weapons. And they had strode along a busy commercial street. There were security cameras on that block, some belonging to a bank that had a shot of part of the street, but a review of those had shown nothing in the moments leading up to the robbery. And the cameras inside the gift shop were low-res and only told them what they already knew.

Nate was convinced there was a shot of the suspects somewhere, in the background of someone's selfie, or in the periphery of the dashcam of a passing car. The police had already put out a general request for information from witnesses who might have been in the area, but those never reached more than a small percentage of the people in the city. Regardless, he'd suggest to the Captain to make a specific plea for dashcam footage from anyone driving down that avenue between those hours on that day and previous days. The men had to have cased the street, taken note of where the blind spots were where they could do their quick change without being on camera. And if she complained about manpower, he'd volunteer to do it. He'd be sidelined for several months at least, longer depending on the outcomes of his coming shoulder surgeries.

He started his list and could sense Max rolling his eyes at that moment. But, lists worked. Nate always said Santa Claus would make a great detective because he made his list and checked it twice. Max countered that Saint Nick would be a great detective because he sees you when you're sleeping and knows when you're awake.

The list started on a legal pad. Nate liked having the extra three inches to work on. He started off with the suspects. What he knew about them. The physical description, things they said and then a list of questions about them. Were they local, or from out of town? Was this a onetime heist, or part of a spree? Had they done the same type of robbery elsewhere in the city? The state? The country?

Nate found he was able to write with his right hand as long as he didn't move his arm. The constraint caused him to twist his entire body as he scrawled his list down the legal pad until he realized it was just easier to move the pad.

He started a second list inventorying all the evidence and witness statements that seemed at all potentially relevant. Normally, he would be able to coordinate the officers who were doing the initial canvassing and give them some direction on the type of questions they should be asking. They would have been instructed to call him in immediately if they came across anyone who had anything resembling the type of information Nate was looking for. But this time around, he had to rely on Max organizing those initial interviews. And he was obviously distracted with Nate's condition and the fact that there were two armed and dangerous fugitives on the loose.

The results were substantially below Nate's expectations, but he wasn't going to be hard on anyone for it. It was a tough situation. He made tick marks next to the names of witnesses he'd want to question himself. The passage of time and the right questions could often reveal important information that initially seemed irrelevant. What he didn't include in either of his lists were the details of the strangely vivid dreams he had experienced. Those he knew were inventions of his subconscious. While he'd often had revelations on cases after going to sleep thinking about a case, this was not the same thing. It was different, strange. And that, in Nate's mind, made it something not to be trusted.

He spent some time going over the photographs. Initially, seeing the bloodstain on the store's floor where he had been shot was difficult. It was a reminder of how reckless he had been. If it had been Max instead of himself launching his body into the path of a bullet, he would have chewed out the younger detective with a furious tirade about taking chances. But having been in that situation where his instincts just took over and squashed any rational thought or analysis, he knew that anger would have been misplaced.

Nate put aside the fact that it was his own blood smeared on the floor and analyzed the photographs as he would any other crime scene. He wasn't sure what he was looking for. There was little to discover in any regard. The blood was smeared and had been trampled by several people, including Max and the paramedics. The robbers hadn't been anywhere near him at the time, so it wasn't relevant to them in any manner except that the bullet fragments the doctors had pulled out of his chest might identify the gun used if one was ever found.

Then he realized what was nagging at him. Why he was spending so much time looking at those photos. When he viewed the wide shot, he realized that when he tried to get up, he was facing Max. He was facing the rear of the gift shop. His back was to the door. There was no way he could have seen at any point what the men were doing when they left or known if either said anything. This confirmed in his mind that the dream was indeed a fantasy, wishful thinking on the part of his subconscious that he held some critical piece of evidence in some dark corner of his memory.

No, that was clearly not possible. He actually felt relieved.

Nate checked his watch. The light outside had long ago faded from the dimness of dusk to the blackness of night and he was surprised to find it was closing in on three a.m. The revelation unleashed a wave of fatigue. He stepped back from the table and took in the collage of evidence and lists and sticky notes he'd been working on for hours. It felt good to be doing something. All those days in a hospital bed had left him anxious. Now, with a sense of accomplishment at the front of his mind, he found sleep came easily, and he drifted off and did not dream of getting shot.

CHAPTER TWELVE

Dave sat at a small table that served as his desk and sorted the contents of a file box. There were several dozen other similar boxes stacked behind him. A light bulb hung above him from a cord, barely giving clearance to Dave's head and he could feel the heat of it on his forehead.

Emily sat cross-legged in an old executive office chair that swallowed her up, reading a book and occasionally jotting notes down on a laptop perched precariously on one of the arm rests. The cracked leather was patched in places by duct tape.

"Aren't you going to help me?" Dave asked.

"I have to study," Emily replied.

"And I have a thesis to research and write."

"Yeah, so why are you sorting through all those old files?"

"Dr. Daye lost her space in the archives." He leafed through a stack of photos, flipped them over. "Jeez, she's got stuff from ten different incidents in this box. This isn't a filing system, it's a hoard."

"You can always say no to her," Emily suggested.

"Yeah, right. You can, but every time I try I end up doing what I said I wouldn't plus half a dozen other things."

"Like organizing all her old files?" Emily asked.

Dave screwed up his face and mimicked Emily's question in a whiny voice, "Like organizing all her old files?" He dropped the file he was looking at into its box. "Why doesn't she ask you to do this?

You like doing research."

The lights went out. The only illumination was a dim glow from Emily's laptop.

"Great," Dave muttered. "We're stuck down here in the musty, dusty dark and I'll bet she's sitting at a Starbucks sipping a seven dollar coffee."

Then there was a sound that raised the hair on the back of Dave's neck, an unearthly screech.

"What the hell was that?" he asked, a note of fear creeping into his voice.

"Pipes," Emily answered, unfazed.

"That didn't sound like a pipe." Dave fished his phone out of his pocket and switched the camera flash into flashlight mode. He started scanning the perimeter of their area.

The basement office was nestled among a network of water, steam and sewage pipes. There were also old steel filing cabinets packed together like shipping containers at a dock, with broken bits of chairs, desks and tables stacked on top of them. It was like a Sargasso Sea of obsolete office furniture.

They shared the space with the occasional building engineer and what Dave estimated to be at least twenty rats. Rats the size of cats, as he described them. No one else ever saw them. And the traps he laid went unsprung.

Emily had another explanation.

Pipes.

They were everywhere. And they each had their own particular noises as various fluids at varying temperatures rushed around in them. The sounds didn't seem to bother Emily, but Dave found them unnerving and distracting. Ironically it was more comforting to blame it all on a population of giant, invisible rats.

"Is there a fuse box around here?"

"I think I saw some electrical stuff in the back corner," Emily offered.

From her tone, Dave had no idea if she was being helpful or sarcastic but decided to put his faith in the former and picked his way through a random placement of shelves until he found what looked like some sort of metal electrical box with a large lever on one side. The lever was in the off position. He reached out to touch it, but then his paranoia held him back. He pulled his arm back up into the sleeve of his sweatshirt and used it as a thumb-less mitten, then pushed the lever back to the on position.

A nearby light came on.

Standing at the edge of its cone of illumination was a man, his face shrouded in shadow.

Dave was surprised and opened his mouth to ask who he was and what he wanted. But before he could, the man stepped forward. He had the head of a pig.

"Oink," grunted the pig-man.

Dave screamed and backed up into a shelf. A dusty stack of empty boxes fell on him and he collapsed to the floor. "Who are you? What do you want?" Dave screamed.

Emily walked over to see what was going on. She saw Dave on the floor, then looked over at the pig-man. "Hey, Bits," she said to him. "You finally found us, huh?"

The pig-man took off the latex mask, revealing the face of a skinny, twenty-something guy with red hair and a specked band of freckles across his cheeks. "How did you know it was me?" Bartholomew "Bits" Bigelow asked.

Emily cast a glance down at his shoes. He was wearing moccasins, with white sweat socks.

Bits looked down at his feet. "Oh," he said.

"Besides, you're too skinny to be a real pig-man," Emily added.

"I could be a pig-man who was down here, starving for years," Bits suggested.

"Oh, that's where all the rats went."

"Ha, ha," Dave said, getting up from the floor and dusting himself off. "Very funny, but I knew it was you."

"You did not."

"You didn't," Emily confirmed.

"You guys are going to miss me when I graduate," Dave said as he made his way back to the file sorting table. He knew better than to get into a three-way conversation with Bits and Emily.

"This place is awesome," Bits said, looking around.

"Yeah, I know. Doc Daye's not a fan, though. She's working on getting us something less subterranean," Emily replied.

"Where is she?" Bits asked. "She asked me to meet her here."

"She probably wants you to set the place up with WiFi. There are absolutely no bars down here. It's like the middle ages."

"The nineties?" Bits joked.

They walked back toward the main office area. Off in its own little nook was Jennifer Daye's workspace. Her Harry Houdini poster was propped up against the back wall hiding the pipes and dusty masonry. The Mysterious Professor poster was positioned as it had been in their previous office, across from Houdini.

The wooden desk from her upstairs office was situated directly in front of it. The moving men didn't have it on their manifest, but Jennifer was able to talk them into bringing it down with the rest of her belongings and files, gleeful at the rage she imagined Crenshaw would display when he found a folding table in its place.

"You guys got a fiber optic line down here?" Bits asked.

"I don't think so," answered Emily. "We do have a phone line."

"Yeah, that won't do." Bits inspected the conduits that led to a sparse arrangement of electrical outlets. "I might be able to piggyback a signal on the power lines. You should have some pretty decent bandwidth if I plug you directly into the main switch."

"Sweet," Emily said. "I hate it when I have lag on Fortnite."

"Hey, if you're interested, I have a build of the game with some cheats built in."

"We'll talk later. I have mid-terms. Can't get caught up in any time-eating battle royales just now."

"I admire your restraint," Bits said. Emily knew the older guy had a crush on her, but he wasn't really her type. If she could ever figure what that was exactly.

"Great news everybody!" announced Jennifer as she entered the "office," carrying a cardboard tray populated with coffee cups.

"You got us out of this death trap?" Dave guessed, hopeful.

"No, not yet." She held up the tray. "I have coffee for everyone."

Emily and Bits each helped themselves to the cup marked with their name. Dave reluctantly approached and took the one for him. He sipped at it, then grimaced. "Yuck, is that Stevia?" he asked.

"It's better for you than sugar," Jennifer told him. She took her cup to her desk, sat down and took a sip. "You'll thank me for it when you're eighty and don't have diabetes." She noticed Bits staring at her. "Hey, Bits. Welcome to our office cave."

"Yeah, very cool. Internet?" he asked.

"Internet, and how are you coming on those new speaker boxes?"

"Oh, I gave up on those."

"You did? I need those."

"No, you don't. I've got something better." He handed her what looked like a small ring box.

"For me?" Jennifer said. "This is so sudden, Bits. You haven't even met my parents."

"Just open it," he said, unamused.

Jennifer opened the small box and found what looked like one of a pair of Bluetooth earpieces inside. "Explain," she said, looking at Bits.

"Well, it looks like a Bluetooth earpiece, and it is, essentially, but instead of connecting to your phone, it connects to the box. You can have a bunch of them all synced up. And I wrote a new noise suppression algorithm so you won't get an earful of static, only the audio patterns that represent possible DVs."

"Yes," Jennifer said, looking at Bits longingly, "I will marry you."

"Careful, he'll take you up on that," Emily warned.

Bits blushed.

"This is spectacular," Jennifer said. "Great job, Bits."

"You can also sync the feed with the video recordings. Oh, and it does connect to your phone as well."

"Great. Now all we need is a good case to investigate. I thought we'd be getting more calls after the Palace Theater piece in the paper."

Bits looked down at her desk phone. He reached over, unplugged the cable from one socket and moved it to another. The phone's display came to life, booted up and then rang.

"Oh," Jennifer said in surprise. "That's better." She looked to Emily, who rolled her eyes, and answered the phone.

"Dr. Daye's office." She listened for a while, then put the mouthpiece of the phone against her shoulder. "Do you want to do the Moe Hogan Podcast? They saw the article in the paper and want to know if you'll come by for an interview."

"A podcast?" Jennifer asked suspiciously.

"Moe Hogan?" Bits asked. "Holy shit, that guy's got like two million subscribers."

"Yeah, even I've heard of him," Dave added.

Jennifer shrugged. "Okay. When?"

Emily put the phone back to her ear. "When?" She listened a moment. "Tonight. Six o'clock-ish."

"What does my calendar look like?" Jennifer asked.

Emily put the phone to her shoulder again. "It's a big piece of paper with a grid on it that hangs on the wall."

Jennifer raised an unamused eyebrow.

"You're free," Emily confirmed.

"Then yes."

"Yes," Emily said into the phone. "Yeah, I don't have a pen on me. Just email it over. Okay, thanks."

"This might be the kind of thing that will help get the word out and get my research into high gear."

"Yeah," confirmed Dave, "it's also the kind of thing that's going to leave us stuck in this dungeon."

Jennifer ignored Dave's pessimism. "I should probably listen to some of his podcasts to prepare."

"You can watch them on YouTube," Emily suggested.

She turned to Bits. "How long until we get WiFi down here?"

"I can probably sneak in a patch to the main switch tonight."

"Great. I'll be at Starbucks if you need me."

She got up from behind the desk and wove her way toward the

freight elevator leaving her faithful staff behind.

"Do you think Moe will ask her to smoke pot with him?" Emily asked Bits.

"Hell, yeah. He asked the Governor."

"Really? I gotta download that one."

CHAPTER THIRTEEN

Diane lit the bundle of dried herbs and the smoke quickly filled the apartment with the overpowering scent of sage. She was grateful she heeded the advice of the woman at the shop to take the batteries out of her smoke detectors. Once the white cloud was delivered to every corner of the apartment, she left the remainder of the bundle to smolder in a clay bowl. She pulled some crystals from a small paper bag and started placing pairs of pink and black rocks on the window sills throughout the apartment, including the small window in the bathroom.

It was the first time Diane had been back at her place in a while for anything more than grabbing a change of clothes. Even though her friend would never admit it, Diane knew she had worn out her welcome on Julie's couch.

She had stopped by a local New Age store that specialized in the spiritual and occult. The owner did not seem phased when Diane explained her situation. In fact, she seemed to be familiar with the ghosts of the Oakley Arms—though in her experience, they were mostly benign. Nevertheless she showed Diane a selection of items known to repel spirits and encourage them to move on from a particular location. Most of it seemed like nonsense to Diane, but on the other hand, until a week ago when she had seen an actual ghost with her own eyes, she thought psychics and mediums were mostly frauds and scammers.

Now, she didn't quite know what to believe. The shop she visited was highly rated on Yelp, so Diane decided to put her faith in the unconventional wisdom on the subject, and educate herself, hoping to better discern the truth from the fiction.

She settled in on the couch wrapped up in a crocheted afghan. She grabbed her phone off the coffee table, tapped it awake and scanned the news feed. She had watched the Hollywood version of a few supposedly "true stories," but none of them seemed true to Diane's experience. The ghost she saw was not interested, it seemed, in possessing her or throwing things around her apartment. When she thought back to that night he didn't seem threatening, but rather concerned.

But the mere fact that he was in her apartment was what disturbed her. Moving was not an option. She had almost nine months left on her lease and there was a strict subletting clause to prevent Airbnb rentals. Hopefully the sage and crystals would have the advertised effect, but just that one encounter had already changed the way she lived.

Diane read through a few links to stories about different paranormal encounters. There were a lot of reported hauntings in San Francisco. Many of them were attributed to the Gold Rush, and the Great Quake, and of course Alcatraz. It struck her that so many hauntings were associated with famous people and events.

There were a lot of YouTube videos that had caught her attention as well. In this era of special effects on your phone, she was wary of almost all the shadowy photos that claimed to represent the presence of spirits. There were so many self-styled "ghost hunters" out there purporting to have hard evidence of the existence of the supernatural.

All Diane wanted was to be able to sleep through the night without waking at the sound of every creak and groan of the old building that she previously found charming and even soothing.

A notification at the top of her screen caught her attention. It was an alert that a new episode of the Moe Hogan Show was streaming live right now. The guest was a parapsychologist. It was a name she had seen a few times in the dozens of stories she had read over the last week.

Dr. Jennifer Daye.

Diane clicked on the view button and the YouTube app opened. She grabbed the television remote, turned on the set and switched the input to the little dongle she had bought a while back to be able to watch stuff on her television rather than the tiny screen of her phone. She tapped on the casting icon and after a couple seconds, the independent podcast came to life on the big screen. She enjoyed the casual nature of Moe Hogan's show. It was just two, sometimes three people talking around a table. It had started out as an audio only show, capitalizing on Moe's celebrity and the audience he had built up as a stand-up comedian. Just a few friends joking around, exchanging stories and debating various topics.

As the popularity of the show grew, so did the quality of the people who appeared on it. Moe was a sincerely curious person, who was friendly and congenial with anyone anywhere on the political or socio-economic spectrum. He had a knack for finding something interesting to talk about with Nobel Prize-winning scientists or conspiracy theory talk radio hosts or athletes, entertainers and fellow comedians. But it wasn't like the talk shows on television. The podcast medium allowed for a long form presentation that often lasted two or three hours. There were no commercials—except for the occasional sponsors pitch at the beginning of the show or product placement. His audience had grown from the thousands to the millions, rivaling many cable television shows. And now thanks to a tiny thumb-drive sized device plugged into one of the sockets on her television, Diane could watch it in stereo sound and hi-def video.

The show began with Moe thanking his sponsors and introducing his guest for the next couple hours, parapsychologist Jennifer Daye.

"Dr. Daye, welcome to the show."

"Please, call me Jennifer," she said with a disarming smile.

"Okay, Jennifer," Moe replied, just as charming. "I'm so glad you're here. I've been reading about you and your investigations for years. But I have to say, the one about the Palace Theater was a little different. You actually debunked a haunting."

"Well, I would say that most of the cases I investigate turn out to not be supernatural or paranormal in nature."

"Really?"

"Yes, cases with genuine ghosts, or apparitions as most of us call them, are relatively rare—at least the type that people associate with Hollywood movies and TV shows."

"So, no Poltergeist type kidnappings of young girls through the television."

She laughed. "No, nothing like that. But that is a cool movie."

"In the top ten scariest movies, ever," Moe agreed. "But before we get into all that 'Ghostbusters' stuff, tell me about you. Did you grow up fascinated with ghosts and the supernatural?"

"No, not really. I was a pretty typical kid. Played with dolls, liked boy bands—still do—loved books. As I got older I became fascinated with history and later anthropology. I stole my brothers Legos and built a model of Stonehenge. I idolized Mary Leakey—"

"Right, she and her husband found like some crazy old human ancestor," Moe interrupted.

"She was amazing. I watched and read everything I could find about her. A lot of it was old PBS and BBC documentaries. It was a little confusing to my parents that my hero had died in the early seventies."

"That is a little strange, Jennifer."

"It was. When I dressed up as her for Halloween, most people thought I was Jane from Tarzan."

"Yeah, I don't think they sell Mary Leakey costumes at Walmart."

Jennifer smiled. "No, I had to cobble it together with stuff I found at thrift shops."

"But it stuck with you."

"It did. When it came time for college, there was no question that I was going to be an anthropologist. I was going to make some Earthshaking discovery like Mary Leakey, and someone would make PBS and BBC documentaries about me."

"Well, will a podcast interview do?"

Jennifer looked around, nodded, "Yeah, this is good. I have arrived."

Moe laughed again. "And we're glad you arrived here. Anyway, did you do any of that dusting bones with paintbrushes in the desert stuff?"

"Hardly. Turns out anthropology is not that exciting."

"But the PBS and BBC documentaries…"

"Few and far between. Turns out most of the anthropologists just read what other anthropologists have written and try to poke holes in it. It seems we've found most of the old stuff people have left lying around already. King Tut's tomb has been opened and all the ancient hominids have been dug up. I was fortunate enough to be at a school with a decent anthropology archive and I started digging through it looking for some longstanding theory I could poke holes in."

"Did you find it?"

"No. Turns out you can only look at the birth of agriculture so many ways. But what I did find was this sort of common theme throughout pretty much every culture I studied."

"Which was?"

"Death."

"I should've seen that coming."

"I know a woman down in Los Angeles who says she can."

"Sounds like she's a lot of fun at dinner parties. 'Thank you for a lovely time, I'd say I'm looking forward to seeing you again, but that's not going to happen.'"

Jennifer laughed. "Yeah, she can be a bit of a downer."

"Well, what do you mean by death? Obviously we all die. And I'm guessing every culture has something to say about that."

"What's interesting is how similar they are. How many independent cultures came to have a belief in an afterlife. The Egyptians, the Greeks, the Chinese, Native Americans, the Mayans, the Norse. Eventually that belief evolved into the concepts of Heaven and Hell that most people in Islam and Christianity are familiar with. But each one encompasses the idea that some part of us goes on after death."

"Wow, I never thought of it like that. That's pretty interesting."

"Yeah, I thought so, too. So, that became my thesis. How this near universal conviction came to be. What was the evidentiary basis for it?"

"Did you get any resistance for tackling the subject from that point of view?"

Jennifer took a deep breath and sighed. "Well, a bit. And by a bit I mean I was almost universally shut down."

"But there is a Ph.D. after your name."

"Yes, I did eventually find an adviser willing to work with me on the topic. I spent more than two years doing the research. I finally got to do some field work."

"I'm guessing it didn't include any dusty bones or paint brushes."

"Not quite. A lot of interviews with people from widely divergent cultures, all telling basically the same story."

"Ghosts are real."

"More or less. At least the idea that the spirit or the soul lives on in some way after the body dies."

"And did you find any evidence of this during your research?"

"I did," Jennifer said plainly.

"You met ghosts."

"I've met many. During my research and in the years since."

"But no selfies with any of them," Moe challenged.

"No, not quite. But we have some videos with interesting visual events—"

"Any headless horsemen or weeping brides traipsing across the moors?"

"No, we're sadly lacking of moors here in Northern California."

Moe laughed. "Okay, let me ask you this. I was reading that you also believe in things like precognition, astral projection, and other psychic abilities. How does that tie in to your research as an anthropologist investigating afterlife belief systems?"

"Well, let's think about it. If there is a part of us that continues on after we die, then it must be with us while we're alive."

"Makes sense."

"And if we have this aspect to ourselves, this consciousness, then why couldn't it, under the right circumstances, exist outside of our living bodies as well as our dead ones."

"I've never heard anyone explain it like that."

"Chances are it's not bound by the same laws of time and space that we are in our corporeal bodies. Couldn't that explain psychic abilities, precognition, astral projection, remote viewing?"

"Yeah, I can see that."

"So, evidence of psychic phenomena would support the existence of the spirits. If we have a consciousness that can exist in another plane that sometimes intersects with our mortal reality, it opens up a whole other realm of possibilities and perceptions."

"I can't argue with that. Let's go back to this story about the Palace Theater."

"Sure."

"What happened there? The article I read said that the manager of the theater—by the way, if anyone in the San Francisco area wants to have a truly great art house movie experience, I saw 'Citizen Kane' there myself. Bit of a scratchy thirty-five millimeter print, but still amazing to see it on the big screen."

"I agree, it's a beautiful theater, and it has a long and rich history."

"There was even supposedly a murder or suicide there?"

"Several."

"And the manager was convinced that he was being haunted by some spirit attached to the place."

"He was. He was afraid that if word got out, people wouldn't want to come and he'd have to shut the place down."

"I actually would pay more to go to a haunted theater," Moe said.

"Well, Mr. Nagel didn't have your marketing foresight."

"So, he asked you to come and investigate."

"He actually was hoping I could get rid of the ghost for him."

"How do you deal with someone like that?"

"Well, he's not unusual in that regard. It may seem cool to be haunted, that it's some kind of fun 'Beetlejuice' type experience. But it's rather disconcerting to share your home or your workplace with a ghost."

Diane perked up at this point in the conversation. She cast a glance toward the bathroom, half expecting to see the sad young man standing there, looking at her. But there was nothing. Maybe the sage and crystals were doing their job.

"We start off by just looking around, asking questions, getting a feel for the place."

"I kind of picture you wired up with all sorts of gadgets and sensors."

Jennifer smiled. "My assistant, Dave, carries the bulky stuff. I have a tech guy who made me a smaller sensor array that I connect to my phone with Bluetooth."

"Cool."

"Yeah, we've come a long way from ouija boards."

"So, you go in, scanning for ghosts, skip to when you realize this isn't one."

"Well, it was a combination of things. There was a periodic nature to the events we were experiencing—"

"So there was something weird going on, it wasn't just his imagination."

"Definitely something real. Physical vibrations and a feeling of nausea."

"Which led you to believe what?"

"That it was something mechanical rather than paranormal in nature."

"And not to spoil your story, but it turned out to be something rather mundane."

"A washing machine."

"A washing machine?"

"A very large washing machine. You know how your washing machine makes a horrible noise when it hits the spin cycle and the load is unbalanced?"

"I don't really do laundry. I have people. But I've heard stories."

"Well, imagine a washing machine ten feet tall."

"Yeah, that's all kind of scary without being a ghost. Okay, changing subjects on you. So, what do your parents think of all this?"

Jennifer paused. She didn't expect this question and was not prepared to talk about her family.

"Sore subject?" Moe asked.

"No, not at all," Jennifer lied. "Just not very interesting."

"Well, now you've got me curious as to why it's not interesting."

Jennifer smiled. "Let's just say they had other plans for me."

"Yeah, that sucks when parents don't support their kids. I mean, look at you, a Ph.D., a professor at a state university, two published books... No wonder they're disappointed."

Jennifer smiled again. She always did that when she was nervous, or didn't want to answer a question. She was an attractive woman who hated trading on her looks, but sometimes a disarming smile was the only weapon she had to get out of a tight spot.

Moe studied her, trying to figure out what she was hiding. "Is it kids? Grandkids? They wanted to see you married to some rich prick with a mansion in Palo Alto?"

Jennifer laughed at the image of her, the socialite wife of a silicon valley executive. She also laughed because he was so close to the truth.

"All right," Moe said, sensing he had mined that topic for all she was comfortable to give, "moving on. I also read that you're somewhat of an accomplished magician."

"I am," she said proudly.

The video feed switched to a version of Jennifer's "The Mysterious Professor" poster.

"Ooh, you look kind of scary and sexy all at the same time in that picture," Moe said.

"I had fun with that," Jennifer confessed.

"Isn't magic kind of cheating?"

"What do you mean?"

"Well, like when I go to see Penn and Teller. They tell you right up front that everything they do is a trick. There is no real magic. The psychic stuff they do is fake."

"That is true. I'm a big fan of theirs."

"Yeah, but aren't they kind of in the tradition of The Amazing Randi? I mean they would call bullshit on anything you might sincerely present as evidence of the paranormal."

"Oh, I'm certain they could replicate anything I've seen with straight up magic tricks. But I saw a movie about the moon landing that they did with special effects. That doesn't mean we didn't go to the moon."

"Don't get me started on that!" Moe warned humorously. "But, fake moon landings aside, that's an interesting point. They can make a digital dinosaur rampage through San Diego and it's obviously not a real dinosaur, but that's not to say that there weren't real dinosaurs."

"Exactly."

"Okay, I see what you're saying. But let's get back to the magic thing. Who's to say that you aren't tricking people with your skill at illusions?"

"I guess at some point it's a matter of faith. I learned magic so I could more easily spot the scams, attention seekers and outright frauds."

"Are there a lot of them out there?"

"Yes. Maybe more than the real deal. But I know the difference because I've lived in both worlds. The one of magic, and the one of the paranormal. They both can exist simultaneously."

"Not to put you on the spot, but I'm going to put you on the spot. Can you do a magic trick for me right now?"

"How about a little telekinesis?" Jennifer offered.

"Sounds cool."

Jennifer looked at the assortment of items on the table between herself and Moe. She put a hand up to the side of her face, pushing her hair behind her ear as she thought.

At the same time, she scraped off a small piece of wax she had placed behind her ear earlier, one attached to a virtually invisible strand of black thread, the other end of which was wound around a button on the jacket she wore over her turtleneck.

She picked out a pen and placed it on the table between them. As she did so, she stuck the waxy end of the thread to a point at its center and gave it a spin so it whirled around like a mini propeller.

She held her hand over the pen and slowly raised it. As she did so, the pen followed. The thread lay between her fingers. As she leaned back, the pen rose even higher. The dark clothing she wore created the perfect background for the thread to be undetectable. And the spinning of the pen made it certain that no one would notice the small ball of sticky wax that connected it to the thread.

Jennifer grabbed the pen out of mid-air and quickly scraped the wax off with a practiced move.

"Let me see that!" Moe insisted.

Jennifer handed him the pen.

Moe inspected it, regarded her suspiciously. "You are good, lady," he said. "How did you do that? I swear, we did not talk about this in advance, and that is definitely my pen. And it never did any crazy shit like that before."

"Well, unlike Penn and Teller, I try not to give away all my secrets."

"That was probably the coolest thing anyone has ever done on this show. That's going to go viral, I predict that right now. That clip is going to light up the tubes!"

Jennifer smiled.

They spoke for over two hours. Much of it was a spirited debate in which Moe took on the role as devil's advocate and he and Jennifer genially sparred on topics ranging from spoon bending to near-death experiences.

Diane watched the whole interview without once getting up from her spot on the couch. As the show drew to a close, she picked up her phone and quickly Googled the parapsychologist's name. There was a link to a website that she clicked on. It was fairly slick as such sites went. And she'd seen a lot of them in the last week. She wondered how Dr. Daye's had escaped her attention. It wasn't filled with advertisements and click bait like most of the others. She had a very orderly catalog of her published works, some online tests to determine your psychic abilities, and what Diane was particularly searching for, a contact page.

Diane filled out the simple online form, unconcerned about disclosing her address and phone number. Dr. Daye did not seem like some kind of cable TV huckster. Jennifer Daye had a Ph.D., she taught at a state university, major newspapers published stories about her, hell, she was on the Moe Hogan show!

When it came to the portion of the form where she was asked to describe the situation she wanted to have investigated, she paused to think of something that would not make her sound crazy.

There was a crash in the bathroom. Diane put her phone aside and suddenly felt like she had just entered a walk-in freezer as a wave of cold washed over her. She looked down at her arm and was surprised to see the hairs standing straight up, and goosebumps from her wrists to her shoulders. She got up and tentatively walked across the room to the open bathroom door to investigate. On the floor was a small broken bottle of rosewater perfume. She couldn't remember leaving it near the edge of the vanity. She looked around, half expecting to see the shadowy figure of the man who had scared her that night.

But there was nothing.

The scents from the rosewater and sage made for a pungent combination. Diane grabbed a dustpan and broom and a roll of paper towels to clean up the mess.

Once she was finished, she plopped back down on the sofa and picked up the phone. In the box marked "Paranormal phenomena you want investigated" she wrote:

"There is the ghost of a man in my apartment at the Oakley Arms. It is a very old building, and he appears to be from at least fifty years ago. He frightened me one night, but I don't think he meant to. Nonetheless, I would like to see if he can be encouraged to leave somehow—if that's something you do. Please help, I don't know where else to turn."

Diane tapped the send button and the text from her phone screen disappeared, off to the cloud.

She put the phone back down, switched her television back to her regular cable feed and flipped through the channels until she found a movie that would hopefully lull her to sleep.

CHAPTER FOURTEEN

Nate didn't want to risk driving, so he hailed an Uber through his phone and rode to the police station in the car of a very talkative woman named Naomi. Naomi, Nate learned, was a developer for a startup in town, but drove for Uber before and after her day job. She seemed to think it was Nate's fault he was taking her further from the office she needed to get to after this ride, and at one point even asked Nate if he would mind getting out about a mile from his destination so she could get back across town before nine. He couldn't tell if he genuinely felt sorry for her, or just wanted to get out of the car and away from her complaining, but agreed to get out a few blocks from the police station. Once she had driven away, he gave her a two star rating and started walking the rest of the way to the tenth precinct.

The streets were busy, equally so with cars, bikes, pedestrians and buses. Nate never really had time to take a walk and just enjoy the city. Usually, he was in his car or Max's and in too much of a hurry to pay attention to anything but the task of getting from one place to the next.

On the occasions he did get outside for a run, his mind was on a case, and he would often listen to audio recordings he made of his notes, hoping something would jump out at him and break the case. But now, there was no urgency. The bullet had given him an unplanned vacation from the hectic pace of the job.

Today, he wasn't running, or rushing or even thinking about the robbery case. He had left the file at home—technically, he wasn't supposed to have it, though he expected the Captain assumed Max would slip him a copy at some point.

When he got dressed that morning, he was able to wriggle into a t-shirt, but trying to manage one of the dress shirts he usually wore let alone a neck-tie was too much to attempt at this point in his recovery. He did put on a clean and pressed pair of slacks and a sport jacket. It was more the type of ensemble Max would wear, except his partner would definitely substitute a pair of high-tops for the loafers Nate was wearing. Either he was starting to heal, or the pain pills were becoming more effective because moving his arm in and out of the sling was much less painful than it had been the previous days. He felt even more like a civilian without his gun and badge. Those were in the bottom of the robbers' duffel bag or more likely at the bottom of the bay. He would have to fill out a rather large stack of paperwork to get replacements.

As he drew closer to the station, the concentration of police increased. Some recognized him and offered cheery hellos and welcome backs. Nate knew most of the officers in the precinct by name. It was something his Uncle Bill had always drilled into him. "Make every cop your friend, you never know when you're going to need him to be one." Of course, these days "him" was just as likely to be "her." But the axiom still held. Nate made a point of remembering the name of every patrolman, officer and detective he met. When the hat was passed for gifts, or donations, he always had his wallet out and was as generous as he could be.

The station was set a bit back from the street. There was a small plaza in front of it, and more officers were gathered there. Nate returned their greetings with a smile and a nod and made his way into the precinct.

Everything was on one floor. Normally he would park around back and use the rear entrance, but it felt more appropriate to come in the front since he was technically a civilian. Max would certainly tease him about being such a stickler for the rules. He approached the desk sergeant and started to print his name awkwardly on the visitor's log.

"Detective Raney, no need to do that. Go on back, I know the gang is anxious to see you."

"Thanks, Roy," Nate said. He finished filling out the log regardless, then walked to the door that led to the detectives' bullpen. Sergeant Roy buzzed him in. Nate pulled open the door with his left hand, careful not to twist his torso in such a way as to tweak his injury.

Inside, he walked down a short hallway, flanked by offices, conference rooms and storage areas. It opened up to a nest of desks, arranged in pairs facing each other. He saw Max sitting on his desk, chatting up one of the female patrol officers. Nate caught his eye. Max stood up straight and began applauding.

Nate thought it was a joke at first, a sarcastic response to his premature return to the department, but soon others joined in and all other noises in the room ceased as it was filled with the sound of applause.

Captain Bode stepped out of the partitioned area that served as her office, joining in on the accolade.

Nate shook his head and raised a hand for them to stop. It took a while for the clapping to end. When it did, they all looked at him, expectantly.

"Go ahead, say something," Max said.

"Well," Nate began, "thank you. It's nice to be back. Good to see all of you."

"Jeez, never mind," Max interjected, "I thought you were going to say something interesting, or at least funny."

"Sorry, I left my prepared remarks at home."

"Yeah, along with your shirt and tie. You're going all Miami Vice on me, Nate. I like it."

"Purely temporary until I am once again bi-dexterous."

"That anything like bi-curious?" Max asked.

Some in the room laughed.

Nate looked around and then teasingly said, "Hey, aren't you guys supposed to be out there finding the guy who did this to me?" he asked.

"We're waiting for your lists," his partner joked.

Nate smiled. "You know, I could get you your own legal pad. A couple pens. It's not that hard."

"I'll leave the thinking to you, partner. Just point me in the right direction once you've found them," Max said.

"Raney, Lee, my office," Captain Bode shouted across the room.

The impromptu celebration of Nate's return broke up as Nate and Max wound their way through the maze of desks to the captain's office. By the time they reached it, she was sitting behind her desk, her attention on a file open before her.

Nate and Max entered. Max closed the door, and they both took seats in front of the desk.

Captain Bode looked at Nate and smiled. "Welcome back, detective. How are you feeling?"

"Not too bad, all things considered."

"You mean the thing where you were shot and nearly died?" Max asked.

"That's one of them."

"How's the shoulder?" she asked.

Nate knew the meaning behind that question. Was he ever going to be able to come back? "It's good. The doctor says with a minor surgery or two it'll be like new."

"I'm glad to hear that," Captain Bode replied with relief. "I expect that your partner has been keeping you up to date on the developments in the case."

"He filled me in," Nate said.

The captain regarded both of them with a suspicious look. "I have a feeling he did more than that." She turned to Nate. "Is there anything else you can tell us? Anything you remembered, something you might have seen or heard them say?"

Get in the catty, echoed in the back of Nate's mind. The words from his dream. The words he couldn't possibly have heard or even known that they were said. It was pure imagination, a fantasy of his mind. Nothing to share with the captain.

"No," he said plainly. "But I did have some thoughts about making a call for dashcam footage."

"Already on it," the captain replied.

"I haven't seen anything."

"Went out on the late newscasts a few days ago."

"It needs to go out every day. TV, radio, the papers, on the web, Twitter, Facebook—"

"Slow down, detective," the captain said. "We're chasing every lead and idea we can think of. You know the stats on something like that. It was a long shot that someone captured anything useful, and that that person heard the request and they still have the footage."

Nate sagged. She was right, they'd be better off committing their resources to other avenues of investigation. The more time that passed, the likelihood that such evidence existed diminished exponentially. He just wanted something to do.

"I appreciate that you want to help, but what we need you to do is heal. The investigation is our job," the captain said.

Nate nodded. For a moment he considered telling her the robbers had a Cadillac and were hiding out in the Tenderloin. But that was just a desperate reaction to being shut out. He didn't want to pollute the case with random dreams, no matter how eager he was to be a part of it. "I know," Nate said.

"Make sure nothing interferes with your recovery. I can't afford to lose you for longer than I have to."

"Thanks," Nate said.

"That said," the captain continued, "I also can't afford to do without your instincts and talents as a detective. So, I do want Detective Lee to keep you apprised of any developments in the case with the expectation that anything you might think of, remember, or any inspirations or revelations you have you bring directly to me. Don't try to investigate this on your own, or even with your partner. Do I have your word on that?"

Nate nodded. "Yes, ma'am."

"I'll keep him in line," Max promised.

Nate and Captain Bode exchanged a worried look.

"What?" Max asked. "I can wrangle a one-armed old dude."

The captain waved them away and returned to her file. "Oh, by the way, thanks for the gift. Max said you helped pick it out." She indicated a set of hammered copper planters on the credenza. The very thing Nate had told Max not to get.

Nate and Max left the office and returned to their desks.

"You got the planters?"

"You said over your dead body. I figured getting shot was close enough."

Their workspace was a study in contrasts. Nate's desk was orderly and clean, Max's was buried under an inch of paper, fast food wrappers and empty energy drink cans and bottles.

"Come on, I want to show you something," Max said. He led Nate to one of the conference rooms they used when working on a complicated case. There were photos, reports and notes on one wall. On a white board was a list similar to what Nate had written down on his legal pads.

"I thought you didn't do lists," Nate said.

"Yeah, don't be so surprised."

"I am," Nate confessed. "I didn't think this was your style."

"Hey, just because I let you take the lead on our cases doesn't mean I can't. You actually have been rubbing off on me. I mean, I'd have to be an idiot not to follow your lead considering how good a detective you are."

"I can't tell if you're serious or if you're mocking me," Nate said.

"Really? The great Detective Raney can't figure something out?" Max teased.

Nate had to laugh at that one. "Touché," he said.

"So, why don't I walk you through what we have and you can fill in any gaps you see," Max suggested.

"All right, lead on," Nate said.

Max took him through the timeline he and the other detectives had put together. Like Nate, they had assumed the suspects had spent some time casing the job and had gone back to canvass the other businesses on the street, checking for security camera footage or any loose ends the robbers may have left behind. There were none. At least none that they had found so far. One would think that on such a busy street, someone would have seen something, but it actually worked the other way. There was so much going on, that none of it registered.

Nate offered a couple suggestions for lines of inquiry Max could pursue, but it was all long shot stuff. The squad had come to the same conclusion he had. Unless the suspects made some stupid error, they weren't going to be found. Their best shot was the fact that they had stolen so many personal items. They had inventories from the shoppers of what had been stolen and the team distributed the lists to every pawn shop in town. Chances were they had an out-of-state fence to launder the proceeds of their crime through, but they may have tried to unload some of it before they left and one slip would be all that was needed to catch a break in the case.

After spending most of the morning comparing notes, Nate could tell that Max was getting bored. Max wasn't a sit-in-a-room-and-think-about-the-case kind of cop. He preferred being out in the street, but a lot of police work was done at a desk. And Nate was glad to see that Max was starting to appreciate that fact. But he also could appreciate that there was a point of diminishing returns with Max and he had squeezed as much out of him as he was going to get in one morning and walked him back to their desks.

"I think I'm going to call it a day," Nate said.

Something Nate said triggered a memory for Max. "That reminds me," he began, "Daye, Professor Daye..." he shuffled some papers around on his desk.

"Dr. Jennifer Daye?" Nate asked.

"Yeah, that's it. She's from some university. Came by saying she wanted you to be a part of some study she's doing. Something about people who nearly died."

"Near-death experiences."

"Yeah, how did you know?"

"She paid me a visit in the hospital."

"Really? She's pretty hot for a teacher, right?"

"Max, she's a professor of anthropology at a prestigious state university. Granted she does have a potentially unhealthy interest in some borderline macabre topics, but you go straight to 'she's hot'?"

"Yeah. Did you get her number?"

Nate shook his head. "Just when I think you're making progress..."

"Is that a no? She left her address, but not her number. But if you're not going to call her..." Max continued flipping through papers on his desk.

Nate laughed. "Okay, I'm going to go home now. I've reached my max Max for the day."

"Yeah, you don't want to overdo it. You heard the captain, you need to heal. And listen, don't hesitate to call if you need anything. Seriously."

"Thanks, Max. I appreciate that."

"Need a ride?"

"No, I'm good." He holds up his phone. "Meeting new and interesting people in the gig-economy."

"Yeah, Uber is a great way to meet women," Max added.

"Is everything about meeting women with you?"

Max considered. "No. Not all the time."

"Let's leave it at that," Nate suggested. "I'll catch up with you tomorrow."

"Okay, boss. Take care of that arm."

"I will," Nate promised.

Max started gathering papers and came across a sticky note with a name and address on it. "Wait! Here it is." He handed the paper to Nate.

Nate took the yellow paper square and without looking at it, slipped it into his jacket pocket.

Max walked him out to the front of the station. They exchanged words with some other officers on the way, everyone promising that they would get the guys who shot Nate, but at this point his expectations were that it would become a cold case if it wasn't already.

Nate pulled the slip of paper out of his pocket and tried to decipher Max's illegible scrawl. He did make out an office number and building name he recognized from the times he'd been on the campus of Cal State Hayward. He wasn't interested in pursuing her romantically, nor was he buying into her near-death nonsense. But in his experience, someone who went to this much trouble was bound to keep on hounding him, and it was better to head it off early, rather than letting it get out of control.

CHAPTER FIFTEEN

Nate found himself standing in front of an imposing building on the Hayward campus. It was not the building he was heading for when he arrived at the university. That was an office building that housed among other departments, professors from the Anthropology Department. But when he located the office number that was written on the scrap of paper Max had given him, he found a man in his mid-thirties, sitting behind a folding table who flew into an incoherent rage about "that nut job" stealing his desk when Nate asked about Dr. Daye.

Eventually, Nate was able to discover that she was currently lecturing at a nearby hall. He followed the directions of a friendly student and entered the auditorium where Dr. Daye was conducting her Introduction to Anthropology course.

The auditorium seated a few hundred people at maximum capacity. It was a bowl shaped room with a circular stage at the front. An array of large, curved LED screens showed digital slides behind the speaker.

Jennifer was wearing her usual tweed pants along with a dark turtleneck, her hair pulled back. She looked very professional—aside from her bright red Vans. It was a contrast to the flirtatious disguise she wore when she visited Nate in the hospital. She had a commanding presence as she spoke, the students hung on her every word.

Jennifer had a reputation for delivering an interesting and fun course and it filled up fast at registration. It was actually a source of conflict with her colleagues in the anthropology department. Many accused her of resorting to cheap parlor tricks to garner attendance at her lectures—which was true. She shared her love of magic with her students, often incorporating a volunteer into her weekly demonstration of legerdemain. But five minutes a week of tricks and illusions alone were not enough to capture the attention of undergraduates, especially when she had to fight with the duo of social media and smartphones for their attention.

Many students where surprised that she didn't enforce a no phone policy like other classes. But those who thought they might need the distraction to pass the time quickly discovered that putting the phones away for an hour and a half a few times a week was worth it. It may have been the magic shows that drew them in, but it was Jennifer's knack for making her subject matter relatable and relevant that kept her attendance rates among the highest at the university. She'd even been invited to give a Ted Talk on the subject of the anthropological links to the afterlife.

Nate took a seat in the back, trying to be as inconspicuous as he could. He managed to squeeze into a spot surrounded by enraptured undergrads. He bumped his arm a couple times which caused him to wince, but once he was seated, he settled into a pain-free position. He glanced at the image displayed on the screens behind Jennifer. It showed a corridor lined with statues representing the gods of ancient Egypt.

"The concept of an 'Underworld' is an idea that is common to many civilizations." Jennifer cycled through a few more slides depicting Egyptian murals illustrating various stages of death and the afterlife. "The Egyptians believed that you were guided to the underworld through a corridor by the Gods." The slides moved on to artistic renderings of Charon ferrying souls across a dark ribbon of water. "And the Greeks believed that souls were escorted across the river Styx to the entrance to Hades. And the Chinese have stories of a realm called Diyu, a sort of underground afterlife maze where your soul is judged.

"A common thread in many of these myths is a journey from the world of the living to that of the dead, a transition that takes place. Crossing a river, being guided down a corridor, entering a maze. In each of these belief systems, and even embedded in the concepts of reincarnation is the existence of a soul, or spirit. A part of a person that moves on either to the next life, or a new life. Even Native American cultures have a belief in spirits, ghosts and an afterlife. They certainly weren't influenced by the Greeks or Egyptians. What could inspire so many divergent civilizations to come to believe in such similar ideas?"

"Because ghosts are real," said one student somewhere near the front.

Jennifer smiled. "Maybe. A lot of cultures have deities associated with the sun, the moon, the earth. The things that make up their world. They have creation myths because they see life being created all around them and simply extend it to the whole of the world. They see sick children cured by a shaman or a priest and they believe in miracles. What caused them to believe that the soul exists beyond the life of the body? Maybe there are ghosts. Maybe every culture has experienced encounters with spirits and like other elements of their belief system, constructed the concept of an afterlife to explain it."

A young woman in the middle of the auditorium raised her hand. Jennifer nodded to her. "Couldn't it just be hallucinations? I mean, that's something all human beings are susceptible to, visions, seeing things that aren't there as a result of mental illness or psychotropic drugs. Certainly the existence of commonalities between cultural belief systems isn't by itself evidence of the existence of ghosts or a soul."

Jennifer nodded. "That's correct. The human mind is very susceptible to deception."

"That sounds like a segue," another student said.

An excited murmur spread through the hall.

Jennifer held up a hand until there was quiet. Then she checked her watch. After a brief moment, she clapped her hands together.

"All right," she said, "who wants to help me out today?"

Nearly every hand in the room went up.

Jennifer scanned the students. Nate shrunk into his chair as her gaze swept past the area where he was sitting, but she noticed him instantly, fixed her gaze on him and smiled. "Detective Raney, I didn't know you were auditing my course. Would you care to help me out with my demonstration of psychic ability?"

Nate adjusted his posture, then smiled back. "I don't think so. Seems like you have much more eager volunteers to pick from."

Jennifer nodded and continued scanning her audience until she pointed at one young man casually raising his hand near the left aisle. "Jeremy, come on up."

Jeremy got up from his seat and walked up to the low stage while Jennifer got a box from a hiding spot in the rear of the platform. She set the box next to her lectern, then began pulling out stacks of books, and placing them precariously on the podium. There were well over thirty volumes of different sizes, colors and thicknesses.

Jennifer stood aside, looked at Jeremy and waved her arm at the books. "Pick a book, any book."

Some students laughed at her paraphrase of the beginning of every card trick ever.

Jeremy crossed over and inspected the hardcovers stacked in front of him. He pulled out a thick one in the middle of one of the piles and read the title, "Harry Potter and the Goblet of Fire."

"Not my favorite book of the series, but certainly a more than adequate movie version. But you kind of ruined the trick. Pick another one, but don't tell me the title this time." Jennifer turned her back on Jeremy and the stack of books.

Jeremy grabbed another book, this one not as thick and replaced the previous choice. "Okay, got one."

"Good. Now I want you to just flip through it and put your finger on a page without looking at it, just pick one at random."

The student held the book so that he could flip the pages with one hand while he selected a random page with the other. "Okay," he said. "Now what?"

"I want you to take the highlighter from the podium and highlight any sentence on that page."

"This isn't a library book, is it?" he asked.

The students chuckled.

"When you're done, I want you to read the sentence to yourself. Don't read it out loud, just say it inside your head, slowly, clearly, distinctly."

"Okay," Jeremy made a show of staring at the page and moving his eyes over the words, mouthing them as he read.

"And don't move your lips," Jennifer added.

More laughter. Jeremy resumed reading, concentrating intently.

Jennifer put a finger to her temple, as if trying to remember something. "Do it one more time. I almost have it."

Jeremy took a breath and silently read it again.

"Okay, got it," Jennifer said. She crossed over to a whiteboard mounted on a wheeled stand, walked behind it and scribbled something with a squeaky marker. "Now, without losing your place, hand the book to someone in the front row."

Jeremy passed the book to a girl in the front row, who stood up.

Jennifer emerged from behind the white board. "Hi, Meredith. Would you read the highlighted passage out loud?"

Meredith turned to face the other students and cleared her throat. "'Some people,' said Humpty Dumpty, looking away from her as usual, 'have no more sense than a baby!'"

"'Alice Through the Looking Glass,'" Jennifer said knowingly.

Meredith consulted the cover of the book. "That's right."

Jennifer went to the white board and spun it around. Written on it in big bold letters was the sentence from the book.

The class broke into applause.

Nate leaned forward, playing back the performance in his head, trying to see the trick.

"Are you really psychic?" Meredith asked.

"A magician never tells."

A tone sounded indicating the end of the class period. Students started gathering their belongings and exiting the lecture hall. Some of them passed by Jennifer, begging her to tell how she did it, but she just smiled in reply.

Nate waited for his row to clear before attempting to make his way out. A couple students had to squeeze past him, but he didn't get his sore shoulder jostled this time. Once the way was open, he got up, sidled out into the aisle and walked down the steps toward the stage.

"Detective Raney, I'm so glad you could make it," Jennifer said.

Nate finished walking down the aisle, waiting for all but a few students to leave before replying. "You say that like you were expecting me."

"Well, I figured if I showed up at the police station looking for you, you'd either give in and agree to talk to me about your near-death experience, or you'd track me down and tell me to stop bothering you. I'm hoping it's the former."

"Stop bothering me," Nate replied with a hint of a smile.

"You could have told me that over the phone."

"You only left me an address. And a wrong one at that."

"Right, that was before we moved. Sorry about that. I may be a mind reader, but I'm not so good at precognition."

"You're not a mind reader, you're a magician. And a good one at that."

"Thank you."

"But seriously, you cannot go to the police station to try to question me for your so-called research."

"Hmm, we're still at 'so-called.' I would have thought since you sat through my lecture you'd realize that death is a serious topic of academic inquiry."

"Only caught the last five minutes. And I'm not completely convinced that you didn't slip that in when you saw me enter to try to persuade me that your academic inquiry is legitimate."

"You caught me. I switched out my slides in mid lecture. I was actually talking about primitive body mutilations before you walked in. Interesting that no one else noticed. Students these days." Jennifer finished putting the books back in their box. Then she turned back to

Nate. "So, you really just came all the way down here to tell me to back off? You're putting a lot of effort into not talking to me."

Nate ignored her comment. "We're in the middle of a very time-sensitive investigation and I don't need any distractions."

"Interesting. A moment ago I was a bother, now I'm just a distraction. I think I'm growing on you, Detective Raney."

"Just stay away. I have a lot on my mind."

Jennifer put the box aside and stepped off the stage to speak to Nate directly. "That's exactly what I want to know. You may not see any connection to what you went through, but I've talked to hundreds of people who've been in your situation, and there's always more to it. And I can promise you, keeping it bottled up is not going to make it any better."

"You have got to be the most arrogant woman I've ever met."

"Really? You should get out more."

Nate shook his head. "You think you know me? Know what I'm thinking? Know what I'm going through? I'm not some volunteer in one of your magic tricks."

"I know," Jennifer said, gently. "I also know that part of you came here today because you have questions that you can't answer on your own. Things you may have experienced, or seen that you can't explain."

"I came here because you left me an address and no phone number."

Jennifer smiled, busted. "But I bet you're also wondering if just maybe I'm not a complete charlatan and maybe I might have some answers."

"I've seen your show. I know the answer to that. I'm a cop. I deal in facts. If I can see it, I believe it."

"So, you're making the assumption that our sensory organs allow us to perceive everything that happens around us."

"What's your point?"

"Have you ever been in love?"

"I think we're getting a little off topic."

"Haven't you ever felt that rush when you meet a woman you're instantly attracted to, your heart races, your palms sweat." She stared directly at Nate. "Your eyes lock, and for a moment, the rest of the world just dissolves away. Maybe it's love at first sight. Maybe it's just lust. But in either case, you do feel something."

"And?"

"Can you see it? Can you see love? Can you touch it?"

"No, of course not."

"Then you don't believe it exists?"

Nate seemed offended at her accusation. "I can't see the abstract concept, but I saw the way my mother treated my father. I saw how she sat by his bedside while he wasted away from cancer. I saw her mourn his passing, missing him so much that she turned to shysters and con artists disguised as mediums and psychics who bled away all of his insurance money with promises that she could speak with him again. She still..." Nate let his last sentence hang in the air between them.

"I'm sorry," Jennifer said, reaching out with a compassionate touch on Nate's arm. "But I'm not those people."

"You enable them. You perpetuate those ideas, give them credibility."

"I'm a scientist, Nate. I search for evidence the same way you do."

The comment made Nate cringe. *The way I used to,* he thought to himself.

Jennifer sensed his discomfort. "I'm guessing you are going crazy not being able to chase down the men who did that to you," she said, nodding at the sling. "You're obviously not in any physical condition to be doing the work of a police detective. And even if you were, I'm guessing there are policies preventing you from contributing in any meaningful way."

Nate looked away.

"I have an idea. Kind of a challenge, actually," Jennifer suggested.

Nate perked up, curious.

"Me and my team do investigations from time to time. People call us thinking they're haunted, or have a possessed tea set, or want us to check out something some dime store medium told them."

The last bit caught Nate's attention. His mother had spent a lot of dimes on those phony psychics over the years. "Possessed tea sets?" he asked.

"It was just mice. But occasionally we do come across something we can't explain."

"So what's your challenge?"

"Well, you're sidelined from your job as a policeman for a while, why don't you come out with us on the next case we catch. Give it a skeptic's eye."

"To what end?"

"Let's say we investigate some incident and it turns out that there isn't any logical explanation for it. You don't have to agree that it's paranormal, just that you can't explain it with science or chicanery."

"Okay, I'll play along. What if?"

"Then you give me one hour of honesty about what you experienced when you were dead."

Nate paused, then let out a dismissive snort. "I told you. I didn't experience anything."

"Okay, it'll be a short hour. What do you say?"

"And if we don't find something that can't be explained with a little common sense?"

"I'll buy you dinner."

Nate was surprised.

"We can go to Georgio's. They have a great wine selection."

"Oh, are you an oenophile?"

She smiled at his ostentatious use of vocabulary. "Yes, I'm a fan of good wines. In fact, I used to work part time as a sommelier in college. I promise, I won't talk about ghosts or death or anything fun like that."

Nate laughed. He hated to admit it, but she was right. She was growing on him. God, did that mean Max was right, too? Nate shook off the thought.

"What do you say?" Jennifer asked. She extended her left hand so he could easily shake it. "Do we have a bet?"

Nate shook her hand. "All right." The hand shake lasted a moment longer than it needed to, and Nate found himself noticing that her hands were smooth and warm and she gripped his hand firmly.

Jennifer smiled, "Great. I'll need your number. Don't want to have to go through that guy at the police station again. He's a little creepy."

"Yeah, I worry that he has a hash-tag-me-too moment in his future."

Nate broke the handshake, then realized he didn't have his wallet or any business cards with him.

Jennifer pulled her phone out of a deep pocket. "I'll just type it in," she offered.

Nate rattled off the digits of his phone number and Jennifer saved it to her contacts.

"Well, I should be going. I'm supposed to see my orthopedist this afternoon," he told her.

"All right. I'll be in touch. Hopefully soon."

"Looking forward to it—the dinner, that is. With a bottle of Mouton, nineteen-eighty-eight."

"Good choice," Jennifer agreed. "I guess we'll see."

Nate nodded, turned away and started walking up the aisle to the exit.

Jennifer watched him go. She looked down at his name in her phone and smiled again. Not a bad-looking guy, she thought to herself. For a cop.

CHAPTER SIXTEEN

Emily sat at Jennifer's desk, her legs folded up on her lap and her face buried in a book, earbuds nestled in among her piercings. The office chair she was perched on moved slowly away from the desk. Emily looked down and plucked out her earbuds. "Are you done yet, Bits?" she asked.

Bits climbed out from under the desk. He had an LED headlamp on that shone directly in Emily's eyes when he looked at her. "All set," he replied. "You guys are back online. I've got you hardwired and put in a new WiFi router."

"Awesome," Emily replied, shading her eyes from the glare of Bits' lamp. "Can you turn that thing off?"

Bit reached up and switched the lamp off. "Tell Dr. Daye I'll send her my bill."

Emily reached down and picked up a wastepaper basket. "Give it to me now, I'll file it with the others."

Bits smiled. It was an ongoing inside joke that he would someday get paid by Jennifer. The truth was, he was more than eager to provide tech support and hi-tech gadgets to the Professor. He had his own ideas about the nature of the soul and had some wild theories about how he would retain his consciousness inside a robot body when he died. And since Jennifer's research conveniently intersected with his own crazy ideas, he was happy to help her out whenever and wherever. For Bits, the reward was the work.

Which is also why he didn't actually live anywhere. He found it hard to pay rent when he didn't believe in the concept of money. Instead, he used the university gym to shower and change, slept on any number of couches spread across campus and traded his services with various restaurants and roamed the faculty lounges for leftover food.

He had a laptop computer that never left his side. It was a Linux system, protected with his own tweaked VPN and anti-intrusion monitors. He never used off-the-shelf stuff, even the operating system was heavily modified. His files were backed up on a secure server in Norway. Bits liked his privacy.

The stuff he did for Jennifer was mostly hardware. The software coding he could do anywhere, but to build the gadgets Dr. Daye needed for her investigations, he needed a workshop. The details of how he managed to get himself access to the school's electronics labs and the supplies he needed was something he never shared with Jennifer. Like the rest of his life, it was strictly off the books.

Bits reached over and powered on the computer on Jennifer's desk. The monitor cycled through the various screens that took it to the login.

"The password is—" Emily started to say, but Bits' fingers danced over the keyboard and unlocked the system before she could finish. "Remind me to never let you touch my phone," she said.

"It's not me you have to worry about, it's the NSA."

Emily clicked on the icon for the email app. The number next to the inbox reported that there were five-hundred-and-thirty-seven unread messages. "Dave!" she shouted.

Dave emerged from between some shelves. "What?"

"Email."

"You're the undergrad intern, I'm the graduate student teaching assistant. Sounds like an intern job to me."

"I have class." Emily offered an insincere smirk, gathered her book and shoved it in her backpack.

"You do not."

"Study group."

"You hate people."

"Bye," Emily said, and slipped past Dave and Bits toward the elevator.

Dave looked over at Bits. "Don't you have some magic program to sort emails?"

"I never touch the stuff," Bits answered. Then he grabbed his own pack and followed Emily.

"Great," Dave muttered to himself. "I swear as soon as I finish my thesis I'm done with this." He sat down in front of the computer and started clicking through the emails.

Dave had a nagging fear that Dr. Daye's sponsorship of his thesis was contingent on his being her office slave, equipment lugger and errand boy. At the rate his graduate studies were progressing, it was going to take a while and the stipend he got as Dr. Daye's graduate assistant was a lifeline.

The truth was he didn't really mind screening the email. He had a system. Whenever Emily or Jennifer deigned to do anything to help, they ended up making things worse. It would take Dave twice as long to fix what they had messed up. He wondered sometimes if they didn't do it on purpose.

He started sorting through the messages, dragging them into various folders depending on whether they were in the categories of ghosts, poltergeists, people claiming to have psychic abilities, possessions or the inevitable UFO nut who claimed that angels were actually aliens. Sometimes he had to read quite a bit of the email to get to the point. He had pestered Bits about the fact that the website form had a drop down option to categorize the message, but that information wasn't present in the email at all.

It took Dave the better part of an hour just to get through the first one-hundred messages, after which he took a break and did a little web surfing to see if there was any news about Dr. Daye that the dean could use against them. He found a few fringe blogs who had picked up some previous stories, and a few memes had come out from the Moe Hogan interview, most of them featuring Moe quoting a line from "Ghostbusters." "I ain't afraid of no ghost," "Who you gonna call," and "You said crossing streams was bad," among the most popular. How he had worked that into a conversation with Jennifer, Dave didn't want to know.

After a while he returned to the incoming messages and after a few dozen more obvious crackpots, one caught his eye. It was brief, sincere and absent any of the fantastical claims that most of them contained. A woman who lived in the Oakley Arms claimed she was being haunted by a man who appeared to be from an earlier era. She was simply inquiring if they could look into encouraging him to leave. Dave checked the time the email was sent. It was during the live podcast of Moe Hogan's show—which made sense, a lot of the incoming messages were in fact from that time period.

He Googled her name and came up with several entries, but the one that was most likely was a woman who worked on the staff of a local law firm not too far from the address he had found for the Oakley Arms.

Next he did an online search for the Oakley arms and on the second page of results—past the real estate listings and reviews—he found some mentions included in websites he was familiar with that chronicled stories of San Francisco hauntings. Apparently a deceased janitor was the most famous non-corporeal resident. The building was over a hundred years old—which reminded Dave of his trip to the Palace Theater not too long ago. He knew now for a certainty that Dr. Daye would absolutely insist on looking into the case based on the age of the building alone. "History is mostly ghost stories," Jennifer was fond of saying. It was often quoted when she did interviews and she frequently promised to write a book with that title, but had yet to get around to it.

Dave put the email from Diane Collins at the Oakley Arms in the "Interesting" folder and sent the last of the emails to their appropriate destinations—most of them being spam. The badge indicating how many unread emails were in the inbox was now gone. He leaned back, laced his fingers behind his head and put one foot, then the other on the big wooden desk and leaned back for a well-deserved moment of peace.

It had been three years since he began his research under Dr. Daye. He'd had several false starts on his thesis and at present was still searching for a novel approach to his chosen topic. Jennifer's style was mostly hands off—well, entirely hands off. He would come to her with questions, which she would bounce back at him and whatever answer he grabbed out of thin air, was what she enthusiastically endorsed. So, he would sit in front of his computer for months at a time, writing, researching, rewriting only to find that the premise of his thesis fell apart, and he was back at square one.

Of course Dr. Daye assured him it was all part of the process, and would set him about one task or another, grading papers, scouring recordings, scanning photos, logging videos. After a while he would give it another go, but Jennifer never seemed particularly concerned that he wasn't making progress on his degree. He knew, of course, that she didn't care if he finished his studies. The longer he was her grad student, the longer she wouldn't have to find someone else to do what he did for her.

There was many a time when Dave felt he'd had enough. He was going to find another adviser, finish his thesis, get his doctorate and go on to...

And that was where the fantasy would end. Go on to what? He had no desire to teach let alone the aptitude to give the kind of lectures that Jennifer was known for. The truth was, he liked being a student. The pay sucked, but he had access to cheap student housing and Bits hooked him up with free phone and Internet, and he actually liked ramen. Being Jennifer's grad assistant was the perfect job for him. He got to avoid the responsibilities of real life and to be honest, although he complained, he kind of liked working with her. A lot of it was boring, and tedious and she treated him like her own personal servant, but it was also exciting at times. And the things he'd seen.

He was a skeptic at first. He'd been drawn to Dr. Daye like every other undergrad who had taken her course. She made anthropology interesting, accessible and for Dave, very appealing. It was through Jennifer that he had awoken his own love for the field. Being her graduate assistant and doctoral candidate was an opportunity he couldn't pass up. Little did he know at the time, that instead of being a path to his career, it would actually become his career.

"Comfortable?"

Dave jerked at the sound of the voice. He tried to remove his feet from the desk, but ended leaning back past the tipping point of the chair. His arms flailed, but that only made it worse and he ended up crashing backwards in a heap on the floor.

Jennifer walked over to the desk and looked at Dave lying on the ground. His expression was more embarrassed than pained. "Sorry, didn't mean to scare you," she said.

"You didn't scare me," Dave replied. He laid there for a moment, then crossed his arms over his chest as if he was perfectly comfortable where he was.

Jennifer stared at him for a moment, then asked, "Can I have my desk back?"

"Oh, sure," Dave said. He swung his legs up over his head, bumping his feet into the bookshelves behind him. He then dropped them to one side and tried to roll over, but the arm rest on the chair snagged his belt and made it impossible for him to stand.

"Need a hand?" Jennifer asked.

Dave smiled and shook off her offer. He struggled a bit more, then finally managed to get to his feet. He righted the chair, and spun it around, offering it to Jennifer to sit in.

"Thank you," she said, letting out a small laugh. She liked Dave a lot. She knew she took advantage of his easy-going nature and personal insecurity, but she also knew they both had a good thing going and couldn't resist the urge to keep it going for as long as possible by not pushing him to finish his thesis. That time would come, but no need to rush it.

"Did you set up that meeting with the dean?" she asked.

"I did. Tomorrow afternoon. Don't miss it," Dave warned.

"I won't."

"And don't make him any angrier at you."

"Don't worry, I'm going to straighten everything out. We'll be out of the dungeon before you can say—"

"Just be nice," Dave said.

"I'm always nice, aren't I?"

Jennifer sat down at the desk and spied the tidy inbox on her computer screen. "Anything interesting?" she asked.

"Uh, that would be the emails in the 'Interesting' folder," he said, annoyed at having to point out what seemed perfectly obvious.

Jennifer opened the folder and scanned the subject lines.

"The one about the Oakley Arms is the most promising. Old building. Lots of history," Dave suggested.

She found the email he was talking about and opened it up. She read it, knowing that Dave was doing the same over her shoulder. He was right. The woman who wrote it seemed perfectly rational, and the phenomena she described was nothing they hadn't seen before. "Do we have anything in the files on the Oakley Arms? It sounds familiar."

"Yep," Dave confirmed. "I did a quick search when I first saw the email. I think we might have received other tips about spirits there, nothing ever panned out, though."

"Anything about a male ghost haunting young women?"

"Not specifically. The stories mostly concerned an entity that, well, sometimes tidies the place up."

Jennifer raised an eyebrow. "A neat freak poltergeist?"

Dave shrugged.

"Dig a little deeper. See if you can find anything in the newspapers."

"How far should I go back?"

"How old is the building?"

Dave sighed.

CHAPTER SEVENTEEN

Nate finished cleaning up after his takeout meal from Basiano's, a favorite restaurant of his. He didn't mind dining alone, but after all the day's activities and a lot more walking than he had expected to do, he settled for a Grub Hub delivery of an herb crusted snapper with some mushroom risotto. The food had lost some of its luster in its transition from Basiano's rustic dining room to his own home, but was still better than anything he'd be able to rustle up one-handed in his own kitchen, or worse, microwave. Although he had the perfect bottle of wine to pair with the meal in his cellar, his medications forced him to settle for Perrier instead.

He found himself thinking about Jennifer Daye. Ever since her appearance in his hospital room almost a week ago he couldn't quite get her out of his mind. She was obviously intelligent and charismatic—the portion of her lecture he had seen was evidence of that—and there was no doubt that he found her attractive. But at the same time, she was completely and irrepressibly aggravating.

Her persistent prying into what he experienced when he was shot was particularly unnerving. It made him second guess himself. He was certain it was all a crazy dream, cobbled together from the last thoughts his oxygen starved mind had experienced and a life of police work. In his dream, he had clearly seen the men who had robbed the store and shot him. But he had no evidence to support the idea that they were hiding out in the Tenderloin district, let alone what type of car they were driving.

What Dr. Daye had suggested, that he had had a near-death experience, was just a fairy tale. Such things were the province of superstitious or religious people, and he was neither one. He had actually Googled alternative explanations while he was waiting for his delivery from Basiano's and they seemed to him much more rational theories. The fact that when the heart stops beating, the brain is starved of oxygen and starts shutting down, connections misfiring, then the intermittent return of blood flow during his surgery could easily have compromised his memory or engendered the strange dream.

Yet at the same time, parts of it were so vivid, not like the foggy recollections he normally woke with of disjointed scenes and convoluted scenarios. This felt like he was watching a movie—albeit from an impossible perspective. First in the hospital's operating room, and then at the run-down house. Everything was coherent. That's the part that bothered him the most.

But there was an explanation for that as well, wasn't there? He was heavily medicated with analgesics and anesthetics, both of which had the capacity to create hallucinations, and in some cases vivid dreams. It was by far the more likely explanation. And it reassured him that his instincts to dismiss the elements of his dream as pure fantasy were correct.

He returned to his computer with a glass of sparkling water and typed Jennifer Daye into Google. There were thousands of results, and near the top was a YouTube video of a podcast where she was the guest. She was just as captivating in this setting as she was behind the podium on the stage of her lecture hall. He smiled when she performed her magic trick for Moe. The impromptu demonstration of her "telekinetic powers" was slick, but he made a career of noticing things most people didn't, and he could tell the difference between a casual scratch behind the ear and a magician's load.

It was clear why she garnered so much attention and why there were so many links to her on Google. He listened to her stories of hauntings and paranormal phenomena and psychic experiences. None of it he found convincing, but he could see how someone with a predisposition to believing in such things would find her anecdotes to be powerful confirmations of their own biases.

Nate's distrust of the supernatural stemmed in part from his experience on the force. He had spent some time dealing with the shady underbelly of the psychic scene in San Francisco because of his mother's pursuit of communication with her deceased husband. Most of the psychics in town had connections to organized crime. Some, Nate found, sincerely believed in their abilities. From his perspective, however, they were merely natural cold readers, people who were good at sensing body language and micro-expressions and coupled it with an acute, inborn intuition—not unlike what you would find in a good police detective. But regardless of their intentions, if they didn't have the means to get out from under the thumbs of the shady elements that were insinuated throughout the city, they were sometimes strong-armed into doing things that went against their better natures.

Of course, for each of those good-intentioned practitioners, there were ten or more who were simply out to scam people. Unscrupulous magicians who found they could make more money reading palms and Tarot cards than pulling rabbits out of hats at kids' birthday parties, populated the mini-malls and the second floors of storefronts. It seemed like his mother had visited every one of them and probably put many of their children through college. It enraged him when he thought about it. He had made sure the bulk of his father's death benefits were protected. A lawyer friend had helped convince his mother to put the funds through a trust, so no major withdrawals could be made without Nate's approval. However, she still managed to find enough cash in her weekly budget to spend on psychics, and he suspected she was selling off her jewelry and other possessions to fund her quest for spiritual communion with her departed husband.

Nate had tried to cut her off. He would follow her to her

appointments, try to expose the scams the phony psychics were pulling on her, but it only created resentment. She saw Nate not as a loving son trying to protect her, but an obstacle to her relationship with her husband. She and Nate had a tremendous argument, and both said things they would later come to regret. They didn't speak for almost a year.

Then one evening, Nate received a call from one of his mother's friends. She was worried and hadn't heard from Eleanor Raney for more than two days.

Nate went to his mother's house and found her on the edge of life, badly dehydrated. She had been beset by a bad stomach flu, which almost instantly weakened her to the point where she didn't have the strength to even make a phone call.

A couple days in the hospital set things right and provided the impetus for a reconciliation between the two. Nate made the concession that his mother firmly believed she was communicating with Nate's father through the various psychics. He agreed to not interfere, but in exchange, she agreed to let him have a hand in her finances. The detente had endured since then, and Nate swallowed his incredulity whenever she told him of the latest news from his father. He realized it gave her a comfort that she craved. They had spent over thirty years together before he passed. They were childhood sweethearts, and he was the only man she had ever loved.

So, Nate let his mother have her little fantasies, and smiled when she told him how proud his father was of him and groaned when she related how worried they both were that he would never find a nice girl.

The doorbell rang. Nate closed his computer, silencing the video podcast in its final moments. He stood slowly, still a bit weak from the day's exertions. He steadied himself, then walked to the front door and looked through the peep hole.

It was Max, holding up a six-pack of beer. Nate opened the door and a rush of cool, evening air swept in along with Max. "Hey, boss. Am I interrupting anything?"

Max looked around the room, expectantly. Not seeing what—or

whom—he was looking for, he shrugged, disappointed.

"Hi, Max, come on in," Nate offered sarcastically.

"Well, I knew you probably didn't seal the deal, but a guy can dream, can't he?"

"What are you talking about?"

"The sexy professor? You did go see her this afternoon, didn't you?"

Nate didn't answer. He hadn't even thought about checking in on Jennifer until well after he left the police station.

"Don't blame you, boss. She's smart, sexy, pushy just the way you like them. No, wait, that's the way I like them. Did you get her number yet?" He plopped the beer on the coffee table, then himself on the sofa and reached for a bottle and twisted it open. "So, spill. What happened?" he asked, then took a long draught from the beer.

"Nothing," Nate answered. He crossed to the recliner next to the sofa and lowered himself down gently, using his good arm to steady his descent.

"Not buying it," Max declared. "She's interested in you. You should make a move."

"Well, not that it's any of your business, but I only saw her to get her to stop harassing me."

"You really are rusty on the whole dating thing, aren't you?"

"She's an opportunistic, showboating publicity hound and only wants to get me to be a story in her next book."

"Oh, so you have been checking her out."

Nate stammered. "I-I looked into her background. Nothing more."

Max used his beer to point at the laptop. "So, if I open that laptop, I'm not going to see a picture of her on your screen?"

"Not even close."

Max lifted himself out of the couch and started toward the dining room table where Nate's laptop lay closed.

Nate put his arm out to stop him. "Okay, when I was Googling her there was a YouTube video of some podcast she appeared on."

Max collapsed back on the couch, smiling. "I knew it. Is she naked?"

"Of course not."

Max kept on smiling as he drank from his beer. "She is hot, though. You have to admit that."

"She's attractive. But she's also intelligent and accomplished."

"Oh, what happened to opportunistic and nefarious?"

"I never said nefarious. Look, did you really expect to come here and find me with her? I just got out of the hospital. I can barely walk around on my own for more than fifteen minutes."

Max shook his head. "Excuses."

"Reasons," Nate countered. "So, any updates?" he asked, hoping to change the subject.

"Not yet," Max answered, shifting into a more serious mood. "But we will get them. I put out some feelers to some out-of-state jurisdictions. If we can establish that they've been working across state lines, we can get the FBI involved."

"Oh, yeah? The captain is on board with that?" Nate asked suspiciously.

"I just sent some emails."

"If it gets back to her—"

"Don't worry, I'll put all the blame on you. I'll be okay." Max finished off his beer, then cracked a smile.

Nate couldn't help but laugh. The slight motion sent a needle of pain through his shoulder. "Don't make me laugh," Nate said, trying to get himself comfortable again.

"Hey, enough shop talk. If you don't have any deets on your new girlfriend—"

Nate moaned and rolled his eyes.

"—then we can at least watch the Giants' game." Max reached for the television remote and turned it on. He tapped in the number for the local Sports Channel and opened another beer. He offered it to Nate.

Nate declined with a sigh. "Can't, still on the pain meds."

"Oh, right. You probably have all the good pills that keep you from operating heavy machinery. More for me." He put his feet up, and they spent the rest of the night criticizing the performance of the team and the decisions of the manager.

It was exactly what Nate needed.

CHAPTER EIGHTEEN

Dave and Emily sat in front of two ancient microfiche readers, paging through old editions of the San Francisco Chronicle. Dave had found a story about the completion of the Oakley Arms just after the turn of the last century in the digitized version of the archives. He was lucky. Most of the scans of the old newspapers were barely legible, and the technology that read the blurry text to create the index was invented years before any machine learning algorithms added their smarts to the task. He did have some key dates that he was able to identify and articles that mentioned the Oakley Arms. Some headlines were legible, and he was able to create a hit list of issues of the old paper he'd want to start with. But without looking at the actual pages and scanning for other contemporary stories, they wouldn't really be able to get a complete picture of the history of the building.

Emily actually enjoyed this kind of work. She liked scrolling through the past on the large, grainy projector and had an uncanny ability to pick out relevant stories from the full sheet newspaper pages on the screen. The political incorrectness of many of the stories and the advertisements was amusing to her.

Dave, on the other hand was not a fan of such an analog throwback. He was of the growing generation that felt if it wasn't on Google, it wasn't worth knowing.

"How far back do we have to go?" Emily asked.

Dave tapped a date on a notepad he kept next to the microfiche reader. "January fifteenth, nineteen-twelve. It was built after the great Earthquake of nineteen-oh-six."

"I thought that was in the eighties."

"You know, things did happen before you were born."

"That is before I was born."

"Okay, before your parents were born."

"Nothing interesting," she commented, scanning sheet after sheet of poorly photographed newsprint.

"Why did you ever become an anthropology major if you're not interested in history?" Dave asked.

"I prefer my history ancient," Emily replied. "Bingo," she said matter-of-factly.

She pressed the copy button on the Microfiche reader and the output of the display was optically redirected to an equally outdated photocopying mechanism that spit out a smudged copy of the page she was looking at. Dave leaned over and looked at her screen.

The headline read, "Axeman Meets His End From Atop Oakley Arms."

"That sounds promising," Dave commented.

"Can I go, now?" Emily asked.

"We've got two more decades to search. See if there's any other stories about this 'Axeman' in the weeks before."

Emily raised an eyebrow. "You want me to go back?"

"Yeah, it sounds like there was a killer slashing people. Violent deaths mean restless spirits. If we don't get it now, Dr. Daye is just going to make us go back and do it later."

Emily sighed and did a quick rewind of the spool of microfiche.

"Ooh," Dave exclaimed while paused on a page on his own machine.

"Find something?" Emily asked.

"Sale on suits. Only twenty dollars. For two."

"You know people made like twenty dollars a year back then."

"You really need to get a better perspective on contemporary history."

Emily hit the copy button a couple times in a row.

"Hey, easy with that. It's a buck a copy."

"You want the goods on the local axe murderer or not?"

Dave glanced over at her screen. "Carry on."

CHAPTER NINETEEN

Jennifer sat in one of the uncomfortable leather chairs in the Dean's outer office flipping through her Twitter feed. After an appearance on something like the Moe Hogan show, she was usually inundated with a mix of compliments, lewd offers, religious warnings about trespassing on God's domain, random memes and the occasional inquiry for her to look into some ghost or paranormal situation. She was specifically focused on the latter category, though she did take a moment to reply to some compliments on her appearance on the podcast.

Specifically, she was looking for something she could use to open Detective Raney's mind. She knew that his experience with his mother and storefront psychics made him a more resistant skeptic, but the right experience might be able to shift his thinking.

"He'll see you now," June, the dean's assistant said abruptly.

Jennifer looked up at the middle-aged woman who was always nice to Jennifer despite being fiercely loyal to the dean. "Thank you, June," Jennifer said. She tucked her phone away and strode purposefully toward the door to the inner office.

Inside, the dean was sitting at his desk with what looked like a hand-written letter unfolded in front of him. Jennifer strode up to the desk and stood in front of it with her arms crossed.

"Have a seat," the dean offered.

"I'd rather stand," she replied. "That way I can look down on you like the cowering rat you are. What are you trying to achieve by putting me and my staff in that crypt?"

"Seems to me you might enjoy that kind of environment," the dean said.

Jennifer ignored his insult. "I'm a tenured member of this department. I conduct one of the most popular classes on this campus."

"The drunken Bacchanalia the frat houses host are popular as well, that doesn't mean either of them contribute to the academic mission of this institution. Look, I appreciate that your little magic shows bring students into the program, but there comes a time when you have to put the fun and games aside and stick to science instead of voodoo."

"You realize that Anderson actually teaches a course on voodoo," Jennifer countered.

The dean shook her comment off. "I'm talking about your extra-curricular activities. The ghost hunting and mind reading and teleportation—"

"I think you mean astral projection."

"I mean this department cannot reward such blatant disregard for the standards and the academic mission we need to uphold. You're not studying an acknowledged field of legitimate academic value."

"How can you call yourself an educator and be so close-minded? Just because my research doesn't involve sorting through dusty bones and broken pottery doesn't mean it's not a legitimate avenue of inquiry. We have a Theology department at this school. They believe in omnipotent deities, an afterlife, miracles. Does that mean they should be drummed out of the university?"

"That's different," the dean insisted. "They are not representing the sciences."

"But isn't that why we draw a line between the hard and soft sciences? When we study the past, there's no experimental process we can rely upon to support our hypotheses. We look for evidence and try to interpret it. And to pretend that there is no evidence for the supernatural with all the thousands of stories and accounts ranging across all civilizations is counter to our responsibility to question everything."

The dean sighed and sat back in his chair. "There is a line, Dr. Daye. We can't just take every crackpot idea and turn it into a college course. Your colleagues are trying to provide a serious educational environment for our students."

The dean rose from his chair and leaned forward, his fingers tented on his desk blotter. "And," he said emphatically, "I know that you and your staff use the university's resources for your... 'investigations.'"

"My 'investigations' are a continuation of the work in my thesis, the document upon which I was awarded a PhD. The university hired me and granted me tenure knowing full well the direction my research would go."

"I was not the head of the department at that time, otherwise you never would have had the opportunity to contaminate the corpus of work generated by this department."

Jennifer shook her head and took a step back. "Have you forgotten that we started teaching here together? You used to be interesting. A little lacking in confidence, but I liked you. You had promise, you just needed to believe in yourself more."

The dean stood up straight and lifted his chin. "I don't need your back-handed compliments. I accepted a position in the administration because I knew I could do more as a leader."

Jennifer laughed. "The only reason you're dean is that you couldn't get published. You were always jealous of me when we were colleagues. And as you climbed your way to this office, you've been trying to keep me down every step of the way."

"I've only acted in the best interest of the department," the dean insisted.

"Well, is it in the best interest of the department to be a constant obstacle to the member of your staff who consistently gets the highest student ratings?"

"Teaching is not a popularity contest."

"Well, what does it matter how the university gets attention as long as it attracts students and donors."

The dean is surprisingly silenced by Jennifer's question. "Look," he began in a more conciliatory tone of voice, "I didn't ask you here to get into an argument." He sat back down in his chair, then waited for Jennifer to seat herself in one of the chairs in front of his desk.

"The fact is I did have some space open up that you and your staff may use," he said.

"I'm sensing a but," Jennifer replied suspiciously.

"There is no but, I just need you to fulfill all the responsibilities of your position."

Jennifer grinned. "And which of those responsibilities exactly am I being expected to fulfill?"

The dean hesitated. "There is a donor..."

Jennifer sensed he was reluctant to continue. "Go on," she urged. "What is it about this donor that involves me?"

"Well, it seems he caught wind of you and is considering making a sizable donation contingent on meeting you."

"Ah, and you can't have your precious money man thinking you keep me in the basement. So, who is this philanthropist who is so interested in my work that you needed to swallow your pride and maybe a little crow along with it."

The dean picked up the letter on his desk and handed it over to Jennifer. She took it and started reading. It was a short note, expressing his desire to set up an endowment for the department where Dr. Jennifer Daye was a professor. It ended with a request that he have a chance to meet with Dr. Daye and discuss topics he was sure she would be of help on. It was signed Daniel Worthington.

Jennifer raised an eyebrow at the name and grandiose signature. "Daniel Worthington, the restaurateur?" she asked.

The dean nodded.

"The one who married into the Kirkwood family?"

He nodded again.

"The Kirk-Mart Kirkwood family?"

"Yes, that's the one," he said with an air of frustration.

"A lot of money there," Jennifer said, realizing that the balance of power in the room had suddenly shifted in her favor.

The dean just nodded, avoiding her eyes.

"So, tell me about this new office suite you have for me."

"Office suite?" the dean asked.

Jennifer sat back and smiled, quite pleased with how the day was starting off.

CHAPTER TWENTY

Nate arrived at his mother's house in his second Uber in as many days. He still wasn't comfortable driving himself and certainly wasn't going to take Max up on his offer to chauffeur him around. He had been thinking about his mother since the night before and realized he hadn't seen or spoken with her since he had been discharged from the hospital.

He was only marginally afraid that something unfortunate had happened to her. One compromise he had convinced her to accept was a smart watch, which had the ability to detect if she had fallen, or was experiencing any cardiac irregularities. Twice he had had to replace the device when she reported that she had given them to her friends—the psychics knew the value of the gadget was far more than Eleanor gave it credit for having—so he convinced her that the latest model was tied to her DNA and if she gave it to anyone else, it wouldn't work. A ridiculous claim, but she either believed it, or realized he really wanted her to wear the watch and this last one had remained in her possession for nearly a year now.

He had checked in on the monitoring account linked to the watch, but there were no incidents reported, and the GPS history showed that she hadn't left home for a few days—that was one feature he never told her about, but he also never used it to just check in on her.

Nate walked slowly up the path to the front door of the old frame house. He rang the bell.

There was a crash, then another sound. Barking?

He peered into the window. A black nose set amid some dirty white fur bumped up against the glass. Nate almost took a tumble backwards. A dog? His mother didn't have a dog. He double checked the address to make sure he was at the right house, then looked around to make sure he was on the correct street. There was no doubt. This was his mother's house. The one he had grown up in. The one where pets were never allowed despite the begging and pleading of a young boy, an only child, desirous of a best friend.

Then he heard his mother's voice. "Madge! Madge! Get away from there! Move, move. Get down. Get off me!"

The door finally unlocked and opened.

Madge, the standard poodle who was responsible for Eleanor Raney's frazzled state, squeezed out of the door, took a lap around the front yard, toyed with the idea of chasing a car that passed by, then bounded back toward Nate.

Nate instinctively turned his left side toward the oncoming dog, protecting his damaged arm.

Madge reared up and put her paws on him with a weight he wasn't expecting. Fortunately, she merely pushed him into the house rather than knocking him over. The impact on his injury was painful, but he was more upset that he had allowed himself to be taken by surprise. It was just so unexpected. A dog was the last thing he thought he would find at his mother's house.

Nate steadied himself, then shouted a single, stern command. "Off."

Madge took her paws off of Nate, set them on the ground and looked up at him.

He took a step toward her and said, commandingly, "Sit."

Madge obeyed.

"Oh, my, how did you do that?" Eleanor asked.

"We have dogs on the police force, Mom," Nate told her, leaving out the part where he had briefly dated one of the K-9 handlers. "The better question is where did she come from?" he asked.

"Well, you remember Beverly Simmons? She broke her hip, and they don't take pets at the facility they moved her into, and, well, she didn't want Madge going to a shelter, so how could I say no?"

"Why didn't you call me? You can't take care of a dog."

"I thought I could. Beverly said she was such a good girl, but she just doesn't listen to me."

Madge whimpered, then started to get up and move toward Nate.

Nate shushed her and held up his hand.

Madge stopped her whining, sat back down and lowered her head.

"Maybe you could take her?" Eleanor suggested.

Nate looked at his mother with a shocked expression. "Oh, now I can have a dog? After asking you and Dad for twelve years?"

"Yes," Eleanor said. "I give you permission to have a dog, and here she is."

Nate started to say something, but realized that any other course of action would be even more effort on his part. And he did always want a dog. Since he was stuck at home for a while, he could properly train her.

Eleanor saw Nate hesitate and smiled knowingly. "I have some food and her toys on the back porch."

Nate grunted. "Until we can come up with a permanent situation, I guess I can take care of Madge temporarily."

Madge got excited hearing the words "toys" and "Madge" so close together.

Nate glared at her and she quieted down. "I can tell you right now, if you don't behave I'll lock you in the basement."

"Oh, you'll do no such thing. She's a very good dog," Eleanor stated firmly. Then she looked down at the confused but still obedient poodle. "Except for the food stealing. Poor thing must be starving."

Nate shook his head, instantly regretting his decision.

"Why are you here?" Eleanor asked, suddenly concerned. "Is everything okay?"

"I'm fine. Still a few months away from active duty, and—"

"Oh, you're not going to go back, are you? You nearly died? I couldn't take it. Both your father and you gone? I'd give up and starve myself if I wasn't afraid I'd go straight to hell and never see my boys again."

Nate refrained from expressing his thoughts on the subject of an afterlife. "Let's go inside. I want to talk to you about something."

Eleanor held open the door. Madge looked at it, then up at Nate. Nate gave her an approving nod, and the dog ran inside, directly toward the kitchen. "I hope there isn't anything on the counter," Nate warned as he entered the house and closed the door behind him.

They walked into the living room and Nate took a seat on the couch, while Eleanor perched herself on the paisley upholstered armchair next to it. Nate avoided looking at the empty recliner across from his mother, the chair his father had spent much of his life in.

"What is it, dear?" Eleanor asked.

"Well, I met someone—"

"Oh, my, is she nice? Is it that pretty nurse from the hospital? Oh, Nate, I'm so happy for you."

"No, I'm not dating anyone. She's an anthropology professor at the state university, and she also investigates things."

"Like what?" Eleanor asked, suspicious.

"Like fake psychics."

"Oh, pshaw," Eleanor said, posturing herself to face her body away from Nate.

"Mom, it's not… She actually believes in all that stuff, but she investigates to find out whether they're real."

"Of course they're real," Eleanor insisted. "I talk to your father every week, just like I talked to him for thirty years. I would know if I was actually speaking with him or not."

"People can be very clever," Nate suggested. "Sometimes they find out things that make it seem like—"

"I don't want to argue about all that. I want to know why you don't want to ask her out? She's a college professor. You always liked the smart ones."

"What if we all went out some time?" Nate found himself asking, as much surprised as Eleanor was.

"All of us?"

"Sure. As long as you listen to what she has to say."

Eleanor considered. It was a small price to pay to see her son out with a nice girl. And it would give her a chance to talk him up to her. Any mother would kill to tag along on a date with their son. "All right. I'll listen. But we go somewhere nice, where you have to dress up. Wear that blue suit you have, and that pink and silver tie."

"Sure, Mom. We'll go someplace nice."

"Good. Are you staying for dinner? I have a fresh meatloaf."

There was a crash from the kitchen.

"How about I take you out?"

CHAPTER TWENTY ONE

Jennifer breezed into her office. "Good news," she announced, but then realized there was no one there to hear it. She looked around. No Dave, no Emily, no Bits.

She walked around the desk and sat down. She turned on the computer and logged into her Twitter feed to continue sorting through the growing list of responses to her appearance. It looked like the Moe Hogan interview was paying off. There were a few more direct messages from people reaching out to her with claims of ghosts, one woman insisting she was possessed by the spirit of a dead cable car driver, and another who asserted she had precognitive visions and needed to speak with Jennifer as soon as possible. She forwarded each to Dave to look into, then noticed a folder on the corner of her desk.

Jennifer picked up the bulky packet and read the label across the tab. It was written in Dave's precise printing. "Oakley Arms Research." She tried to remember why he would be compiling information on something called "Oakley Arms," then remembered one of the possible cases he had flagged. She opened the folder and started flipping through the pages.

Her staff's work, as always, was methodical and thorough. The material was organized chronologically—likely Emily's contribution—starting with stories about the laying of the building's cornerstone, up through the opening which attracted the attention of

141

the mayor, and a couple local celebrities. The building's elevators were state-of-the art for the time, and the spacious apartments and pleasant views attracted an upscale clientele as it was one of the first buildings of its size to go up after the great quake.

There were a couple of articles through the early part of the twentieth century about the building's owner falling on hard times during the depression, and the property changed hands a few times during and between the World Wars when it became a popular residence for military personnel.

During the fifties, it saw a renovation that was sparked by a series of electrical fires in the building. Each one was relatively contained, but the original wiring had never been replaced, and hungry rodents had chewed through much of the cloth-clad wire causing blazes that fortunately hadn't killed anyone. The fires did, however, catch the attention of city inspectors who, after decades of either malfeasance or indifference, had no choice but to insist that it be replaced and sprinklers installed.

The next time the Oakley Arms made the news was in the sixties. A headline screamed, "Axeman Falls To Death off Oakley Arms." Jennifer sat down to read this saga in detail. A violent death, actually two of them, the Axeman's last victim and himself, made the old building a strong candidate for a haunting. She read the additional material Dave had included about the Axeman's killing spree that left young women across the city wracked with fear. For over a year, the serial killer had struck seemingly at random throughout the city, with the only commonality among his victims being that they were all attractive, young women living on their own.

Jennifer reread the article detailing the Axeman's demise, the reporter captured the harrowing moments when the murderer was trapped in the building, driven to the roof, and found dead from a fall onto a neighboring building.

And there it was. She couldn't believe it hadn't stood out to her the first time she read it. One of the policemen who found the body was named William Raney. Same spelling on the last name as Nate. It was common for police work to be a generational vocation, and she wondered if there was a connection between Officer William Raney and Detective Nate Raney.

The elevator opened at the far end of the basement offices. Jennifer looked up from the pages and saw Dave approaching, a sandwich in one hand that he was hungrily eating.

"Dr. Daye," he said with a mouthful of tuna salad and a bit of surprise.

"Hi, Dave." She held up the folder. "Great work."

Dave finished chewing and swallowing before speaking again. "Thanks. Looks like it checks a lot of boxes."

"It does. Old building, lots of history, violent deaths, a police officer named Raney..."

"I was hoping you'd spot that," he said, smiling.

"Can you find out if he's any relationship to Nate Raney?"

Dave dropped his backpack and fished out a printed page. It showed a graduation ceremony at the Police Academy including a young officer, Nathaniel Raney, attended by his great-uncle, Detective William Raney—retired.

Jennifer's smile matched Dave's.

CHAPTER TWENTY TWO

Madge jumped up on Nate's bed and started licking his face.

It was late morning, but Nate was still exhausted from a restless night and it took him a moment to return to consciousness and realize what was happening. "Madge," he commanded sternly, "off!"

Madge pulled back and stared at Nate, quizzically.

Nate wondered if this dog had received any training at all. Then he remembered that he had left Madge locked in a large, wire kennel he had purchased and paid to have delivered and set up the previous night.

"Off," he repeated more sharply. Madge backed up half a step, looked down at the carpeted bedroom floor, then back at Nate.

Nate nodded his head toward the floor.

Madge reluctantly jumped down and then jumped right back up again.

Nate used his good arm to prop himself up to a sitting position and shifted his leg under the covers to nudge Madge to the edge of the bed. The dog tried to maintain her position on the increasingly shrinking sliver of bed between the edge and Nate's leg until she unceremoniously toppled over and crashed to the floor. She scrambled to her feet and peered up at Nate with sad eyes.

"How did you get out of your crate?" he asked rhetorically.

Madge looked at him, then turned and trotted away, walked to the other side of the bed where she hopped up and then curled up on the corner out of Nate's reach.

Nate decided to put off any further attempted discipline of his new house guest until after breakfast. He checked his watch and was surprised to see it was already a quarter past nine. The doctor had warned him that the side effects of his medications could include fatigue, but at the same time he had trouble sleeping. Despite the pain pills, there was always a persistent, dull ache in his shoulder, and headaches that would come in waves. That, coupled with the vivid dreams, left very little time during the night for actual sleep. He found himself turning on a late night radio talk show and letting it distract him until he couldn't stay awake any longer.

Now he could add worrying about what Madge was up to while he was asleep to the list. That notion jolted him to full wakefulness. He made his way downstairs and to the kitchen where he had left Madge securely locked away—or so he had thought.

He stopped and took in a deep breath as he surveyed the mess. The garbage was strewn around and everything that could be shredded, was torn into tiny, wet, smelly pieces. Fortunately, he hadn't left any food out and she hadn't managed to get into his refrigerator—though there were some scratch marks on the large cabinet that served as his pantry.

He inspected the steel wire crate he had left Madge in the previous night. It had a latch that required squeezing two handles together to release the door. The door was shut. There didn't appear to be any way she could squeeze her snout between the steel wire, or the gap between the door and the crate. And even if she had somehow undone the latch, how could she have managed to lock it back up again? Nate began replaying the events of the night before, wondering if he had merely dreamed locking up Madge. Regardless, it was a puzzle that could be put off till later. He opened the locked door of the crate.

"Madge, breakfast," he called out, gently, hoping to lure her with the promise of food.

A few seconds later, he heard a thump, and the pad of her feet on the carpet, then the click of her nails on the wood floor of the hallway. She poked her head into the kitchen. Nate glared at her, and she bowed her head, sheepishly, as if trying to explain it was out of her control. He stood next to the open kennel and Madge, head still bowed, trudge slowly to her incarceration as if accepting her sentence.

"Just until I get things cleaned up," Nate promised her, "maybe you need to go for a walk."

At the word "walk," Madge's ears perked up, and she excitedly turned around in the cage.

"Soon," Nate promised, then started a pot of coffee while he set about trying to sweep and mop up the mess on his kitchen floor with one good arm. It took a while, but when he was done, he made himself a heavily creamed cup of coffee and carried it out to the living room.

"Madge!" he shouted, once he saw that every single throw pillow had been shredded and relieved of their stuffing, and all the cushions yanked from the chairs and sofa. He heard an apologetic whimper from the corner of the kitchen. Nate set the coffee down, found the cushion for his chair and set it in place. He lowered himself into it, forcing his mind to ignore the storm of stuffing blanketing his living room, and took a satisfying sip from his coffee.

The doorbell rang.

Nate waited for Max's familiar voice to shout through the door, but it obviously wasn't his partner. Max didn't have the patience to wait for anyone to answer the door. He'd be shouting for Nate to open it and trying the knob by now.

Who else could it be? He wasn't expecting anyone. It wouldn't be his mother. Perhaps a delivery?

Nate set the coffee down, then lifted himself from the chair and stepped around the cushions. He was partially aware that he was barefoot and only wearing a t-shirt and some loose pajama pants and had his arm in a sling. He opened the door.

"Good morning, Detective Raney," Jennifer Daye said with a smile. Without waiting for Nate to ask, she squeezed by him into the house, and then froze when she saw the state of the place. "I'm not sure I want to know," she said, looking to Nate who was still in a state of shock.

"What are you doing here?" Nate asked. "And how do you know where I live?"

Jennifer ignored his questions, fished a thick file folder out of her bag and handed it to him. "I have a case for us."

"Us? I never said I would—"

"Actually, you did. We have a bet. I find a case that convinces you that the paranormal is real, then you talk to me about your near-death experience."

"I never had a—"

"And this is the case," she said, flapping the folder in front of his face. She sniffed at the air. "Do I smell coffee?"

Nate felt completely off guard. Part of him was embarrassed to let someone into his house with the state Madge had left it in, while another part was embarrassed to have Jennifer see him essentially undressed, with an unknown degree of bed-head. But oddly, he found himself glad to see her. Despite the disaster he had woken up to, her free-spirited personality assured him somehow that it was all good.

"Lots of sugar, no cream. I don't know how people can drink coffee with cream in it," she said as she placed the file on the coffee table next to Nate's cup, filled with an almost-white liquid. She smiled an awkward apology. Then she caught something out of the corner of her eye. "Who's this?" she asked.

Nate turned and saw Madge standing in the kitchen door. The dog trotted around the minefield of cushions and deflated pillows and sniffed at Jennifer's outstretched hand. She then stepped forward and slipped her head under the hand and allowed Jennifer to scratch her behind the ears.

"I, um," Nate stammered, still in shock at Jennifer's unexpected entrance, and Madge's repeat performance of her escape artist act.

"Need to get dressed?" Jennifer suggested. "I thought you might be up by now. I know it's a Saturday, but I didn't take you for one to sleep in."

"A lot on my mind lately, plus the meds are really messing with me," Nate explained, nodding toward the sling.

"No worries," Jennifer said scratching the dog behind its ears with one hand, while reading the tag attached to its collar with the other. "Madge will keep me company. Go make yourself pretty," she teased.

Nate grimaced at the comment, but decided the opportunity to get out of this room and into some clothing that made him feel comfortable instead of powerless was the best move for the moment. He grabbed his coffee cup. "The coffee's in the kitchen, cups are next to the sink, sugar's on the counter." At least he wasn't going to be corralled into waiting on her as well.

"Thanks," Jennifer said while giving Madge a two-handed neck scruff that made the dog squeeze her eyes shut in delight.

Nate left the room. Once he was gone, Jennifer looked down at the poodle. "Did you make this mess? Was this you?"

Madge moaned.

"It's okay. Let's clean it up for your daddy." Madge looked around, as if not quite understanding what Jennifer wanted her to do. "By us, I mean me. You just stay out of trouble for a little while, can you do that?" Madge answered by jumping up onto the chair recently vacated by Nate—as it was the only one with its cushion. Jennifer smiled and started gathering up the stuffing.

After a look in the mirror, Nate decided he needed to jump into the shower before any further dealings with Dr. Daye. He had mastered putting on and taking off both t-shirts and dress shirts around his injured shoulder with minimal pain. The steamy warmth from the shower seemed to provide a level of relief from the constant discomfort that his medication couldn't quite reach. He had intended to do just a cursory rinse rather than a full shower, but the momentary bliss supplied by the stream of hot water cascading over his shoulder was too good to rush.

Once he was clean and carefully toweled dry, Nate slipped into some chinos and a casual polo shirt. He ran his electric razor over the previous night's stubble, dreading the possibility of a compliment from Jennifer, while at the same time not wanting her to think he was a slob who lived in a house that looked like a war zone.

He slipped on some socks and loafers, checked to make sure his hair looked presentable, and walked down the stairs and through the hall to the living room. When he got there, he was somewhat surprised to find it was restored to a respectable state of order. The cushions were all back in place, the empty pillow cases were stacked on one of the chairs, and all the stuffing had been cleaned up and removed.

Jennifer and Madge sat on the sofa. The dog rested its head in Jennifer's lap while she scratched behind its ears with one hand and navigated something on her phone with the other.

"Thanks, you didn't need to do this," Nate said.

"Not at all. Besides, I figured if I did something nice for you, I could guilt you into listening to my proposal and convince you to investigate this case with me."

Nate lowered himself gingerly into his chair and glanced at the folder before him on the coffee table.

"I think you'll find this one interesting."

"Why's that?" Nate asked, unconvinced.

"Because it may involve a serial killer from the sixties who was caught by a young police officer named William Raney."

Nate shot her a look. "Uncle Bill?" he asked.

"Oh, is he related?" Jennifer asked, innocently.

Nate smirked at her heavy-handed attempt to play dumb. He picked up the folder, laid it in his lap and opened it up.

Jennifer had placed the newspaper article detailing Nate's uncle's role in ending the Axeman's reign of terror at the top of the stack. She sipped at her cup of coffee while she watched him read it. If he was curious, he didn't let on. One by one, he read carefully through the pages of the articles, then the incident report Dave had compiled based on Diane Collins email and subsequent phone interviews. Once he got to the other historical information about the Oakley Arms, Nate became less careful of his inspection of the documents, reading only the first few paragraphs to see if it was of any relevance and then skimming the rest.

Jennifer sat and watched Nate read, while ruffling Madge's curly hair absently much to the dog's delight.

After nearly an hour, Nate closed the folder and set it down.

"She has a stalker," Nate declared confidently. "Tell her to call the police."

"What are the police going to do about the apparitions in her bathroom, the unexplainable cold spots in her apartment, the sounds and disturbances?"

"Nothing. It's a job for the building superintendent. There's nothing supernatural about an old building having drafts, or creaking and groaning. As for the 'ghost' she saw? Come on, she admitted it was a in a steamy bathroom."

"Okay, so it's an easy bet, then."

"It is."

"But you have to prove everything you just said to win," Jennifer insisted. "And I get a chance to prove to you that there's something paranormal at work here. It has all the earmarks of an apparition."

"And you think the ghost is the lost soul of this Axeman that my great-uncle chased off the roof of her building sixty-some years ago?"

"Could be," said Jennifer. "Why is that so impossible?"

"Because there are no such things as ghosts."

Jennifer smiled.

"What's so funny?" Nate asked.

"We'll see," she answered confidently.

"You think just because there's a connection to my Uncle Bill that I'm going to jump at the chance to look into it," Nate accused.

Jennifer shrugged innocently.

Nate had to admit, he was sincerely curious about looking into something having to do with a case his great uncle had worked on. And there was that promise of taking his mother to dinner with Dr. Daye he had made. "Tell you what, I'll look into this with you, if you do me a favor."

"What did you have in mind?"

"Dinner."

"I thought that was after I lost the bet."

"No, I want you to have dinner with my mother and me. I told you she's been taken advantage of by a lot of psychics in town."

"Unfortunately there are a lot of con artists who thrive on taking advantage of the vulnerable," Jennifer admitted.

"So, explain that to her. Let her know that she can't trust every storefront palm reader who tells her that my dad wants her to buy them a new iPhone."

Jennifer nods. "I can do that. You do understand that even though I acknowledge there are frauds out there tricking people, I also believe it is possible to communicate with the dead. And I've done it myself."

"If you could just convince her to be more careful—and I can't believe I'm saying this—maybe refer her to someone you trust not to bleed her dry..."

Jennifer nodded, a serious look on her face. "No problem. I get it. You care about her. And maybe you think you can trust me."

Nate considered. "Well, you aren't the typical grifter. Most of them aren't tenured professors at state universities."

"Have you seen the job market for anthropology majors these days?"

Nate laughed. "Okay, Challenge accepted. When do you want to visit Miss Collins?"

"She's expecting us right about now. I didn't know you would spend an hour reading that file."

"Us? Now? You were that confident I'd agree?"

Jennifer rose to her feet, causing Madge to sit up. "As you'll find out soon enough, never bet against me."

Nate directed his gaze at Madge. "I think you, my friend, are going into the yard. I can't trust you in the house."

Madge looked up at Jennifer. "Don't look at me, I'm on his side on this one. You made a big mess."

The dog stepped down off of the sofa and walked through the living room, then into the kitchen, all the way to the back door.

Nate and Jennifer exchanged curious looks.

"Smart dog," Jennifer commented.

"After we debunk your noisy pipes case, I need you to figure out how she's been getting out of her kennel."

"Oh, you keep her locked up?"

Nate rolled his eyes, reminding her that she spent quite a bit more than a few minutes cleaning up after that "smart dog."

"Right," Jennifer acknowledged. "I see your point."

Nate rose and walked to the back door and let Madge out, then locked the door behind him. "All right," he called out to Jennifer, "let's not keep Miss Collins waiting."

CHAPTER TWENTY THREE

Jennifer pulled the van up to a spot near the entrance to the Oakley Arms. Nate let out a breath.

"Come on, my driving's not that bad." Jennifer protested.

"It wasn't so much the driving as this thing we're riding in," Nate told her. "I always wondered what happened to the Scooby Doo Mystery Machine."

"I love that show. And Fred wishes he had a van as cool as this one," Jennifer said.

"You liked Scooby Doo? But they always found out that the ghost was really old man Jenkins trying to scare people away from the old mine because he found there was really gold in it."

"Nice summary of every episode ever, but there was something about Fred that just made me swoon." Jennifer looked at Nate, sizing him up. "Have you ever considered wearing an ascot?"

"No. Please do not project your cartoon fantasies on me."

"Oh, come on, you know you had a thing for Daphne."

"Nope. I was a Velma guy, always liked the smart girls."

Jennifer nodded approvingly. "Good answer. Shall we?" she asked, looking out at the façade of the stately old Oakley Arms.

They exited the van and walked up to the front door. The outer door was open, and there was a beat up security phone hanging on the wall with instructions for looking up the tenants posted next to it. Jennifer had the information already and merely dialed Diane's apartment number.

"Hello, who is it?" a female voice asked.

"Hi, Diane, it's Jennifer Daye and Detective Raney. Can we come up?"

The door buzzed. Nate pulled it open with his good arm and held it for Jennifer. She hung up the phone and entered the lobby and Nate followed.

Jennifer paused to admire the architectural details in the old building. Despite the renovations over the years, much of the ornate plasterwork had been preserved. The counter where a concierge would have once served stood empty, home to brochures and notices about the proper procedures for requesting maintenance. She tried to imagine what it had been like when it first opened. A tall, uniformed doorman out front, the obsequious yet efficient concierge tending to the tenants' needs as he surreptitiously tracked their comings and goings. She saw couples dressed up for an evening on the town, the women in long furs, the men in dapper overcoats and top hats.

"Nice," Nate said, taking in the surroundings.

Jennifer slowly turned, sending her gaze into every corner and toward every light fixture and the framed painting on the walls. "At one time, this was the place to be. A lot of the people who made this city run lived in this building."

"Progress. Things change," Nate commented.

"Come on, the elevators are over there."

Jennifer pushed the button to call the elevator and Nate watched the old-fashioned metal needle swing in an arc over the numbers of the floors as the elevator descended. He couldn't remember the last time he'd seen anything like it outside of a movie.

One of the set of elevator doors opened and a middle-aged couple stepped out. They regarded Jennifer and Nate suspiciously. "Are you the Silvermans" Jennifer asked them.

Nate looked at her quizzically, not knowing what the question had to do with what they were doing there.

"No," answered the man. "I don't know who that is," he added for good measure.

"Great," Jennifer said, turning to Nate. "They're probably still up there, we can catch them before they skip town." Jennifer guided Nate into the elevator and pushed the button for the tenth floor. "Bye, thank you," she said to the couple as the doors closed.

"What was that all about?" Nate asked.

"I don't know, sometimes I just feel like being goofy. They'll be talking about the Silvermans for weeks. Don't you ever just mess with people for fun?"

"No," Nate answered firmly, and turned his attention to the elevator doors.

"Okay, but don't blame me if the Silvermans get away again," she said.

Nate rolled his eyes and tried to contain a smile. He had to admit, it was kind of funny, but he wasn't about to let her know he thought so.

Jennifer pulled a rumpled paper bag from her pocket. She poured a small pile of candy corn into one hand and offered it to Nate. "Candy corn?"

"No thanks," Nate answered, adding yet another item to the list of Jennifer Daye's quirks he was mentally compiling.

The elevator doors opened up on to a hallway with the smell of stale carpeting. The rug that ran the length of the hall was getting threadbare in places, and the wall paper was also showing its age. Jennifer checked the apartment numbers, then turned to the right and led Nate to the far end of the hallway. She knocked on the door for apartment ten-H. Almost instantly, the one behind them opened up.

"Oh, hello," said the old woman who poked her head out. "Are you here to see Diane?" she asked.

Nate and Jennifer exchanged a puzzled look. "I thought she lived here," Jennifer said, pointing to the door they had just knocked on.

"She does, she does," the old woman assured them. "I didn't know she was expecting any visitors."

Diane's door opened. Nate and Jennifer swung their attention to the attractive young woman standing there, but she sighed and spoke to the nosy woman from across the hall. "Hi, Rose, just some friends, visiting."

"I didn't know you had any friends, dear," Rose said, then she explained to Nate and Jennifer, "she's always working—or so she says," she added teasingly.

"Thanks, Rose, have a nice day." Diane ushered Jennifer and Nate inside her apartment and quickly closed the door.

"Well, you won't have to worry about anyone robbing the place," Nate observed.

Diane laughed uncomfortably. "I guess not," she said.

"Hi, I'm Dr. Jennifer Daye," Jennifer said, "and this is Detective Nate Raney."

"Yes, you mentioned that on the intercom. You think this is a police matter?" she asked.

"I'm not currently on active duty. I'm just consulting with Dr. Daye on this investigation."

"Oh, okay," Diane said. "Well, please, come on in. Have a seat." She closed the door, locked the bolt and fastened the chain, then directed them to a sitting area in front of the television.

Jennifer took in as much of the place as she could and settled down on the couch. "I love this place. Such tall ceilings, it has a lot of character." She pulled out her cell phone and activated a recording app.

Nate continued walking around the apartment, taking in details with his detective's eye.

"Yes, that's one of the reasons I liked it, too. It is a pain to dust up there, but it just feels less like living in a box and more like a home." Diane sat down next to Jennifer and took a deep breath, "So, where do we start?"

"Let's go back to the beginning," Jennifer suggested. "When did you move in?"

"It was just over six months ago, now," Diane began. "I had gotten a promotion at my job, and with that came longer hours. My living situation at the time was a little tense, and I wanted to be closer to my office, so I found this place. The rent was reasonable, and I fell in love with the big windows and the wooden floors.

"For the first few months there were things that seemed odd, stuff not where I expected it to be, new noises. The things that are just different enough to notice until you don't anymore. There were a few electrical problems, but the superintendent was always very responsive with any issues I had."

Nate listened as he continued walking slowly around the apartment, looking out the windows, running his fingers over the ridges of the radiator, taking in the photographs that were displayed in various places.

"Then I started noticing that there were some spots in the apartment that were always cold. I must've rearranged the furniture a dozen times. The super told me that it was common in an old building like this with radiant heat and tall ceilings and that a lot of the tenants got space heaters to help out, but to make sure I got one with a timer because if you left it on for too long, it could flip a breaker."

"Sounds like my old office."

"Sometimes I'd wake up at night thinking I heard a voice, but I didn't think anything of that. It could have been someone's TV too loud on the floor above or below me, or just a dream. I didn't start putting it all together until the night I saw him."

Nate stopped his survey of the apartment and casually jumped into the questioning. "Him? You saw a man in your apartment?"

"Well, yes and no. I saw something, but I'm always very fastidious about locking my apartment door."

"Have you always been? Or is that a more recent habit?" Nate asked.

"To be honest, now that I'm living alone, I have been more cautious."

"Go on. Tell me about that night," Jennifer urged.

Diane positioned herself so she was facing Jennifer directly, putting Nate to her back. "Well, I usually like to relax in a hot shower, you know, where you let the bathroom get steamy like a sauna."

"So good for the pores," Jennifer said.

"Right. So I was finishing up, drying off, and I started feeling strange. Like I was being watched. I thought I saw something behind me reflected in the mirror. When I turned around, there he was, standing in the middle of the bathtub. I think. I had the feeling he was maybe floating."

"Did you see his feet?"

"What?"

"Do you remember if you could see his feet?"

Diane thought back, "I don't know. I couldn't be sure, I mean if he was standing in the tub, I wouldn't have seen his feet, so I guess, I don't know. Is that important?"

"Go on."

"Anyway, he said something to me. Or he tried to, I didn't hear him, but I could see his lips move. I was so surprised that when I was turning, I slipped and fell and hit my head. I don't know exactly how long I was out, but when I woke up he was gone."

"Did you see a doctor?" Nate asked.

"No," Dianne confessed, "I had a cut, but it didn't need stitches. I took a few Tylenol and went to bed. After that, I started staying with a friend from work. I didn't want to sleep here. I was scared."

"I don't blame you," Jennifer said. "How long did that last?"

"About a week. I would come back here to change clothes, but after a while, I felt like I was paying rent for a closet. So, I went to one of those shops that sells crystals and stuff and bought some sage and some other things to ward off spirits and I returned home."

"Did it work? The sage and crystals."

Diane laughed. "I have no idea, but I haven't seen the man again. There have been other things. The night I saw you on the Moe Hogan podcast a bottle of rosewater I had on my vanity fell and broke. And I know for a fact that it was no where near the edge."

"What else?" Jennifer asked.

"I don't know, a lot of little things. A bouquet of flowers will wilt quickly, except for a single bloom. I told you about the cold spots, but sometimes, it feels like I'm walking through a freezer when I'm standing perfectly still. I get actual goosebumps. And a few times, now, I think I've heard the same words, but I can't be sure. It sounds like someone saying, 'ouch it froze.'"

Jennifer raised her eyebrows at that one.

"Does that make any sense?" Diane asked.

"Not yet, but we don't have all the pieces."

"Did you save them?" Nate asked.

"Pardon me?"

"The pieces of the bottle. You said it broke?"

"Why, do you want to check for fingerprints or something?"

"No, but he's got a point. It could mean something."

Diane thinks. "It's probably still in the waste basket in the bathroom."

Nate was the closest and crossed over to the bathroom and turned on the light. He reached for the waste basket and lifted it up on top of the vanity. Then he pulled out some makeup stained tissues, cotton balls and put them into the sink. He carefully retrieved the broken glass at the bottom and laid the pieces on the flat surface of the vanity, like a puzzle. Diane and Jennifer joined him just as he reassembled the glass fragments into a raised pattern of a rose.

Jennifer pulled out her phone and snapped a photo. "Tell me more about the man you saw," she suggested, now that they were in the room where the apparition had appeared. "What did he look like? What was he wearing?"

Diane looked at the tub, then turned and looked at it in the reflection in the mirror. "He was about as tall as Detective Raney, short hair, clean-shaven. Blue eyes—he had the bluest eyes. He was wearing a raincoat. The old fashioned kind. Thick rubber, with metal clasps."

Jennifer and Nate exchanged a look. The Axeman had been a fireman.

"Like a fireman would wear?" she asked.

Diane considered the question, then after a moment answered, "Yes, it could have been. I think so."

Jennifer crossed to where she had left her bag and fished out a compact version of the magnetometer she used for full scale investigations. She turned it on and walked around the bathroom. The LEDs lit up and grew brighter.

"What does that mean?" Diane asked.

"This device detects unusual variations in magnetic fields. Like the kind we sometimes see when there is paranormal activity."

"Or in a bathroom full of metal pipes," Nate suggested.

Diane and Jennifer ignored him.

Nate continued his reconnaissance of the apartment while Jennifer had Diane direct her to the places where she had felt cold spots or heard voices.

Nate noticed a collection of magazines on a table near the front door. Some of them were addressed to Diane Collins, others to Jerry Henderson at an address that was not the Oakley Arms. He inspected the lock on the door. The chain seemed unusually long. "Has Jerry ever been to this apartment?" Nate shouted across the room to Diane.

Diane and Jennifer both looked at Nate.

"He's your ex-boyfriend, right? The one you were living with before you moved here."

"I didn't tell you I had a boyfriend."

"You said you were in an uncomfortable living situation, and you've got magazines with his name and your old address on it. Not quite Sherlock Holmes, but I am a detective."

"See why I brought him along?" Jennifer asked.

"Yes, he was here once to collect some things. But he hasn't been since."

Nate nodded, accepting her explanation. "I would recommend you get a police lock installed. I know a guy who will do it for free if you pay for the hardware."

"Thank you."

"Is he still living at this address?" Nate asked, holding up one of the magazines.

"Yes."

"Does he have a car?"

"He does. A black Civic."

"You wouldn't happen to know the license plate number."

"I do. Better Get Busy To Afford Some Gold."

Jennifer regarded Diane quizzically.

She clarified, "B-G-B-2-4-S-G. It's a little thing I do to remember phone numbers and license plates."

"I do the same thing," Nate said with a smile. Then something tickled the back of his mind. A memory. But the thought was banished at the sound of Diane's voice.

"Are you going to check up on him?"

"I am—if you don't mind."

"I don't at all. If he is behind any of this, I want to know and I want him to stop. But I don't think he would do something to scare me. It wasn't an ugly breakup, we're still friends."

"Well, I have some friends on the force who won't mind doing me a favor," Nate said.

Jennifer put a reassuring hand on her shoulder. "I'd like to do some full scale surveillance, bring in some more sensitive equipment and see if we can determine the nature of the phenomena you're experiencing."

Nate turned away, returned his attention to the door.

Jennifer noticed, and continued, "Detective Raney and I would like to spend twenty-four hours here, see what we can find out."

"Okay, if that's what it takes. Should I find someplace else to stay?"

"No, you may be more a part of this than you know. It'll take a few days for me to get everything together, plus I have classes, so how's next weekend? Saturday, around noon? That'll give us time to talk to your neighbors beforehand."

"Oh, is that necessary? I don't know if I want them knowing I asked you to look into this."

"We're discrete," assured Jennifer. "My team is very experienced at getting people to talk about any strange things they may have seen without betraying any confidences."

"Okay," Diane said, still concerned. "Does this mean you don't think I'm crazy?"

Jennifer smiled warmly. "Not at all. Listen, I would not be devoting the resources of my team to investigate this if I didn't think there was a good chance this is a legitimate paranormal incident."

Nate let out a barely audible sigh.

Diane and Jennifer turned their attention to him.

He realized the room had fallen silent and turned around to face them. He addressed Jennifer. "I thought I was here to offer my expertise."

"You don't think I'm being stalked by a ghost?" Diane asked.

"I believe you may be being stalked, but not by a ghost." Nate opened the door and stepped outside the apartment. "Close the door and secure the chain," he said to Diane.

Diane stepped forward and did as Nate instructed. She closed the door on him, then slipped the chain into its slot.

Nate opened it. The chain kept it from opening all the way. Then he closed it so it was open just enough for him to slip a pencil through the crack and push the end of the chain out of its groove. He opened the door again. "You don't need to be able to walk through walls to get in here. Your deadbolt is a little out of line. If it hits the strike plate, you can think it's locked, and chained, but..." He stepped inside.

Jennifer smiled to Diane. "Between the two of us, I think we can help you find out what's going on."

Diane nodded. "Okay, let's do this. What else do you need?"

"My staff will be in touch to do some follow up."

"Okay. Can they call me at home instead of work? I don't want people at the firm to find out that..."

"No problem," Jennifer assured her. "I think we have what we need for now. If you experience anything, the slightest sound, temperature change, if anything is out of place, write it down. Keep a diary. Anything you notice will help."

"Okay, I can do that."

"Great. We'll see you next Saturday."

"Thank you," Diane said, giving Jennifer a grateful hug. She turned to Nate, and he offered her his good hand for an awkward handshake.

"I do want to send someone around to secure this door."

"You don't have to convince me any further on that," Diane admitted. "Thank you."

Jennifer and Nate nodded their final goodbyes and stepped out of Diane's apartment. She closed the door behind them. At almost the same moment, the door across the hall opened, and the old woman stuck her head out. "Oh, it's you again."

"Yes," Jennifer said. "We're just leaving."

The woman harrumphed. "Young people today," she said without any further explanation, then disappeared and closed the door.

Jennifer looked to Nate and then tried unsuccessfully to contain a laugh. "Come on," she said to the implacable detective as they walked down the hallway to the elevators. "That was funny—in a weird, creepy kind of way."

"You didn't tell me I'd be giving up my weekend," Nate said, changing the subject.

"You have somewhere else to be?" She asked.

"I have a dog that eats my house even when I'm there."

"Oh, right. I forgot," Jennifer admitted as the elevator door opened. "If you don't mind a small detour to my new offices, I might be able to help you with that."

CHAPTER TWENTY FOUR

Dave exited the elevator and stepped into the lobby of a modern building that smelled of new carpeting and fresh paint. He was carrying a trio of bankers boxes, while also clasping a collection of shopping bags in his hands, making it difficult to see let alone walk.

"Nine-oh-nine, nine-oh-nine," he kept muttering to himself so he wouldn't forget the number of their new office he had so carefully memorized before loading himself up with the boxes and bags. He found the small signs posted indicating which direction to go to find the office number he was looking for. He made a right turn and found the correct door. While he supported the boxes with a knee, Dave turned the knob and pushed it open. He re-secured his hold on the boxes, backed into the office, then set the boxes and bags down once he was inside.

It was nice. There was a single desk in the center of the room, and the entire space was somewhat larger than the office they had before they were banished to the basement. "Not bad, a bit smaller than I expected, but at least it has a window," he said out loud.

Two doors on either side of the office opened and Bits and Emily poked their heads out.

"Finally found the place, huh?" Emily asked.

"Don't plug anything in until I finish rewiring," Bits warned.

"What? We have our own offices?"

Bits and Emily exchanged a look.

"Well, *we* have our own offices," she answered with an emphasis on the "we." "You get this desk."

"Why? I see four doors," Dave said, referencing the other two doors that were still closed."

"That one is for Dr. Daye," Bits said.

"And what about this one?" Dave asked, as he crossed to the fourth door and pulled it open. It was a small office that had been hastily converted into a storage space. Inside were file cabinets, boxes, equipment cases and shelves filled with miscellaneous items.

"A closet? Why does this have to be a closet?" Then he looked at Bits and Emily. "I've been with Dr. Daye longer than either of you two, why do you get offices and I'm stuck at the receptionist's desk?"

"I need a secure environment," Bits answered, then closed the door. Dave and Emily heard the sound of locks whirring into place and the beep of what was likely an alarm system activating.

"He's going to be living in there," Dave said.

Emily nodded.

"You know I should have that office," Dave said to Emily. "I deserve that office."

"Yeah, well," Emily countered, "the thing is I got here first. So, I'm afraid there's nothing I can do, really."

"That's not a reason. We'll sort this out when Dr. Daye gets here," Dave challenged, crossing his arms with a look of defiance on his face.

"Sort what out when I get here?" Jennifer asked.

Dave turned around and saw Jennifer and Nate standing in the open doorway.

Unperturbed, he pointed to Emily. "I want her office."

"Why?" Jennifer asked. "It's a lot smaller than this is," she said waving her arm around the common area. "Besides, she got here first."

"But—"

"And, you're my number one guy. I can't be traipsing all the way across the office whenever I need you. You're my right hand, Dave. I can't cut you off from the rest of me."

Jennifer walked up to Dave and put an arm around him. His demeanor changed immediately, and he smiled.

"Okay," he said. "I'll make it work."

She turned to Nate and introduced the members of her team. "Detective Nate Raney, I'd like you to meet my most valuable team member, Dave. And that back there poking her head out is Emily. You've met before."

"Right. At the hospital."

"That was all her idea," Emily said.

"It's nice to meet you both," Nate assured them.

Jennifer turned her attention back to Dave. "Oh, by the way, we're doing a stakeout at Diane Collins' apartment next weekend and Nate needs a dog-sitter. I was hoping you wouldn't mind having Madge at your place. She's a bit of a terror, and if we left her alone at Nate's, she'd tear the place up. Thanks!"

Dave's mouth hung open. In the span of less than a minute, he had gone from staking his claim to some private office space, to being demoted to dog-sitter.

Jennifer crossed to her office door and went in.

Nate walked up to the shell-shocked Dave. "Thanks. She said you loved dogs."

Dave nodded blankly.

"Great. I'll pack up some food for her. Do you have a yard?"

Dave shook his head.

Nate hissed a wordless warning. "Just take her for lots of walks. Hopefully that will work."

Dave nodded and offered a meek smile.

The detective stepped into Jennifer's office. The room was rather spacious with the same desk that had followed her to the basement at its center. Two large, framed posters adorned the walls, one of "The Mysterious Professor" and the other the vintage poster of Houdini. Jennifer was seated behind the desk in a high-backed leather chair, sitting back and enjoying her new office courtesy of the dean's pandering to donors. She smiled at Nate. "Nice, huh?"

"I'm guessing this is an improvement from your last office?" he asked.

Jennifer shivered at the memories. "Vast improvement, you have no idea how long it's taken me to fight through the academic prejudice and get some respect from my peers. Turns out all it took was a philanthropist with an interest in parapsychology and a checkbook."

"I should get going," Nate said.

"Well, don't go without me," Jennifer warned.

Nate looked at her, puzzled.

"You are going to visit your uncle, right?"

"I was thinking about maybe seeing him later this week."

"Well, I have a free afternoon. Let's do it now."

Jennifer stood up from behind the desk. "He's at the Atwood Home, right? Where all the retired cops go?"

"Yes, how did you—never mind."

"Besides, in your condition you'll want me around to help out. I used to work at a nursing home when I was in college. Taught ballroom dancing. I can catch a falling octogenarian faster than a short-stop can snag a line drive."

Jennifer breezed by Nate back into the common area where Dave was unpacking his things onto the desk. Emily had already vanished into her office. "I'm going out to do some research with Detective Raney," she informed Dave. "Probably won't be back today. See you Monday!" She continued out of the office, not bothering to wait for Nate.

Nate looked over at Dave, suddenly realizing how he felt. "She does that a lot," Dave warned.

Nate nodded, then turned and followed Jennifer.

CHAPTER TWENTY FIVE

The Atwood Home was nestled on top of a hill, surrounded by a green garden criss-crossed with walking paths and dotted with benches. Nate and Jennifer escorted William Raney down one of these paths, and when they reached a bench across from a bed of chrysanthemums, they sat down.

"So, she's obviously not your girlfriend," the older man observed.

"Why not?" Jennifer asked, with mock offense.

"Not saying you shouldn't be. If I was fifty years younger—"

"She wouldn't have been born yet," Nate interjected, preventing his uncle from inadvertently creating an actual offense.

Bill smiled and shook his head. "It's a different world," he commented. "So," he said, directing his comments to Jennifer, "why are you here if not to invite me to a wedding?"

Nate rolled his eyes and dropped his chin in embarrassment.

"Well," Jennifer began, gently gripping the retired detective's hand. The gesture certainly got his attention. "I wanted to ask you about an old case you were involved in about sixty years ago."

Bill looked to Nate, then back to Jennifer. "Sixty years ago? I was just a rookie, then. I didn't get my detective's shield for another five years."

"This was the Axeman case," Jennifer said.

Bill sat back as if hit in the chest. He whistled through his teeth.

"Haven't thought about that one in a while. Certainly wasn't my biggest case, and it wasn't even really mine. I just happened to be on duty that night when the call came in. Why are you asking about the Axeman?"

"It's related to a case Nate and I are investigating."

"It's not related," Nate countered, "there's a woman who lives in the same building who's being harassed by an ex-boyfriend."

Bill smiled warmly to Jennifer. "He can be stubborn, can't he," he said.

Jennifer smiled back and nodded.

"That's part of what makes him a good cop, but keeps him from becoming a great one." Bill glanced back at Nate to see if the remark would engender a response. But it didn't. This was a criticism that was not new to Nate. "Well, since you came out all this way, I'll tell you what I know, and then you can tell me if it helps you at all."

"Okay," Jennifer responded.

"Well, it was a crazy time to be a rookie on the force. I was about three months out of the academy when he started killing. The last one, the one he murdered at the Arms, was the only victim I actually saw. A lot of the guys threw up when they viewed the body. Her head was almost completely cut off. So much blood." Bill realized he was painting a rather gruesome picture and continued on with his narrative.

"Anyway, there was this call into the station from someone who claimed they saw a man carrying an axe and heard a woman scream at the Arms. Everyone was on high alert. There was a lot of political pressure. So it wasn't unusual to see a dozen cars converge on the scene. We didn't have walkie-talkies in those days, but most of the cars had radios. Me and my partner were the second to arrive. We had been instructed to secure the building and wait for the detectives to get there.

"Maroney and Jackson went around to the back, and me and my partner, Kendall, took the front. More cars arrived and filled up the streets. But no one was allowed in or out of the building until the detectives got there. The building superintendent had told us that there was another door to the basement, used to be for the coal that heated the place when it first went up. Before they could send anyone down into the basement to check it out, the detectives arrived.

"There was a lot of confusion at that point. Orders being shouted about, policemen wanting to be close to the action in case this was it. We almost didn't notice him.

"He came into the lobby from the stairs. I don't know exactly what bothered me about him. He was a fireman and was wearing his turnout coat—a lot of them used them as winter jackets back then. Neither the police department or the fire department paid all that much. But it was the kind of thing that made someone invisible in a crowd like that. We weren't looking for an off duty firefighter, we were looking for a bloodthirsty killer, some monster of a man wielding an axe with a crazed look in his eyes. This guy was none of that, just the type of guy I'd run into a hundred times before. I remember seeing him, and he looked at me and nodded. You know, just the kind of nod you give a fellow when you're passing to be polite.

"But there was something about the way he was walking. The way he held his hands. The sleeves of his coat were long, and you couldn't even see his fingertips. I didn't even think to look down at his shoes. I had it in my head that his pants would be so long that you couldn't see his shoes, either, like when a kid dresses up in his dad's clothes. But I had reached into my pocket to grab my notebook. I thought I should write down that I had seen this guy in case it was important later—they always told us to write everything down. Anyway, someone bumped my arm, and I dropped my notebook, bent down to pick it up and while I was down near the floor, I glanced over at this guy. I could see his shoes. I could see blood on them even though I didn't immediately recognize it as blood. I just thought to myself, 'wonder what he stepped in?'"

Bill paused at this point. "I stood up and looked back up into his face, only his expression had changed. He saw me looking at his shoes, and the friendly smile he had was different. Forced, somehow.

He looked like he just wanted to get out of there. I asked him to stop, and he did. Then I asked him to put his hands behind him, and I saw the blood there, too. It was unmistakable. I must've loosened my grip on his arm at that point, because the next thing I knew he had twisted around, grabbed my wrist and forced me to my knees. He let go, then ran off back in the direction he came.

"Bullets were flying, men where shouting. The detective in charge, Hoffman, was the only one who remained calm. He asked me what had happened, and I told him about the blood. He gave some orders, then had me join him as we went up the stairs. The guy was fast, and by the time we got there, the stairwell was empty. We checked each floor on the way up to make sure there was an officer on guard and kept going up and up.

"Before I knew it we were on the roof. It was threatening to rain all day, but now it meant it. There was a stiff wind up there, and I made sure to steer clear of the edge of the building. As we were looking around, it was during a flash of lightening that I saw him, standing on the parapet. I let Detective Hoffman know what I saw, but when we got there, he was gone. He had fallen to the roof below.

"It was some time later that we found his last victim. We did a door-to-door search. Hoffman kind of took me under his wing that night. Whenever he worked a scene I was at, he invited me to offer my observations, and he was always encouraging me to take the detective's exam. Eventually I did."

"Did the Axeman know any of his victims?" Jennifer asked.

"The last girl was the only one he had any connection to. According to her neighbors, they dated. He had pursued her for a while before she agreed to go out with him. Her friends said she thought he was wonderful, and they were even talking about getting married. But there were also rumors that she was seeing someone else. A married man in the building."

Nate entered the conversation. "That would give him a motive for the last victim, but what about the others?"

Bill shrugged. "We never did figure that one out. Later on when profiling became a thing, I remember some FBI guys came out and asked about the case, most of them were sold on some theory about how his killing of the other women was some kind of release, so that he could maintain a normal relationship with his girlfriend. Something to do with how they all kinda looked alike."

"Most of them?" Nate asked.

Bill grinned. "There was one guy who didn't think Luther Laramie had killed the other girls. In fact, he suggested he hadn't killed any of them."

"Then who did?" Jennifer asked.

"Who knows? There never were any other suspects," Bill replied.

Jennifer continued her questions. "Did Luther live in the building?"

"No, the girl did. He lived in a tenement with his mother in the Tenderloin. The mother was adamant that he hadn't killed anyone. Even tried to offer alibis for the other murders. But after Luther Laramie fell to his death, the killings stopped."

"Fell? You don't think he jumped?" Jennifer asked.

"I guess he could have. In fact, that was the theory at the time since there really wasn't any other reason to go up there."

"There were no fire escapes or ladders leading down?" Nate asked.

"There were, but there were cops at the bottom of each one." Bill turned to Jennifer. "Did I help you out at all?"

"Yes, very much. Can I ask you one more question?"

"You can ask me questions all day," Bill told her.

"What floor did the victim live on?"

"The tenth floor," Bill answered without hesitation. "Apartment ten-oh-eight."

Jennifer looked over at Nate. "That's the same apartment Diane lives in. They must've switched from numbers to letters at some point. Ten-H was ten-oh-eight."

"They might not have renumbered them in the same order. It could be any of the twenty other units on that floor."

"Remember the first rule of investigation," Bill admonished his great nephew. "There is no such thing as coincidence."

"You know we have DNA now, we don't have to rely on old sayings."

"I lost count of the number of cases I solved because of some stray fact that someone else discarded as a coincidence."

"I know, I know," Nate assured him. "But those were real crimes, not ghost stories."

"There's a ghost?" Bill asked Jennifer. "Is that what this is about?"

"Possibly," she answered with a sly grin. "I'm a parapsychologist."

Bill smiled. "Nate's mother says she speaks with her dead husband. I talk to Lillian all the time, but she never talks back."

"Maybe you're just not listening the right way."

"All right, enough with the psychic mumbo-jumbo. I don't need two relatives chasing seances," interrupted Nate.

Bill ignored his nephew and continued his conversation with Jennifer. "Anyway, I don't think she can hear me. If she's hanging around anywhere, she's in my house."

"Well," Nate added, "if she gives me a message, I'll let you know."

Jennifer perked up, shifted her attention to Nate. "You live in your uncle's house?"

"Great uncle," Nate corrected.

"Did Lillian pass away in the house?" Jennifer asked Bill.

"She did. She loved that place. I couldn't stay there anymore after she passed. I was glad Nate was able to take it off my hands. Though if I'd known at the time how high property values would go, I would've just rented it to him," he added jokingly.

Jennifer gave Nate a suggestive glance.

"What?" he asked.

"You have described some impossible things happening at your home."

"I don't have a ghost."

"You said there was no way the dog could've gotten out of that cage—"

Bill jumped back into the conversation. "You locked a poor dog in a cage? Your aunt would never have allowed that." He turned to Jennifer. "She loved dogs. We had one when we were first married, but after it died, she didn't have the heart to get another one. It was too painful for Lillian to lose a pet."

Jennifer took the ammunition offered by Bill and aimed it back at Nate. "Your aunt, who died in the house where you live, loved dogs so much she would have never allowed one to be locked up."

Nate rose from the bench. "You two can continue weaving your paranormal fantasies. I need to get home and feed that dog before she chews up any more furniture."

Jennifer turned to Bill with a grateful smile. "Thank you, Uncle Bill," she said, purposefully adopting the familial reference, "it was really nice meeting you."

"And you, my dear. Please, come back any time."

"I will. I want to hear all about what Nate was like as a child."

"Oh, in that case I have some good stories for you. But it'll take more than one visit."

"Deal," Jennifer said. She leaned over and kissed the older man on the cheek.

Bill's eyes widened.

"You're going to give him a stroke if you keep that up," Nate warned.

Jennifer rose and held her hand out to Bill. "Can we walk you back to your room?"

Bill took her hand, but instead of pulling himself up, he kissed it gently. "No, I want to sit out here for a while. It's such a nice day."

"It is," Jennifer agreed. "Thank you again."

"I'll see you next week," Nate promised.

"Not if you don't bring her with you," Bill warned.

"We'll see."

Nate started walking away.

Jennifer squeezed Bill's hand one last time, then turned to catch up with Nate.

CHAPTER TWENTY SIX

Nate opened the door to his house. Jennifer strode past him and made her way to the sofa.

"Would you like to come in?" he asked sarcastically as he closed the door.

Madge trotted in from the kitchen, jumped up onto the sofa and laid her head in Jennifer's lap. "Hello, gorgeous," she said, rubbing the dog between its ears.

Nate shook his head. "How in the world did she get in? I don't have a doggy door." He closed the front door.

Jennifer lifted Madge's head so she could look into the dog's eyes. "You're not an outside doggy, are you?" she asked.

Madge whined her agreement.

"I'll bet it's my mother. She comes by from time to time to clean and buy groceries."

"Or, it could be your great aunt."

"Ha-ha," Nate laughed sarcastically. He crossed over to the easy chair and carefully lowered himself down, taking care not to jostle his shoulder. "We're not going to do this," he declared.

"Do what?"

"You know. This whole thing where you try to convince me there are ghosts everywhere."

"Not everywhere. But certainly you have to admit, sometimes strange things happen," she said, gesturing at Madge. "And sometimes they happen in the house where a woman who loved animals lived and died."

"I should never have brought you to meet my Uncle."

"He's a real sweetheart. You should visit him more often. Maybe it'll rub off on you."

Nate smirked at her.

"Maybe you're right," she said. "Maybe there is a perfectly reasonable explanation of how your dog escaped from a locked cage."

"There is."

"And I'm sure it's just as reasonable as the explanation of what's happening with Diane."

"It's the ex-boyfriend," Nate says.

"Is that what your gut is telling you?" Jennifer asked.

"It's what the evidence is telling me. He's trying to spook her, make her afraid, then swing in to rescue her."

"She's not interested, they're just friends."

"Is that your gut telling you that? Or your woman's intuition?"

"She had no pictures of the two of them. At least not anywhere out in the open. You do that, get rid of the photographic evidence when you've written a guy off."

"He may not have gotten the message."

"Maybe, I'm just saying if he tries to rescue her, he's going to find out he's trapped in the friend zone."

"I hope that's all it comes to," Nate sighed. "Sometimes guys don't know how to take 'no' for an answer."

Jennifer shrugged off his response, changing the subject. "Anything you want me to add to the shopping list?"

"Shopping list for what?"

"Snacks for the stakeout. At Diane's."

Nate shook his head. "Oh, no. I'll bring the food."

"Ooh, cop stakeout food. Let me guess, Red Bull and Red Vines? Donuts?"

Nate shook his head. "Nothing of the kind. You won't be getting my full culinary repertoire," he added, lifting his bad arm slightly, "but I can assure you, any pastries that may or may not be present will not be deep-fried nuts of dough."

"Ah, a chef. Well, then, it's a date. I'll bring the motion sensors, infrared cameras and electromagnetic field detectors, you bring the food."

CHAPTER TWENTY SEVEN

Dave walked through the large office that had been converted to a storeroom, mentally imagining how it would look with his desk, maybe a television on the wall, a nice bookcase, perhaps a small couch. He shook off the daydreaming and returned to inventorying the items on a clipboard, the list of equipment Dr. Daye had requested for the Diane Collins case. He picked up one device he didn't recognize. Something new from Bits, he suspected. It looked like a camera, but instead of a lens, there was a circle of metal, perforated with hundreds of holes. It kind of reminded him of what you might find covering a shower drain.

"Careful with that, it'll make you sterile," said Bits from the doorway, surprising Dave. He almost dropped the device, and in the process, accidentally switched it on. It made a pinging noise. He fumbled to find the off switch, holding it as far away from himself as he could.

Bits stepped into the supply room, took the device from Dave and pressed a button that silenced the machine. He placed it back onto the shelf. "Trust me, that one's not on Dr. Daye's list."

"Thanks," Dave said. He was sometimes wary of Bits. The guy never gave him the impression that they were actually friends, but there were times when he helped him sort out a computer issue, or upgraded his cable when it felt like they were more than just coworkers. Bits was a bit of a puzzle to Dave, but then again most people were. Ironically, everyone else—especially Dr. Daye—had Dave figured out completely.

"Dave!" Jennifer shouted from her office.

"Just a minute," Dave shouted back. "I'm in the supplies office." He called it that to bring attention to the fact that even the filing cabinets had a higher priority than he did around here. He set the clipboard down on the shelf, then he slid past Bits and headed for Dr. Daye's office.

Emily was there, seated in one of the modern library chairs that were positioned in front of the desk.

Jennifer looked up at him and smiled. "Come on in, have a seat. I was just going over the canvassing checklist with Emily."

Dave stayed where he was. "Great. I'm sure she'll do a wonderful job. I'm going to go finish up the inventory."

"I asked Bits to finish that up. I need you to help Emily."

Dave started to back out of the office. "She's so much better with people than I am," he insisted.

"Don't be silly, you're my top guy and this is an important case. I need it done right."

Dave froze in his tracks. Damn, how did she do that? How did she make the one job he hated most feel like the one thing she was depending on him to do? He sighed and walked up to the seat in front of the desk next to Emily and sat down.

"So, as I was telling Emily, I want you to talk to as many of Diane's neighbors as you can. See if you can get them to tell you if they've seen anything strange or unusual, things out of place, weird noises—"

"Why don't we just cut to the chase and ask them if they've seen any ghosts?" Emily asked.

"You can't do that," Dave explained, "they may have witnessed something irrelevant to them, but relevant to us. You know it's extremely unlikely the phenomena they may have witnessed is going to be a full on visible spirit."

"Exactly," Jennifer agreed. "You should do Diane's floor, and the ones directly above and below her. And if you run into the building superintendent, or a janitor or someone like that, see if you can get them talking."

"You really are picking the two worst people to try to get other people to open up to them."

"Speak for yourself, weirdo," Emily said, deadpan.

Dave shrugged while casting a sideways glance at his coworker.

Jennifer smiled. "You two are exactly the type for the job. People are suspicious if you're too slick, or come off as disingenuous."

"No danger of that with us," Dave confirmed.

There was a knock on Jennifer's open office door.

"I hope we're not bothering you," the dean said with a surprisingly deferential tone.

Jennifer looked up from the desk. She saw that there was an elderly man a step behind the dean, wearing a suit that matched his gray hair and eyes. Even his skin had a monotone pallor. The only color was the violet necktie and matching pocket square. "Not at all," she answered.

Her mind instantly connected the dean's guest to the cursory research she had done on the donor whose largess was overflowing into her professional career. She stood and made her way around the desk, smiling. "Mr. Worthington, I presume," she said, extending a hand to the older gentleman.

He smiled back, the effort accentuating a web of creases and wrinkles in his skin. "Professor Daye, it is an honor to meet you," he said, shaking her hand gently yet warmly.

"Please, call me Jennifer," she said.

"I was just showing Daniel how some of his donation will be put to use," the dean interjected.

"Yes, I'm very pleased to see that Professor Daye has such a befitting space to engage in her important work."

"Of course," the dean assured. "She's not only one of our top teachers but also a cutting edge researcher."

Jennifer could see the effort the dean was making to choke the words out. Doing it in front of her certainly added to the pain. "Yes,

Robert has pledged his ongoing and unconditional support. We're lucky to have him as our dean."

Dave barely stifled a laugh.

Emily muttered under her breath, "Are we in one of those sci-fi body snatcher movies?"

Jennifer shot them both a warning glance. "Mr. Worthington, the dean tells me that there's something I might be able to help you with."

Worthington nodded. "Yes, indeed. I certainly hope you can. That would be so reassuring."

They all waited a moment for him to explain, but no additional words were forthcoming.

Jennifer cleared her throat. "What is it?"

"Oh, I don't want to get into it here." He turned to the dean. "Have you not told her of my plans?" he asked.

"Not yet," the dean answered. "I thought it would be better coming from you."

"Ah, yes, quite," Worthington stuttered. "I'm having a party, you see, in your honor," he said to Jennifer.

"My honor?" Jennifer asked, casting an inquisitive glance toward the dean who was conspicuously avoiding making eye contact. "I'm flattered."

"It will be at my home Wednesday evening. My personal chef has a spectacular seven-course meal planned. He has two Michelin stars and a James Beard award as well as being an extraordinary sommelier. Oh, I meant to ask. Do you have any food allergies?"

"No, though I'm not fond of cilantro."

"Who is?" Worthington replied, laughing awkwardly. "I will explain everything at the party. You're welcome to bring a guest if you like."

"Thank you," Jennifer said. She instantly thought of Nate, perhaps bringing him along to a gourmet meal would help grease the wheels.

"I'll have June send over the details," the dean assured. "Come, Daniel, I want to show you the archives. I think you'll find them very impressive but sadly in need of some financial attention."

Worthington allowed himself to be steered out of the office by the dean who seemed relieved that the episode was over.

Once they were gone, Emily turned to Dr. Daye. "What was that all about?"

"That was our benefactor, the man who got us out of the basement," Jennifer answered.

"What do you think he wants?" Dave asked.

Jennifer shrugged. "I don't know. Maybe he wants me to sign my books."

Emily shook her head. "It won't be anything that simple. It never is."

Jennifer waved off Emily's paranoia. "You two should get started on canvassing Diane's building."

"It's almost six o'clock," Dave complained.

"I have a test I need to study for," Emily added.

"Fine," Jennifer conceded. "But first thing tomorrow evening."

"Evening?" Dave asked.

"Right, you want to do it when people are home."

"And in such a good mood because we interrupted their dinner," Emily added. "I've always wondered what it felt like to be a telemarketer."

CHAPTER TWENTY EIGHT

Nate stood in front of his house, alternately staring at his phone, and the street as he waited for the tiny car icon on his Uber app to become a real car on his street. He had spent the rest of the weekend and all of Monday recuperating from his Saturday with Jennifer Daye. And even then, his respite was interrupted by a call from the persistent professor. She had insisted he accompany her to some function for the University. He had tried to beg off, claiming that he was not physically able to endure a formal event, but then she told him that the event was being catered by an award-winning chef—one whose fare he had been lucky enough to enjoy some years earlier. The promise of a gourmet meal after a week of hospital food, and the tepid takeout he had endured since returning home won him over.

He glanced at the phone again. The small black car on the map hadn't moved for the last couple of minutes. But then suddenly, it zoomed down the line representing a nearby street. He looked up and spotted a black Prius as it turned the corner and quickly pulled up in front of him. The driver rolled down his window.

"Name?" he asked perfunctorily.

"Nate, you?"

"I'm Boris. Get in."

Nate mentally reminded himself to take a star off of the driver's rating. The man could have offered to open the door for a passenger wearing a sling. He wrangled the door open himself and slid into the back seat on the passenger side. No complimentary water bottle or phone charger. *Just lost another star,* Nate thought to himself. "You have the destination?" Nate asked.

"Yeah, yeah, I got it," the driver answered in an annoyed tone as he tapped the screen of the phone mounted on his dashboard by a clip on the air vents. A navigational map took over the screen, and they were on their way.

Nate sat back and stared out the window. He'd spent most of the morning cleaning up after a mess Madge had made after she had gotten out of her cage and into the garbage. And she'd needed a good hosing off as well, which was difficult to impossible for a one-armed man to do. She kept on trying to bite the stream of water that was attacking her. After a while, he managed to rinse off the worst of it and dry her off with an old beach towel.

After exerting himself all morning, Nate was rethinking his plan to head down to the police academy shooting range and test his left-handed shooting. His Uncle Bill had always stressed that it was important for a policeman to be proficient shooting with either hand, but he hadn't really focused on his marksmanship the last few years. He had a personal revolver he usually kept locked up in a safe in his bedroom nightstand, now tucked discretely in a holster under his jacket. He'd had to reconfigure it so the gun sat under his right armpit rather than the left, and then further adjust it so as not to interfere with his injury. A feat almost as difficult as bathing Madge.

He stared out the window, not focused on the surroundings, but rather on the facts of the case he was working with Jennifer—with Dr. Daye, he corrected himself—in his mind. He had realized this morning that he was now thinking of it *as* a case. It was as if the cop part of his brain needed a crime to solve, so adopted this situation and started breaking it down as he would an official investigation. He reminded himself to start compiling his notes later, maybe even construct a timeline on a whiteboard. It actually felt good to be in detective mode. It was the kind of thing that he didn't realize how much he missed it until it was gone. Now a part of him had reawoken, and the depression that was beginning to set in was pushed aside by his renewed purpose.

There was also a part of him that was admittedly flattered by Dr. Daye's flirtations. He wasn't quite sure if she was serious, or was just trying to get close to him to worm her way into his mind. He found himself hoping it was the former. She was undeniably attractive, but Nate was even more drawn to her intellect.

He'd downloaded one of her books the previous night. Most of the material he found on the fantastic side, but the research was well referenced and the writing style cogent and even entertaining. She obviously wasn't some new-age kook he could easily dismiss. He'd have to do some of his own research to provide counterpoints to the assertions she made.

Regardless, reading her liturgy of suspected paranormal cases had put him in a strange state of mind. His dreams included fragments of the robbery, and more disturbing, that eerie vision he had during the fog of anesthesia. In some ways, his recollection of that dream seemed more vivid than what he could recall about the actual shooting.

He toyed with the idea of telling Jennifer about the dream, just to get her off his back about the whole near-death experience thing, but he knew it would just fuel her curiosity rather than quench it.

After a while, Nate realized he had been lost in thought so deeply that he had lost track of his surroundings. He looked at the landmarks passing by and realized he was in the Tenderloin and not anywhere close to the police academy. "Hey, I think you're going the wrong way," Nate said to the driver.

Boris looked at Nate through the rearview mirror, then glanced at his phone. "This is the destination you put in. It's not wrong. No refund."

"I wasn't asking for one." Nate pulled out his phone and checked the address he had submitted for the ride. The driver was right. He had put in an address in the Tenderloin, and it wasn't even something that could be mistaken for the police academy. Somehow, he had entered a completely random address. And they were almost there.

The driver pulled up to the small, rundown house and put the car in park and tapped the confirmation prompts on his screen that ended the ride. "You want me to take you someplace else? That's a new ride."

"Yeah, give me a second," Nate said as he started typing in the address for the police academy. He glanced over at the house, frustrated that he had made such a time-wasting mistake.

He froze.

He recognized that house.

It was the one from his dream. The one in which he had imagined a conversation between the two men who had robbed the store and shot him.

"Wait," he told the driver. "I'm getting out here."

"Suit yourself," the driver said as he sat behind the wheel, waiting for Nate to struggle to get out of the back seat. The second the door closed, the Prius was on its way.

Nate stood at the curb looking at the house.

It was the same house. He looked to the driveway where there had been a car parked in his dream, but there was nothing there now.

Nate scanned his memory, trying to remember when he was last here. It must have been on some other case. He never worked patrol in the Tenderloin when he was a uniformed officer, so he wouldn't have been here for a domestic disturbance or to serve a warrant. But he couldn't recall any cases that he had in the Tenderloin that ever took him to a place remotely like this one. He would've remembered the low, stone fence. That is something that would have stuck in his memory.

He walked up the path to the front door. A chill ran down his spine as he recalled again the dream and the sensation of floating. When he reached the front door, he extended his good hand to the door knob and turned it. It moved freely. He pushed on the door, but the deadbolt prevented him from opening it.

Nate took a step back and surveyed the property. He walked around to the back of the house and spied another door. He tried it as well, but no luck. Then he noticed a bedroom window partially obscured by weeds that appeared to be open. He looked around to make sure no one was watching, then walked across the scrubby yard to the window. It was indeed open a few inches, and the screen was torn away. He tentatively pulled up on the window and with a bit of force, it slid upward creating an opening large and low enough for Nate to enter.

He hesitated. Technically, this was breaking and entering. If he was conducting an official investigation, he would need a warrant to enter, otherwise anything he might find inside would be tainted. But he was currently inactive as a police officer and not acting in any official way. He was committing a crime and would be arrested—if he was caught. But, if he found anything, he could call it into the department tip line anonymously.

He lifted his leg, stepped inside and ducked under the window sash. The place smelled stale, a combination of rotting food and cigarette smoke.

There was a crash from another part of the house.

Nate drew his gun. It was uncomfortable to reach under the sling, but he managed to pull the gun free and hold it firmly in his left hand. He stepped slowly and quietly through the bedroom toward the hallway, listening.

There was a scratching noise. Then a sort of chittering sound.

Nate continued down the hallway until it opened into the living room. There was no one there. He moved cautiously into the kitchen.

On the floor was a broken jar with some remnants of jelly in it that a hungry raccoon was eagerly licking up.

"Shoo!" Nate shouted, waving his gun at the animal. It looked up at him as if to say, "Find your own jelly, I got here first."

Nate pointed his gun at the raccoon. Apparently, this was a gesture the creature recognized, because it dropped the broken jar segment it was holding, and scurried into one of the cupboards. From the sound of it, there was some kind of tunnel to the outside. Nate didn't bother to investigate the creature's egress. Instead, he holstered his weapon and started looking around the kitchen for any clues the previous occupants might have left behind besides their favorite flavor of jelly.

He put on a nitrile glove, one of a pair that he always had stuffed into the pockets of his suit jackets, then started opening cabinet doors. Most were empty, but there were some that had canned goods that were still within their expiration date. There might be fingerprints on them, but Nate wasn't equipped to gather that type of evidence. He needed something that would link the residents of this house to the robbers.

He stopped and shook off that thought. It was crazy for him to think that the robbers had actually used this place as a hideout. There was another explanation. Maybe he had never been here before, but had come across this address while reviewing another case, or one that he had been consulted on. The notion that he had dreamed it was too fantastical for him to take seriously.

He found a receipt tucked in a drawer, but it was from two years earlier. Nothing else gave him any clue as to who might have lived here more recently.

Nate moved back to the living room and looked around. It was sparse. There was furniture, and again, it was eerily similar if not identical to what he had seen in his dream when the two men were arguing. But it was also generic, the furniture was the kind of cheap, discount stuff you could find lots of places.

There was a fireplace. Nate walked over to it and kneeled down.

It was a gas fireplace, but there were ashes in it. He sifted through them and found something solid. A piece of unburnt paper. Or rather, a small photograph. He picked it out and shook off the ash.

It was a photograph of a baby.

His mind instantly snapped back to the robbery. The young couple, and the locket the woman was so eager to hang onto. When it opened as the skinny guy was inspecting it, there was a photograph of a baby. This same photograph.

Nate felt his heart stop. He dropped the photo into the ashes and covered it back up. He knew he couldn't be the one to discover it.

That would bring up too many awkward questions. From Captain Bode and Dr. Daye. Besides, was he sure it was the same photograph? All babies looked alike to him. Best to let the crime scene guys sort it out. Max would know to check with the robbery victims to see if it was something that belonged to any of them, and he was certain that analysis of the ash would reveal that it contained the remnants of id cards. Anything the robbers would want to get rid of that could link them to the crime.

Assuming, of course, that this was connected to the same robbery. It could easily be a flop house used by any number of criminals who used the convenient fireplace to destroy evidence.

Nate took one more look around the house, searching the bedrooms, the closets, the bathroom. Nothing jumped out at him—figuratively or literally—and he decided he had spent enough time in the place. He exited the way he came in and closed the window completely. He pulled out his phone, and summoned a new Uber to take him to the police academy, then walked up to the corner to wait for his ride and placed a call to the police department tip line.

A figure, just down the street from the house, leaned against a light pole and watched Nate with intense curiosity. It was the skinny guy, his features now hidden behind a beard and sunglasses. He pulled out a burner phone and dialed a number from memory.

"We have a problem," he said as soon as the call connected. "He was at the house... What do you mean, who? The cop we shot... Okay, the cop I shot. Deuce's guy Julio tipped me off that someone was snooping around... I don't know what he was doing or how he found it, but we gotta move again. And we gotta clear our debt with Deuce soon so we can get out of town already."

He ended the call, broke the phone in half and dumped it down a storm drain grate, then walked away in the opposite direction from Nate.

CHAPTER TWENTY NINE

Emily and Dave stepped off the elevator onto Diane's floor. Emily looked bored, while Dave wore a mantle of anxiety.

"So, you want to split up, or—"

"Yeah, let's split up," Emily answered before Dave was able to finish the question.

"What are you going to tell them?" Dave asked.

Emily shrugged. "I think I'll go with the building department rodent infestation story. Figure if they have heard any weird noises, the prospect of an invasion of rats might open them up to admitting it."

"Can't you get arrested for impersonating a building inspector?"

Emily gave Dave her best, "are you kidding me?" look, and walked down toward the end of the hall. He followed.

They stopped in front of Diane's apartment. Emily looked at the door, checked it against her notes. "I'll take this side," she said. "We already know this one has definitely seen something."

Dave watched as Emily moved on to the next door and knocked. A middle-aged man answered. She said something to him, and the man invited her in. Dave worried for a second about Emily disappearing inside a strange man's apartment, but then remembered it was Emily. Good luck to the strange man.

He turned to the door that was directly across from Diane's, took a deep breath and knocked. He waited a moment, then let out a sigh of relief. They probably weren't home. One fewer stranger for him to have to interact with.

Dave turned and took a step when he heard a faint voice from inside the apartment. "Just a minute. I'm coming," it said. About a minute later, the door opened a crack. "Yes?" asked the elderly woman inside. "Can I help you?"

"Hi, I'm Dave…" Then he froze. The carefully worded script he had crafted and rehearsed blanked from his mind. Instead, he just blurted out, "have you heard any strange noises or anything that might be strange or unusual or out of the ordinary?" He braced himself, waiting for the door to close in his face. Instead, it opened wider.

"Oh, you must be with that woman who's helping poor Diane. The ghost lady."

"Parapsychologist," Dave corrected.

"Yes, some funny name like that. Please, come in." The old woman stood back and made room for Dave to enter, then she gingerly closed the door, taking one last look out into the hallway as she did so. "I do hope she can help Diane. She reminds me of another young woman who used to live in that apartment. Living alone, working long hours… What did you say your name was?"

"Dave. And the woman I work with is Dr. Jennifer Daye."

"Such a pretty name. I'm Rose."

"That's a pretty name, too," Dave offered, nervously.

"Thank you. Aren't you a charming young man? Make yourself at home. I just have some tea on I need to tend to. Would you like some?"

"No thank you."

"Oh, I'll bet you're a milk and cookies man. I'll fix some up for you."

"That's quite all right. I'm fine."

"It's no trouble," Rose insisted, waving off Dave's refusal.

Dave started walking around Rose's living room. It seemed like every other old lady's apartment he had been inside—and working with Dr. Daye, that had been quite a lot. Old ladies seemed to be particularly sensitive to paranormal activity. Dave had no hard and fast statistics to back that up, but he wondered if it might be because they were so close to death themselves.

There were shelves filled with various collectibles and antique photo frames filled with portraits. There was a black and white wedding photo that held a prominent place. He could see the resemblance in the bride's face to Rose. She had been quite an attractive woman in her day.

There were other portraits of her over the years, but none of the man from the wedding photo. She didn't seem to be one to display vacation photos, either.

"Here we are," Rose announced as she returned from the kitchen with a tray laden with a cup of tea and a tea pot, a glass of milk and a plate of Girl Scout cookies. She set them down on a low coffee table and took a seat in an embroidered arm chair protected with doilies of varying sizes.

Dave took a seat on a small sofa next to the table. "Girl Scout cookies, I love those."

"Yes, there was a young lady in the building who was trying to sell enough to go to camp. I felt so sorry for her, her mother was barely able to afford the rent. I ended up buying ten cases of them."

"Wow, that's a lot of cookies. It's going to take a while to get through all of those," Dave supposed as he picked up a cookie and placed it into his mouth.

"Four years and counting," Rose declared proudly.

Dave crunched down on the cookie. It felt as if he had bitten into plaster. He reached for the glass of milk and took a sip, trying to let the milk soak into the cookie in his mouth to soften it up a bit. It didn't help. He ended up crunching the thing into small pebbles and swallowing them with the rest of the glass of milk.

Rose sat and smiled at him.

He wondered if she knew that the cookies had petrified and if this was some kind of test. He smiled back and dabbed the corners of his mouth with a napkin from the tray.

"How can I help you, dear?" Rose asked.

Dave thought he detected a hint of darkness in her tone, but shook off that notion. "Well, we're just trying to find out if anyone else in the building has experienced anything like what your neighbor, Diane, has. Strange sounds, people who are there one second and gone the next, things out of place..."

"Oh, of course. All of them. This place is quite haunted, after all."

Dave couldn't help betraying his surprise. "Really?"

"Indeed. There's old Mr. Shoetensack—but he's pretty harmless. He was the building superintendent for over fifty years. Still hangs around and fixes little problems, tidies up little messes."

"What else?" Dave asked, as he grabbed his notebook and started scribbling.

Rose leaned back in her chair, staring upward as she fished information out of her voluminous memories. "Well, there is some mischievous spirit in the elevators. Sometimes you'll press a button for a floor, and it'll take you to a different floor. Or you want to go up, but instead you go down. Or it just stops altogether."

Dave continued writing. "You don't think it's just old elevators?" he asked.

"I think I know the difference, young man." Rose glared at Dave, scornfully, then continued her litany of strange occurrences. "Mrs. Green on the eighth floor hears strange bells in the middle of the night. Mr. Howard in four-G says that he hears a couple making whoopee in his spare bedroom every Saturday night. Dozens of people have been helped by Mr. Shoetensack of course, he's all over the building."

Dave scribbled furiously trying to keep up with the roll call of spirits inhabiting the Oakley Arms.

When she finished, he had filled up nearly six whole pages of unexplained sounds, spirits, ghosts and other miscellaneous "mysterious" happenings. Dave shook out the writer's cramp in his hand. "Thank you, Rose. This is all very helpful." He started to fold up his notebook, but then she leaned forward and spoke to him in a low, conspiratorial tone.

"Of course, the real nasty one is the Axeman."

Dave froze at the mention of the serial killer who had met his demise in this building. He flipped his notebook back over and picked up his pen. "Were you here when that happened?" he asked.

Rose sat back and nodded solemnly. "It was the same year I married and lost my husband," she said, glancing over at the wedding portrait.

"Can you tell me anything about the girl? Sarah Montgomery, the Axeman's last victim? She lived across the hall, didn't she?"

Rose became suddenly disgusted. "Oh, that hussy? She got what was coming to her, if you ask me."

"What do you mean?" Dave asked. He was sitting on the edge of his seat, the pen nearly poking a hole through his pad. He noticed how tense he was, set the pen down and reached for the glass of milk, but his hand was shaking and the glass rattled against the table as he picked it up.

The noise broke Rose from her spell. A reassuring smile returned to her face. "That was such a horrible time. Gregory—my husband— and I had just gotten married, and it seemed like he immediately lost interest in me. And then when Miss Montgomery moved in across the hall, well, the way she carried on with my husband. It was shameful. He left me shortly after she died. Sometimes I don't know what I ever saw in that man.

"Anyway, ever since he killed himself—the Axeman that is—he's been haunting this building. People say he shows up sometimes before bad things happen, as if he's causing them." Rose shuddered. "If there's anything your Dr. Daye can do to get rid of that one, I know we'd all appreciate it. And that's all I have to say about that!" Rose declared, crossing her arms.

Dave got the feeling that he wasn't going to get any more out of Rose. He closed his notebook and put his pen away. "Thank you for your time, Rose. You were very helpful."

Rose took on a sad, pouty expression when she saw that the remaining cookies were still untouched. "You didn't like the cookies?"

Dave reacted instinctively, answering, "They were fine. I just wanted to make sure I wrote down everything you had to say."

"Oh, I'm so glad to hear that. Let me give you a case."

Before Dave could decline the offer, Rose was on her feet and scurrying back to the kitchen. She returned a moment later struggling with a case of Girl Scout cookies. Dave rushed over to help her. "Thank you," he said, taking the box.

A moment later, Dave left the apartment with the case of cookies and the remaining ones from the tea tray in a plastic baggy.

Emily walked out of the door next to Rose's on Dave's side of the hall. "You were taking so long I decided to do your side as well. What's with the cookies?"

"Don't ask."

"Okay. Two more floors to go. I'll take the one above, you take—"

"No," Dave said, with a surprising level of confidence. "We're finishing this together. I'm not going into one of these apartments alone again."

Emily shrugged and headed back to the elevator.

Dave stopped at the garbage chute and tossed the cookies down the dark hole, listening to them bang against the metal walls all the way down.

CHAPTER THIRTY

Nate aimed his gun at the target at the far end of the range. He squeezed off six shots in quick succession, then set the gun down and pressed the button that caused the paper silhouette to fly toward him on its track.

The sight of the dark shape floating in his direction caused his mind to flash back for the second time that day to the dream he had coming out of anesthesia. Only he was the silhouette, floating back to rejoin his body in the operating room.

"Jeez, were you even aiming at it?" Max asked.

Nate took off his ear protectors and set them on the counter next to the gun. "I used to be able to get a good grouping with my left hand. Just need more practice."

Max pulled the target down and poked a finger through a hole in the upper-right corner. "Well, if this was a bad guy, he certainly would have heard it whizzing past."

"Very funny. Did you get that file for me?"

"Which one? The one where I had to violate procedure to secure a police file for a civilian?"

"Oh, all of a sudden you're Mr. By-The-Book?" Nate asked.

"All of a sudden you're not?" Max asked back.

"It's a favor for a friend," Nate explained.

Max regarded Nate suspiciously. "A blond friend with the letters P-H and D after her name?" Max teased.

Nate changed the subject. "How's the case going?"

"As a matter of fact, we got a tip on the robbers. Someone saw a couple of guys matching their description hiding out in the Tenderloin. The crime scene guys found some unburnt items in the fireplace. They're trying to get prints from the scene. Could be from the robbery."

"That's good," Nate replied.

Max smiled to himself, realizing. "Of course, you already knew that. You phoned in the tip."

Nate's sheepish expression was his admission. "I just did a little leg work on my own, didn't want to make it complicated," he explained.

"A little legwork? How in the world did you track those guys down to a house in the 'Loin? We've had the entire force working on getting a lead for weeks, and you just happen to stumble across their hideout? What am I missing here?"

"Did you get that file for me or not?"

"I got it," Max confirmed. He fished out a thumb drive from his pocket. "I know you like paper, but us new kids don't like to carry around big folders. Feel free to print it out yourself, though."

Nate accepted the thumb drive and shoved it into his pocket. "Thanks, I owe you one."

"Great, I'll collect right now. How did you find that hideout?"

Nate didn't respond.

"Come on, Nate. If you're holding out on me, you could be putting the investigation at risk. You know that. How can we find the guys who almost killed you if you keep information from me?"

"It's not important how I found out. It has nothing to do with the case."

Max raised an eyebrow. "Really? You know, if the situation was reversed, you would say something like, 'I'll be the judge of that.'"

"You really want to know?"

"Yeah, I really want to know."

"I put the wrong address in for my Uber ride, it dropped me off in front of the hideout, it looked familiar so I checked it out."

"What do you mean, 'looked familiar'?"

"I don't know. I can't explain it. It was a hunch."

Max stared at his old partner. "A hunch?"

"Yeah. Hunches are just educated guesses based on experience and—"

"I know what a hunch is, but this was a hell of a hunch. Based on a random incorrect address?"

Nate nodded.

Max crossed his arms and looked into Nate's eyes.

Nate looked away.

"There's something you're not telling me."

Nate remained silent.

"Nate, it's me, Max. I trust you with my life. You're the best detective I know. If you colored outside the lines a little, I'm not going to hold it against you."

Nate shut his eyes and squeezed his temples between the thumb and middle finger of his good hand. The image from his dream appeared behind his eyelids. The house with the car in the driveway. The two men inside the dilapidated house. He dropped his hand and looked back into Max's demanding eyes. He knew Max was right that knowing the source of the information was critical to the investigation, but he couldn't rationally explain how he knew that that house was connected to the robbers. None of it made sense.

"Hypothetically," Nate began, "if I was to tell you that I saw it in a dream, what would you make of that?"

"Hypothetically?" Max asked. "I'd first ask if you were crazy, then maybe if you were psychic."

"Hypothetically the answer to both questions is 'no.'"

"Hypothetically, I would probably have to assume there was some kind of explanation," Max said. "Maybe you've come across these guys before, and you knew there was a connection between them and that address."

Nate shook his head. "I thought of that. I've never worked a case in that neighborhood."

Max was out of ideas. "Okay. So, is there any other information you have that can help us?"

"No," Nate answered without conviction.

"But if there was, you'd tell me."

"Of course," he replied embarrassedly.

Nate looked down the range.

"So spill," Max coaxed.

"They might be driving a Cadillac, a cream-colored Seville, maybe a two-thousand."

"Same dream?"

"Hypothetically."

Max considered. "Okay, partner. We'll leave it at that." He eyed the target again. "You better move in here if you're going to get certified shooting lefty."

"I'll be fine. The doc says all I need is time to let it heal and I'll be one hundred percent again."

"A hundred percent? I always had you pegged at around seventy, seventy-five," Max joked.

Nate smiled. "We'll see. I'll be kicking your ass up and down this range before long."

"Why wait?" Max placed a box of ammunition on the counter. He set up a new target and sent it down the lane, then pulled out his sidearm and switched it to his left hand. "Batter up."

CHAPTER THIRTY ONE

Jennifer drove her van up the long driveway to the Worthington estate. She wore a version of her usual wardrobe—a white turtleneck sweater and black slacks with a matching jacket, but she had swapped the Vans for a classy pair of flats. The ever-present psi necklace hung about her neck.

Nate sat in the passenger seat, fighting a yawn. He had managed to wriggle into his tuxedo on his own, but needed Jennifer to help him with the bow tie. She had assured him the invitation was solely because he was the only person she knew who would appreciate it. A gourmet meal to Dave or Emily would be the Cheesecake Factory. She assured Nate that she wouldn't use it as an opportunity to probe him about the shooting, though if it earned her a couple goodwill points toward him keeping an open mind about Diane, she'd take it.

Nate yawned again.

"Not sleeping?" Jennifer asked. "Is it the shoulder or the dog?"

"Both," Nate answered. He wasn't about to tell her about his Uber adventure that led him to discover the robbers' abandoned hideout, and the strange dreams that made him reluctant to want to sleep. "I'm going to have to weld that kennel shut."

"Or you could just let her sleep in your room. Get a doggy bed."

"She's temporary. I'm just doing a favor for a friend of my mother."

Jennifer smiled. "That's a shame. She's a sweet dog. You two make a cute couple."

Nate smirked his reply.

As they drew closer to the main house, they came upon a circular driveway. A pair of valets rushed up to the van and opened the doors for them.

Jennifer and Nate stepped out onto the walkway that led to the front door of the mansion. They paused to take it in.

"Wow," Jennifer said. "Imagine all the history in that place."

"Imagine the property tax bill," Nate countered.

"I thought you would be more excited."

"I am," Nate assured her. "Thank you for inviting me." He was genuinely grateful. The opportunity to enjoy a meal the caliber of which Worthington's chef would provide was a rare one for someone like him. He was a pretty good cook himself, but some people are artists. And he was guessing the meal he was about to have would cost hundreds of dollars—and that would be before the wine. His medication was still an obstacle to enjoying whatever vintages would be presented, but maybe he would take a sip here and there. Certainly that would be okay.

They walked up the steps to the stately home. A butler was there to hold the door open for them.

The foyer was like something from a Hollywood set. There was a large spiral staircase, marble floors, and a vaulted ceiling.

"Aperitifs and amuse-bouches are being served in the library," the butler announced and pointed in the direction of a large, arched doorway.

Jennifer and Nate headed in the direction of the promised appetizers, the scents of which were already teasing their noses.

It seemed they were the first to arrive. Or maybe the other guests were somewhere else. Regardless, a table was set with various bites set on ornate plates. A waiter appeared with a tray of glasses. There were two choices, one that had a slice of orange on the edge, the other with a sprig of mint. "Could I get a sparkling water with a splash of lime?" Nate asked the waiter. The white-gloved man nodded, set the tray down alongside the food and disappeared through a cleverly hidden door.

Jennifer tasted one of the hors d'oeuvres and a look of utter joy crossed her face. "You have to try these, they're amazing!" she said with her mouth still full.

Nate smiled at her reaction. He approached a plate with small, breaded ball, swiped it through an artful smear of sauce and popped it into his mouth. The sauce provided an initial tangy, acidic taste, but once he bit into it, a savory wave washed over his tongue. Sweetbreads if he had to guess, seasoned to perfection with the breading providing a perfect contrasting texture.

"Dr. Daye, I see you actually did bring a date," a voice said from behind them.

"I'm not her date," Nate said reflexively.

Jennifer gave the dean a cool stare. "Hello, Robert. This is Detective Nate Raney," she added, taking a step closer to Nate.

"A police detective?" the dean asked.

"Currently inactive," Nate explained, lifting his sling.

"You seem surprised," Jennifer added.

"I didn't know the police were big supporters of anthropology," the dean said.

Nate smiled. "From your lack of imagination, I'm guessing you must be an administrator," he said matter-of-factly.

Jennifer unsuccessfully tried to stifle a laugh.

"I'm the dean of Dr. Daye's department," he replied.

"Ah, the one who's been playing musical offices. Interesting."

"What's interesting?"

"How the stereotype of an academically deficient pedagogue who turns to a career as a power driven administrator can be so accurate."

Jennifer covered her mouth to hide her amused smile.

The dean hemmed and hawed. "I'm sorry Dr. Daye's arm-twisting took you out of commission. The force must miss your Holmesian logic."

Nate didn't reply, so Jennifer answered for him. "Detective Raney was injured when he threw himself in front of a bullet meant for a young couple."

The dean was caught off guard by the revelation. "Excuse me, I think the other guests are arriving. Nice to meet you, Detective," he said, then quickly scurried away to say hello to a couple entering the library.

"Thank you," Jennifer said to Nate. "I rarely see Robert knocked back on his heels like that."

"Don't mention it. I deal with people like that from City Hall all the time. They hate when you hold a mirror up to them."

"Maybe they're vampires," Jennifer suggested.

The room filled up with about a dozen other people, some of whom Jennifer knew. She made introductions and some of them were familiar with Nate's story, but all of them were very interested in the famous Dr. Daye. Those who were close confidants of Worthington mentioned that he was very excited to have her here.

"What do you think the dean signed you up for?" Nate asked.

"I thought I was here to sign a book or two to get an extra zero on his donation, but now I suspect there's something else at play."

A door at the far end of the library opened and Daniel Worthington made his entrance. He scanned the faces of the guests, and when he spotted Jennifer, he walked straight toward her.

Behind him was a much shorter man, dressed in a jacket that looked like it was made from a carpet. His hair was tucked up into a ridiculous looking man-bun. He wore a shirt buttoned all the way to the neck, but no tie. Instead, there was a collection of chains, some gold, some silver, some adorned with various gems. A goatee framed the thin lips of his mouth, and he seemed to be wearing mascara giving him a somewhat goth look that reminded Nate of Emily from Jennifer's office.

He also reminded Nate of someone else. Who, he couldn't quite recall, but something about him was familiar. Where had he met him before?

"Professor Daye, I'm so glad you could make it," Worthington said to Jennifer as soon as he reached her. He extended his hand and Jennifer shook it. "My wife will be so excited to meet you," he said.

"Your wife? I thought I read that she had passed away recently," Jennifer said. Then she noticed the man standing behind Worthington. A man she recognized, also.

"Yes, she did," Worthington replied with a sly smile. "May I introduce my dear friend, Meyer Krazinski. He too is a student of the paranormal," the old man informed them.

Suddenly, Nate remembered where he had seen the small, oddly adorned man before. He was one of the psychics his mother had visited, one he had confronted personally, the very conflict that had created a year-long rift between himself and his mother.

Krazinski smiled and bowed slightly to Jennifer, then Nate. If the man recognized Nate, he didn't betray it. "Jennifer, it's nice to see you again."

"Meyer," Jennifer replied simply.

Nate noticed that the tone of her voice was not friendly.

"Oh, you know each other?" Worthington asked.

"Our paths have crossed," Jennifer replied.

"I had no idea Ms. Daye was going to be here, Daniel," Krazinski said to his host.

"I wanted to surprise you," Worthington answered. "I know if Dr. Daye endorses your work, you'll get the attention you so richly deserve."

Krazinski smiled. "Thank you, Daniel, that's very generous of you."

Worthington grinned proudly. "Now, if you'll excuse me, I must say hello to the rest of my guests before we get started." He walked away and Krazinski followed like a loyal puppy.

"You know that guy?" Nate asked Jennifer.

"Oh, yes," she admitted, watching him inflict his Californian Swami act on Worthington's guests. "I debunked a seance he conducted a few years ago. It was a cheap magic show. My client wasn't happy to find out he had been taken. Meyer's the kind of con artist that turns my stomach."

"When I met him his name was Murray."

Jennifer turned to Nate.

"He took my mother for nearly ten grand," Nate said.

"I'm sorry," Jennifer said. "Despite the ridiculous getup, he can be very charming and persuasive."

"Any chance he's anything but a complete fraud?" Nate asked.

Jennifer shook her head.

"And your dean wants you here to please Worthington?"

She nodded.

"Sounds like a classic rock and a hard place you got yourself caught between," Nate said.

"Now I remember why I invited you, I needed someone to remind me of the obvious."

"Glad I could help. Just try not to blow everything up before the soup course."

The clink of a silver spoon against the side of a crystal wine glass silenced the conversations taking place in the library. "Everyone, may I have your attention," Worthington announced from the center of the room. "Before we sit down to the wonderful meal our chef has planned for us, I'd like all of you to participate with me in an attempt to make contact with my dear wife, Hazel." He waved an arm toward an enormous portrait high on one wall of an older woman, a lively smile on her face.

"Maybe you better fill up on the appetizers," Jennifer advised Nate.

Nate scanned the room. If there was going to be some sort of show put on by Krazinski, he likely would need confederates. All the guests were transfixed by Worthington and his psychic sidekick. The only other people in the room were the waiters, who were circulating the appetizers—except for one. He wore the same tuxedo-like uniform and white gloves, but he didn't carry anything, nor did he seem interested in Worthington and Krazinski.

Jennifer sidled up close to Nate so she could whisper discretely in his ear. "Now it makes sense to get everyone gathered in the library. I'm guessing Meyer has had time to hide a few gadgets, maybe a projector among all the books and art. He's probably working with someone…"

Nate subtly nodded toward the suspicious character he had identified. "Check out that waiter over by the door."

Jennifer looked in that direction, but not directly at him. "Yep, I know him, too. Damn it, here I am trying to get you to open your mind to the paranormal and I lead you directly into a nest of phonies."

"On the bright side, at least I have some evidence that you do actually agree there are frauds and scammers."

"You're also going to have evidence that I'm completely willing to screw up my academic career in order to call them out. No wonder Worthington wanted me here, he wants validation that whatever Meyer has been feeding him is real."

"Won't Krazinski know you'll try to call him out?"

"He seemed surprised that I was here. But after our last run-in, I have to assume he's upped his game. And with Worthington's money behind him, I suspect he's not playing with invisible threads and blue-tooth speakers anymore."

"Ladies and gentlemen," Krazinski began. "If you can put aside your plates and glasses for a moment, I'd like all of you to form a circle and join hands."

The waiters—except for Krazinski's man—collected the plates and glasses from the guests and they formed a circle extending from Worthington and Krazinski around the center of the library. Conveniently, the pattern of the large rug on the floor was a circle that served as a guide.

Jennifer placed her left hand on Nate's right shoulder and held hands with the person on her right. She caught the dean looking at her. He obviously wasn't buying the whole seance thing, but his glare conveyed a warning that if Jennifer wanted to keep her nice offices, she should play along until Worthington's check cleared.

Nate reluctantly accepted the hand of the woman to his left, all the while keeping an eye on Krazinski's stooge.

"Everyone, please close your eyes," Krazinski said in a commanding yet ethereal voice.

Nate left his open. The fake waiter walked over to the light switches for the room and turned them all off, plunging the room into darkness. Then he closed the doors, blocking out any remaining light. The sudden shift from a brightly lit room to near pitch black left a faint afterimage in Nate's vision. He lost track of Krazinski's helper.

Krazinski continued. "I want all of you to fill yourselves with love, with openness, make yourselves welcome to accepting the presences of our dear friend. Those of you who knew Hazel, think of your happiest memory with her, think of her smile, those beautiful, friendly eyes..."

Nate detected a faint ozone smell, then could feel the hairs on the back of his neck and hands standing up. Somehow, Krazinski was filling the room with an electric charge. Jennifer lifted her hand from his shoulder and reached for his ear. A spark jumped from her fingertip to his earlobe. "Ow!" Nate exclaimed in a whisper. The woman to his left shushed him.

Krazinski chuckled as if he had just heard a funny story. "Is someone thinking about the time Hazel dressed up as her husband for Halloween?"

A woman gasped.

"He's got them," Jennifer whispered to Nate. "Anything they see or hear from this point on they'll believe is Mrs. Worthington."

Although Jennifer probably couldn't see him in the dark, he nodded his agreement. It only took a sliver of confirmation to reinforce people's biases. And of course by now everyone was feeling the effect of the electrical charge leaking into the room, attributing it, no doubt, to the presence of spirits.

He took the hand of the woman to his left, stepped back and laid it atop the hand Jennifer had placed on his shoulder. "Cover for me," he whispered to her.

"Okay," Jennifer whispered back.

The woman shushed them both.

Nate stepped back, trying to remember the layout of the library as his eyes slowly adjusted to the tiny amount of light leaking in under the doors. At least he knew where the doors were, he could orient himself on that thin, white crack in the black.

He continued moving backwards until his feet found the edge of the rug. Then he traced the edge, remembering that it was clear of furniture. All the guests where locked in a circle in the middle of the rug, so he probably wouldn't bump into any of them.

Then his foot passed over a lump under the rug. He slowly and quietly kneeled down and reached out with his left hand to find out what it was. He found a cord snaking under the rug. It appeared to be taped down to the exposed wooden floor, likely with a tape the same color of the wood to help it escape notice. He assumed it was the source of the electrical charge.

Krazinski continued his act, asking if anyone had questions for Hazel. After a hesitant pause, one of the guests volunteered a query, and Krazinski made a big production of trying to pull the answer out of a psychic onslaught of images and words that were assaulting his sixth sense, getting the questioners to answer the very questions they were asking.

Nate ignored the communion with the spirits and continued making his way toward the door. As he got closer and his eyes further adjusted, he could see that the dim slit under the door was throwing up a slight reflection from the polished floor. It was clear that the man who had switched off the lights was no longer standing there.

Reaching out in the darkness, Nate found the panel where the switches were located. He was about to turn the lights on when he heard a noise, an eerie tone that sounded like a woman's voice holding a high, soft note.

"Hazel!" Worthington shouted from his position in the circle. "I hear you my darling. I hear you."

There were murmurs and gasps among the guests.

Nate almost switched the lights back on at that point, but a part of him wanted to see the show Krazinski had prepared for them.

His patience was rewarded by a very dim blue light that appeared to hang in the air above the circle of Worthington and his guests.

"Oh, Hazel. Please speak to me," Worthington begged.

Nate knew the old man wouldn't get an answer in words. That would be too easy to screw up. Instead, as if in response, the blue light appeared to travel across the room.

It was clear at this point, that Krazinski had orchestrated a cloud of vapor upon which his confederate was shining a diffuse blue light. Nate couldn't make out the source, though, wondering where they might have concealed it, or by what means they were orchestrating the show. A gust of wind had sent the cloud across the room making it appear as if it was an ethereal body floating across the library.

The light settled upon the portrait of Hazel Worthington, dimly lighting her face. There appeared to be a thin layer of smoke or fog clinging to the surface of the painting. The face appeared to lift off of the canvas, shimmering in the haze.

"Oh my, her eyes are closed," one of the guests observed. The others reacted with a mixture of awe and a little fear.

Nate looked up, and sure enough, the eyes of the face dancing on the wisps of smoke had its eyes closed. It was an effect he recognized from a trip to Disneyland his mother had taken him on when he was a boy. For a suggestive mind it was quite convincing.

The singing stopped. The eyes of Hazel Worthington's spirit sprung open. A woman screamed and Nate could hear sounds consistent with someone fainting and falling to the floor. He switched the lights on.

Everyone covered their eyes.

Krazinski was still in his place, clutching Daniel Worthington's hand. Nate scanned the room for Krazinski's accomplice. He heard a moan from above and looked up. He was perched atop a ladder used to reach the books on the upper shelves. He wore night vision goggles and turning on the lights had temporarily blinded him. On the shelf behind him was a gap in the books where a tiny projector was mounted, aimed at the portrait of Hazel Worthington.

Daniel Worthington angrily cast his eyes toward Nate. "What is the meaning of this? Why did you disrupt the connection? She was going to speak to me. I know she was."

Jennifer stepped forward into the center of the circle of guests that was now looking more like an amoeba on the verge of dividing. "Mr. Worthington, I'm afraid you've been deceived. What you just witnessed was not the spirit of your wife. It was a show put on by Mr. Krazinski and his associate. She pointed up to the spot where the accomplice had been perched, but the gap in the books was now covered up and the man had slid quickly and silently back to the floor.

"This is outrageous," Krazinski exclaimed. He turned to Worthington. "Daniel, I didn't want to say anything before, but this woman and I have a history. I was hoping she wouldn't try to disrupt the proceedings, but her professional jealousy, I'm afraid, has gotten the better of her."

"But Hazel was such an admirer of Professor Daye. I can't believe she would—"

Worthington's protest was cut off by a gasp from Krazinski as he suddenly sucked in a lungful of air, grabbed both of Daniel's hands and threw his head back with his eyes closed.

"Meyer, are you okay?" Worthington asked in concern.

"Oh, brother," Nate said, just loud enough for some guests near him to hear.

The dean entered the circle and stepped toward Jennifer. "What are you doing?" he asked her in a hushed voice. "You're here to butter the old man up, not upset him."

Krazinski's head tilted forward. His eyes opened just enough to reveal the whites. Nate knew the trick of hooding your eyelids while looking up as far as you could. Sometimes perps he had taken into custody used it to fake a seizure.

Worthington gasped.

"She's a fraud, Daniel," Krazinski said in a what Nate assumed was his attempt at a female voice. "She... oh Daniel... I'm going... I love you..."

"I love you, too, Hazel," Worthington said into Krazinski's blank eyes.

The psychic's eyes closed, his head fell forward and his knees buckled. Worthington caught him. "Help me get him over to that chair," he said to one of the men nearby. They dragged his limp body over to the chair and gently sat him down. Jennifer watched him closely. One eye opened a crack, looking directly at her and his lips betrayed a slight smile.

The dean rushed up to Worthington. "Daniel, I'm so sorry. I had no idea Dr. Daye would be so rude. Please, let me apologize on her behalf, and on behalf of the university. I'm sure Hazel would still want you to make sure your legacy at the school remains in place."

Worthington looked to Krazinski. The man looked around as if listening to some faint, far away voice. He looked at Worthington and shook his head.

Worthington stood up straight and addressed the dean. "I'm afraid I'm going to have to reconsider our arrangement," he declared. He turned his attention to Jennifer. "Professor Daye, I must ask that you and your guest please leave."

"Mr. Worthington," Jennifer said, walking toward him, "I'm sorry if I upset you, but I cannot in good conscience allow Mr. Krazinski to take advantage of you in this way. I can show you how he did everything you felt and heard and saw. But it wasn't your wife. If you really want to try to make contact, there are some psychics I trust who can—"

Krazinski cut her off. "I knew it. She's after your money, Daniel. Nothing but a con artist."

Worthington nodded his agreement.

Nate couldn't believe what he was seeing. "Mr. Worthington, she's right—at least about Murray faking the whole thing." He pointed at the ladder. "I saw his accomplice up there, they have equipment hidden behind the books, I would guess there's a fog generator in the vent in the ceiling and another behind the frame of your wife's portrait. And there's a cord leading under the rug that—"

"Enough. Please, both of you, just leave. I've known Mr. Krazinski for months. He has never been anything but truthful to me."

Nate sighed. It was his mother all over again. He knew there was nothing he could say to convince Worthington. Even if he revealed the hidden projector and the other equipment, he was not going to let go of that connection to his wife—no matter how phony it was.

"I'm sorry, Mr. Worthington. We'll go," Jennifer said as she walked across the room toward Nate. She turned back to the old man. "I hope you do really find what you're looking for. Thank you for the invitation." She took Nate by the arm. "Come on, there's nothing more we can do."

Nate nodded. "Do you think he'd be willing to give us a couple of plates to go?"

Jennifer laughed at the notion. She pulled her rumpled bag of candy corn from her jacket pocket and offered some to Nate.

"You brought dime-store candy to a gourmet dinner?"

Jennifer nodded and helped herself to a couple of the colorful kernels.

Nate reached in the bag, pulled one out and popped it in his mouth.

CHAPTER THIRTY TWO

Jennifer sat at her desk, perfectly still, her hands resting on its glossy surface. The computer was off, but she stared at its dark screen, wondering when the dean's hammer would come crashing down on her once again.

Emily entered and plopped herself in one of the chairs in front of Jennifer's desk. "So, did you and the detective have a good time last night?," she asked.

"Ha, ha," Jennifer answered.

Emily smiled. "Come on, it must've been awesome to see that Worthington guy tell the dean he wasn't getting the money."

"That money is what was supposed to pay for these offices."

"So we go back to the basement. Big deal. This place smells too new."

Jennifer leaned back and sighed. "Things were going my way for a minute. Then I had to screw everything up."

"I thought it was Detective Raney who broke up the seance."

"I could have stopped him. But I wanted him to do it. I couldn't stand the idea of having my name associated with that crackpot Krazinski."

"How long do you think we have before they move us out?" Emily asked.

"I'm sure we'll get to the end of the month," Jennifer replied. "There's no reason to kick us out before then."

Dave popped his head in. "Dr. Daye, there are some guys outside who say they're here to move us?" he announced questioningly.

Jennifer and Emily exchanged a look, then laughed.

Dave was confused. "Is this another joke I'm not a part of?"

"No," Jennifer sighed. "The joke's on me this time. I thought I had finally gotten out from under the dean's prejudices, but it's back to the bottom of the totem pole."

"Oh," Dave said with the implicit message, "What else is new?" He consulted the sheet of paper in his hand. "Well, at least we're not going back to the basement. I don't recognize the address on this moving order, but I think it's on the other side of campus." He stepped into the room and placed the paper in front of Jennifer. She looked it over.

"I guess we'll find out where they're sticking us soon enough. Sorry guys."

"What are you sorry for? The dean is the asshole," Emily commented.

"He certainly is. World class," Nate added.

Jennifer, Dave and Emily looked over at the police detective who was suddenly standing next to Dave, his free arm gripping a large envelope. He wore a necktie and a suit jacket that covered his sling with the right sleeve hanging limply. Obviously, he was regaining some mobility from the injured arm.

"Hi Nate, we were just absorbing the fallout from last night," Jennifer sighed. "What are you doing here? You're a little early for the stakeout, it's not until Saturday."

"Well, I didn't want to bring this up last night. You seemed to have enough to deal with."

"That's an understatement," Emily commented.

Nate continued. "We might not need to go through all that nonsense," Nate said. He stepped over to the desk and dropped the packet in front of Jennifer.

"What's this?" she asked as she removed a sheaf of papers from the gray envelope.

"Your ghost."

Jennifer looked at Nate, then back at the papers in her hands. She flipped through the first few pages of the sizable stack. "Jerry Henderson? The boyfriend?"

"Ex-boyfriend," Emily added.

"The ex-boyfriend with a police record, arrests for domestic violence and a little B-and-E."

"So you think this explains everything that happened to Diane?" Jennifer asked.

"It fits. Couple his record with her stress at work and case solved."

"You're good," Emily said sarcastically. "You got the location of Jimmy Hoffa's body in that envelope, too?"

"I thought you wanted to get my cop's perspective on this case. Are you afraid I'm right?" he asked.

"Ooh," Emily said in her millennial monotone. "Looks like he's calling you out, Dr. Daye."

"What are we supposed to do with this information?"

"Talk to him," Nate suggested. "Once people know you're on to them, they tend to make mistakes. When he does, we'll know we have our man."

"Right now?" Jennifer asked.

"Do you have anything better to do?"

A couple of burly movers pushed their way into the office past Dave. "Excuse us," one of them said as they walked up to the large poster of Houdini and lifted it off its mount.

"No, I don't," Jennifer answered. "And it looks like I'm just in the way here," she added. She stood up, put the papers back in the envelope and grabbed her bag and coat.

"Should we wait up for you?" Emily asked, deadpan.

"I'll check out the new offices later. Make sure they don't damage my posters," she said. "Come on Nate, let's go ghost-bust this guy."

CHAPTER THIRTY THREE

Nate sat in the passenger seat of Jennifer's van, belted in securely. They approached an intersection, and it appeared that Dr. Daye was determined to go straight through it.

"You'll want to turn here," Nate suggested.

Jennifer quickly consulted her side-view mirrors, cut across the mostly empty lanes and barely made the turn as her worn tires squealed and slid across the pavement.

Nate sat through the reckless maneuver unperturbed. Compared to Max's driving, she was a little old lady on her way to church.

"Would it reassure you to know I've never had a traffic accident? Not even a ticket?" Jennifer asked.

"No," Nate replied. "Though I suspect you've gotten more than your share of warnings."

Jennifer became offended. "What is that supposed to mean?"

"It means that there are a few patrol cops who pull over women doing anything ticketable to flirt with them. Not something I ever did or endorse, but I know it happens, and it must be frustrating for you."

Jennifer relaxed. She was still on edge about the previous night's events. The glare the dean had given her as she left the dinner party was beyond any look of disdain she had seen from him in the past. "Okay, I may have talked my way out of a speeding ticket or two."

Nate smiled. "So, judging from last night and the fact that movers

216

were carrying your stuff away, I'm guessing there's a bit more to your relationship with the dean than just the typical teacher-administration conflict."

"Can't pull one over on you, detective," Jennifer said.

"Anything I can do to help?" Nate asked.

"How could you help?"

"He may have unpaid parking tickets, or some building code violation at his home. That kind of stuff can tie a person up in bureaucratic knots for quite a while."

"Detective Raney, I'm shocked that you would suggest such a thing."

"Yeah, I guess my partner's been rubbing off on me. I know I shouldn't want to boot his Mercedes, but I met the guy. What is his story?"

"How do you know he drives a Mercedes?" Jennifer asked suspiciously.

Nate shrugged. "I may have looked him up," he confessed.

"Thanks," she said.

"So, did you two date or something?" Nate asked.

"God, no," Jennifer replied adamantly. "We started as associate professors together. He was a big get from Columbia, I was a grad student who moved to the faculty after I was awarded my doctorate. There's a big east coast-west coast rivalry in the anthropology world."

"I had no idea it was so rough."

"Oh, you should see the registration line at the annual conference. You can cut the tension with a spoon."

Nate laughed. "I'll take your word for that."

"Anyway, it was clear from the start that he wasn't cut out for teaching. And almost the entire administration for the department were on the verge of retiring with no one waiting in the wings to take over. So, all he had to do was kiss the right butts, whisper in the right ears, and before you know it, the youngest dean in the department's history."

"So what's he got against you?" Nate asked.

"He doesn't feel there's a place in our field for the type of research I do."

"The ghost stuff."

"There's actually more to it than that. But yeah, the 'ghost stuff.' Ever since I got tenure, he's been trying to get me to leave, trying to cut back my classes, criticizing me for associating the university with all my 'superstitious mumbo-jumbo.'

"But, I have one of the most popular undergrad classes across all the departments, it's the top elective among the engineering and computer science students as well as many of the athletes—and before you ask, no, I'm not an easy A.

"Of course, now he has me tied to the loss of a major donor. That may sway some higher-ups."

"You think he set you up?"

"I think he saw a win-win situation. Either he would get a big donation, or be able to scapegoat me."

"Wow, what a douche."

It was Jennifer's turn to laugh. "It's strange to hear that from a man wearing a tie and jacket."

"I could have worn my 'Animal House' t-shirt. It's got the 'this situation absolutely requires a really futile and stupid gesture' quote on the back."

Jennifer laughed harder. "I can't imagine you wearing a t-shirt with anything on it besides a Calvin Klein tag."

"You should see my collection of concert tees. I've got a great faux black velvet of Celine Dion. It's got the complete lyrics to 'My Heart Will Go On' on the back. I cry every time I wear it."

"Stop!" Jennifer warned as her laughter grew. "I'm trying to drive."

"Stop," Nate said.

"No, you stop."

"No, stop here, this is the address," Nate told her.

Jennifer looked around for a place to park and found a spot that would accommodate her van.

"That building over there." Nate pointed to an apartment

building abutting the sidewalk.

Jennifer peered through the windshield at the building. "So, what's the plan here, Detective? A little good-cop-bad-cop?"

Nate looked at Jennifer. "We're just going to ask him some questions. No TV cop stuff. Nobody does that. It doesn't work."

"If you've never done it, how do you know if it works or not?"

Nate answered her with a raised eyebrow and then let himself out of the van.

Jennifer followed him to the door of the apartment building. There was a row of buzzers with worn nametags next to the dirty buttons. He found the one for J Henderson and noted that the name D Collins was also still there.

He pressed the buzzer, then waited.

Nothing happened.

"Should we press all the buttons and see if someone lets us in and then go check out his place?" Jennifer asked.

"Again, not doing any TV cop stuff, especially anything illegal like breaking and entering." Nate judiciously omitted mentioning he had done just that earlier that week.

"All right," Jennifer said, shrugging. "I saw a little Indian place on the corner. Should we grab lunch while we wait for him to come home?"

Nate took a step back from the building and looked up to the third floor, trying to guess which apartment was Henderson's. He looked up and down the street, then turned around and saw Jerry Henderson jaywalking through the parked cars carrying a tattered plastic shopping bag stuffed with groceries and heading right for him.

Henderson checked the traffic and walked across the street. He looked over at his building and noticed Nate staring at him.

Jennifer realized Nate's attention was focused on something, and followed his gaze to Henderson, who stood frozen in the middle of the street. "Is that him?" she asked Nate.

Nate nodded slightly, but he knew Jerry had made him. Now it was just a matter of waiting for Jerry to make the next move. Nate prayed he wouldn't run.

A cab screeched to a halt next to Henderson, its horn blaring. Jerry looked at the cab, then back at Nate.

"Don't do it," Nate whispered under his breath.

Henderson turned around and ran.

"Damn it," Nate said as he chased after Henderson.

Jennifer watched Nate's pursuit, took note of where Henderson was going and got into her van.

Henderson had a good lead on Nate, and Nate was nowhere near his peak physical condition. The doctors hadn't cleared him for running yet, fearing it would aggravate his recovery. Instead of trying to chase Henderson down, Nate just tried to stay close enough to keep him in sight, hoping that the guy was at least as out of shape as he was.

The street met up with a much busier thoroughfare, and Henderson, instead of trying to cross it, backtracked into a nearby alley that paralleled it. Nate followed and saw him turn down a junction. He jogged after him, hoping the man would make a mistake.

Nate turned the corner and saw Henderson, still running. Nate slowed down, feeling the painful effects of the jog on his shoulder.

Henderson turned back, saw that Nate had given up and smiled. He turned up the speed toward another junction in the alley just as Jennifer's van appeared. Henderson crashed into it. He bounced off the side of the van falling backward, cracking his head on the pavement and spilling his groceries. He was dazed, but not unconscious.

Jennifer got out of the van and stood over the stunned man. She looked down the alley and saw Nate walking briskly in her direction.

Henderson managed to sit up. Blood was pouring out of his nose. He pinched it shut with one hand and looked up at Jennifer.

Nate caught up and looked down at him. "Jeez, Jerry, that looks like it might be broken."

Jerry looked over at Nate. "Who are you guys?"

"I'm Detective Raney, and this is—" Nate hesitated introducing

Jennifer. He wasn't officially an active law enforcement officer, and he didn't want to entangle Jennifer in his little off-the-books investigation more than he already had.

"I'm his partner. Didn't your mother ever tell you to look both ways before you cross the street?" she asked in a thick, pseudo-northeastern accent.

Nate looked at her quizzically.

"Whatcha got in the bag, there, Jerry?" Jennifer asked.

"My groceries," he replied.

Jennifer looked in the bag and pulled out a dripping carton of eggs. "Looks like you'll be having omelets for lunch."

"What do you guys want?" Henderson asked.

"I want to know why you're harassing Diane Collins," Nate answered.

"Diane? I'm not harassing her."

"That's not what she said," Nate told him. "She says you got into her apartment and tried to scare her. You think that's going to make her come running back to you?"

"I don't know what you're talking about. If she said I broke into her place, she's lying."

"Come on Jerry, you can do better than that," Nate said.

"I'm telling you, if someone is bothering Diane, it's not me. I wasn't that hung up on her."

"Why was you runnin'?" Jennifer asked.

Henderson paused before answering. "I thought you guys were Jehovah's Witnesses."

Jennifer and Nate exchanged a look.

"I hate those guys. I took a brochure from them once and they won't leave me alone," Henderson explained.

Nate crouched down and looked Jerry straight in the eyes. "I don't believe you, Jerry. I think you're still upset that Diane left you and is doing well on her own. I think you're having trouble making rent on that crappy apartment of yours and you think if you can scare her, she'll come running back to you."

"Well, you think wrong. She didn't leave me, it was a mutual thing. We parted on good terms, and we're still friends," he said, echoing everything Diane had told them. "Besides, I'm living with my new girlfriend now, wouldn't be much room for Di if she did come back."

"You already moved in with someone else?" Jennifer asked. "Were you cheating on Diane with this woman? That's disgusting."

"Who are you, her new BFF?"

Jennifer was about to answer, but Nate cut her off. "I'll be checking out your story, Henderson. And if I find you within a mile of Diane, you'll be heading toward your third strike."

"Look, I don't know where you got the idea that I'd want to scare Diane, but I'm telling you, everything is cool between us. She got a great place closer to her job, and she's doing well in her career. I'm happy for her."

Nate regarded Jerry skeptically. He didn't sense that there were any underlying feelings of enmity between him and Diane, but some men were good at disguising their feelings, lying to everyone about the true state of their relationships. It was possible he was being straight with Nate, but it was equally likely, in his experience, that his denials were just a performance.

"Yeah, we'll see," Nate added, staring down Jerry until the man looked away.

Jennifer placed the broken eggs back in his grocery bag and handed it to Henderson. Then she reached in her pocket, pulled five dollars from a collection of bills and tossed it at Henderson. "For da eggs," she said in her ridiculous accent.

Henderson got up and started walking away, holding his nose tight with his head back to try to control the bleeding.

"What was that?" Nate asked Jennifer.

"What, the accent? Pretty good, huh? I used to do a bit of dinner theater when I was in college."

"No, the money."

Jennifer shrugged. "I felt bad about the eggs. Wasn't sure if I was the good cop or the bad cop, though."

"You're not a cop," Nate reminded her. "And where did you

come from? How did you know he was coming this way?"

"Oh, that was easy. I knew he wasn't going to cross Fifth, it's too busy this time of day, so I figured he'd try to double back around to the alley."

Nate was impressed. "Nice," he said.

"Thanks," Jennifer replied. Then she added, "I saw it on TV."

Nate shook his head. He walked around to the passenger side of the van. As he stepped on his right foot, a twinge of pain lit up his ankle. He almost stumbled.

"Are you all right?" Jennifer asked.

"Yeah, I must have tweaked my ankle," Nate said. He had no clear memory of doing so, though. When he was running after Henderson, he was fine, and he only did a quick walk when he was catching up to him after he ran into Jennifer's van. Maybe the adrenaline from the chase had masked the injury until now.

"Do you need to see a doctor?" Jennifer asked.

"No," Nate answered reflexively. Then he heard a voice in his head. Not as if someone was talking to him, but more like an echo. It was a familiar voice, but he couldn't place it. He could only make out a part of what was being said. "Hot dog," Nate said aloud without thinking. He realized he was now sitting inside the van, and they were now driving down the street. Nate had no memory of getting into the van let alone Jennifer starting it up and driving them out of the alley.

"Hot dog?" Jennifer asked.

"What?"

"You just said 'hot dog.'"

Nate shook his head.

"Are you sure you're okay? You kind of tuned out on me for a minute there."

"I'm fine," Nate reassured her.

"Probably low blood sugar," Jennifer guessed. "It's after lunch. A hot dog actually sounds good right about now."

"I didn't say 'hot dog,'" Nate protested.

"I think I saw a place that sells them next to that Indian

restaurant."

Nate grimaced and shook his head. "If you want a hot dog, we're not going to some greasy hole-in-the-wall. Head over to SoMa StrEat," he said. "I'll get you a hot dog to die for."

CHAPTER THIRTY FOUR

Diane exited the elevator, grocery bags in both hands. As she walked toward her apartment, she shifted one batch of bags from her right hand to her left, then fished out her keys from her purse to unlock the door.

Her phone rang just as she fitted the key in the lock. She paused opening her door to check the screen which identified the call as "Work." She tapped to answer. "This is Diane," she said, then listened while she squeezed the phone against her ear and shoulder and finished unlocking her door.

Across the hall Rose poked her head out and saw Diane juggling her groceries, phone and keys. "Diane, dear, what are you doing home so early?"

Diane turned around and offered Rose a neighborly smile. "I can't talk now, Rose. Excuse me." Then, into the phone she said, "Sorry, you caught me just as I was walking in the door, hang on for a second." She opened her door, entered the apartment, set her bags down and pushed it shut behind her, leaving the building busybody frustrated.

Diane flopped down into the nearest chair. She put the phone back to her ear. "Okay, sorry about that. What's up?" As she listened, she became aware of an unusual odor—or rather a combination of odors she couldn't quite place. She started to get up, but the person on the other end of the phone conversation said something that brought her attention back to the call. "What? I just got home. I've been putting in sixteen-hour days for the last two weeks. Rob told me I could take the rest of the day off. You were there."

Her demeanor shifted from exhaustion to frustration. "I can't. I have people coming over this weekend and I haven't been home long enough to do anything but sleep for a week." She closed her eyes and listened for a minute. "All of that can wait until tomorrow, and if it can't, Eric can handle it. I'm not the only paralegal in the firm."

Diane tried to open her eyes, but found the lids heavy. She rubbed the back of her neck, feeling a headache coming on. "All right. I'll be there early, but I'm not staying past six. Goodbye."

She could hear the voice on the other end continue to talk, but hung up anyway, and then turned the phone off. She took a deep breath and settled down into the chair, letting sleep overtake her.

There was a crash from the kitchen.

Diane awakened, startled. She leaned forward and started to raise herself out of the chair. She found herself light-headed. Her vision was blurry and dim around the edges. She looked over toward the kitchen and saw something on the floor. "Who's there?" she asked.

There was no answer. She reached for her phone, then remembered she had turned it off. She pressed the power button, and the phone started its boot process.

Suddenly, a part of her recognized the odor she had detected when she entered her apartment. It was hidden by some kind of floral scent, something like the rose scented lotion she used, but still there, unmistakable.

Gas.

There was a gas leak in her apartment. The kitchen?

Diane pushed herself to her feet and made her way across the living room to the kitchen. On the floor were the shards of a coffee cup. She looked over at the stove.

There was a man standing there.

She blinked, rubbed her eyes and looked again, but the figure was still there.

But then again, he wasn't. There was something strange. He

seemed to be occupying some of the same space as her stove. And there was something else. It looked like he didn't have any feet.

Diane stared at him. His face was pleading, desperate. "Who are you?" she asked. "What do you want?"

He turned toward the stove.

Diane noticed that the knobs were missing. She could hear the gas hissing out of the stove, but none of the burners were lit. She rushed to the kitchen window and tried to open it. She managed to get it open a crack, and bent down to get some fresh air into her lungs.

Then she looked at her phone. It was ready to unlock. She did so and opened the phone app and dialed nine-one-one as she made her way back through the kitchen.

The man was gone.

She stumbled through the living room, the phone to her ear. She heard a voice on the other end identify itself and ask what her emergency was.

"I have a gas leak in my apartment. Oakley arms, tenth floor, apartment ten-H." The voice recommended that she get out. "I'm trying," Diane assured the operator. She dropped the phone and headed for the front door. She tripped over the groceries, fell to the floor and banged her head against the door.

Stars filled her dimming vision. She pushed herself onto her hands and knees and reached up for the door knob. She grabbed it with both hands and twisted and pulled until it opened.

Fresh air filled her lungs, but not enough to clear her head. Diane crawled out into the hallway, making her way toward the elevators, sucking in as much fresh air as she could.

The elevator opened. A middle-aged couple exited and saw Diane on the floor. They rushed to her aid.

"There's a gas leak in my apartment," Diane told them. "We have to get everyone out."

"Pull the fire alarm," the man instructed his wife. He nodded to the small red box across from the elevators.

The woman pulled down on the alarm and a loud ringing filled the hallway. Some of the doors opened, most people were likely still at work where Diane would have been if she hadn't demanded some downtime after working nearly around the clock for the last week.

"Can you walk? We should take the stairs," the man said to Diane.

"I think so," Diane replied. He helped her to her feet and held her by her arm. His wife grabbed her other arm, and they started toward the stairwell.

"Wait," Diane said. "Rose, I didn't see her come out."

"The old lady at the end of the hall?" the wife asked.

Diane nodded.

The man left Diane with his wife and rushed toward Rose's door. Diane's door was open, and he covered his mouth with his sleeve reflexively when the odor of the gas grew stronger. He pounded on Rose's door. "Rose," he shouted. "Are you in there? There's a gas leak. We have to get out." He knocked again, then tried the knob. The door was locked. He knocked one last time, then hurried back to Diane and his wife. "I think she's gone," he reported. "Let's get out of here."

The couple guided Diane to the stairs.

CHAPTER THIRTY FIVE

Nate and Jennifer wandered among the tail end of the lunchtime crowd enjoying dishes from the array of food trucks and booths set up serving a variety of gourmet street foods at the SoMa StrEat Food Park. They stopped in front of a truck painted with photo-realistic "portraits" of hot dogs ornately framed as if they were hanging in a museum. The name of the truck was subtly displayed as if carved in stone along the top. "The Art of the Dog."

Jennifer eyed the line of people starting at the ordering window of the truck and disappearing around a corner. "Is this really worth the wait?" she asked.

"Oh, yeah," Nate said. "You'll never want a hot dog from anywhere else after you taste these. She makes the actual hot dogs herself, the buns too. Fresh baked every morning. I don't know what her secret is, but it's not like anything you've ever tasted before. Definitely worth the wait."

They found the end of the line and took their place. More people quickly filled in behind them.

"Can't you use your badge to get us to the front of the line?"

"Nope. Wouldn't insult the woman by trying."

The line moved fairly rapidly, and Jennifer found out why when they reached the order window. There were five options on the menu. Each hot dog was paired with a side dish, and the menu explicitly stated that there were no substitutions allowed.

"What do you recommend?" Jennifer asked Nate.

"Number five, if only for the sweet potato frites."

Jennifer checked out the last item on the menu. It was advertised as a "Windy City Dog," and consisted of a plump hot dog resting in a bun that was more like a cradle than the traditional hot dog buns she was used to. On top of it was a sort of salsa made from all the ingredients of a traditional Chicago-style dog. Tomatoes, dill pickle, a chunky pickle relish, coarsely chopped onions, sport peppers all drizzled with brown mustard then liberally sprinkled with something the menu identified as celery salt.

"Okay, sounds good," she said.

"Two number fives," Nate told the order taker, handing him two twenty-dollar bills, and stuffing another ten into the tip jar. The cashier handed over two bottles of ice cold sparkling water. Nate gave one to Jennifer.

"Wow, a twenty dollar hot dog," Jennifer commented. "Glad it's your treat."

"Trust me, it's as good as any gourmet meal you can get in a Michelin star restaurant." He directed her to a table a few yards away.

"How long does it take to get it?"

Nate shrugged. "Could be a few minutes, could be an hour. She's an artist. You can't rush her."

They sat down at a cafe table within earshot of the food truck. Nate stared at it and for a moment, all the surrounding noise was gone. He had an eerie feeling, and the notion that there was a voice in the back of his mind saying something he couldn't quite hear, was back.

He looked around, and from the corner of his eye saw a silhouette that was somehow familiar. He looked directly at the man. He'd dropped a few pounds, shaved his head and grew a beard, but it was the fat guy from the robbery.

Maybe.

He couldn't be one-hundred percent sure from this angle, but there was something about the way he carried himself.

"Nate? What is it?" Jennifer asked.

With the sound of her voice, his ears opened up to the rest of the world. The chatter from the crowd flooded in. His eyes remained focused on the back of the man.

Even with his attention devoted to the potential suspect, it didn't escape Nate that this was the second time in as many days when a seemingly random choice brought him within proximity of the men who shot him. First it was their recently vacated hideout. Now one of them was standing in front of him, possibly waiting for a hot dog from the very food truck where Nate had placed his order.

No, it couldn't be. It was just a man who bore a passing resemblance to the fat guy from the robbery. His mind was playing tricks on him. The blackout in the van, the one just now. Maybe there was something wrong with him. Was he having a stroke?

A voice from the food truck called out, "John Smith, number two."

The man turned and walked over to the pickup window of the truck. Half of his face was now fully visible to Nate. The profile, the shape of his head and the way his nose sat a little too high on his face leaving room for a tall mustache, were all very distinctive.

It was definitely him.

And yet it couldn't be.

"Are you all right?" Jennifer asked.

Nate kept his eyes on the suspect. He took a deep breath and reached into his pocket for his phone. "You see that guy over there picking up his dogs?" he asked.

Jennifer picked out the man he was referring to and nodded, then said aloud, "Yes," when she realized Nate was intently focused on his target.

"I think that's one of the guys from the robbery."

"Are you sure?"

"No," Nate said, but he was. "I'm going to call it in." He glanced at his phone for a couple seconds as he tapped on the shortcut for Max. When he looked back up, he found the fat guy staring directly at him.

Their eyes met.

The plate the fat guy was holding loaded with a hot dog surrounded by handmade potato chips fell to the ground.

Nate stood, the man looked quickly around, then took off running at a speed Nate wouldn't have imagined the overweight man capable of.

"Hello? Nate, you there?" Max said from the other end of the phone call.

Nate ignored it and started after the heavyset man. But the first full step on the ankle he had tweaked earlier caused him to pull up in pain. He lost sight of the fat guy, then spotted him again heading toward a street where cars were parked. He took a few tentative steps, then did his best to give chase, running with a limp as each step felt like there was broken glass in between the bones of his ankle.

He almost shouted, "Stop, police," before remembering he was not currently active duty. Then he remembered the phone in his hand. He lifted it to his ear. "Max, are you there?"

"What the hell is going on?" Max asked.

"One of the guys from the robbery. He's at the SoMa Food Park."

"What are you talking about?"

"The guys who shot me. I found one."

"Okay, you said you're at SoMa?"

"Yeah, the west end. He's got a beard now, lost a few pounds, but it's him, I'm sure of it. Looks like he's heading for a car."

"I'll alert any units in the area. Jeez, Nate, are you sure? What are you doing at SoMa?"

"Getting a hot dog."

"A hot dog? You?"

"Long story."

"I'll bet twenty it includes a pretty professor. Are you all right? You sound like you're about to pass out."

"I twisted my ankle. Can't keep up with him. I still got eyes, but he's so far ahead."

Then Nate noticed another figure rushing through the crowd

ahead of him and catching up to the fat guy. It was Jennifer.

"Oh, shit," Nate said into the phone.

"What, is he gone?"

"No, but Dr. Daye thinks she's Cagney *and* Lacey today."

"My dream girl," Max commented.

Nate took the phone away from his face and shouted after Jennifer. "Daye, let him go!" But she was too far away to hear him.

Then a group of people passed by, obscuring his view of the scene ahead and after they passed he had lost sight of both of them. He continued limping toward the street, desperately scanning the crowd for Jennifer or the fat guy. He spotted Jennifer standing on the sidewalk next to a line of parked cars. One spot was conspicuously empty. She waved at him, then started walking toward him.

"What were you thinking?" Nate asked her.

"I was thinking you were never going to catch him. Here," she added, handing him a sticky note with some letters and numbers written on it. "That's his license plate number."

Nate took the paper and looked at it. He lifted the phone back to his ear. "Max, you still with me?"

"I am. Sounds like you caught up to the prof."

"Yeah. She got a plate number. Got a pen?"

"Shoot," Max said, then, "sorry, poor choice of words."

Nate ignored the comment and read the letters and numbers off to Max. "Mike, Romeo, eight, two, two, echo, echo."

There was a moment of silence, then Max asked, "Is this a joke?"

"No. Get a BOLO on that plate."

"You're sure this is the license plate number?"

Nate looked to Jennifer. He held the phone between them and switched it to speaker mode. "You got this right?" he asked her.

Jennifer nodded. "Absolutely. I got a good long look at it."

"You heard her," Nate said to the phone. "Why?"

"My Rabbit ate twenty-two Easter eggs," Max replied.

"What?" Nate seemed confused.

The phrase triggered a mental connection for Jennifer. "Oh, like the memory trick Diane did for Jerry's license plate."

"And," Max added, "the first thing you said to me after you woke up in the hospital. 'My Rabbit ate twenty-two Easter eggs.'"

Then Nate realized what they were getting at. The phrase was a mnemonic. A way of remembering a random sequence of letter and numbers by associating them with words in a sentence. The brain was much more likely to remember something like that than a straight up license plate number. It was a trick he had used countless times on the job and had even managed to get Max to make it a habit.

My rabbit ate twenty-two Easter Eggs.

M-R-8-22-E-E.

"Jesus, Nate, what the hell?" Max asked over the phone.

"Just put out the BOLO," Nate said.

"Nate, take me off speaker."

Nate switched back to handset mode and put the phone to his ear.

"What is it?"

"He saw you?" Max asked.

"Yeah," Nate confirmed.

"I'm going to send a unit to pick you up."

"Max, they're not going to go after me, certainly not right now."

"I'm not taking that chance. You may think it's all a big coincidence, but do you think they do? The guy they shot, a cop, just happens to run into them at a food truck?"

"If they're smart they'll leave town," Nate replied.

"Yeah, well, they haven't done that yet so we can rule out them being smart. They're sticking around for some reason. And now they think you're on to them, what would your next move be?"

"I don't need a police escort. They're not going to try anything here."

"I'm going to get the captain to put a unit outside your house. I insist."

"I don't think—"

"Hey, it's that or I'm sleeping on your couch tonight."

"All right," Nate sighed.

"And Nate, if you get any more... weird thoughts, or crazy urges, give me a call."

"Sure," Nate replied, relenting to his partner's pressure. He ended the call, then looked to Jennifer. He half expected her to give him a big, "I told you so."

But instead, she looked back at him with concern.

Her phone rang.

Jennifer looked at the screen, but didn't recognize the number. "Now what?" She answered it. "Hello, this is Jennifer Daye."

Her expression changed from concern to worry, then something close to fear.

"All right, Diane, I'm with Detective Raney. We can be there in half an hour. Are you safe?" She listened for a moment. "All right, we'll be there as soon as we can."

It was Nate's turn to be curious. "What was that?"

"There was a gas leak at Diane's building. She says the ghost was there."

"A gas leak, huh? Henderson did a stint working for the gas company. I knew if we tweaked that guy he'd make a mistake. But I didn't think it would happen so fast."

"I told her we'd be there as soon as we could. We'll have to come back another time for the hot dogs."

A short woman, with literally fiery hair dyed yellow, orange and red, walked up to Nate with a couple of cardboard to-go boxes. "You forgot these," she said with the voice of a woman who smoked too much and didn't care.

Nate smiled at the sight of her. "Thank you, Maddy. That wasn't necessary."

"Nobody walks away from my truck unsatisfied," she grunted. "And what were you doing paying? You know your money's no good at my joint."

"You're the cook?" Jennifer asked.

"The artist," Nate corrected, allowing the aroma of the dogs to seduce his nostrils.

"Hey, sweetie," Maddy said to Jennifer, sizing her up with a maternally critical eye. "Eat those before they get cold." Then she turned around and started trundling back to the Art of the Dog.

Nate handed Jennifer one of the boxes. "She's right, they taste best right off the grill."

He started limping in the direction they left the van.

"How about you wait here and I pick you up? I promise, I'll eat this on my way to the van." To fulfill her vow, she picked up her dog from the to go container and bit off one end. She chewed for a moment, then her eyes widened as she continued chewing and swallowed. "Oh my god, that is amazing."

"I thought you were getting the van," Nate said, taking a bite from his own dog.

"I'm going, I'm going." She took another bite and started walking. Then she turned back to Nate and said, "We are definitely coming back here when we don't have to chase after bad guys and ghosts."

"Deal," Nate answered with a grin.

CHAPTER THIRTY SIX

Seymour and Freddie sped away.

"Slow down," Seymour snarled at his skinny companion.

Freddie eased off the gas and continued driving. "What the hell? You had to get your stupid twenty dollar hot dog. How did he know you were there?" Freddie asked.

"I don't know. I guess the same way he knew we had been at that house."

Freddie thought about it for a moment, then reached a conclusion. "He knows who we are."

"Yeah, that's obvious. But how does he know *where* we are?"

"Maybe the cops got us under surveillance."

"Nah, they would've grabbed us by now."

"I should've put two bullets in him. They said on the news he was on medical leave from the department. You think he's working on his own?"

"Not unless that arm in a sling is an act. And the way he was running, he's not in any shape to write parking tickets let alone chase us down. And if he knew anything, he'd tell his buddies on the force."

"So what's his game?"

"Whatever it is, I'd bet he's got every cop in the city looking for this car. We gotta ditch it. Pull into this parking garage."

Freddie drove the car into the garage. He put on a baseball hat and a pair of glasses before rolling down his window to take a ticket and entering the structure."

"Head to the roof. Less of a chance anyone will spot it."

"So, what are we going to do?" Freddie asked. "Get out of town?"

"We still need to pay off Deuce. If he gets word that we skipped town, we won't be safe anywhere. We have to get that cop off our backs." Seymour considered their options. "We have to finish what you started."

Freddie looked at his partner. "Maybe Deuce can help. After all, he won't see any money if we end up behind bars."

They arrived at the top of the parking garage and pulled into a corner spot. They got out of the car, emptied a couple of large duffel bags from the trunk and headed for the nearest stairway.

CHAPTER THIRTY SEVEN

The scene outside of the Oakley Arms was chaotic. The entire building had been evacuated when the fire alarm was pulled. At least six fire engines and ambulances were present, and twice that many police cars had set a perimeter around the building.

Diane sat inside one of the ambulances, a mask supplying oxygen covered her nose and mouth. A paramedic monitored her vital signs.

"How are you feeling?" the young ambulance attendant asked.

"A little nauseous," Diane replied.

"That should pass. How long were you in there?"

"Just a few minutes. I almost fell asleep."

"Lucky you didn't."

"I guess," Diane replied. She hadn't told anyone about the ghostly figure in her kitchen except for the brief phone call to Dr. Daye she made from her neighbor's cell phone. She remembered having hers in the apartment, but couldn't recall when or where she had dropped it after dialing nine-one-one.

"Di, are you all right?" a new voice asked, concerned.

Diane turned to face the speaker and smiled weakly. "Jerry, what are you doing here?"

"Can't an old flame stop by for a visit?"

"Usually they call first," she said.

"I did, you didn't answer."

Diane remembered her lost phone. "Oh, right. Lost my phone

somewhere in the confusion. You could have left a message."

"I did that, too. But then the news was saying there was a fire in your building, and I just wanted to make sure you were okay."

Diane retained a degree of skepticism that Jerry could easily sense.

"And," he continued, "I wanted to find out why you were telling some cop that I was harassing you?"

"What?"

"Some guy, dresses really nice. And a blonde woman. I'm not quite sure what her story was, to be honest."

"Detective Raney and Dr. Daye? They talked to you?"

"They paid me a visit."

"I'm sorry, I didn't tell them anything like that. They must have…"

"Must have what?"

"I've just been having some problems at my apartment. They're looking into it for me."

Jerry became suddenly concerned. "What problems?"

"Just strange things. And this afternoon I came home to a gas leak in my kitchen."

Jerry shook his head. "These old turn of the century places are death traps."

"I hardly ever touch that stove, I usually use the microwave."

Jerry felt a hand on his shoulder. He spun around to find Nate and Jennifer standing behind him, accompanied by a uniformed police officer.

"Hi again, Jerry," Nate said. "I thought I told you to stay away from Diane."

"And I told you we're friends. I was concerned about her."

"It's okay," Diane said. "Jerry was just worried. It wasn't him."

"Did you see your… guest again?" Jennifer asked.

"You mean the ghost?" Diane asked, not caring if anyone else knew at this point. "Yes. I think he saved me."

"You had a gas leak in your apartment," Nate said. "Hypoxia can cause hallucinations—"

"It wasn't a hallucination. I left work early—I'd been putting in sixteen-hour days—stopped at the grocery store, and I got a phone call as I was coming in the door. I smelled something, but it didn't register as gas right away. I was upset because the call was from work, they wanted me to come back in. I remember just wanting to close my eyes for a minute.

"Then there was a crash. He broke a cup. In the kitchen. The noise woke me up. If he hadn't, I'd be dead now."

"I believe you," Jennifer said, stepping forward. "You're not the first person to be helped by a spirit."

"Why are you talking about ghosts? I want to know who the cops think started the leak," Jerry said.

"Are you volunteering to go to the top of the list?" Nate asked.

"Look, I told you I came here to see if she was okay, not to try to kill her."

"Stop it," Diane said. She turned to the paramedic. "Am I okay to go?"

The young man frowned. "Your vitals are fine. But if you feel any light-headedness, or if the nausea gets worse, get yourself to the ER," he advised.

Diane took off the mask and stepped out of the ambulance. "I think I'm going to find a hotel for the night."

"Ms. Collins," Nate said, "can we have the keys to your apartment? I'd like to have a look around if that's okay with you."

Diane considered, then realized she had left everything in her apartment. "I left my keys, my wallet, my phone... everything inside. I guess I have to go back in there after all."

"We can go for you," Jennifer offered. "I can grab some clothes for you, too, if you like."

"Actually, I have an earthquake bag in my front closet. If you can grab that for me, I'll be fine. There's a motor lodge up the street, White House, White Fence—something with White in it. You can't miss it."

"We'll find it," Nate promised.

"Come on," Jerry said, "we can put your room on my credit

card."

"Thanks," Diane said. "Thank you all."

"We'll talk more later," Jennifer replied. "When you're ready, I want to hear everything about what you saw."

Diane nodded a promise to do so, then walked off slowly, allowing Jerry to support her by one arm.

Nate got the attention of a nearby uniformed officer. "Detective Raney," the officer said, surprised. Nate didn't know the young man, but obviously getting shot had came with a degree of notoriety.

"Would you mind making sure Ms. Collins gets to where she's going safely?" He nodded at Diane slowly walking away with her arm draped over Jerry's shoulder.

"No problem, sir." The officer fell in step behind the couple and Nate felt relieved.

"You still think he's the source of her problems?" Jennifer asked him.

"More than ever," Nate responded. He turned to Jennifer. "She has a gas leak not more than a couple hours after we talk to him? Then he's here to comfort her afterward? Some crazy Munchausen-white knight thing going on here. I don't trust him one bit."

"Or, he's a friend concerned for her well-being just like he said."

Nate shook his head. "I think I've seen a bit more of the dark side of humanity than you have. Trust me, people are seldom what they seem."

"That's a very cynical point of view. No wonder you're such a skeptic."

Nate ignored her comment and searched for a familiar face among the gathered first responders. He walked up to a man in a white shirt with black epaulets and a badge pinned to his breast pocket. "Gary, how's it going?"

Gary Fitzhugh, the fire inspector, turned toward Nate and smiled. "Nate Raney! How are you? More importantly, how is that old uncle of yours?"

"He's doing well, just saw him the other day."

"I heard what happened to you."

"Yeah," Nate answered, glancing down at his slung arm. "Forgot to duck."

Fitzhugh laughed. "What can I help you with?"

"Is the building cleared yet?" He nodded at Jennifer. "We know the woman from ten-H. I was hoping to take a look around—after you've done your thing, that is."

"Oh, we're done."

"What did you find?"

"Looks like someone was cleaning the stove, the knobs were off and the burners got turned on without igniting. We see that quite often."

"Diane didn't say anything about cleaning," Jennifer said.

Gary shrugged. "Maybe she had a careless cleaning lady? Maybe the super stopped by?"

"Could it have been intentional?" Nate asked.

"Certainly," the fire inspector answered. "But there was no sign of forced entry. Ms. Collins said that her door was locked when she got home. She might have done it accidentally before she went to work, and just forgot about it. She seemed to be under a lot of stress."

"You check for prints?"

"Yeah, but the stove was wiped clean. That's why we think someone was cleaning and didn't realize they had turned on the gas."

"Or they were hiding their trail," Nate suggested.

"Well, CSI took a look, and unless we find any evidence to the contrary..."

"Thanks, Gary. So we can go up?" Nate asked.

"Sure, but you'll have to take the stairs. The elevators got locked down when the fire alarm went off, and we haven't reset them yet."

Nate winced at the notion of climbing ten flights of stairs with his tweaked ankle.

"You could try the service elevator?" a voice suggested.

Nate and Jennifer turned around. Rose was standing behind them, smiling warmly, her hands knotted together in front of her.

"Hi," Jennifer said. "Rose, isn't it? You're Diane's neighbor."

"Yes, I was also on the tenants' board when we put the freight elevator in. It wasn't put on the same fire controls since it wasn't publicly accessible. You should be able to get to it through that doorway in the corner of the lobby. Mr. Dingle, the current superintendent, leaves it unlocked during the day. I'll show you."

"Thank you, Rose," Nate said. He turned to Jennifer. "Let's go take a look."

CHAPTER THIRTY EIGHT

The fire inspector sent a rookie under his command to accompany Nate and Jennifer and Rose through the barricade, then the old woman led them to the door discretely tucked away in one corner of the lobby marked "Employees Only." As she predicted, the door was unlocked. A short hallway led them through a utility corridor and then to a loading dock with a roll-up door on one end, and a service elevator on the other.

"Thank you, Rose", Jennifer said to their guide.

"You're welcome, deary," Rose answered. "If you don't mind, I'm going to wait until the regular elevator is in order. I like it when my elevator plays music." She turned around and shuffled away.

Nate and Jennifer approached the old service elevator. It had a manual door that opened vertically rather than horizontally.

There were buttons for each floor inside the car.

Nate reached for the handle of the door to pull it open.

"Hey, watch it there. You're not in any condition to be straining yourself like that," Jennifer warned. She stepped between Nate and the handle, grabbed a hold of it and easily flung it open.

"If I knew you were so strong, I would have just had you carry me up the stairs."

Jennifer looked around inside the dingy interior of the elevator. "It may still come to that."

They entered the car, and Jennifer pulled the door shut. Nate pressed the button for the tenth floor. After a second, the elevator started making noise, then jerked into motion, carrying them slowly upward.

Jennifer noticed the elevator inspection certificate. "Ah, inspector number forty-three. I'm familiar with his work, but it seems like he hasn't been here in a while."

"You could have pointed that out before we pressed the button."

The elevator creaked skyward. The numbers of the floors passed by as they ascended, visible through the slats of the elevator door.

"You still think Henderson was behind all of this?"

"He had plenty of time to get here after we talked to him, sabotage the stove."

"You don't believe the fire inspector that it was an accident?"

"Diane said she has barely been home long enough to sleep. I very much doubt she decided to give her kitchen a good spring cleaning."

"Maybe it was the building super."

"Too many maybes," Nate said. "When you have to work that hard to explain something away, chances are you may want to give it a second look."

"Jerry seemed genuinely concerned about Diane."

"Yeah, he shows up to comfort her after she nearly dies. How convenient. Maybe the ghost turned on the gas," Nate suggested sarcastically.

"I don't think so," Jennifer replied. "When they interact with the physical, it's usually something like what Diane mentioned, knocking over a cup, blowing out a candle."

"Sounds like ghosts and the wind have a lot in common."

Jennifer smiled, realizing Nate was not making a serious suggestion. "Well, either the wind or Diane's ghost saved her life. I'm guessing the gas was so strong in her apartment because the windows were closed, so I'm betting on the ghost."

Nate shook his head. He watched the numbers go by and saw the elevator car pass nine and then ten. "Hey, didn't we press ten?" He jammed his thumb against the button over the number twelve, but the elevator kept on moving.

"Press the stop button," Jennifer suggested.

Nate jabbed at the red button, but the elevator continued its upward trajectory.

There was a loud bang.

The car stopped suddenly, throwing Nate and Jennifer off balance.

The motor for the elevator kept on grinding away, humming and screeching, but the car wasn't moving.

"Looks like we're stuck between floors," Nate said.

"Why is it still trying to move?" Jennifer asked.

"I don't know, but I don't like the sound of that."

The elevator jerked up about a foot, made another loud bang, then something snapped off the bottom of the car. They couldn't see it, but they could hear something large hitting the sides of the elevator shaft as it fell to the basement.

Nate pulled out his wallet and fished out a metal rectangle with various shapes cut into it. He used one corner as a screwdriver and removed the screws from the cover of the elevator control panel.

"Do you have any idea what you're doing?"

"Nope, but I'm hoping we can shut it down before that cable snaps."

"Okay, I'm all for that. Can I help?"

Nate inspected the collection of wires leading from the buttons. "What's your favorite color?"

"Blue," Jennifer answered.

Nate reached for the blue wire with a recessed wire snipper on his wallet tool.

"No, red," Jennifer shouted.

Nate looked at her and she shrugged. "I'm discovering I'm not very confident in life-threatening situations. Of course, this is the first one I've been in, so I don't have a lot to go on."

"Don't worry, we'll get out of this," he said calmly.

Nate reached for the green wire and sliced through it.

The elevator motor died with a whine.

They both breathed a sigh of relief.

"Let's see if we can get out of here," Nate suggested.

He and Jennifer both grabbed the door handle and slid it open. They were between floors, but could get enough of a grip on the second door to open it wide enough to make an opening they could fit through.

"You go first, then you can help me out," Nate suggested.

Jennifer nodded. She climbed up to the opening and pulled herself through. Then she reached back to give Nate a hand.

The elevator slipped and jerked down a few inches.

Nate was knocked off his feet. He got back up and reached up with his good arm to grab Jennifer's outstretched hand. She pulled on him and he managed to get most of his body through the opening and onto the twelfth floor.

The elevator groaned again. Nate's feet were still inside the car. Jennifer grabbed the collar of his jacket and pulled back while he brought his knees up to his chest.

The elevator cable snapped, and the car dropped down the shaft, screeching and sparking until it crashed into the basement floor.

Nate found himself with his head in Jennifer's lap. He looked up at her.

She smiled.

"Thanks," Nate said.

"Any time." She replied. "And by any time, I mean I hope we never do anything like that again."

CHAPTER THIRTY NINE

Nate and Jennifer exited the stairwell on the tenth floor. The journey obviously took a toll on Nate's ankle and he walked with a pronounced limp at this point.

"Let me help you," Jennifer said. She took his good arm and wrapped it around her shoulder so he could use her for support.

"Thanks," Nate acknowledged reluctantly. It wasn't that he felt emasculated by accepting help from Jennifer, but rather that he needed help at all. This physical recovery wasn't exactly speeding along, and now with his ankle hurt, there would be more delay.

"You sure you still want to take a look at Diane's apartment?" she asked. "We should get you looked at."

"We need to wait for them to get the elevators operational, so we might as well use the time to investigate."

They arrived at Diane's door. It was unlocked. Jennifer pushed it open, and they walked into the apartment.

Nate took his arm from around Jennifer's shoulders and supported himself on the back of a chair.

Jennifer found Diane's phone, gathered up the groceries and carried them to the kitchen. Her nose caught a scent. "You smell that?" she asked.

Nate sniffed. "Smells like flowers."

"Roses," Jennifer replied. "Do you see any flowers around here?" She crossed to the bathroom and returned with an empty bottle.

"Looks like Diane replaced that bottle of rose water that broke, but it's empty."

"She did mention she didn't immediately recognize the gas smell. Maybe someone used the rose water to hide the scent of the gas?"

"Maybe it was Diane. I have a friend who sprays it on her bed linens. But I can't believe she'd use the whole bottle."

"I certainly don't think your ghost did it."

"Yeah, I think Diane was right, he was trying to warn her, not harm her."

Nate smirked.

"Oh, right, more sarcasm."

"Look, this is getting serious. She could have died."

"The fire inspector thinks it was an accident."

Nate limped his way into the kitchen. The stove was pulled away from the wall to access the shut-off valve for the gas. The knobs for the stove were lined up on the counter. There was a roll of paper towels and a spray cleaner next to them.

Jennifer came in behind him. Her foot crunched a shard from the coffee cup.

Nate stepped aside, and she spotted the cleaning supplies.

"Well," she said, "I can see why the fire inspector thinks it was an accident."

"Maybe," Nate said.

"You know how you assume that I'm always looking for evidence to confirm my belief in the paranormal? I think you might be doing the same with Henderson."

Nate stood there, silent.

"And we still need to talk about how you knew that guy was going to be at the hot dog truck. And how you knew that license plate number."

Nate looked up. "You think that was something more than a coincidence?"

"Someone's uncle once told me there is no such thing as coincidence. Listen, you had some kind of spell in the van, then the first thing you said was 'hot dog' and we go to SoMa and there's the guy. Then, I get his license plate, and it turns out you already knew it because it was the first thing you said when you woke up after a near-death experience. That's a lot of coincidences."

"And that's *all* it is."

Jennifer stared at Nate. She nodded, and bent down to pick up the pieces of the shattered coffee cup. "Well," she said, placing the shards on the counter, "I guess we'll settle this once we find out exactly what's going on in this apartment. I have a feeling this is going to be an interesting stakeout."

CHAPTER FORTY

Nate had Diane Collins' case organized on a large whiteboard in his living room. Well, half of the whiteboard. The other half he had devoted to notes and thoughts on the Axeman case and Luther Laramie. He wasn't willing to admit yet that the two were related.

Madge lay on her spot on the sofa, watching him. He was resigned to the fact that he had a dog now and found himself enjoying her company. She actually behaved rather well when she could see him.

He stepped back from the board, the medical walking boot he had been given at the doctor's office made a hollow clunking sound against his wooden floors. Jennifer had insisted he go to the hospital after they had reported their experience with the freight elevator. The building superintendent didn't seem surprised at the news. He rarely used the old thing himself and the tenants all knew it was a death trap.

Nate talked Jennifer into going to an urgent care clinic instead of the E.R. They did an X-ray, and some blood tests, and the physician's assistant told Nate he had a severe sprain but nothing appeared to be broken. A week in the boot was prescribed, and Jennifer drove him home insisting that his injury was not serious enough to serve as an excuse to get out of their stakeout at Diane's place.

When he got home, he realized that he had spent the better part of the day with Jennifer. They had passed the time in the waiting room at the clinic exchanging stories of childhood injuries. She had offered to treat him to dinner since he had bought lunch, but he was exhausted and he accepted a rain check instead. She recalled that while she was running around with Nate, her staff was being relocated to yet another office, and she was not anxious to see which level of hell the dean had condemned them to.

Nate changed clothes before making himself a sandwich from what he could scrounge from his relatively bare pantry and refrigerator. He still hadn't had time to shop since he'd gotten back from the hospital. He ended up with a marmalade and cream cheese sandwich, something akin to what his mother used to pack in his lunch box for school. It wasn't bad, but he made a note to get some meats and cheeses in the morning when he went to the market for the stakeout supplies. He enjoyed cooking, but decided that he wouldn't purchase anything that needed an elaborate preparation since he was effectively down one hand.

He regarded the whiteboard. A portion of a map showed the location of Diane's apartment, her office, and Jerry Henderson's place. Between them he had a small sticky note indicating the travel time between Diane's and Jerry's homes.

On another part of the board, he had a timeline for the day: when he and Jennifer encountered Henderson, when Diane made her nine-one-one call, and when they saw Henderson with her outside of the building.

Jennifer was right. Nate wanted to believe that Henderson was behind all of Diane's trouble. And the timeline fit, but barely. There was time for Henderson to get to Diane's place after Nate and Jennifer had confronted him and before Diane got home to stage the stove to appear that she had accidentally turned on the gas while cleaning.

But the logic didn't fit.

Why would Henderson risk showing up at Diane's place so soon after his encounter with Nate and Jennifer, let alone try to scare her with a gas leak? How did he even know she'd be home early? Or did that change in her schedule throw his plan off? He considered that

Henderson wasn't trying to scare her, and actually wanted her dead, but as much of a deadbeat loser Nate thought Jerry was, he didn't figure him for a killer. Besides, Jerry had worked for the gas company. He likely would have made his sabotage a little less obvious. He could have easily moved the stove away from the wall, loosened the gas line and moved it back. Staging a careless cleaning accident didn't fit with Jerry's character. He doubted Jerry had ever cleaned a stove in his life.

Which led back to the fire inspector's explanation. Diane had accidentally turned on the gas while cleaning the stove, got distracted, and then came home to a gas-filled apartment.

Was it possible it was all Diane? Was she unintentionally or even subconsciously responsible for everything that had happened so far? The result of an over-active imagination and over-stressed work life?

If that was the case, maybe this stakeout Dr. Daye and her team wanted to do was just the thing she needed to put her mind at ease. It would reassure her that there were no supernatural entities at work, and she could process the stress of her job without the notion that she was haunted by a ghost.

His phone rang. It was Jennifer. "Raney," he said as he answered.

"I know," Jennifer replied, "I called you."

"Sorry, habit," he explained.

"I just wanted to give you the new address for our offices. Can you meet me there Saturday around eleven? We can head to Diane's from there."

"Sounds good," Nate answered. He wrote down the address she gave him. "Hey, how is the new office?"

"I have no idea. I won't get a chance to check it out until Saturday myself. How are you?" Jennifer asked. "Is your ankle feeling better? I keep picturing you hobbling around with your foot in a boot and your arm in a sling and Madge trying to trip you up."

Nate laughed at the image. "I'm getting by fine. Thanks for asking. I think I'm going to sit out that marathon next weekend, though."

It was Jennifer's turn to laugh. "I feel bad. I got you involved in this investigation and it's turning out to be a lot more physically demanding that I expected."

"That's all right," he reassured her. "I've been through worse."

"Really?"

"Well, no, actually. I've never been shot before, or nearly killed by an elevator. I have had my share of foot chases, but seeing Henderson smash himself into your van was a first."

"That was pretty cool," Jennifer said.

Nate laughed again. "Yeah, it was. I need to watch more TV cop shows."

There was a beat of silence. Nate had the urge to thank her for a wonderful day, but as he formed the words in his mind, it sounded like something he would say at the end of a date. Before he could say anything, Jennifer spoke up.

"Well, I'll see you Saturday."

"Yeah, see you then. Good night."

"Good night."

Nate ended the call, slipped the phone into his pocket and hobbled into the kitchen. Madge slid off the sofa and followed him.

Out of habit, Nate absently poured himself a glass of red wine from a bottle on the counter. He let the aroma tease his nose. Then he set the glass down and pulled a prescription bottle from his pocket and glanced at the label where a warning sticker admonished him about mixing it with alcohol.

Madge whined at him from the floor. She was sitting next to her food and water dishes. Nate noticed Madge had her gaze focused on his wine.

"You want some of this?" Nate asked.

Madge whined again.

Nate leaned down and poured a splash of the scarlet liquid into Madge's bowl, curious to see what she would do. The dog sniffed at it, then started lapping it up.

"You've got expensive tastes, pooch," Nate told her.

She looked up at him and whined for more.

"I don't think that's a good idea, Madge." He reluctantly poured the rest of the glass down the sink.

The coffee maker beeped.

Nate reached into a cabinet with his good hand. He grabbed a couple of travel mugs, opened the tops and filled them with hot coffee. To one he added a dash of cream from the refrigerator, screwed the tops on the cups and tucked them inside his sling. He crossed back through the living room to the front door and walked outside.

Directly in front of his house was a police cruiser. The passenger side window rolled down as Nate approached. "Good evening, Moore, Amari," Nate said to the man and woman sitting inside the car. They smiled a greeting. He held up one of the travel mugs.

"You didn't have to do that, Detective." Amari held up a styrofoam coffee cup.

Nate caught the scent of the coffee from the car. "Smells like I did. Here." He passed them the thermos cups.

Moore opened his and took a sip. "Can't argue with you there."

"Hey, you didn't bring one for me?" Max asked.

Nate turned and saw his partner standing on the sidewalk behind him.

"Don't you have a robbery and attempted murder to investigate?"

"Well, I figured since you're catching all the breaks in your case, I'd stick as close to you as I can, maybe one will come my way."

"I have a feeling that whatever luck I had earlier has run out."

Max moved a little closer and lowered his voice. "Nate, have you considered that you didn't accidentally run into these guys, but they've been tailing you?"

"You think I was a target?"

"No. Not initially at least. But maybe something's changed. Jeez, if this was any other case, you'd be telling me all this."

Nate nodded. It was the same point Jennifer was making. He was too close to this investigation to have an objective viewpoint.

"Come on, I want to do a walk-through of your house. Make sure everything is locked up tight."

"Thanks, but that's not necessary. I'm not an invalid."

Max made a point of glancing at Nate's sling, and the boot that encased his foot.

"I can still kick your ass," Nate asserted.

"Just make sure no one can sneak in while you're sleeping. Do you have an alarm system in that old place?"

"I have Madge," Nate answered.

"What the hell is a Madge?"

"My dog."

Max laughed. "I tell you to get a girlfriend, you get a dog. Well, I guess that's better than nothing. Keep your phone and your gun nearby. These officers are instructed to check on any lights that come on, so if you have a weak bladder, expect a knock at the door."

Nate sighed.

"Now you know what it's like to be on the other side of that Raney stubbornness."

"I'm not stubborn."

"Said the man who made me pee in a Pepsi bottle on a stakeout."

"No one told you to drink a gallon of coffee."

Max turned to the officers in the car. "I want status reports every fifteen minutes."

"Ten-four, Detective," Amari answered.

Max wished everyone a good night and walked back to where he parked his car.

Down the street, in a black Mustang convertible with the top up sat Seymour and Freddie.

Freddie watched the interaction between Nate and his body guards in the side-view mirror. "What do you think?" he asked his partner.

"I think the longer we wait, the harder it'll get."

The headlights of Max's car lit up the inside of the convertible as he drove by. They both ducked down until he passed.

Freddie looked to his partner and gave a nod.

CHAPTER FORTY ONE

Nate woke with a start. He glanced at the glowing numbers on his alarm clock.

Three-oh-five.

He slowly and quietly sat up and pushed aside his bedding. He paused to listen.

There was a faint bump, as if someone was trying to navigate an unfamiliar room in the dark.

He reached down to the gun safe under his night table and pressed his thumb against the fingerprint sensor. The safe popped open, and he took the gun out. Holding it in his left hand was still a bit awkward. He swung his legs down onto the floor and silently got to his feet.

Nate always saw well in the dark, the faint red glow from the alarm clock was enough for him to make his way from the bed to the door. He cautiously peered into the hallway toward the stairway. He thought about the squad car outside, and turning on a light to alert them, but that would likely alert the intruder as well.

The hallway was empty. He waited a moment, listening and watching. There was nothing.

He stepped out of his bedroom and made his way toward the stairs. One at a time, he descended the steps, keeping his eyes and ears open.

Another sound caught his attention. A tapping, as if someone was rapping against something wooden. It stopped.

Nate continued down the stairs to the hallway. There was a faint light from a street lamp slipping in through a crack in the curtains. He peeked into the living room. The front door was closed. Considering there was a police car parked in front of his house, it was unlikely any intruder would have tried to enter through there.

He turned in the opposite direction, toward the kitchen.

The clicking sound echoed in the darkness again.

Followed by a plaintive whine.

Nate reached for the kitchen light switch and turned it on.

Madge looked up at him.

Nate looked over at her kennel in the corner of the kitchen. The door was still closed.

"You know, one of these days you're going to have to tell me how you do that."

There was a knock at the front door. Nate was startled until he realized he had turned on the lights. He crossed back into the living room and unlocked and opened the door. Amari stood in the doorway, her hand resting on her gun.

"Everything all right, Detective?" she asked, eyeing the gun in his own hand.

"Yes, just the dog."

On cue, Madge trotted up to the front door and walked up to Amari. The officer smiled and scratched the dog on her head.

"Okay, sorry to disturb you."

"No problem, Max will be glad to know you're on the ball."

"We all want to catch the guys who shot you," she affirmed.

"Well, they're not here tonight."

"Goodnight, sir."

Amari turned and walked back to the police car.

Nate closed the door and walked back to the kitchen. He reached down to open the kennel door and Madge whined again.

"All right, but just tonight," Nate told her.

He turned off the kitchen light and led Madge back upstairs to his room. He returned his gun to the safe as Madge curled up on the floor next to the bed.

CHAPTER FORTY TWO

Dave was sitting at a desk that was nothing more than a card table with a folding chair pulled up next to it. Sweat beaded on his brow and soaked his shirt. Of all the locations they had been stuffed into over the years he'd been working with Dr. Daye, this one was the bottom of a very deep barrel.

They were in a corner of an athletic supply room. There were shelves filled with various types of balls, gloves, helmets, track and field paraphernalia, and a caged off area held the more valuable assets of the university's athletic department. If there was any ventilation, he couldn't find it. The room was swelteringly hot— though between himself, Emily and Bits, he was the only one who was suffering.

Emily was peddling slowly on a stationary bike while reading a textbook. Whatever was playing through her earbuds was successfully blocking out the sounds of yelling and grunting college athletes in the adjoining gym.

Bits had cleared out a corner of the equipment cage. The fenced off section was locked when Dave had first arrived, but locks and other security measures never seemed to impede Bits when he wanted to be somewhere others didn't want him. He had said something about it being a near-perfect Faraday cage and once he had crawled inside, he dropped his normally guarded demeanor and seemed one or two degrees less paranoid than normal. He was lost in a screen full of code, while a random techno soundtrack battled the sound of Emily's exercising and the shouts from the adjoining gymnasium.

The only part of the "jock closet"—as Dave now thought of their newest office—that remotely resembled anything professional was a corner that had been cleaned out for Dr. Daye's desk. The two over-sized posters leaned against the walls so that it looked as if the haunting eyes of Harry Houdini were staring into the seductive glare of "The Mysterious Professor." Dave knew the dean was especially mad at Dr. Daye. They hadn't received the usual barrage of angry messages, just silence and banishment to this equipment room.

Things had been going well—despite Dave being relegated to the receptionist's desk at their last office—it had been an office. Here he barely had room for his keyboard on the folding table and the sole phone line ended on an outdated handset on Dr. Daye's desk. Fortunately, Bits managed to set it up so that the calls also went to Dave's cell phone.

Jennifer entered.

Dave looked up from his computer. He tried to get her attention, but she seemed not to see him. Her attention was focused on a rack of basketballs.

Jennifer stepped back outside. She checked the number on the door against the one on a slip of paper she held and then reentered. She scanned the room and saw Bits huddled over a laptop in the cage, Emily peddling away on a stationary bike, then Dave seated at his card table. He offered her a welcoming smile and wave. He nodded his head toward the corner where her desk and posters were situated.

Jennifer spied her corner. She closed her eyes, took a deep breath and stayed that way for nearly a minute.

"Are you all right, Dr. Daye?" Dave asked.

"I'm hoping when I open my eyes I'm going to be back in our old offices instead of the athletic department's closet," she answered. She opened one eye, then the other. But when she looked again, the racks of equipment were still there. She crossed over to her desk, placed her hands on it, then tilted her head back and howled. The primal scream released a torrent of anger, frustration and despair in one ear-splitting screech.

Dave was uncertain what to do. He had never seen her like this. She was usually a roll-with-the-punches sort of person. It was Dave who usually felt hopeless enough to scream. Dr. Daye was the one who always gave him a compliment and made unrealistic assurances that somehow made it all better. He wasn't sure how to do that for her.

Jennifer spun around. Her shriek had garnered the attention of Emily and Bits as well. They too were unaccustomed to the fury and rage that now showed on Dr. Daye's face.

She spied a soccer ball on the floor nearby and gave it a kick that would have put it into orbit if they were outside. It bounced off a wall, knocked into a rack of basketballs sending all of them to the floor bouncing and rolling.

Emily ceased her spinning, Bits turned off his music, and the room fell silent. Even the activity from the gym next door seemed to take a break.

The soccer ball rolled back toward Jennifer, stopping just short of her feet. "This," she said in a voice devoid of her usual cheery optimism, "is unacceptable." She turned to Dave. "Get the dean on the phone."

Dave automatically searched his desk for the phone, but then remembered the sole handset for their current location was on Dr. Daye's desk. He stood up from his table, then crossed over to the desk in the corner against which Jennifer was now leaning, regarding the equipment room with a steely, furious glare. He picked up the handset and dialed the extension. It was one he was unfortunately very familiar with.

"It's ringing," he told Jennifer.

She didn't even look at him. Her jaw was clenched and her arms were folded tightly across her chest.

"Hello, I have Dr. Daye for Dean Patterson." Dave listened to the voice on the other end for a moment, then asked, "When do you think he'll be available?"

Jennifer spoke up. "Tell her that if she doesn't get the dean on the phone right now, I'll go to the media instead."

Dave put his hand over the mouthpiece of the phone. "The media?" he asked.

Jennifer turned to Dave. "Tell her," she ordered.

Dave repeated the message to the dean's assistant.

"The media?" Emily asked, curious.

Jennifer ignored her, focusing her attention on Dave.

"Yes, I'll hold," Dave said into the phone. He turned to Dr. Daye, hoping for some guidance as to what to say next. But Jennifer had returned her stare to some unfortunate spot on the opposite wall.

"Hello, Dean Patterson," Dave said.

"Tell him this so called office he's stuck us in is not suitable for a tenured professor."

"Um," Dave said tentatively into the phone, "Dr. Daye wanted to tell you she's not happy with—"

Jennifer cut Dave off and repeated her message. "This so-called office is not suitable for a tenured professor."

Dave took a breath. "She wanted to tell you that this so-called office is not suitable for a tenured professor." He listened for a moment, then said, "He's sorry, but the funding for the other office fell through and there's nothing else—"

"Tell him I know exactly why the funding fell through, and so does he, and if he's going to be such a petty bureaucratic nincompoop, he should resign and let someone who cares have the job."

Dave put his hand over the mouthpiece again. "Can you repeat that one?"

Jennifer snatched the phone from his hands. "Robert, do I really need to take this to 'Dateline'? There's a producer over there who's dying to do a profile on me, and I'm sure she'd love this angle. Professor punished for dean's disastrous fundraising attempt." She listened for only a second before cutting him off. "Of course it's your fault. I did the right thing. You're the one who let the dollar signs blind you to an untenable situation. Did you even know that his wife was dead? Did you even care?"

Dave's mouth hung open. He'd never heard Dr. Daye let loose on the dean like this before. Usually she deflected his complaints with a joke. This was an altogether different side of her.

"I don't know. You're the administrator. Find some other rich widower you can sweet-talk out of a few million. I do my part. You know that my classes bring in more students than—" Jennifer bit her upper lip listening to how the dean was answering her. "My work in that area does not interfere with my responsibilities to the department. You know that. And if you had told me Worthington was under the influence of that dime store Svengali, I maybe could have done something to help and keep your precious donation."

Jennifer fumed as she listened to the dean's reply.

"You are a pompous, arrogant idiot, Bobby. I hope you rot in Hell." She smashed the handset back into its cradle and buried her face in her hands.

There was a knock at the open door to the supply room. Everyone's heads turned to see Nate standing there, neatly dressed despite having his arm in a sling and one foot in an orthopedic boot. In his good arm, he carried what looked like a giant basket. He offered a friendly smile. "You guys don't like to stay in one place, do you?" The joke didn't elicit the reaction he was expecting. There was a seriousness among Jennifer and her staff that didn't take a detective to discover. "Should I come back later?" he asked.

"No, come on in," Jennifer said, wiping the start of a tear from one eye as she walked around the desk and took a seat behind it. "Dave, would you and Emily mind getting the equipment over to Diane's apartment?" She tossed Dave the keys to her van.

"I can help out," Bits offered.

"You can?" Dave asked, surprised that Bits would volunteer to do anything.

Jennifer smiled. "Thank you, Bits. I'd appreciate that."

"I can also see about transferring Worthington's liquid assets to a Cayman bank account under the dean's name, leak it to the

University president and the press. A kill two birds with one stone kind of deal," Bits added.

"That's okay, Bits. Thanks for the offer, though. I'll keep it in mind," Jennifer replied.

The three of them grabbed some equipment cases, and a dolly loaded with other boxes and left the equipment room, leaving Jennifer and Nate alone. He limped over to her desk and looked around. "I'm not saying it's the Taj Mahal, but it does have possibilities."

Jennifer laughed. "It doesn't matter. He won. I give up. I can't fight this battle anymore. Maybe I should move on to someplace else where I'm not constantly in someone's crosshairs."

"If you find such a place, let me know. I could use a break from office politics myself." He sat down on the edge of the desk across from Jennifer. "You know, I'm not usually one for giving people pep talks. I'm probably not very good at it, but in your case I'm going to give it a try."

"Oh, why's that?"

"Because, I just saw three young people who you mean the world to soldier on in the face of the biggest adversity they're likely to see. Until maybe they get married."

Jennifer chuckled. She was determined to stay in a bad mood, but Nate was making that difficult.

"What would happen to them if you left? Bits would probably be okay, but Dave would have to start over on whatever it is he's doing. And Emily would be forced to try out for the cheerleading squad."

Jennifer couldn't hold it in any longer. "Oh god, that would truly be an earth-shaking disaster for all involved."

"And it would be all your fault."

"Wow, you really didn't undersell sucking at pep talks."

"Listen, I may not be on board with all the ghost-hunting stuff, but I've seen you teach, I've seen the loyalty that your staff has for you, I saw you do the right thing at Worthington's house despite knowing it would land you in this godforsaken wasteland of an office. And I respect that. I don't think this university can afford to lose you."

"I can't fight this battle alone."

"You don't have to," Emily announced.

Jennifer and Nate turned and saw Emily and the guys standing in the doorway.

"We're all behind you, Dr. Daye," Dave added.

"Doesn't sound like you're alone at all," Nate said.

Jennifer considered. "Okay. I'm in." She looked around the equipment room. "Don't get used to this place, I promise we won't be here long." She took a deep breath and stood up. "Diane is expecting us to help her find out what's going on at her apartment, so let's get that done." She straightened up, wiped away a tear running down her cheek and grabbed her bag. She nodded at Nate's basket, "I hope that's food in there, I haven't had lunch."

CHAPTER FORTY THREE

Nate stood out of the way and watched as Jennifer directed her crew to place a variety of sensors and cameras around Diane's apartment. Diane stood next to her, nervously watching the technical invasion of her home.

Bits set up a portable workstation that had an array of three monitors displaying camera feeds and visualizations of different instruments measuring electromagnetic activity, temperature and a host of other parameters.

"Dave," Bits called out, "tilt that bedroom camera to the left a few degrees."

One of the video screens shifted.

"That's it," Bits said. He turned to Jennifer. "My work is done. You've got the standard setup, cameras on visual spectrum as well as infrared. Motion detectors are here," he added, pointing to an area on one of the monitors, "and the ambient sound monitors are over here. I worked on the algorithm to minimize the noise and amplify the anomalies. Had to put in my own hotspot—Ms. Collin's WiFi was too slow. Everything is streaming to the cloud with a local SSD backup."

"Thanks, Bits," Jennifer said.

"Ping me if you need anything," he said, then closed a laptop, stuck it into a backpack and slipped quietly out of the apartment.

"He's an odd one," Nate commented. "Where did you find him?"

"I didn't. He found me. Just showed up one day at my office with some gadgets and asked if I would test them for him. I don't know if he's even a student at the University. He just comes and goes, brings me new toys and handles all the data, so I don't ask too many questions."

"I'm guessing that's how you found my address and my uncle."

"I'm outta here, too," Emily said. "I am a student and I've got homework to catch up on." She stuffed some leftover devices into one of the cases, grabbed her backpack and left the apartment.

Dave entered from the bedroom carrying a mostly empty crate. He looked around and saw that Bits and Emily were gone and sighed. "Anything else you need?"

"Looks like all the sensors and cameras are in place. Can you put the cases and crates over in that corner?" Jennifer asked.

Dave nodded, then collected the containers all the equipment had been brought in and stacked them neatly in the corner.

"What's next?" Diane asked.

"Well, we wait. Make the apartment as welcoming as possible for whatever presence may be inhabiting this space."

Nate hobbled over to the sofa and lowered himself down. "Weirdest stakeout I've ever been on," he said. "Usually we're not in the same room as whoever—or whatever—we have under surveillance."

"Do we sit in a circle and chant or something?" Diane asked.

"No, this isn't a seance, and I'm not a medium. We're just going to record everything we can so we can try to capture some evidence of what you're experiencing and maybe discover what we can do to mitigate it. A lot of times, paranormal phenomena is generated by living people rather than spirits."

"You think it's me?"

"Or possibly connected to you," Jennifer said.

"I'm voting for the living people angle," Nate added.

Diane turned to Nate. "It wasn't Jerry. I know you don't like him, and I can understand why, but we are friends and he just wants to make sure I'm okay."

"Did you tell him we were coming tonight?" Nate asked.

"Dr. Daye asked me to not mention it to anyone."

"You didn't exactly answer my question."

Diane smiled. "No, I did not tell Jerry you were going to be here." Her phone rang. She peeked at the caller ID and frowned before answering. "Hello," she said. Her expression grew aggravated as she listened to the voice on the other end. "All right. I'll be there in fifteen minutes." She hung up the phone and turned to Jennifer. "There's an 'emergency' at work," she explained, giving the word "emergency" a sarcastic inflection. "I need to go for at least a few hours. Is that okay?"

"Of course," Jennifer assured her. "It'll be good to get a baseline off the sensors while you're not here."

Diane grabbed her bag and threw some papers from her desk into it, then slipped into her coat. "Help yourself to anything in the fridge," she offered. Then hurriedly walked out of the apartment past Dave.

"Everything's all tidied up," he told Jennifer. "I'll be back in the morning."

"Aren't you forgetting something?" Jennifer asked.

Dave turned around, a puzzled look on his face.

"Nate's dog," Jennifer reminded him.

Dave reacted with shock and surprise. "I kinda hoped you were kidding about that."

Nate reached into a pocket and tossed Dave a key on a souvenir San Francisco key chain. "Her name is Madge."

Dave tried to catch the keys in mid-air, but dropped them. He stooped over and reluctantly picked them up. "I don't know if my apartment is the best place to keep a dog. Isn't there anyone else—"

"You don't have to take her home," Nate said. "I set up the guest room for you. There's a note on the kitchen table explaining everything you need to do. She has a kennel, but I wouldn't bother trying to keep her in there. She's a notorious escape artist. I left you some money and some local takeout menus, too. Treat yourself to something nice. I really appreciate you doing this."

Dave's demeanor suddenly changed. He wasn't used to being rewarded with anything beyond a kind word for his efforts. "Thank you," he said.

"Oh, and there's probably a police cruiser parked out front, they know you're coming, if anyone tries to break into the house and kill you, let them know."

A look of panic washed over Dave's face. "Why would they want to kill me?" he asked.

"Oh, they don't want to kill you, they want to kill me. It's nothing for you to worry about, forget I mentioned it."

"Okay," Dave said sheepishly. He stuffed the keys into his pocket and turned slowly to the door, his short-lived enthusiasm had evaporated.

"Thanks, Dave," Jennifer added.

Dave grunted. He opened the door and jumped in surprise when he saw Rose from across the hall standing there.

"Hello again, young man," she said. She peeked around him and spied Jennifer and Nate sitting in the living room. "Is Diane here?"

"Sorry, no, she had to go to work," Jennifer explained. "She'll be back later tonight. Anything we can help you with?"

"Oh, no, I was just wondering what all the commotion was. A lot of coming and going going on."

"We're just—"

Nate cut her off. "We're going to be leaving soon ourselves. Sorry for the bother."

"Oh, all right," Rose said. "Have a nice day." She turned around and shuffled across the hall to her open door and disappeared inside.

"One more thing, Dave," Jennifer said.

Dave turned around, his usual defeated demeanor hanging on his face. "Yes?"

"Could you bring Nate's basket over here?"

Dave looked around and spotted the basket nestled between some other containers. He pulled it out and carried it over to where Jennifer and Nate were seated and placed it on the coffee table.

"Thanks," Jennifer said. "You're the best."

"I know," Dave answered, unconvinced. He headed for the door, picking up his own backpack on the way and closed it behind him.

"Well," Jennifer said cheerfully. "Looks like it's just you and me. And I don't know about you, but I really am starving. Shall we see what you brought?"

Nate smiled and sat back as Jennifer began unpacking the basket.

CHAPTER FORTY FOUR

Jennifer placed a hand over her stomach as she reclined, satisfied. "Okay, two questions, where did you learn to cook like that and how is it that you're not married?"

"Did my mother put you up to that second question?"

"Well, in my experience, it's rare to find a man whose kitchen repertoire goes beyond the microwave."

Nate shrugged. "I always liked good food, and after a while I decided it would be easier on my wallet to learn how to make it on my own instead of always paying someone else to do it."

"Well, my compliments to the chef. I'm going to hire you to cater all of our stakeouts from now on. I can't imagine the meal at Worthington's would have been any better."

Nate cast a glance at the workstation monitors. Several of the video windows showed different angles of the living room, most of them with either Nate or Jennifer or both of them in view. Others showed the kitchen, the bedroom and even some discrete views in the bathroom.

"So," Nate casually asked, "what do you expect to see?"

"Hard to say," Jennifer answered.

"Have you caught a lot of ghosts on video?"

"I wish," Jennifer answered. "It's not that easy. There's even debate on whether a video or even a film camera can see a ghost. There may be a psychic component that cannot be captured electronically or chemically."

"Then why all the cameras?" Nate asked.

"What we're more likely to capture is our phenomena interacting with physical objects. Diane described in two of her major encounters that our ghost broke a perfume bottle and then a coffee cup. Hopefully we'll catch something like that," Jennifer explained.

Nate pointed out one of the other sections on the monitor. "Electromagnetic activity?" he asked.

"Yes, we often detect various electromagnetic anomalies during paranormal events."

"What about the microphones?" Nate asked, pointing at some displays that danced in sync with the sound of their voices.

"Sometimes we get audio artifacts."

"Got all your bases covered," Nate remarked. "What happens if you don't record anything?"

"If Diane lets us, we'll leave behind one of Bits' omni-boxes." She held up her hand. "Little device about this big, a scaled down stakeout in a box, And we keep looking.

"There's just too many examples of unexplained phenomena. Eventually we're bound to capture some definitive proof of one sort or another. It may be that we just haven't developed the tools to capture the evidence. Bits is always coming up with different sensors and cameras and microphones. It's just a matter of time."

"Or maybe it's just a big waste of time," Nate suggested.

Jennifer assumed the air she projected in her lectures. "At one point scientists thought that atoms were the smallest unit of matter. Then we discovered electrons and protons and neutrons and developed the tools to smash them together into even smaller pieces and record their existence. We can't see them with the naked eye, or even with a video camera, but once we discovered how to detect them, no one doubted their existence."

"Interesting argument," Nate conceded.

"You're not convinced."

"Well, if you're saying a human brain is required to see a ghost, then no. I'm not. The way the mind interprets information from our senses bears little resemblance to what most people would consider reality. We're evolutionarily designed to be susceptible to confirmation bias, and memory is notoriously fallible."

"That's true. But the fact that the human mind is a mystery that we are still a long way from fully understanding just means that there may be room for the possibility that it can be receptive to thoughts from others, that it can perceive physical objects beyond the reach of our senses, that we can even sense events that haven't happened yet."

"That's a stretch."

"But if we can get there, if we can conceive of a mind that reaches beyond the physical, then the concept of a soul isn't far behind. After all, what is a soul but a human mind that exists beyond the impermanence of our physical selves?"

Nate smiled politely.

"You can't tell me that you've never had a 'gut feeling' about a case you were working on."

"That's different," Nate insisted. "That's merely the mind processing information on a subconscious level."

It was Jennifer's turn to smile politely.

Nate shifted uncomfortably in his chair. "You're going to bring up the license plate thing again."

"What's your explanation?"

"Simple," Nate said. "When Max and I were driving to the store, my subconscious mind took note of a suspicious car, maybe even noticed the two robbers inside it. When I was asleep after surgery, my brain connected the events of my being shot with that sub-textual memory and it surfaced as a mnemonic phrase."

"That doesn't sound very simple."

"You think it's more likely that my soul took a little vacation from my body, gathered intel on the robbers and delivered it to me when I woke up?"

"Out of body experiences are fairly common to people who are receptive to them. And it's also an element of near-death experiences."

"Are we really going to go there again?"

"No, not if it makes you uncomfortable."

Nate ended the conversation and started cleaning up the remnants of their meal. He sealed up the plastic containers he had brought the food in and stacked them up, laying a half-empty package of crackers on the top. He stood up and picked up the pyramid of Tupperware with his good hand.

"I can help you with that," Jennifer offered.

"I got it," Nate said.

He started hobbling toward the kitchen to store the leftovers in Diane's fridge. About halfway there, the crackers started to slide off the top. He tried to rebalance the load, but the crackers fell off and he was barely able to maintain control of the containers.

The package hit the floor, and the crackers smashed into crumbs.

"Are you okay?" Jennifer asked.

"I'm fine, I'll clean that up in a minute."

He continued walking to the kitchen.

The lights flickered.

Nate stopped and looked back at Jennifer. "Is that the best you can do?"

She held her hands up to show she had nothing to do with it. "I was just sitting here."

"Probably all the electronics Bits has plugged in here."

"Actually, all of his stuff runs off a battery. He's very particular about isolating his systems from stray signals and power surges."

Nate nodded suspiciously then continued into the kitchen. He set his containers on the counter, then opened the refrigerator and placed the leftovers onto a free shelf. Diane didn't appear to be the type of person to keep a lot of food on hand.

He closed the fridge, then looked around for something to clean up the mess. He spotted a tall, narrow cupboard and found a broom and dustpan inside and carried them out to the living room.

"You just missed it," Jennifer said.

"Missed what?"

"One of the magnetometer windows just went nuts."

"Probably because I opened the refrigerator door." Nate approached the spot where he had dumped the crackers.

Instead of being spread out across the floor, the crumbs were gathered up into a neat little pile. Nate looked over at Jennifer who was staring at the screens. "Very funny," he said.

Jennifer looked up from the screens at Nate. "What's funny?"

"The mess."

"What about it?"

"I may have only one good arm, but I can still use a broom."

Jennifer stood up and peered over to the area of the floor where the neat pyramid of cracker parts was sitting. "Schoetensack," she said.

"Shoeten-what?"

"One of the ghosts Rose told Dave about. It's in the advance notes, didn't you get a chance to read them?"

"Right," Nate said, "and he just happened to amble by while I was in the kitchen. Too bad I didn't get a chance to see him in action."

"He was the building's first superintendent. Apparently, he still hangs around and tidies up random messes. I told you there was a spike in electromagnetic activity."

"How convenient," Nate said dismissively as he clumsily swept the crackers into the dustpan.

"I can rewind the video for you. I swear, I didn't leave this sofa."

"Uh huh," Nate replied, unconvinced. He carried the dustpan back to the kitchen and dumped it into the trash before returning it and the broom to the cupboard. When he got back to the living room, Jennifer was sitting with her arms crossed, glaring at him.

"What?" he asked.

"Do you approach all of your investigations with such a closed mind?"

"I never think the neat-freak ghost did it," Nate said. He shuffled over to the sofa and sat down next to Jennifer. "Besides, whatever this is, it isn't an investigation."

"Why? Because there's a possibility of discovering something you can't explain?"

Nate shook his head. "I just think there's another explanation."

"Look, I deal with skepticism every day. My office isn't in a jock strap closet just because I didn't play along with the dean. I've been battling with the administration and my colleagues for years to gain acceptance for my work. And I understand how difficult it is to convince people to open their minds to something that is so easy to fake. That's why I study magic. That's why I chase down every possible opportunity to find proof. I just want you to be open-minded."

"Okay," Nate said. "If you do the same."

"Fine. Convince me that everything Diane experienced was Jerry Henderson."

"I don't have to."

"Oh, really. Sounds like a bit of a double standard going on here."

"You saw her when she was here earlier. That job of hers is a stress factory. It's much more likely to believe she accidentally left that stove on than some supernatural explanation."

"And the apparition she saw in her bathroom?"

"In a steamy bathroom, in the reflection of a steamed up mirror? Stress, anxiety, maybe paranoia. A move into a new building across the hall from a nosy neighbor full of gossip and ghost stories. You don't need to resort to the supernatural to see a woman on the brink of a nervous breakdown. Throw in the emotional roller coaster of an ex-boyfriend—and don't try to tell me he's just a good friend. He's keeping her close to him because he thinks he can catch her in a vulnerable moment."

"Okay," Jennifer said, "I might agree with you on that last point. He is kind of a slimy guy."

"Thank you," Nate said smugly.

"But I also don't think he's smart enough or motivated enough to pull off some paranormal sideshow just to get her back in bed."

Nate considered. "Well, I can't argue with that. But it doesn't rule out that it was all in her head."

Jennifer shrugged. "It doesn't rule out that it was a ghost, either."

"All right, truce," Nate said decisively. "You helped me track down Henderson—"

"—and catch him," Jennifer added.

"—and catch him," Nate agreed. "So, I will do my best to keep an open mind tonight."

"Thank you," Jennifer said. "So, what's for dessert?"

Nate reached over and pulled out another container from his basket. He set it down on the coffee table between himself and Jennifer and peeled back the lid.

The aroma of the tiramisu inside brought an instant smile to Jennifer's face. Nate produced a couple of forks and handed one to her. "I have to share?" she asked.

CHAPTER FORTY FIVE

Nate and Jennifer were both asleep on the sofa. Nate had his booted foot up on the coffee table next to the empty tiramisu container. Jennifer had her feet tucked up under a pillow on the sofa while she leaned against Nate, her head resting on his good shoulder.

The room was nearly dark except for the glow from the monitors of Bits' workstation. Most of the cameras had switched to a night-vision mode, casting the room into an eerie, ghostly version of itself.

In the window that showed the front door, the words "Motion Detected" superimposed themselves over the image. The door silently opened and the light from the hallway overloaded the night vision, causing the view to washout completely.

A subtle alarm sounded from the workstation.

Nate stirred. He checked his watch. It was nearly midnight. He looked at the monitors.

The view of the front door had returned to its night vision mode, but he caught a movement in one of the other monitors. A glowing figure that passed from frame to frame.

"Daye," he whispered, "there's something going on."

Jennifer stirred. She realized she was leaning against Nate and sat up, squinting at the monitors.

"Anything happen yet?" Diane asked.

Nate and Jennifer jumped at the sound of their host's voice.

Diane let out a short scream. She collected herself and turned on a nearby lamp. "Sorry," she said, "I should have called you to let you know I was heading back. Work took longer than I expected and I just wanted to get home."

"No apology necessary," Nate said. "This is your home."

Jennifer grabbed the mouse connected to the workstation and clicked a button that showed a log on one of the screens. There was nothing except for the motion detected at the front door when Diane entered. "Looks like it's been quiet."

"Should I just stay with a friend tonight? I don't want to be in the way," Diane said.

"No, I prefer for you to be here. There may be a link between you and the apparition."

Diane sighed. "All right. I think I'm too tired to pack up anything and go anywhere, anyway." She looked at the monitors and noticed the ones showing her bedroom and bathroom. "You're not going to be watching me, are you?"

Jennifer clicked on the control that minimized a couple of the cameras. "Privacy mode activated," she said. "Well, we're still recording, but I promise we won't look at it unless something happens."

"Thanks for the warning," Diane said. "Good night." She turned around and headed into her room.

"I hope she doesn't think she walked in on anything," Jennifer said.

Nate laughed. "I'm hardly in any shape to try anything," he said, lifting his bad arm slightly.

"Does that mean you would if you were able?" Jennifer asked playfully.

Nate felt suddenly uncomfortable. "Let's get back to the stakeout," he suggested.

Jennifer ignored his attempt to change the subject. "Well, you did make me the most amazing tiramisu I've ever had. And you did that with only one hand."

Nate smiled. He usually didn't pull out the tiramisu unless he really wanted to impress a woman. "I like tiramisu," he lied.

Jennifer sensed his discomfort and backed off. She liked Nate, maybe even more than that, she respected him. It was obvious the history with his mother was putting up walls to accepting the paranormal, but she still believed that she could tap that skepticism to open his mind as well.

"If this guy who you think is haunting Diane jumped to his death, wouldn't his ghost be flat?" he asked.

"First of all, a haunting is different from an apparition. Diane's ghost appears to be interacting with her, but in the case of a haunting, it's more like there's an impression of a person or event embedded in the environment, playing out an unchanging scene. And no, the injuries to his corporeal form that caused his death would not show up in his psychic representation.

"Our best guess is that the apparition projects their self image. Like if you were to close your eyes and imagine looking at yourself in a mirror. That is the form that they share with us. Fun fact, most people report that the apparitions they see don't have feet."

"What?" Nate asked in surprise.

"Think about it. How many people remember to include their feet when they picture themselves?"

"You're just making this up, now," Nate accused.

"I'm not. It's just one of those things that makes sense when you consider it and tilts more to the idea that an apparition is working outside of our normal senses. It also explains why some people can see them and others can't in the exact same situation, and why we don't have any photos."

"Okay, let's put the ghost talk aside for a moment and talk about why this Luther guy would want to 'interact' with Diane. He was allegedly a serial killer who targeted women of her specific physical appearance."

"Allegedly?" Jennifer asked. "I thought the police had evidence that he had killed his girlfriend."

"Yes, but there are parts of it that just don't fit."

"You mean despite evidence to the contrary, you have a gut

feeling that he wasn't the killer?" Jennifer goaded.

"Okay, point made," Nate said. "I guess my biggest question is why would a fireman use an axe to kill someone."

"Because he's a fireman?" Jennifer suggested. "And they have fire axes?"

"Yes, firemen use axes, but they don't carry them around with them like a cop carries his gun." He pulled a file out of a stack of papers he had on the coffee table and opened it up. He handed a photo of an axe to Jennifer. "This is a pick head axe, it was standard equipment for every fire station in the city sixty years ago."

"Looks pretty deadly."

He pulled out another photo showing a different type of axe. Instead of the end opposite the blade ending in a sharp pick, it was blunted. "This is a flat head axe, the type that was found next to Sarah's body."

Jennifer looked at Nate with shocked surprise. "Wow, you did a lot of research on this."

"Force of habit. The point is, it's not the axe a fireman would have had easy access to. But someone else could have bought or found it and used it to kill Sarah Montgomery and the other girls."

"And do you know who that was?"

"No, but I did find a common thread among the other four. They all had connections to the financial district."

"That sounds kind of thin. The financial district is fairly big, there are thousands of people there."

"True, but it is a connection. They lived in different parts of the city, but the one other thing they had in common was that they had nothing in common with Luther Laramie."

"A fireman meets hundreds of people."

"He worked in the station in this neighborhood, presumably that's how he met Sarah. His station wouldn't be involved in calls to the financial district, or any of the neighborhoods where the women lived. Serial killers generally prefer areas they're familiar with. The only woman he had any familiarity with was Sarah. And the way she was killed... it's not the type of thing someone does to a person you love. It's too messy. It doesn't make sense. I don't think Luther was the Axeman."

"Why did he attack your uncle? Why did he run from the police? Why did he kill himself?"

"He found the love of his life brutally murdered. He had her blood all over his hands and clothes. But I'm not sure he killed himself."

"Because he jumped to the next building instead of the street."

"Exactly. A fireman would be very aware of what type of fall could kill someone. The one that killed him could have just as easily left him with just a couple of broken legs, but the full twelve stories would have done him in without a doubt.

"I think the real killer was still here. I think he followed Luther to the rooftop, and either chased him off the edge or pushed him."

"That's a lot of 'I thinks' in there."

"Yeah, and absolutely no proof. But it makes sense," Nate said setting down his folder.

Diane picked out a comfortable pair of pajamas from her dresser, mindful of the camera placed in a corner of the room. It did make her uncomfortable that Dr. Daye and her crew would be recording her sleeping, but she wanted to do everything she could to find out what was going on. She trusted Jennifer and her staff to be discrete, but she also knew of a few videos from her college days that were still floating around the internet that she hoped her future children would never see.

She opened the closet door and used it as a screen between herself and the camera as she changed. She normally wouldn't skip brushing her teeth, but she was so tired, and her bedroom didn't have a direct doorway to the bathroom. She'd have to go back out into the living room and interact with Dr. Daye and the detective. She'd just brush first thing in the morning. Right now, after an extra ten hours of soul-sucking work at the law firm, she just wanted to crawl under the covers and fall asleep.

Diane closed the closet door and looked over at the camera. She froze. Standing there, mouthing words she couldn't hear was the man in the fireman's coat. He moved toward her.

She screamed.

Jennifer and Nate both got to their feet immediately when the shriek from Diane's bedroom reached their ears.

"Diane?" Jennifer called out. "Diane, are you okay?"

There was no reply.

Nate rushed over to the bedroom, refusing to let the orthopedic boot slow him down. He grabbed the knob and tried to open the door, but it was locked. "Diane," he shouted, "open the door!"

Pressing his ear to the door, Nate could hear part of what sounded like a conversation, but he couldn't make out the words. Then there was a shout, followed by a thump.

Nate reared back and slammed into the door with his good shoulder, but the old oak was too strong and he was too weak.

"Let me try," Jennifer said. Nate stepped back, and she aimed a surprisingly powerful front kick at the door near the knob.

"Where did you learn to kick like that?" Nate asked.

"I used to be a Martial Arts Instructor in college." She landed another powerful kick. The door didn't budge. "Hang on, I have an idea," she said. Jennifer raced out of the apartment into the hallway. She returned a few seconds later with an axe. "It was in that box with the firehose across from the elevators," she explained. She hefted the tool and took aim at where the door met the jam just above the door knob. The axe bit into the solid wood. Jennifer pried it out and after a few more blows the door jamb was starting to splinter.

"Give it another kick," Nate suggested.

Jennifer set aside the axe and assumed a martial arts stance and launched all of her weight behind a front kick that shattered the door jamb. The door swung open.

Diane was lying unconscious on the floor. A ceramic bowl lay broken next to her. Jennifer rushed to her side while Nate scanned the room. The window was open. He went to it and cautiously stuck his head out. The fire escape was just outside. He looked down the iron steps, but there was no one there.

He looked up. That was the only direction the assailant could have gone in such a short time. "Henderson!" he shouted.

Nate pulled his head back in and went to check on Diane.

Jennifer drew his attention to a bleeding wound on the back of Diane's head.

"Diane, Diane," Nate said as she started to drift back into consciousness. "Was it Jerry? Is that who hit you?"

"I saw him," Diane said weakly.

"Who? Who did you see?" Jennifer asked.

"I'm not letting him get away," Nate said. "Call nine-one-one." He headed for the window and stepped out onto the fire escape. He pulled out his phone, put it into flashlight mode and pointed it skyward. There was no sign of the attacker. He started climbing the iron steps between floors, scaling the fire escape upward toward the roof.

Jennifer grabbed a pillow from Diane's bed and gently lifted the woman's head to place it underneath.

Diane cringed and let out a weak moan.

"What happened?" Jennifer asked. "Was it Jerry?"

"Jerry?" Diane asked, confused. "No, it was the man in the coat."

"Luther? He hit you?"

"No." She said, frustrated. "He was trying to warn me."

"Warn you about what?"

"Whoever hit me from behind."

CHAPTER FORTY SIX

Nate pulled himself up the fire escape. The steps were too steep to climb like stairs, he had to use his good arm to pull himself up one step at a time. His bad ankle grew more painful with each step. He had crawled through the window on instinct, chasing the bad guy was automatic. It wasn't until he was on the final landing before the roof that he realized he wasn't wearing his shoulder holster. He had his cell phone, but right about now he was wishing he had at least grabbed the axe before he chased after Henderson—if that's who it was.

He didn't need to catch him, just catch up to him. But staring up the ladder leading to the roof, he wasn't sure that was an option.

Nate tentatively reached for a rung on the ladder, then stepped up with his good foot and lifted himself up. He let go with his hand and grabbed for the next higher rung, then stepped up, straightened his leg and repeated the maneuver until he could peer over the parapet. It was dark and storm clouds were obscuring what little moonlight there was. A distant flash of lightning illuminated the rooftop. There was no one to be seen, just a sparse forest of vents and smoke stacks and in one area a collection of dilapidated lawn furniture surrounding what looked like a charcoal grill.

Nate loped the rest of the way up the ladder and swung his booted foot up onto the gravelly surface.

Rain drops started to fall. Nate silently cursed himself again for rushing into a situation so ill-prepared. But it was too late now. He took out his phone and turned on the camera. He switched it to video mode, started it recording, then tucked it into the breast pocket of his jacket with the lens facing outward as a makeshift body camera. He may not be able to effectuate an arrest, but he could do his best to gather evidence.

He walked toward the stairwell entrance that poked up in the center of the roof like a tiny house.

The rain transitioned from a drizzle to a light shower. Nate made a wide path around the stairwell entrance, scanning for any signs of Henderson. He peered over the side. Below was the rooftop of the building where Luther Laramie had fallen to his death. It was about four stories below. A flash of lightning showed him that Diane's attacker had not gone that way. There was no sign of anyone dead or alive.

He continued walking around the edge of the roof, coming upon the front of the building. A fall from this side, he confirmed, would most certainly be fatal.

A gust of wind blew, and along with it came a sheet of rain that instantly drenched Nate. He started walking back toward the stairwell entrance and just as he was about to reach for the door knob, he saw it slowly start to open. He hurriedly limped to one side so that the opening door would hide him.

His hand brushed against something leaning against the wall. It was a broom handle. He grabbed it in his good hand and held it in front of him.

The door swung closed.

Standing there in the rain, looking out across the rooftop was Jennifer.

"There's no one here," Nate said.

Jennifer jumped and let out a surprised shout. "Nate, you scared the hell out of me."

They both sighed with relief as their hearts settled back into their chests.

"Sorry, I thought you might be Henderson. Did you hear or see anyone else in the stairwell?"

"No," she answered.

"You left Diane alone?" Nate asked.

"I took her to Rose's place. The police and an ambulance are on their way. Let's get you back inside, you're drenched," Jennifer said. She grabbed the door knob and twisted. But the door was locked.

"I guess that's what this is for." He tossed the broom handle aside. "Come on, we can go back down the fire escape," Nate suggested. They trudged through the rain toward the fire escape Nate had climbed. "This must be the way the attacker got into Diane's bedroom tonight—and maybe that's how they tampered with her stove."

When they were about ten feet away a flash of lightning cut through the darkness revealing a figure standing in the rain between them and the fire escape. It was wearing a hooded raincoat. And in its gloved hands was the axe.

"Henderson," Nate shouted. "Don't even think about it. The police are on their way."

"Henderson?" the figure asked in an ancient, creaky voice. Rose Walton lifted her head so that Nate and Jennifer could more clearly see her face. "Who's Henderson?"

"Rose?" Jennifer asked. "What are you doing up here? I thought you were watching Diane?"

"Oh, I'll take care of her in good time."

Nate slapped his forehead. "Of course. It was you. You're the one who killed Sarah Montgomery and those other girls."

"I rid the world of those evil temptresses, you mean. Those hussies who flaunted themselves in front of other women's men."

"Your husband worked in the Financial District," Nate guessed. "That was the connection."

"Well, finally a policeman with half a brain," Rose said.

"Luther never killed anyone. It was you."

"They had it coming," Rose insisted.

"But Diane doesn't," Jennifer said. "Why would you want to hurt her?"

"She's just like them. Coming and going at all hours, it's not respectable. Do you really think she's working late all those evenings at her office? I know what goes on between young women and their bosses."

"The fire escape. The platform stretches from your bedroom window to Diane's. You could come and go as you pleased."

Rose smiled. "No one thinks to lock their bedroom window ten stories up."

"And the axe," he said. "You didn't need to buy one, they're all over the city, on every floor of every apartment building."

"They made it so easy to punish those husband-stealing hussies."

Nate took a step toward Rose. "Put the axe down, Rose. You can't get away."

"Well, that's the beauty of it, isn't it?" Rose said with a smile. "I don't need to get away if you two aren't alive to tattle on me."

Rose raised the axe and lunged toward Nate. She was surprisingly quick and strong.

Nate moved backward and raised his arm to fend off her blow, but his plastic boot slipped on the loose gravel and he fell hard. The axe blade swooshed through the air above him, another flash of lightning glinting off the steel blade.

The momentum of the missed blow put Rose off balance. Jennifer rushed at Rose, grabbing her from behind in a bear hug.

"Get off me, you witch!" Rose shouted. "You think I don't know what that girl does in that apartment? You think I didn't know what she did with my husband?"

Jennifer realized that Rose was somehow conflating Diane with the woman who had been murdered there sixty years earlier. The old woman squirmed in Jennifer's grasp like a greased pig. Both of them were wet and slippery and Rose managed to get herself in a position where she could stomp on Jennifer's foot, loosening the bear hug enough for Rose to slip away.

The old woman swung at Jennifer with the axe.

The blunt side of the axe head hit Jennifer in the side. Nate could hear the ribs crack from where he was. He struggled to his feet, a rush of adrenaline offsetting the pain in his ankle and shoulder.

Jennifer backed up toward the edge of the roof as Rose swung wildly with the axe. She was out of space, no where left to run, and was leaning precariously over the edge.

"Luther," Nate shouted, "help us!"

Rose spun around to face Nate, searching the roof for Luther's ghost. "Where is he? I'll knock him off this roof for good this time."

While she was distracted, Nate aimed a crescent kick with his booted foot at Rose's head. The hard plastic of the orthopedic device connected with her skull and she fell limply to the rain-soaked gravel.

Jennifer tried to stop herself, but she lost her balance and teetered then tipped over the edge.

Nate saw her fall and lunged forward. He caught her belt with his good hand, but her momentum carried him over the edge with her. He dropped to his knees, trying to put his waist at the same height as the lip of the parapet and use his body as an anchor. But everything was wet and slippery. He had a good grip on Jennifer's belt, but she was dead weight. There was nothing she could do to help him save her.

Nate shook his injured arm out of the sling. It was sore from disuse, but he could move it. He grabbed onto the parapet and managed to stop himself from sliding any further, but the strain on his shoulder was excruciating. "Jennifer," he shouted. "Can you grab my arm?"

Jennifer was hanging face down, wondering why she hadn't hit the pavement yet. She twisted her head around and saw Nate straining to keep the two of them from falling. She reached one arm behind her and found Nate's hand clenching her belt.

"I think so," she said. She found his jacket sleeve and pulled on it, but since his other arm had been tucked inside the jacket, foregoing the sleeve altogether, the jacket slipped off Nate's back and fell onto her face.

Nate grunted as the maneuver put more strain on his mending ligaments and muscles. Then a sharp pain lit up his shoulder as he felt something tear. He screamed in agony, but he held on.

Jennifer pushed the jacket aside and grabbed onto his shirt. She managed to swing her other arm around and grab onto the rain-soaked fabric, then pulled herself up enough to grab Nate's belt, lifting herself higher until she could swing a leg up and over the lip of the roof.

Once her weight was on top of Nate and not hanging off of him, she was able to roll her entire body back over the parapet. Jennifer kept a firm grip on his belt and shirt, pulling him with her as they dropped onto the gravel and rolled away from the edge. They lay panting for a moment, rain pelting their faces as they tried to catch their breath.

Jennifer tilted her head and saw Rose lying face down, a trickle of blood at her temple mixing with the rain. "What happened to her?"

Nate lifted his bad foot into the air. "I gave her the boot," he said.

Jennifer couldn't help but laugh. "Ow, don't make me laugh. I think she broke my ribs."

Nate laughed too, but the motion sent a searing wave of pain through his shoulder. "Yeah, I'm not in much better shape," he said.

Jennifer sat up, suddenly aware that Nate's arm was out of its sling. "Your arm. Are you all right?"

"You're alive. I'm alive. That's all that matters."

The sirens of approaching police cars cut through the sound of the rain.

Jennifer put her arm over Nate, careful to avoid his injured shoulder and drew him into a hug. She kissed him gently on the cheek. "Thank you," she whispered into his ear.

Nate knew the pain in his shoulder meant that his recovery had just been set back—if he could even make a recovery now. The doctor had cautioned him about moving the arm let alone stressing it with the weight of two people. He was grateful that the rain hid the tears forming in his eyes. He put his arm around Jennifer and returned the hug. "Anytime."

CHAPTER FORTY SEVEN

The rain had stopped a few minutes earlier, but the street was still slick from the storm.

Rose was strapped to a gurney when she was read her rights. Two uniformed officers got into the back of the ambulance with her. Once the doors were closed, it wound its way through the maze of gawkers and police cars that had gathered in front of the Oakley Arms.

A second ambulance loaded Diane into the back. Jennifer was at her side. "I can't believe it was Rose," Diane said. "She was a bit nosy, but she seemed so harmless. Do you think that's why the ghost—what did you call him?"

"Luther Laramie," Jennifer answered.

"Do you think that's what Luther was trying to tell me?"

"It's as good an explanation as any. Unfortunately, he wasn't cooperative enough to make an appearance on any of our cameras."

"Well, I for one am a believer," Diane said. "Do you think I'll see him again?"

"Hard to say. We did manage to clear his name, so maybe he will feel free to move on to whatever is next for him."

"I hope so," Diane added.

Nate approached. His bad arm was bound tightly to his body to prevent any further injury and he had a blanket draped over his shoulder. "How is she doing?" he asked.

Jennifer reached out and squeezed Diane's hand before answering Nate. "She's going to be fine."

"Thank you," Diane said to Nate. "I don't know what would have happened if you two hadn't been there."

"You don't need to thank us. In fact, I think it was we who gave Rose the impression you would be alone."

"Well, if you hadn't, she might have tried to attack me when I actually was alone."

"I don't understand why she didn't try to kill you when I left you with her," Jennifer said.

"I don't know. She was acting strange after you had gone. At first I thought she was worried that the attacker would come after her next, but then I realized she was angry. She asked what a man and woman were doing in a single girl's apartment so late at night.

"Then she grabbed a rain coat from her closet, but instead of going out the front door, she went into her bedroom.

"After a while, I went to check on her, but the room was empty and the window was open. She must have gone back to my apartment using the fire escape to get the axe."

"It was obvious she had used one before," Jennifer added, feeling her cracked ribs.

"You're lucky she didn't kill you," Diane exclaimed.

"I think we can thank Luther for that," Jennifer added.

Nate rolled his eyes.

"Come on, how much more evidence do you need?" she asked him.

"I'm just saying, everything that happened didn't need any supernatural explanation to happen. It was the fact that Diane locked her bedroom door that forced us to use the fire axe to break it open which is what connected everything together."

The paramedics loaded Diane into the back of the ambulance. She smiled knowingly at Jennifer, then said to Nate, "my bedroom door doesn't have a lock."

The doors closed, and Diane's transport flashed its lights to clear the way.

Jennifer gave Nate a "what about that?" look.

Nate rolled his eyes again. "Seriously? A stuck door?"

"And," Jennifer added, "you saw Luther on the rooftop. I heard you call out to him."

"That was just to distract Rose so I could save you."

Jennifer raised an eyebrow.

"I swear. If I had actually seen a ghost, I would've fallen off that roof after you and we'd both know whether there is an afterlife right now."

Max approached. "Okay, I swear I saw at least two ambulances leave here, but you two apparently didn't get the memo."

"I'm fine," Nate said without thinking.

"No, you're not." Jennifer and Max said together.

Max turned to Jennifer. "And judging by the way you're breathing, I'm guessing you have a couple broken ribs. Come on, I'm taking you both to the E.R. No arguments. Besides, I gotta hear this story. An eighty-year-old axe murderer? Jeez, Nate. Wait till the cold case guys hear about this."

Max led them to his car and held the passenger door open for Jennifer while Nate let himself into the back seat.

"Buckle up," Nate advised.

Max turned to Jennifer. "Nate has a problem with my driving," he told her. "And I have a problem with his passengering."

"That's not a word," Nate said.

"This is what I'm talking about," Max said to Jennifer. "He's such a know it all."

"He is, isn't he?" Jennifer agreed. "How long have you been his partner?"

"Too long."

"Oh, brother," Nate muttered.

Max turned on the police lights in the car and blasted a piercing note from the siren. A path cleared, and he drove them away from the thinning crowd. It wasn't raining, but the sky was still thick with clouds.

Seymour and Freddie had been staking out the tall apartment building ever since they saw the detective and his girlfriend arrive earlier that day. The squad car that was ever present outside his home hadn't followed him—evidently, his body guards weren't concerned about protecting him when he went out, assuming the two robbers wouldn't try something in public.

But their situation had grown desperate. They were boxed in. The man they owed money to had contacts far and wide and was known for never letting someone get away with cheating him. It made sense to Deuce. He didn't mind spending a lot of money, even more than he was owed in some cases, to chase after anyone who dared to cross him. It made the others fall in line.

Freddie and Seymour were in an impossible situation. The shooting at the high-end store that promised to be filled with a lot of rich people with expensive fencible items had prevented them from maximizing their haul. Instead of coming out of there with enough cash to pay off Deuce and set themselves up for a while, they came up short and had an attempted murder charge waiting for them.

The plan was to lie low, the cop wasn't dead and once he recovered and some time passed, they would be able to plan another score and get out from under their current situation.

But somehow the cop had tracked them down. They were no longer anonymous robbers, but wanted cop shooters with names and faces.

How he had managed to find them at the SoMa food trucks, or the safe house was still a puzzle. They had ditched the old car and likely wouldn't need the convertible they had boosted from the long term parking at the airport for very long.

Deuce had put the idea into their heads that since they couldn't do anything with Detective Raney on their tail, they had to get him out of the way. If they proved that they could advance to the next level, he might have a position in his organization where they could work off their debt—and get protection from the police.

They hadn't expected the detective to spend so much time in the building. It wasn't where the girlfriend lived, and they had started to worry that he had made them yet again and had moved into some sort of safe house.

When they heard the first sirens converging on the building, their first assumption was that they had been spotted and they were cornered. But the police cars and ambulances drove right past where they were parked on the street. One officer even asked them politely to move their car—which they did. The activity drew a crowd, all trying to catch a glimpse of some drama playing out on the roof of the building.

Freddie drove their car down the block and found a loading zone to wait in. The police were busy with whatever was going on at the building. Seymour had gotten out of the car and went to find out what exactly that was. From what he could piece together from conversations between the first responders and onlookers, there was supposedly a murderer living in the building who had been caught.

Eventually, two women were wheeled out of the building on stretchers. One was old, easily in her eighties and the other was younger. Shortly after they were carted out, the detective and his girlfriend appeared. Both seemed injured as well. Seymour watched them for a while, but nearly left when it looked like they would leave in one of the ambulances.

Instead, they got into the car of another police detective, the other one who was at the store during the robbery, and who they had also seen outside of Raney's house. Seymour hurried back to where the car was parked and got in.

"They're coming this way. The detective, his partner and the girlfriend."

"Is this a good idea? Shouldn't we wait until, you know, there are fewer cops around?"

"It's the perfect time. The cops are all busy back at the building and we'll be heading away from them. Just put a shot into the driver's head, then we can take out the other two and be on our way before anyone even knows what's going on. Deuce wants to see us take things to the next level, this should do it."

Freddie nodded. He pulled a gun out of the glove compartment.

Seymour started the car.

They watched Max's Volvo emerge from the crowd of people and emergency vehicles crowded around the Oakley Arms. When the car drove by, he pulled away from the curb directly behind them.

As Max turned the corner, a black convertible with its top down pulled in behind them.

Nate eyed the car. "Max, did you spot that Mustang that caught our tail?"

"Yeah. That who I think it is?"

"Our friends from the robbery," Nate confirmed.

"What do you think they want?"

"Well, I don't think they're dropping off a cake. Jennifer, you buckled up?"

She nodded nervously.

"Lean your seat back as far as it will go and stay as low as you can."

Jennifer lowered her seat back so that her head was practically in the back seat with Nate. She nervously looked over at him.

Nate offered her a reassuring smile, then he gave Max a determined look in the rearview mirror. "Hit it," he said.

Max stepped on the accelerator and the wheels spun on the wet pavement before the car raced down the street.

The convertible easily kept up. The fat guy was driving, and the skinny guy was sitting high on the passenger side. He lifted a gun and aimed it at Nate.

"Hang on," Max warned. He down-shifted and spun the car into a sharp turn that took them into a narrow alley.

The skinny guy fired three shots. One of them hit the car, but the others went wide. It took the fat guy a few seconds to catch up to Max's maneuver.

"You thinking what I'm thinking?" Nate asked.

"Yeah, I'm on it," Max answered.

Another shot. This one punched through the rear window and smacked into the rearview mirror. Nate threw his body over

Jennifer's.

Max spun the car around into another high-speed turn.

A fifth shot missed the car completely.

Max reached for the radio mic hanging off the dashboard. "Captain Bode, you still at the Arms?"

A voice crackled back. "Is that you, Lee?"

"Yeah, Cap. I'm coming in hot with a couple of angry wannabe cop killers. Can you whip up a welcoming party?"

"How fast?"

"About a minute."

"Jeez, Lee. Didn't I see you leave with Raney?"

"Yeah, I was taking him and a civvy to the hospital."

Another sharp turn.

Two gun shots slammed into the trunk of the car.

Nate could feel Jennifer tense underneath him. "You're going to be fine," he reassured her.

"All right, we'll be ready," Captain Bode said over the radio.

"Can you go any faster?" Nate asked Max.

"I don't want to lose them." Max made a quick succession of lane changes.

Nate couldn't see what was going on, but heard the squeal of brakes and the crash of metal on metal. It wasn't Max's car that crashed, likely some other motorist who was in the wrong place at the wrong time.

Another bullet whizzed over Nate's head and he could feel broken glass falling over him.

Max didn't flinch. He drove with a purpose. "Hang on," he said and swung the wheel sharply. He sped up, then slammed on the brakes.

Nate pressed himself firmly against Jennifer, using his good hand to pull her close. He could feel her arms wrap around him.

The Mustang didn't have time to react to Max's sudden stop and smashed into the car.

Nate heard a thump against the roof of Max's car and then something rolling across the hood. He lifted himself up and saw the skinny robber writhing in pain against the shattered windshield.

The fat guy was dazed, his face was bloody from the impact with the air bag. Half a dozen police officers stood around the car aiming their guns at the robbers.

Jennifer sat up and looked around.

"Are you okay?" Nate asked her.

She nodded nervously. "Yeah, are you?"

Nate nodded, then turned his attention to his old partner.

"Max, don't take this the wrong way, but I'm never riding with you again."

Max gave him a look of surprise. "Hey, you just cleared two cases in one night. I'm your lucky charm."

Jennifer laughed. "He's got a point," she said.

Nate smiled. He looked at the two robbers who nearly took his life and suddenly realized how much had been weighing on him.

The events of the last month had pushed his life off the track he thought it was on. He knew his shoulder would keep him from returning to active duty even before he aggravated it saving Jennifer.

And the feelings he had for Jennifer. What were they? He certainly liked her and respected her even if he found some of her ideas incongruous with her academic background. She had pressed him about what he had gone through, and even though there was some of it he couldn't explain, he still wasn't willing to credit anything supernatural to it.

Jennifer reached out and slipped her hand into Nate's for comfort.

Was her interest in him purely as a subject for her research? If he didn't play along with her notions about near-death experiences and astral projections would she want to be a part of his life?

There were moments when they were together that Nate felt a connection with Jennifer. Yes, working on Diane's case felt like he was filling the void of police work with something that made him feel useful. And to some degree, she was a replacement for Max— although much more intelligent, interesting and attractive and a lot less annoying. Was all of that just because of the bet she had somewhat forced on him? Was there a part of whatever relationship they had formed that would go on? Even just as friends?

"Nate," Jennifer said. "There's another ambulance. We should go."

He nodded.

"Hey, you kids," Max said, "don't stay out too late."

Nate slid out of the back seat, then turned back to his old partner. "Max, you saved our lives. Thank you."

"You're welcome," Max answered. "Now go take care of yourselves, or I'll get behind the wheel of that ambulance."

Jennifer walked up to Nate and took his hand again. She squeezed it and led him toward the ambulance. "I wonder how Dave and Madge are getting along?" she asked.

CHAPTER FORTY EIGHT

Nate sat in front of Captain Bode's desk, his arm back in a sling. He handed her a sheaf of papers.

Bode flipped to the last page and saw Nate's signature.

"Are you sure about this?" she asked.

"The doctors say I'm looking at a couple years of surgeries and rehab. With this shoulder, I'm a liability. I had a good run. No regrets."

Bode nodded. "Well, you certainly went out in style. Closing a case your uncle worked on. That's quite a victory for the Raney family."

"Yeah, Uncle Bill couldn't believe it. He always thought there was more to the story, but he never suspected that shy little housewife was a serial killer."

Max knocked on the partially open office door and stepped inside. "Hey, boss, I hope you weren't planning on sneaking out without saying hi."

"Not at all," Nate assured him.

"You heard about the party at the Shanty," Max added.

"Of course. I'll be there."

"What's next?" Bode asked.

"Well, I thought I'd get my P.I. license. Hang out my shingle."

"You're going to be happy surveilling cheating spouses and finding lost dogs?" Max asked.

"It'll keep me busy."

"Keep in touch," Bode said with the tone of an order. "No promises, but I may be able to throw some consulting work your way."

"Thanks. I will."

"Hey," Max said excitedly, "looks like we may be able to keep the band together after all!"

Nate shook his head. "Thanks again, Max. You promised me you'd catch the guys who shot me and you came through."

"Though it did come with a hefty bill for damages," Bode added.

"None of that was my fault. Except the stuff that was. But hey, what price can you put on catching bad guys?"

Bode glanced at a report on her desk. "Two hundred and thirty-nine thousand dollars."

Max whistled. "Well, then, I guess I better get back to work catching some more bad guys. See you around, Nate." He offered his old partner a casual salute.

Nate nodded back and smiled. He got up from the chair, realizing it was now official. His police career was over. Captain Bode reached across the desk with her left hand so Nate could shake it without that awkward cross-handed gesture so many people found themselves making with Nate's right arm out of commission. "Sorry to see you go, Nate," she said. "You were the only one who could handle Max as a partner. I think you actually turned him into a pretty good cop."

"He's going to be fine. And so am I. Thanks for everything."

Nate turned and walked out of the Captain's office. He didn't avoid the maze of goodbyes as he wound his way through the bullpen, he made sure to acknowledge every one of them, from the veteran detectives to the rookie uniformed officers. Many more who weren't on duty he would see later that night at The Shanty, the nearby cop bar.

It took him nearly an hour to leave. When he finally made it out of the building and out onto the street, he pulled out his phone and checked the time. Then he used it to summon an Uber that was conveniently just around the corner. The driver saw that Nate had his arm in a sling and hurriedly got out of the car to open the rear passenger side door for his fare.

Nate stared out the window, a smile on his face as he replayed memories of his time on the force. His first day, his first arrest, making detective. They were the milestones that had marked out the road he had been on for nearly half of his life if he counted his years studying criminal justice in college.

"Are you a teacher or a student?" the driver asked him.

"Excuse me?" Nate asked back, surprised by the question.

"Your destination is the University. I figure you gotta be one or the other."

"I'm visiting a friend," he said. The answer seemed strange when he said it aloud. It was time for Jennifer's Introduction to Anthropology lecture. She had offered him a standing invitation to visit any time, and today was a day he could do with something to take his mind off of the drastic turn his life had taken.

"Is she a teacher or a student?" the driver persisted.

"She's a teacher. A very good one."

"They don't get paid enough if you ask me," the driver said. "And the stuff they gotta put up with. Those overly sensitive students, ungrateful parents, overpaid administrators. It's a wonder anyone sticks with it any more."

Nate nodded in agreement.

The driver sensed Nate's reluctance to engage in conversation and turned on the radio instead. He happened to catch the tail end of a news report following up on the case of the octogenarian serial killer. She had had her arraignment this morning.

The story of Rose Walton and Luther Laramie and Jennifer and Nate's involvement in solving the sixty-year-old case had made the front page of the newspapers not only in town, but across the country. It spread like wildfire across the internet, and he had turned down several requests to appear on various television news programs.

Jennifer was not quite so shy.

From what Nate knew about Jennifer's relationship with the dean, he wouldn't be happy with the publicity she generated, especially since the media was playing up the ghost angle. They made a big thing about how her equipment had captured unusual electromagnetic activity during the moments when Rose had assaulted Diane in her bedroom. But the cameras had all been devoid of any evidence of Luther's alleged presence.

Jennifer hadn't pressed him since that night about the bet. Would she claim she had won and would insist he talk to her about his experience? And if she did, would he tell her about the dreams he had, especially the one during his surgery when he somehow saw the robbers' safe house. He had convinced himself that at the time, he hadn't seen anything specific, and his mind had altered the memory to fit his later experience. Regardless, he was sure she would make a big deal about it.

They had exchanged a few emails and text messages since that night, but the topic of who won the bet was never broached. The more time passed, the more he accepted the idea that what he had perceived as their concern for each other, and the flirting between the two of them was just her usual banter, nothing special.

Nate had toyed with the idea of just asking her out more than a few times, but always backed down. Between the endless hours he had spent in the hospital, and the time reassuring his mother he was really okay, there just wasn't time. His mother, of course, was curious about his relationship with "such a pretty lady," as she referred to Dr. Daye. Nate's promises to follow up on Jennifer's offer to recommend some psychics she trusted kept the bulk of his mother's personal questions at bay.

They hadn't had dinner with Nate's mother like they had planned, and he wondered if that whole idea might fall by the wayside as well.

Either the ride was quicker than Nate had expected, or he had completely zoned out and lost track of time. The driver pulled the car in front of the building that held Jennifer's lecture hall. "Here we are, buddy. Need a hand getting out?"

"Thanks," Nate said. "I've got it." He let himself out and stood waiting on the sidewalk for a while after the car drove away, trying to decide if he was going to chicken out of seeing her or not.

CHAPTER FORTY NINE

Jennifer was holding court in front of her students when Nate sneaked in the back. She was lecturing them about the various cultures who shared reincarnation beliefs while a digital slide presentation served as a backdrop.

She had on the same type of outfit he had seen her wear previously for teaching, a kind of modern, female Indiana Jones, he realized.

Jennifer completed the lecture and opened the floor up to questions. Nearly every hand in the room shot up.

"Any questions that are *not* about the Luther Laramie case?" she asked.

All the hands slowly sank back down.

Jennifer sighed. "All right," she said. "But this is the last time."

The hands flew up again, and she began calling on students who posed various questions regarding the case. Many of them seemed rather well versed.

A few questions in, Jennifer caught sight of Nate in the back row and smiled.

"Professor," one of the students began, "the news reports mentioned that you had enlisted a police detective to help you investigate this case. What did he think?"

"Why don't you ask him?" Jennifer said, casting her gaze to the back of the room where Nate was sitting.

Everyone turned around and looked at him. Nate wanted to flee. He wasn't prepared for a grilling from the press let alone a classroom of Jennifer Daye's students.

"No comment," he said, hoping that would cut off any further inquiry before things got out of hand.

"I think I can safely relay that Detective Raney remains a skeptic on matters of the paranormal. But I can tell you I wouldn't be here if it wasn't for him being there."

The details of Nate's career ending efforts to save Jennifer from falling had never made it into any of the news reports. The whole "hero cop" thing would have made things even more difficult for Nate to deal with and Jennifer had respected that.

"Has Ms. Collins seen Luther since that night?"

Jennifer shook her head. "No. Hopefully his spirit or whatever part of him felt obligated to remain on this plane is at rest now."

"No magic trick today?" Another student asked.

"Here's a trick. All of your questions made the rest of the class period disappear."

A buzzer sounded. The students groaned in disappointment.

"Okay, that's enough for now. Remember, you have papers due this Friday. No extensions."

The students started gathering their things and filing out of the lecture hall. Some of them offered a tentative greeting to Nate as they exited, unsure how to treat him.

When about half of them had exited, Nate saw the dean enter.

The administrator made his way against the flow of bodies like a shark cutting through a school of herring. He approached Jennifer and waited for the remaining students to exit and give them some privacy before speaking to her.

"You've been avoiding my calls, Dr. Daye," he said to Jennifer.

"Sorry," she answered. "I haven't been spending a lot of time in my office. It's being fumigated for athletes foot."

"Yes, well, if you had bothered to return any of my calls, you would be aware that those facilities are no longer available to you."

"Thank God," Jennifer said. "Does this mean you're done

punishing me?"

"Dr. Daye," the dean continued, "it's not about punishment. It's about what's best for this institution. And having the name of this esteemed school along with one of its professors demeaned on every front page and website is simply unacceptable. I warned you about bringing this kind of publicity to the school."

"It wasn't that long ago that you tried to use my reputation to land a big donation."

"Yes, and we all know how well that worked out."

"I never mentioned the University when I spoke with the press. They made that association, not me."

"Regardless, it was your actions, your defiance, your self-aggrandizing behavior that instigated the attention and you leave me with no options."

"Really," Jennifer said with contempt. "What's next, the men's room at the stadium?"

"I don't think you understand what I'm saying. Your office privileges are being revoked completely."

Jennifer stared at him in disbelief.

"I'm a full, tenured professor at this school. How am I supposed to do my job without an office?"

"Also, we can no longer support funding for the teaching and research assistants."

"You're going to punish my staff, too? Dave will never be able to find another faculty sponsor this far into his dissertation."

"The blame is completely at your feet, Dr. Daye. You will have access to the department conference room for office hours with your students, but regardless of your tenure, we have no obligation to provide you facilities to perpetuate your extracurricular activities. I'm sure with your popularity you will have no trouble finding alternate arrangements."

"What, you're not taking away my classes, too?"

"We'll evaluate any additional administrative actions at a later date. I expect you to have your belongings removed from your office by the end of business tomorrow." He turned and started walking away.

"It really bugs you, doesn't it," Jennifer said.

The dean turned back. "What bugs me?"

"That I get more attention than you. That you do everything you can to put this department on the map purely with your stuffy old discredited theories, but it's me who gets the press. Me who gets the television interviews. You're just an anonymous cog in the wheel of this institution. You could be replaced tomorrow and no one would remember what you even looked like a week later. How many names of the students who just walked by you do you know? Any of them? Are they just numbers on a spreadsheet to you?"

"You don't know what you're talking about," the dean said. "I am this department, and this department is me and I won't have you sullying its good name."

"You're an ass. That's all you are, have ever been and ever will be. A complete and utter ass that smells, has horrible teeth and probably is awful in bed."

The dean broke eye contact with Jennifer at that point, shocked by her blunt language. "I'll excuse that comment considering the circumstances. I remind you that you always have the option of resigning your position."

"Ah, that's what this is about. You're trying to get me to quit. Well, that's not going to happen, Bobby. Get used to me being around."

The dean looked back at Jennifer, realizing that somehow he was the loser in this particular battle, but with a look of determination that the war would continue. He spun around and headed for the exit.

Nate got up from where he was seated and walked directly at the self-absorbed bastard.

When they met halfway up the aisle, the dean waited for Nate to step aside so he could proceed, but Nate didn't move. He stood his ground and gave the cocky administrator a glare that would have made a hardened criminal pee in his pants. The dean's demeanor changed as he evaluated Nate, and he decided to slink around the detective rather than challenging him.

A wise move, Nate thought.

Nate continued toward the edge of the stage where Jennifer was shoving her notes and some student papers into her bag. Tears threatened to well up in her eyes, but she held them back.

"I'm sorry," Nate said.

"What for? You're not the arrogant prick who's trying to upend my career." Jennifer wiped at her eyes with the back of her hand and forced a smile onto her lips. "I'm sorry," she said. "I didn't mean to take that out on you."

"Be my guest," Nate offered.

"You're sweet," Jennifer said, "but you don't deserve the shit I want to shovel down that man's throat right now."

"Okay. Offer rescinded."

Jennifer smiled again, genuinely this time. Grateful that someone was there to keep her from exploding with rage. "I never thought it would actually come to this." She put her hand over her mouth to keep from sobbing. "Oh, poor Dave. He can't afford to finish his doctorate without this job." Jennifer moved toward Nate and wrapped her arms around him in a comforting hug.

Nate was a bit surprised by the gesture, but he put his hand on her back as he felt her tears soak into his shirt. "You'll figure something out," Nate said reassuringly.

She broke away from Nate suddenly, a look of panic in her eyes. "My stuff. I don't have any room in the shoe box I call an apartment for all our gear. And my posters. And my files."

Without thinking, Nate offered, "you can leave it at my place till you get settled somewhere if you like."

"Are you sure?" Jennifer asked.

"Yeah, no problem," Nate answered.

She grabbed him into another hug. "First you save my life, and now you save my ass. Thank you."

Nate answered with a gentle pat on her back.

CHAPTER FIFTY

Nate woke up to the sound of knocking alternating with his doorbell ringing. He was used to the pain in his shoulder, but he must have slept on it funny because it hurt like hell this morning. He sat up, his vision still blurry and swung his feet onto the floor.

Madge yelped when he stepped on her paw. He should have been used to her sneaking out of her kennel and curling up next to his bed, but the urgency of the knocking downstairs threw him off.

He grabbed a robe from the bathroom, slipped his good arm in its sleeve and draped the rest of it over his other arm and cinched the belt up with one hand, a move he was getting quite adept at.

Madge got underfoot as he made his way down the stairs. "I'm coming," he shouted.

The dog made it to the door before him and started barking at whomever was on the other side. "What's up Madge? Did you order a dog food delivery or something?"

Nate reached the front door and undid the locks. He opened it and saw Dave and Emily from Jennifer's office standing there. Madge jumped up on Dave and nearly knocked him over.

Dave stumbled back a bit. "Hey, Madge. Take it easy."

"Can we get on with this? I need to get back to bed," Emily said. "Where do you want it?"

"Where do I want what?" Nate asked.

Emily waved at someone on the street.

Nate peered out the door and saw that there was a moving van parked in front of his house. A group of what Nate assumed were students started hauling boxes out of the back of it and marching them up to the front door.

"What's going on?" Nate asked.

"Dr. Daye said we're moving in here."

"Moving in? I told her she could keep some stuff here. I thought you'd be putting some boxes in the garage."

"She said you have a bunch of spare rooms."

Some of the students carried their loads up to the door. "Straight in, through the kitchen, the room in the back," Dave instructed.

Nate stepped aside as students marched back and forth through his house.

"Where can I set up my stuff?" Bits asked from behind Nate.

Nate jumped with surprise. He turned and saw Jennifer's tech guy standing in the middle of his living room. "Set up?"

"The attic looks big enough. You mind if I run a two-forty line up there? Thanks." He grabbed a milk crate full of gear and headed up the steps.

"Wait, when were you upstairs?" Nate turned back to Dave. "Where is Dr. Daye?"

Dave shrugged. "She said she would be here."

Two students wielding the enormous poster of "The Mysterious Professor," Jennifer's magician alter ego squeezed in the front door. "Where does this go?" one of them asked.

The larger-than-life image of Jennifer glared at Nate

"Straight back to Dr. Daye's office," Dave answered.

"Office?" Nate asked. "Wait a minute, I just said she could keep some stuff here."

"Sometimes when you say yes to Dr. Daye and you think it's one thing, but it's really something else entirely. You'll get used to it," Dave said. He picked up the cases he had carried to the front door and joined the procession of movers carrying stuff into Nate's house.

Nate turned to Emily. She shrugged and stepped into the house and headed up the stairs. "Everyone, just stop!" he shouted.

The procession came to a halt.

After a moment, one of the students meekly asked. "Can I put this down? It's really heavy.

"Sure," Nate said. "Why not?" He shuffled back into his living room and dropped into his easy chair. The pain in his shoulder flared up. He closed his eyes, hoping he was having a bad dream.

"Why's everyone just standing around?" Jennifer asked.

Nate opened his eyes and saw Jennifer standing in his doorway. She was wearing jeans and a T-shirt, something completely uncharacteristic for her.

"Oh, good morning, Nate," she said.

"Good morning."

"I meant to get here before they did," Jennifer explained.

"Oh," Nate said. "And?"

"And, I was going to tell you—or rather ask you—since you have such a big place, and it's just you and Madge, and the dean took away my office privileges, that maybe you might not mind if we borrowed some of your extra space for a while."

Jennifer looked to Nate, hoping to see some indication that her recitation of the situation had softened the fact that he woke up to an army of volunteers transforming his home into her office.

He merely sat in his chair, stone faced. "Borrowed for how long?" he asked.

"Well, actually, I was thinking. You mentioned that you were going to open up your own private investigation firm. And investigating is part of what we do, and I thought we did a pretty good job working together, so maybe we could help each other out."

Nate nodded. "I see."

"You'd be amazed at the number of calls, and emails and messages we get. A lot of them are people who need a detective more than a parapsychologist, we could create an amazing synergy."

"Synergy."

"I mean, I know it's a big house, but when Bits showed me the floor plan, and how much space you have upstairs that you're not using—and that den off the kitchen would make a terrific office. We could get two big desks, and put them in the middle of the room so they're facing each other, wouldn't that be great?"

"Wait, how did Bits get the floor plan to my house? Never mind. Don't answer that. We're going to share an office?"

"Yes?" Jennifer answered questioningly. "Nate, I'm sorry to spring this on you like this. But after the Dean hit me with the whole office eviction thing, and you offered to let me bring my stuff here, one thought just led to another and I got really excited and I just convinced myself that you would be as excited about it as I was. But I'm thinking that's not quite how it's working out. I'm sorry. Can I still keep some stuff here for a while? Just until I find something."

Nate nodded at the sofa. "Have a seat."

Jennifer tentatively crossed over and slowly lowered herself onto the sofa.

Madge trotted over, jumped up next to her and laid her head in Jennifer's lap.

Nate sighed. "Okay."

"Okay?" Jennifer asked? "Okay which part?"

"Well, the whole sharing an office thing we'll have to talk about, but you're right. I have a lot of room. It never felt empty before I started spending all of my time here. It might be nice to have someone besides Madge for company."

The dog whimpered at the sound of her name.

"Oh, that reminds me," Dave said. He disappeared into the kitchen, then returned a moment later with a small, spherical device. Nate recognized it as one of the camera's Bits had set up at Diane's place. "I left this in the kitchen to see if I could find out how Madge was getting out of her cage."

Nate raised an eyebrow. "You've been spying on me for the last week?"

"No, it's not connected. It was set to motion activation and stored the video on an SD card." Dave popped the tiny memory card out of the camera. "Anyone have a laptop handy?"

Emily appeared and set her computer on the coffee table. She snatched the memory card out of Dave's fingers and popped it into a slot on the side. With a couple of taps on her touch pad, she had the video from the camera playing full screen.

Madge's kennel was full frame. In the video, Nate opened the door to the cage and ordered Madge inside. She obeyed and curled up on the blanket, her chin on her paws looking up with sad eyes at Nate as he locked her in. Nate left the frame and turned off the lights in the kitchen. The camera switched to night vision.

There was a jump in the video and now Madge was on her feet. She peered out through the door of the cage, then moved to the back of the wire frame kennel and squeezed her nose into one corner. The entire frame of the kennel moved as she created a gap between the side wall and the back one. Nate had never checked to see if the corners were all properly connected to each other. He had always assumed she was somehow squeezing out the door.

Madge continued to widen the gap, forcing her entire head through it, then her whole body. Once she had squeezed out of the cage, the side wall snapped back into place, leaving what looked like a securely locked cage behind. She trotted out of the kitchen and the video ended.

"So much for it being Aunt Lillian," Nate said. "I should have gone double or nothing on our bet."

"Yeah, I didn't want to bring that up, but you do kinda owe me a conversation," Jennifer said.

"How do you figure that?" Nate asked. "All you have are some squiggly lines on a screen. Hardly definitive proof."

"What are you talking about? Diane saw Luther."

"Yeah, the woman who got hit on the head."

"He's got a point," Dave chimed in.

Jennifer gave him a reproachful glare.

"Thanks, Dave," Nate said. "You get your pick of the upstairs rooms."

Dave gave an excited fist pump. "Yes!"

"How about we call it a draw, keep it open ended," Nate suggested.

"All right, that sounds fair."

"Does this mean we can keep moving everything in?" one of the volunteers asked.

Nate looked up at the crowd of students. Some of them he recognized from Jennifer's anthropology class. "Bring it all in," Nate said. They started moving again.

"You won't regret this," Jennifer said to Nate. "So, I'm thinking of calling it D and R Investigations."

"D and R?"

"R and D sounds too much like research and development."

"How about Raney Daye Investigations," Dave suggested.

Jennifer and Nate looked to Dave, then back to each other.

"I like it," Nate said.

"Sold," Jennifer added.

Nate extended his good hand to seal the deal, but Jennifer got up and smothered him with a hug instead. As she squeezed him, Nate realized the pain in his shoulder had faded to a dull ache.

"How about you help me make some breakfast for your crew?" Nate suggested.

"That would be perfect," Jennifer said.

Emily appeared again, this time with a tray. On it were four wine glasses and a bottle of red she had found in his kitchen wine fridge.

"Jeez," Nate sighed, "you guys are here five minutes and already you're helping yourselves to my wine? It's seven-thirty."

"Oh, don't act like you weren't going to say yes," Emily commented. "And just because it's first thing in the morning doesn't mean we can't toast this thing—whatever it is you two are doing."

"We're business partners," Jennifer clarified.

"Yeah, let's go with that," Emily replied sarcastically.

Before Nate could respond, Dave grabbed a glass and raised it. "To Raney Daye Investigations."

They all touched glasses and enjoyed a sip of the wine.

"Wait a minute, are you twenty-one?" Nate asked Emily.

"Sure," she said. "Wanna see my ID?"

"No, best that I don't."

"Come on, group hug," Jennifer insisted. She gathered Dave,

Emily and a somewhat reluctant Nate in her arms. "This is going to be great."

"Wait, what about Bits?" Nate asked.

"Bits doesn't do hugs," Emily answered.

"But your WiFi is going to be insane," Dave promised.

EPILOGUE

The sign painter applied the finishing touches to to the frosted glass on the new front door to Nate's house. Simple letters, gold with a black outline. "Raney/Daye Investigations."

The extra upstairs rooms had been transformed by each of Jennifer's staff into their own personal retreats. They weren't there all the time, but sometimes it seemed like it. Nate wasn't quite sure when Bits came and went and learned not to ask too many questions.

Emily had taken the opportunity of them having an office that they were sure they were going to stay in for more than a week to start organizing Dr. Daye's case records. Many of them shared cardboard boxes, but there was no way to reference them except by asking Dr. Daye—or in some cases, Dave—if they remembered something specific. Bits set her up with a sheet-fed scanner and some optical character recognition software that digitized all the related records for each case. Then she categorized them according to a variety of metrics she had developed including the time frame for inciting incidents, type of phenomena recorded, ages and sexes of witnesses.

Nate was impressed by her system, and Jennifer was amazed at how much data they had actually accumulated over the years.

Bits had secreted himself into the attic. Nate had expected to see a spike in his electric bill, but it actually had gone down after Jennifer's team had moved in. What he did up there was anyone's guess, but from time to time he would present Jennifer with an upgrade to some sensor or another, or find a way to reanalyze some dataset. Nate hadn't figured Bits out yet. He was the enigma of the group. He didn't even know the guy's real name.

Dave, with a space of his own and inspired by Emily's work, made a concerted effort to organize the materials he had collected over the last five years of working on his thesis. After several in depth sessions with Jennifer, he realized that all he really needed to do was to write it up. The research was there, it was comprehensive and thoroughly referenced. So, he started writing—or at least tried to. It was hard for him to make the adjustment. Jennifer assured him it would come. One day, he would find himself in front of his computer with thousands of words on the page, and thousands more struggling to get from his brain to the screen.

Nate wondered if Dave needed some level of anxiety in his life. He suspected the graduate assistant's loyalty to Jennifer was related to his insecurity. Despite the outward appearance of him being exploited, working for her had been the most meaningful years of his life, and a part of him probably feared moving on. The longer he could draw out his thesis, the more he could delay that inevitable parting.

Jennifer and Nate did end up setting up the downstairs den as a shared office. Jennifer found an enormous partner's desk that filled the center of the room. It had a kneewell that went all the way through, and each side had its own collection of drawers. Nate had a laptop computer, but Jennifer preferred her desktop model. She didn't want her computer to be portable and preferred the large, curved screen Bits had procured for her.

Jennifer's posters had found a home in the office as well. The remaining wall space was allocated to a few mementos and photographs from Nate's time on the police force, and a few from his great uncle's era as well.

To one side of the desk was a large bay window that opened out onto Nate's backyard, where one could catch glimpses of the San Francisco skyline between the branches of the walnut trees in the yard.

On the other side was a wide couch with a low table in front of it.

Jennifer and Nate sat in their respective office chairs, while their prospective client perched herself nervously on the edge of the couch, clutching her purse in her lap. She was an older woman, immaculately dressed and coiffed, but not ostentatiously so.

Her voice was thin and frail, lacking confidence. "The noises come from the back bedroom, every night at almost nine o'clock exactly," she told Jennifer. "But there's no one in that room. It's been empty for years, ever since my granddaughter moved out. It sounds like…" She paused for a moment, swallowed, then continued in a whisper. "It sounds like someone's being murdered in there."

"Are there any other rooms in the house where you've heard or seen strange things? Do you get that feeling that someone else is in the room, but when you turn around, no one's there?"

"Oh, yes, all the time," the woman replied.

Nate forced himself to keep from rolling his eyes. He turned toward Jennifer. "See, this is the kind of thing I'm talking about. With everyone who comes in here, you leap to the assumption that there's something paranormal going on."

"Her story fits all the elements of a classic haunting scenario," Jennifer replied.

"It also fits the classic granddaughter wants to scare grandma out of her house so she can sell it and get an early inheritance scenario as well—not to mention the squirrels in the attic scenario."

"Oh, my granddaughter would never do that," the old woman declared.

"See?" Jennifer said to Nate pointedly.

"Her husband is the one who wants me to sell."

Nate gave Jennifer a clear "I told you so" look.

Jennifer turned her attention back to the woman. "Well, Mrs. Gladstone. We'll start by checking out your home for anything unusual." She cast a sideways glance in Nate's direction. "And make sure there aren't any animals in your attic," she added.

"Does this mean you're taking my case?" Mrs. Gladstone asked.

Nate gave Jennifer a reluctant nod.

"Yes, we are," Jennifer answered. "Now, tell me everything."

Nate sat back and listened as Mrs. Gladstone poured out her life story to Jennifer.

Jennifer and Nate will return in

AFTER LIFE
a Raney/Daye Investigation

AFTERWORD

One of the things we hope to achieve with the portrayal of all things psychic/paranormal in the Raney & Daye Investigations series is a sense of reality. In other words, my involvement in the series includes making sure the elements of psychic phenomena, abilities, and experiences ring true—even if we have to take some artistic license for the sake of the story.

We also hope that our readers will want to look further into what's portrayed with respect to the paranormal phenomena, to parapsychology (the field that studies such things) and to paranormal investigations.

One place we'll likely have to take more liberties with would be what happens in the actual investigations of ghostly and psychic experiences, as often real investigations don't include the investigators getting to witness or experience things themselves— and contrary to the paranormal "reality" TV shows, there are no devices that can detect ghosts (other than human ones).

For each of our novels, you'll find some additional material after the story that will be informative on the parapsychological elements of the book or related concepts. As the resident parapsychologist of this author team (helmed exceptionally well by Rich Hosek, the main crafter and writer of the novel), it's up to me to provide this.

But first, a bit of commentary on Jennifer Daye, anthropologist-parapsychologist-magician.

Many people may be surprised to learn that those who are officially in the scientific organization of those studying psychic/paranormal phenomena, the Parapsychological Association (the PA), have backgrounds in a variety of social and physical sciences. As there have been very limited opportunities anywhere in the world to get a graduate degree in Parapsychology itself (none since the late 1980s in the US), parapsychologists with rare exception have other advanced degrees. A large number of the PA members have theirs in psychology, but others come from graduate studies in physics, anthropology (like Jennifer), biology, sociology, neuroscience, and even medical sciences.

While I was fortunate, timing-wise, to be able to get a Master's degree in Parapsychology in the early 1980s when John F. Kennedy University (as of 2021, merged into National University) had such a program, my undergrad studies/degree at Northwestern University focused on Cultural Anthropology—and much of my coursework was focused on magic and supernatural beliefs around the world.

Anthropologist Jennifer Daye is also portrayed as a skilled stage magician, with professional experience in that area. Most in the general public—and in the magician community—would be hard-pressed to think of any magician associated with the psychic world other than ones calling themselves "debunkers" and "skeptics." But the reality is that there have been others in and around parapsychology with magical knowledge and performing experience, including Dr. Daryl Bem, and the late Dr. Arthur Hastings and Dr. Marcello Truzzi. And me.

Again, Jennifer's character taps into my own background a bit. I got into Magic because of a graduate course included in our Master's Parapsychology program that focused on basic principles of magic and mentalism (that's mind-reading type stuff) to prepare students for assessing people's psychic claims. Turned out I enjoyed not only learning about it but also performing (especially being paid for performing). I spent the 1980s doing magic at private parties and comedy magic at comedy clubs and corporate events. Around 1990, I was steered to mentalism by Marcello Truzzi and have been in that arena ever since, performing as Professor Paranormal and becoming active in the Psychic Entertainers Association, an international organization for which I'm proud to say I served several years as President. I have performed for college and corporate/business audiences, for private parties, and even performed as part of a bill with a couple of professional spirit mediums.

Performing mentalism/psychic entertainment (and magic) has given me a real grounding in understanding how people can honestly misinterpret what they perceive and experience. It's given me insight into how and why some people who aren't psychic have been convinced that they are, and how phonies convince their clientele that they have "powers." But mainly it has allowed me to separate actual psychic experiences and phenomena from the explainable—just like Jennifer Daye.

Enough about me and Jennifer. Let's talk paranormal.

In the book you just read (or are about to read, if you're the kind of person who jumps to the back matter first) there are three main psychic phenomena involved (spoilers!!!): Near-Death Experiences (NDE) which often include the Out of Body Experience (OBE) as in Nate's experience, and the experiences of the ghostly kind, what we refer to as Apparitions.

But first, in case you're not aware (or have been misled by so many of the paranormal reality TV shows), a little bit on Parapsychology. Lots of dictionary definitions say the field studies experiences and phenomena currently unexplained by mainstream science. That doesn't say much of anything at all.

Parapsychology is the field of study of experiences and apparent phenomena we call "psychic" or "paranormal." These include three major areas: ExtraSensory Perception (information perception outside of the use of our normal senses, logic inference, or guesswork), PsychoKinesis (the mind directly interacting with/acting on the physical world without the use of the body or tools) and Survival of Bodily Death (the mind—consciousness—surviving the death of the body). Back in the 1930s, J.B. Rhine put all of that under the term psi—the 23rd letter of the Greek alphabet, representing psyche (the mind).

In simple terms, we study experiences and phenomena indicating our consciousness can gain information without the physical senses (ESP), can interact/influence the physical (PK) and can exist after the brain has died (Survival).

The term paranormal has been in use since the 19th century to cover it all. It simply means "on the side of normal." Unfortunately, the TV ghost hunters have separated ghostly happenings (apparitions, hauntings, and poltergeists) from other psychic experiences and phenomena (ESP and PK) and have often put forth the notion that these are unrelated things—which is untrue.

ESP is involved in any situation in which someone "sees" a ghost or communicates with an ostensible spirit. Ghosts (apparitions) have no physical eyes and ears to see and hear, so would have to perceive with a non-sensory process (ESP)—and if they move stuff, that's mind over matter (PK). If someone is "out" of their body, they are missing those physical senses, and so would have to perceive with non-sensory processes (ESP).

OUT OF BODY EXPERIENCES (OBE)

An OBE is the sensation or experience many people have of actually leaving their body for a time. In more "occult" language, this is called "astral projection," where the spirit or soul or "astral body" actually leaves the physical body.

Keep in mind that at the base of the definition is the experience, the feeling that you've left your body. I can feel happy, or sad, or detached, or have an experience of feeling as if I'd left my body. This might be considered an OBE, yet this isn't psychic—it's psychological. Only when you add in such factors as "going" somewhere out of body, observing that location or person, and checking the information out later for accuracy (and it does check out) can you term it a psychic out of body experience. Much like what happens to Nate during his near-death experience.

Many experienced OBE practitioners also feel that their soul or spirit does not actually leave the body, but rather that part of the mind or consciousness can split off and travel. According to the late Alex Tanous, a psychic involved in OBE studies at the American Society for Psychical Research (ASPR) for many years, if his soul had left his body, he'd have died. (His death was not, by the way, from an out of body venture.)

One of the interesting categories of apparition (ghost) encounters is that sometimes the "ghost" that is seen is actually a living person having an out of body experience.

NEAR DEATH EXPERIENCE (NDE)

In the near death experience, a person declared clinically dead for a time (or close to it) reports leaving his or her body, perhaps even observing the location and people around the now dead body, then rising up through a sort of tunnel towards a light of some kind. A voice or even a familiar figure (typically a deceased family member or friend, or a religious figure) is seen or heard at the end of the tunnel. The person having the experience is either told it is not yet his or her time or decides that it is not yet time to die. In any event, the body is resuscitated, and the person finds himself or herself back in the body, with a recollection of that near death process. For those who have had such an experience, there is often a lasting impact on their beliefs and personal outlook on life, often on their personality, and sometimes on their ability to manifest psychic abilities.

Many cultures, from Hindus in India to folks in Iceland to people here in the States have similar experiences, many involving that same image of the tunnel and the bright light. In 1991, I visited Japan for a television program that was broadcast on the Tokyo Broadcasting System. The topic of NDEs was a large part of the show (which centered on the reported experiences and abilities of Japanese psychic Aiko Gibo). What I learned was that the Japanese experience involves not a tunnel, but rather a river. There is no particularly bright light, because the one experiencing the NDE essentially crosses the river in "sunshine," and walks down a flower lined path, often with another person (an ancestor or other interested party). As with the tunnel NDE, the person is either told to go back or offered the choice and returns to life.

This discrepancy in experiences is quite interesting, given that diverse cultural and religious beliefs of others (Icelanders, Americans, Hindus, etc.) has not previously made a difference. This river NDE throws a monkey wrench in the explanations some have given for a more physical, biological cause of the NDE—though it's extremely important to note that a large percentage of people declared clinically dead do not have an impactful near-death experience (or even the tunnel/river experience at all) and one or more of the various physical/neurological alternate explanations are more likely at play.

APPARITIONS

My definition of an apparition, or what most people call a "ghost" or spirit of the dead, is what is perceived in ways that seem like it's being seen, heard, felt, or smelled. Apparitions are related to the concept of human personality/mind/soul—consciousness—that can somehow exist in our physical universe after the death of its body (or out of body when we're still alive). The basic idea of an apparition is twofold: that consciousness must survive the body's physical death and it must be able to interact with people.

When I say that the apparition is "seen" or "heard," I don't mean that this is happening through the eyes or ears. Let's remember that our actual perception of the world around us involves a process whereby data is received by the senses, then screened and enhanced by the brain and mind. Perception resides not in the senses, but in the brain (or consciousness itself). Hallucinations, for example, are essentially superimposed images, sounds, smells, etc., that are added to (or in other instances blocked or erased from) the information of our senses.

In the same way, the apparition somehow "adds" information to our sensory input that is then processed with our what our senses pull in and integrated into what we perceive. In other words, the mind of the apparition is providing our own minds with the extra information necessary to perceive the discarnate entity—to "see" and "hear" with our mind's-eye and mind's-ear.

There isn't anything optical about ghosts or hauntings, nor do they make physical sounds to be heard, or touch you with some physical extremity. Those that experience ghosts in various ways perceive them in ways that seem sensory but are actually extra-sensory. And if a ghost were to move something, since they have no physical body, that would have to be via the mind of the entity affecting the physical—the very definition of PK.

What distinguishes an apparition from what I'll cover next, hauntings, is the interaction, some sign that the apparition is conscious.

HAUNTINGS

Hauntings, or what ghost hunters on TV refer to as "residual hauntings," are more familiar to people in that many often experience some form of this throughout their lives. The term now refers to situations in which a person perceives something about a location or object (sees, hears, smells, feels—perceives—something) without there being anything physically there. The observer might see a figure that appears and disappears or hear footsteps or other sounds that seem to indicate someone is physically present or even smell odors that have no apparent source. Others may simply feel something—good or bad "vibes"—about the location. These situations are often confused with apparitions, but what is missing is the interaction.

What operationally distinguishes the apparition from the haunting is the idea that an apparition is conscious, whereas the figure seen in a haunting is some form of "recording" in the environment. Today, many parapsychologists believe that hauntings relate directly to the past of the location or the history of the object. Like a voice or video recorder records information that can be played back (audio and/ or visual), a house, an object, a location, etc. somehow records all the things that have happened in its history. That can be recent or old history.

Under certain conditions, we (that is, living people) can somehow "play back" bits of this recorded history within our own minds. In some way, our brains/minds superimpose this historical playback over our own normal perceptions, so that it, too, seems quite real. What is played back (the event, the recording) may be a random piece of information, or, more often, a happening that has been "imprinted" into the environment with a good deal of emotion.

Most important to understand is the point that the dead don't make these "recordings" (or "imprints" as many refer to them). The actions and emotions of the living are what gets recorded into the environment, and whether someone has died at the location is totally irrelevant.

Another way to understand this factor is to consider movies from the 1940s. All of the actors in those films were alive when the movies were made. Most (but not necessarily all) are likely deceased by now. However, people have been able to watch those movies with those actors since they were released, whether the actors were living or dead. In the same way, hauntings are recordings of emotions and actions made by the living, whether those who made the imprints are still alive or not.

Consequently, just like there are apparitions of the living (when people are seen during an OBE) there are hauntings representing the living. The figures, voices, odors perceived by witnesses can represent people still very much alive. Hauntings are about information in places (and sometimes objects), not about spirits of the dead.

FOR MORE INFORMATION

Lastly I want to mention a few organizations that provide excellent, scientific (and practical) information about psychic phenomena and experiences such as what Raney & Daye encounter in this book (and will encounter in future investigation).

Rhine Research Center: www.rhine.org

The longest running lab and educational organization in the United States, this is the legacy of the Duke University Parapsychology Laboratory founded in the 1930s. The Rhine has a huge media library—videos of lectures by researchers, psychics, and others presented over the last few years. There are a few that are free, but you are encouraged to join, not only to gain access to the media library and get discounts on webcasts of new lectures and discounts on classes and other things, but mainly to help support the work of the Rhine.

The Rhine Education Center (www.rhineedu.org) offers online courses throughout the year (Loyd Auerbach is one of the main instructors).

The Society for Psychical Research: www.spr.ac.uk

The SPR is the oldest psychical research/parapsychology organization, founded in 1882. Lots of good info here for free, especially the Psi Encyclopedia (https://psi-encyclopedia.spr.ac.uk/)—an ever-growing resource on psychic abilities and research.

The Forever Family Foundation:
www.foreverfamilyfoundation.org

Free to join, this non-profit supports the work of evidential mediums in the family grieving process and supports scientific research into experiences suggestive or supportive of the concept of Survival of Consciousness (and Loyd Auerbach is the President)

Loyd Auerbach, MS—October 1, 2020

Follow Loyd Auerbach on Twitter @profparanormal
Visit his YouTube channels at:
www.youtube.com/user/loydauerbach/videos
www.youtube.com/user/profparanormal/videos
You can reach Loyd Auerbach directly at profparanormal@gmail.com

AUTHOR'S NOTE

Almost 30 years ago, I met Loyd Auerbach when I was working in the Paramount Pictures Motion Picture Story Department and was tasked with finding an expert on the paranormal. This was before "the internet" and meant making several phone calls, which eventually pointed me to Loyd. Although the project didn't get made, it began a decades long friendship where we connected on the personal and professional. Sharing holidays – and seances – and creating a seminar for filmmakers to harness a better understanding of the paranormal, "Would a Ghost say that?".

Loyd and I wanted to work on a project together, so we came up with a buddy cop/parapsychologist idea for a series about a skeptical police detective who has a near death experience and the parapsychologist who wants the cop's version of the afterlife. Through years of development, that part has remained to this day. We called the project *Psi Cops*, but the characters were Raney and Daye, who we originally envisioned being played by up-and-coming actors Brian Dennehy and Anthony Edwards. While we got interest in the pitch, without other produced credits, we were advised to spec out the script. First we planned on a pilot, but then we decided to do a "backdoor pilot" movie.

Rich Hosek and I became friends years before, at the University of Illinois, where we met in Julius Rascheff's film class. Rich and I worked on each other's thesis films and made several community cable shows together (pre Wayne's World). When my wife and I moved to California, Rich helped us drive cross country, and then after wasting time at film school in Chicago, he moved out to Los Angeles a year later. We were both writers, and while I worked with various partners – including Loyd – Rich wrote on his own. After exchanging script notes on several projects, Rich and I decided to become an "&", where we teamed up, wrote dozens of television specs, got an agent, went through the Warner Bros Television Workshop, and later worked on several television shows and a few pilots and features.

When we first teamed up, Loyd was happy to have Rich join us to finish the script for what became *Raney & Daye*. By the time we finished the story, we had decided Professor Daye should be female, so we began the painstaking rewrite of changing the character's first name to Jennifer and doing a search and replace for all the hes to shes and hims to hers. When development executives complimented Jennifer Daye, we realized the secret to writing strong female characters – write strong characters. We had several fans, but response on the few submissions was lukewarm. "Good characters and writing, but nobody wants to do a paranormal show." Shortly thereafter, a friend gave me a VHS tape of Fox's new pilot, *The X-Files*. For the next 9 years, Raney and Daye were "too similar" to Mulder and Scully so it went on the shelf.

When I returned to the paranormal with a young adult chapter book, *ESPete: Sixth Grade Sense*, Loyd wrote the introduction. There was occasional interest in the script, but instead of waiting for it to maybe get made, Rich wanted to novelize the script in a Raney/Daye Investigation series, which brought us here. We hope you enjoyed the book and find Raney and Daye as captivating and charming as we have all these years.

Watch for more books in the series, and maybe you'll see Nate and Jennifer on television one day.

ESPecially,
Arnold Rudnick—October 1, 2020

ACKNOWLEDGMENTS

First, I have to acknowledge my two co-authors, Rich and Arnold. The path to this novel began so many years ago with our collaboration on a TV pilot script and series proposal (which really should have sold!!). It is truly a great thing that Rich stuck with the characters and pushed for the novel to be written.

I also want to acknowledge all of the support I've received over the years from my colleagues and students in Parapsychology, as well as the psychics and mediums I have known, several of whom have worked closely with me in one context or other.

Finally, I would be remiss without acknowledging former student (and current member of my paranormal investigations "team") Sheila Smith for all of her support, including providing feedback and edits on*Near Death.*Thank you Sheila!

—Loyd

Anything that takes 30 years has a lot of people to recognize for making it happen. I want to thank Sheldon and Charlotte for making me, and encouraging my creativity. All, or most, of my teachers and educators I've worked with, but especially Sheila Ott from Robeson Elementary, Karen McKenzie from Jefferson Middle School, Adele Suslick from University Laboratory High School, and David Desser, Richard Leskosky and Julius Rascheff from University of Illinois, Urbana-Champaign. In Los Angeles, special thanks to Michael

Palmieri for the early motivation; Ted Gold and Margaret French-Isaac for feedback; Edgar Halley for what only he will know; and Gary Lucchesi and Bob McMinn for their support and the assignment that led to my relationship with Loyd.

Thank you, Loyd, for your insight and excitement about this and so many other projects. And Rich, for your partnership and for literally willing this iteration into existence. And both Loyd and Rich for friendships that have endured more than half my life. And specifically to this publication, thank you to the eagle eyes of Kathryn Balzer and Kathryn Rudnick. And evermore, Kathryn Rudnick, thank you for continuing support before, during and after. There is nobody I would rather spend my life or afterlife with than you.

—Arnold

Thank you to Kathryn Rudnick and JD Mier, the two people I can always count on to read my early, rough work and give the kind of feedback that shapes it into something good.

Thank you to Loyd Auerbach, whose own body of work served as not only an invaluable resource for the parapsychological aspects of *Near Death*, but an inspiration for the story and characters as well.

Thank you to Arnold Rudnick for being my creative partner for the last 30-some years and taking my crazy idea of writing this book and wrangling it into being.

—Rich

THE WRITERS

RICH HOSEK
Rich has written for numerous television series with his writing partner Arnold Rudnick including, *The Fresh Prince of Bel-Air*, *Star Trek: Voyager*, and *The New Addams Family* for which they won a Leo Award for Best Writing for Comedy or Variety. More recently he has been focusing his efforts on novels and short stories. He is a fan of Legos and *Doctor Who* now that there is a Doctor Who Lego set, his life is complete. Be sure to check out his other novels, short stories and non-fiction at RichHosek.com, and follow on Twitter @RichHosek and on Facebook @Written by Rich Hosek.

ARNOLD RUDNICK
Arnold studied film and accounting at the University of Illinois, Urbana-Champaign, then moved to Los Angeles, where he worked in feature development at Paramount Pictures and Gary Lucchesi Productions. Arnold and Rich have collaborated on numerous scripts for film and television, including The Fresh Prince of Bel-Air, Star Trek: Voyager and The New Addams Family. He has also written children's books, including ESPete: Sixth Grade Sense, which won a silver medal in the Moonbeam Children's Book Awards and Reader's Favorite Awards and was a pick in Danny Brassell's Lazy Readers Book Club, and Little Green. He and his wife live in Los Angeles, California.

LOYD AUERBACH
Loyd Auerbach, MS, is a world-recognized paranormal expert with thousands of media appearances and the author or coauthor of nine paranormal books and one on publishing and publicity. He is President of the Forever Family Foundation (since 2013, and Director of the Office of Paranormal Investigations (since 1989). He is on faculty at Atlantic University and JFK University (National University), and teaches online Parapsychology courses through the Rhine Education Center. He is on the Board of Directors of the Rhine Research Center and the advisory board of the Windbridge Institute. He is a past president of the Psychic Entertainers association, and besides working as a parapsychologist, he performs as professional mentalist Professor Paranormal (and occasional chocolatier). Follow him @profparanormal on Twitter.

Made in the USA
Monee, IL
11 October 2020

44210687R00187